THE ODD SEA
CHRONICLES OF THE DAWNBLADE BOOK 3
ANDREW CLAYDON

The Odd Sea

By Andrew Claydon

Published by Andrew Claydon

Copyright © 2023, Andrew Claydon

Edited by Danielle Fine

Cover Design by MiblArt

Written in UK English

Just because you're chosen, doesn't mean you want to be.
Thanks to the dubious gratitude of a Deity, Nicolas Percival Carnegie is now stranded on an island in the middle of the ocean.
But before despair can take hold – for his companions at least – rescue appears in the form of the enigmatic Captain Roberto Ramirez.
Longing to simply go home and forget about notions like adventuring, Nicolas finds his salvation bittersweet; a princess has been kidnapped and war looms on the horizon.
It isn't his country, or his princess, yet his dreams of a quick homecoming have to be put on hold when the seas could run red with blood any day now.
Nicolas may find his sea legs just in time for them to quake in fear as he learns exactly how dangerous the ocean can be.
And soon enough, being stranded on an island may not seem that bad after all.

Dedicated to Rob, the rugged first mate to my dashing Captain.
And to everyone who loves a good adventure.

Guest starring: Hayley Clarke as *Hayley Clarkey (AKA: Hey Sharkbait)*
Thank you for your contribution to my kickstart campaign.

'For a Kingdom that boasts such a large navy, the seas of Merida are practically littered with pirates and privateers, to the point one must wonder if anyone is actually trying to stop them.
These nefarious characters range from the brutal, such as the rightly feared Captain Ezekial Killgore, to the so called 'Gentleman Pirate', Captain Roberto Ramirez. Though how anyone who robs people could be considered a 'gentleman' is a conundrum this author has yet to unravel.'

Etherius, A Travellers Guide – Dieter Von Ostric

Merida Tertius
Merida Secundus
Merida Minor
Meridus
Merid...
N
E
S

CHAPTER 1

Before him, the ocean looked immense, featureless, and worst of all, endless. For as far as the eye could see, there was only rolling water, waves swirling as they rose into being only to crash back into oblivion moments later. Nicolas Percival Carnegie had no idea how long he'd been staring at it, numb with shock. It was the first time he'd ever seen the sea. Was it beautiful or intimidating? Was it even the sea? How would he know the difference?

Of course it's the bloody sea. What else could it be?

Right now, he was supposed to be home, in the village of Hablock with his parents, preferably enjoying a nice hot meal. Nicolas and his companions had gone to great lengths to restore the powers of a Deity that'd been stolen by a jumped-up dwarf gangster. It hadn't been an easy task by any stretch of the imagination, thanks in part to an angry minotaur, a sadistic hunter with a taste for exotic cuisine, and a chicken, of all things, but they'd succeeded. In gratitude, said Deity, T'goth, had granted them each a boon. He'd asked to go home...and instead he'd been dropped in the middle of the bloody ocean.

There had been a beautiful second, in the dockside warehouse after T'goth had agreed to grant his wish, where he'd thought he was done with all of this. One adventure had been more than he'd ever wanted, and the business with the Deity had been his second. He'd acquitted himself pretty well both times, he thought, despite the odd bump in the road. Or, you know, bloody injury. But still...

Maybe I am cut out for this sort of thing, after all?

He quickly shoved that thought out of his mind. The adventuring life was much less enticing than his home and family—which, unless there'd been some major continental shift since he'd left Hablock, was pretty far from where he actually was right now.

'*Dammit!*' he cried out into the ocean.

The sea waved back at him.

Stupid waves. Stupid sand. Stupid...situation.

'Nick,' came a groggy voice from behind him. 'Keep it down. I heard you the first time.'

Swinging around, he saw his companion Shift emerge from some bushes at the edge of the beach and stumble toward him in a drunken fashion. As he watched, the form in which he knew them best rippled slightly before righting itself again. Shift was a shapeshifter who'd named themselves, very unimaginatively, after waking one day with no memory of life before that point. Evidently the trauma of being hurled to...wherever they were was making their ability misfire a little. He knew the feeling; his entire brain was misfiring.

Nicolas found himself running toward Shift, or trying to at least. The sand had other ideas, grappling with his feet constantly and pulling him back. Stubbornly, he continued toward his wide-eyed companion, but the sand had the last laugh as it suddenly sank back underfoot, causing him to fall forwards, half-hugging and half-clinging on to Shift. Thank the Deities he'd avoided—by the slightest of margins—ending up head-first in their cleavage. He was in enough trouble as it was.

'Always throwing yourself at me,' Shift tutted weakly. Still, they were teasing him. It was a good sign.

'You're here!' he cried giddily, using their shoulders to pull himself up so that they faced each other. He'd known that his four companions had chosen to come back home with him, albeit uninvited, but he'd no idea if they'd actually been brought here too. Knowing he wasn't going to be alone on this island made everything slightly less terrible. It was enough, for now.

'Yes.' Shift raised a quietening hand. 'And I have a mighty hangover from whatever method T'goth used to send us here, so if you could please talk more quietly I'd appreciate it.'

T'goth, who had a very strange way of showing gratitude to those who'd saved him from walking the earth as a demented old man for all eternity, had used magic to transport them here. It hadn't been a pleasant experience. Nicolas was sure some of his organs were in the wrong place, and the post teleportation vomiting had been nothing short of epic. Even now, he was still nauseated and dizzy, his limbs alternating between numb and tingly. He was desperate to sleep until he recovered, but he was also desperate not to have to sleep on this island.

'Yes, but you're here.' Though he could barely contain himself, he did manage to lower his voice. A little.

Shift took in their surroundings through half-open eyes. 'I take it from your panicked expression that this isn't your home?'

'No, it bloody isn't,' he replied irritably. 'I've no idea where T'goth's sent us. But now you're here, you can get us out of here.'

Rubbing their hand gently through their short auburn hair, his companion looked at him quizzically.

'You can turn into a bird and fly for help,' he suggested eagerly.

Shift raised an eyebrow, before making an elaborate show of looking at the vast ocean behind him. 'And in which direction would you like me to fly?' they asked soberly. 'We appear to be on an island, and unless you know for a fact which way the help is, I could end up flying until my wings tire and I drop right out of the sky.'

'Oh.' He hadn't thought of that. He'd been so excited to see someone and the hope of rescue that came with them that he hadn't thought over the practicalities. Was this definitely an island? How would he know for sure? He'd been too busy alternating between cursing with vomiting to actually explore the place.

'We are definitely on an island.'

The large green form of Garaz, their magical companion, emerged from the undergrowth. The orc, like Shift, looked worse for wear, his usually bright green skin a little duller than normal, almost grey. Knowing he wasn't the only one to have suffered badly from the way they'd been brought here was strangely comforting.

'I awoke in the bushes a way back. It was very disorientating,' the orc said as he approached, rubbing his head tenderly. A couple of stray leaves still hung from his red cloak. 'Fortunately, I heard you shouting and followed the sound.' Garaz held Nicolas's shoulders thankfully. Or was he just using him to remain upright?

At least the situation seemed to be improving by the moment. He'd been alone on the island, and now he had two of his closest friends for company, and again the glimmer of hope of actually getting off it.

'I don't suppose you have any direction-finding or *'call for help'* spells?' he ventured hopefully.

If he does, then he's in for the biggest hug in the history of Etherius.

'You suppose correctly,' Garaz confirmed, turning Nicolas's hopes to ash with just three words.

It'd been a long shot. The orc's speciality was healing magic with the odd fireball thrown in for self-defence. Better to ask and be sure, though.

A flash of blinding light interrupted their reunion, and a figure appeared directly between the trio, almost as bright as the light itself. Arms flailing in a desperate effort to somehow stave off the inevitable as he fell back, Nicolas landed in the sand with a bump. Bringing his hand up to shield his eyes from the bright light, he saw Garaz and Shift were also lying in the sand around him.

'Aaaaaaaaahhhhhhhhhhhh,' the figure was screaming a lot louder than he had as he'd fallen backwards. Was it a scream though, or a battle cry?

Either way, Nicolas reached for the sword on his belt, the *Dawn Blade*. As it turned out, trying to draw a sword when lying on the floor was somewhat tricky. Another adventurer lesson learned.

As the last traces of light faded, he saw a familiar ethereal form and breathed a huge sigh of relief.

Garaz was the first to speak as he picked himself up, brushing the sand from his red cloak and orange hair. 'Auron? *Auron?*'

'*Aaaaaaaaaaahhhhhhhhhhhhh.*'

The once legendary hero, who'd been recently deceased when Nicolas first met him, stood frozen on the spot—screaming—his fingers clenched and white pupiless eyes wide. The screaming got tiresome really quickly, especially with the state all their heads were in. Nicolas wished he could grab Auron and shake some sense into him, but his hands would pass straight through the light cloud that made up his form. Instead, he stood, brushing the sand from himself as quickly as he could and put himself right in front of his companion.

'Auron, it's me, Nicolas... *Kid*, remember?' he ventured.

Despite his attempt, the empty white eyes wouldn't focus on him, and all the noise the spirit was making made trying to talk difficult. Raising his voice would surely only add more kindling to his fiery headache.

'Let me try.' Shift shoved Nicolas aside. '*Auron? Auron?*' Shift tried to shout over the screaming.

Seeming to lose patience quickly, Shift threw a slap at Auron. Their hand passed directly through the spirit's chin, causing the smoking image to disperse, only to re-form a moment later. It did, however, have the desired effect.

'Okay...okay...' Auron muttered to himself as he looked around frantically, evidently trying to calm down and thankfully not screaming anymore.

When even the undead are panicked, it's really time to worry.

His heart rate jumped dramatically, but instead of giving into it, he copied Auron's method and talked himself down.

'Are we on an island?' the spirit asked finally, looking around with a furrowed brow.

'Yes,' Nicolas replied dryly.

'I thought you asked to get us sent back to Hablock, kid?' The tone was almost accusatory.

'I did,' he replied through gritted teeth.

Auron seemed to need a moment to take in this information properly. Slowly, the spirit walked up and down the beach, turning his head this way and that. Frustratingly, as he moved across the sand not a single grain of it stuck itself to his ethereal form, whereas Nicolas's ratio of sand-to-skin was pretty high right now, making him very uncomfortable.

How did it even get inside my clothes?

'So how are we getting off it then?' Auron asked, returning to the group.

'We were just working on that when you appeared out of nowhere and started screaming in our faces,' Shift replied tartly.

'I think I have an idea.'

Auron spun around, his face dropping to a scowl in an instant. 'Oh, you're alive then,' the spirit remarked coldly.

A lithe, muscular woman approached from the right of the group, wearing armour that could politely have been described as minimalist. The hard, emotionless eyes looked at them all like targets rather than the people she'd travelled and faced danger with. Silva Destrone had been the one responsible for making Auron a ghost—though no one used that word around him—by use of a crossbow while the latter answered a call of nature. She'd also attempted to kill Nicolas several times and Garaz and Shift at least once each, as well as kidnapping them both for a necromancer and his vampiric allies.

However, being thrown into a river wearing the ridiculously over-the-top armour she wore back then had caused a near-death ex-perience, from which she'd emerged with a desire to atone for her past sins. And wear lighter gear. She'd designated Nicolas her role model, seeing as he was responsible for her defeat and therefore her rebirth, and had insisted on joining their party. To say that had caused some friction would be massively understating it, but she'd taken a crossbow bolt meant for Nicolas, which had gone some way to smoothing things over. The scar was still prominent above her right breast. Had it not been for Garaz's ministrations, she wouldn't have been here now, a testament to the orc's skill as a healer. Eventually, Silva had summoned the courage to apologise to Auron, which he'd grudgingly accepted. Or had he? His reaction to her suggested otherwise.

'There's a ship anchored just beyond that treeline,' Silva stated simply without greeting, completely true to form and evidently less affected by their mode of travel than the rest of the group.

Still has sand all over her, though.

Reflecting the big smiles that his other companions, save Silva, now wore, Nicolas ran in the direction the warrior indicated.

They were saved.

****

Following the shoreline, the former mercenary was soon proven cor-rect. Just off the island was a ship, a single-masted vessel that looked dark and old, but there were signs of life on her decks, which meant potential salvation. Even better, there was a rowboat heading away from the island. All they needed to do now was get noticed.

Grabbing the biggest leaves they could find, the group waved and shouted desperately. They were definitely noticed. The rowboat stopped, rising and dipping idly in the water as they ran closer to it. Though it looked too far out to wade to, they could probably swim to it, but Nicolas would rather introduce himself properly before just swimming up to someone's boat, no matter how dire their situation. It only took a moment to be polite.

Cupping his hands over his eyes to keep out the worst of the sun's glare, he looked at the occupants of the boat. They didn't look...savoury. The man manning the oars had a dastardly look to him and the big fellow sat at the fore of the boat looked like an angry ape that someone had shaved and dressed. The man-ape glowered at the group as a figure at the back of the boat stood and waved to them. He was probably about Nicolas's height and build, with short curly hair from which two short horns emerged. That wasn't the only sign he wasn't human. The pointed ears and goat legs were a dead giveaway. Beside him sat a small toadlike creature who regarded them through narrowed eyes.

There was something about them that Nicolas just didn't like, but he chided himself. Who was he to judge anyone? He'd never seen seamen before. Maybe they all looked like this.

'What race is that?' he asked.

'It's a faun,' Shift replied. 'Amiable folk so I'm told.'

'You two should get along fine then.' Auron chuckled.

'Ahoy there,' the faun shouted through cupped hands.

'Um...ahoy,' Nicolas shouted back, wanting to get off on the right foot with these people. 'My name is Nicolas Percival Carnegie. Nice to meet you.'

'Nick would've done,' Shift whispered, mocking his usual, formal greeting, before shouting *'Nick'll do,'* toward the faun.

'I can't hear you very well,' the faun replied with a shout. 'Did you say *Nick Carnage?'*

That name. That bloody name. It seemed to hound him wherever he went. Maybe he should just take the *'real adventurer name,'* as Auron put it, and make everyone happy.

No. Never.

'Just Nick will do,' he shouted back. Going to the trouble of correcting the faun at this distance was a waste of time, but he made sure he glared at Shift as thanks for their input. They seemed eminently pleased with their nonsense.

'Nice to meet you,' the faun replied, not introducing himself in return. 'Are you stranded?'

'Yes, yes, we are!' he shouted back. It hadn't been formally decided that he'd be the spokesperson for the group, but as Auron suggested, he was the most amiable, which meant he was the least threatening and therefore the one most likely to achieve them a lift from this cursed island.

'How?' the faun shouted.

'What?' he asked, his throat, already sore from the sickness, burning with each shouted word.

'How did you get stranded?'

Nicolas thought better of trying to explain that a Deity had sent them here after they'd restored his power from those who'd stolen it because it sounded...well, crazy. It certainly had been crazy. It was also too long-winded to shout. His headache was already raging anew from the volume of his own voice.

'Shipwreck,' he replied simply.

'Bad luck,' the faun shouted back. 'Bit of an odd collection of you.'

'Yeah.' True enough they were a strange group of travelling companions, but the conversation was getting a little off topic. 'I don't suppose you could give us a lift, please?' he asked, deciding to be more direct.

'No,' came the immediate answer.

Well, he hadn't expected that, not even slightly. Even for someone who liked to play out every eventuality of an action in his head before he took it, this surprised him. 'Well...why not?'

'Because I don't want to,' the faun answered, slightly smugly.

'What in the Underworld does he mean *I don't want to*?' Shift cried in disgust.

Nicolas posed the question.

'It's a pretty simple concept, boy,' came the snarky reply. 'I'm sure you can work it out.'

'But we are stranded and require aid,' Garaz interjected, obviously feeling that Nicolas needed some support.

As Nicolas watched, the faun simply shrugged. 'So?' he shouted back.

'Why stop to talk to us at all if you didn't want to help?' Shift shouted, their tone venomous.

'Because I wanted to see if you had an interesting story,' the faun replied. 'And I think that watching your faces as I row away will just be really funny.'

'You dirty troll's ass,' Nicolas roared, overcome by anger at the smug expression on the faun's face. 'You can't just leave us here!'

'I respectfully disagree.'

Shift then levelled a stream of curses at the faun that made Nicolas wince.

The faun only laughed them off. 'I may be most of those things,' he shouted back. 'But do you know what else I am...? I'm eating a proper meal tonight. Enjoy your coconuts.'

With that, the faun clicked his fingers and the rowboat continued towards the ship. The faun, good as his word, stayed standing to watch the expressions of those he was leaving behind. Shift had apparently decided that the most productive thing to do would be to throw any nearby rock at the boat, but they all fell short and only added to the creature's amusement.

This can't be happening. How could he just leave us here, maybe to die?

No, it *wasn't* happening. He wouldn't let it. Nicolas found himself making a run for the rowboat, unsure what he would do if he caught it but determined to try anyway.

Wading into the cold water was all well and good until the icy water touched his quickly retracting tenders. Shivering, he pushed on a few more steps then stopped. The boat was even further away. He'd never catch it; his only achievement had been to get soaking wet and freezing cold, much to the faun's amusement.

'You can't just leave us here,' Nicolas pleaded. 'You can't. Come back.'

The faun pretended he couldn't hear them, putting his hand to his ear theatrically and shaking his head.

Losing his battle against the tide, Nicolas was washed back to shore coughing and spluttering. Garaz helped him to his feet as Nicolas incredulously watched the occupants of the rowboat board their ship again, half angry and half in shock.

'I'm going to say it here and now,' Auron said, glowering at the still-waving faun. 'That's a bad guy if ever I saw one.'

'I'll kill him,' Nicolas cried, his anger overcoming him. 'I'll kill that damned faun.'

'Of course you will.' Shift didn't sound convinced.

'Who just leaves people stranded on an island?' he muttered in disbelief. 'I'll kill him.'

'Of course you will, kid.' Auron echoed Shift's tone perfectly.

Not ten minutes later, the ship had already weighed anchor and was making sail. Twenty minutes after that, it was a speck on the horizon. Nicolas could've sworn he could still hear the faun laughing at them.

CHAPTER 2

*H*ow long have I been staring at the horizon?

The ship was long gone and obviously had no intention of returning. The hope that leaving them had been a poor jest faded into nothing. Looking out at the clear blue sea before him, it became doubtful they had any other hope either. What sort of person left people stranded on an island?

Scum.

Nicolas hoped he'd have a chance to pay the faun back, though it was unlikely their paths would ever cross again.

'So, what do we do now?' he asked nervously.

'Survive.' Easy for Auron to say; he wasn't going to die a second time.

'Fantastic.' Nicolas sighed, removing his shirt in an attempt to cool down in the oppressive heat. The sun glaring on his bare skin made him instantly regret it. 'I was hoping for a bit more of a structured plan.'

The spirit shrugged.

Shift screwed up their face as they looked at him. 'I tell you what I'm not going to do,' they declared. 'Look directly at that pale body of yours. The sun reflecting off it might blind me. Try some chest hair, maybe?'

Nicolas did a faux laugh. Trying not to make it obvious, he folded his arms to cover his chest. 'Great,' he muttered angrily. 'I'm stuck on an island in the middle of nowhere with the funniest person in *all* Etherius.'

'Why thank you.' Shift bowed, only frustrating him further.

'Stupid Deity can't even send people to the right damned place.' Nicolas kicked the sand, sending a cloud of it into the air, some of which blew back on him. Much more went in his boot.

He was about to cry out in annoyance, but stopped dead as he saw Silva watching him with narrowed eyes, head shaking slightly. 'Acting like a pouty child is not constructive,' she chided. 'We need to focus on finding what we need to make a decent camp; a water source, shelter and food.'

True. This isn't my finest hour.

Nicolas dropped his gaze to the sand, looking at the furrow in it made by his kick. Attempting to beat the island into submission would solve nothing. It certainly wouldn't help them survive. *But why do we have to? Why are we even stuck here?*

The frustration was so hard to contain. 'I don't like the sand. It's...annoying,' he cried, only coming up with the words *coarse* and *rough* once he'd failed to properly explain himself. If only T'goth and that stupid faun were here to answer for this then maybe he'd get some satisfaction and not have to resort to kicking sand.

They aren't here. You are. And this isn't helping.

Exhaling deeply, he tried to regain his composure.

'Look, kid.' It was harder than usual to look directly at Auron in the bright sun. 'This is a bad situation, but it isn't going to magically change, so we need to make the best of it.'

'We haven't even properly explored yet. Who knows what we will find,' Silva added. 'There is obviously a river of some sort, so we have water and vegetation. I believe we can survive here for a good long while if needs must.'

'Yeah.' Shift grinned in the way they did just before a snarky comment. 'Give us a week, and we'll have houses and roads and our own currency. I'll give you six bark shavings and two leaves if you put your shirt back on, Nick.'

Before another jibe came his way, he dressed himself again. Though he was more interested in leaving the island than colonising it, at least they had Silva and Auron with them. Their combined experience was much more valuable than any leaf and bark shaving based currency.

Auron looked over Nicolas's shoulder. 'What's he doing?'

Turning, he was surprised to find that Garaz wasn't stood with them any more. Instead, the orc was some way from the group, squatting in the sand.

'If you're answering the call of nature, big guy, then we'd all much prefer it if you went in the undergrowth,' Shift shouted over to the orc.

'I am doing no such thing,' Garaz replied with a distasteful glance. 'I was wondering why that ship anchored here in the first place. As picturesque as this place is, it is also quite unremarkable. They must have been here for a reason, so I intend to follow these tracks.'

Curiosity piqued, Nicolas and his companions went to the orc, who agitatedly gestured for them to slow as they disturbed the sand around him, with the exception of Auron. Sure enough, there were tracks in the sand—several pairs of booted feet and an imprint that was clearly made by hooves. In fact, there were two sets of tracks, one leading into the undergrowth and one leading out again, with a big displacement of sand where the boat had come ashore. Looking towards the large leaves that separated the beach from the jungle environment beyond, Nicolas began to wonder what could've prompted their visit. Maybe the faun had some form of summer accommodation here, complete with stocked larder and a handy scroll containing a magic spell to get them home.

Or maybe the sun is boiling my brain.

'Well, let's see what that little horned asshole was here for, shall we?' Auron said, walking towards the jungle and vanishing through the leaves.

****

The island wasn't large, so it didn't take long for the group to come across the one actual point of interest on it.

Nicolas pushed the last of the foliage out of the way and came to a sudden stop. 'Woah.'

Before the group, at what he guessed was roughly the centre of the island, was a large lake. Though it was surrounded by picturesque jungle and a rushing waterfall, the most remarkable thing about this lake was the giant shipwreck that occupied it. Whatever type of vessel it was—they were all just *ships* to him—it must've looked majestic in its heyday. Now, though, it was a pile of broken wood listing drunkenly aground; it's once proud masts were cracked stumps and regal sails were torn and shredded. There were indents along the side of the ship, like it had been crushed from the outside. The crew was spread across the bank and appeared to have been dead for quite some time.

'Must've been a skeleton crew.' Shift smirked as they stood beside Nicolas and took in the scene.

'Really?' he asked incredulously. 'They're all dead and you're going to make jokes?'

Shift's face became serious for a moment. 'To be honest, this is all pretty unsettling,' they whispered.

For a moment, Nicolas was taken aback by their honesty. Vulnerable wasn't a side of Shift he was used to seeing. Or knew existed. They offered him a thin smile. He supposed it was easy to forget his companions might also be affected by things like this. To him, they all seemed wiser and more experienced, so it didn't often occur to him they would be bothered by things, or scared, or unsure. For a moment, he held their green eyes, about to respond, until Auron called to them from the bank.

'I think this ship only had a skeleton crew.' The ethereal grin accompanying the jest was wide.

Nicolas rolled his eyes and Shift guffawed, adding to Auron's self-satisfaction.

The drop to the bank was quite steep and the footing unsure. Nicolas used trees and vines as handholds while tensing in preparation for a fall.

There was none, and he finally reached Auron, along with the rest of their party. Silva had drawn her sword, presumably as a precaution since Silva liked to draw her sword if someone sneezed too loud. Always respectful of the need for precautions, he drew his sword too.

The *Dawn Blade*, the sword Auron had passed on to Nicolas, was reassuring in his hand. The blade itself was unique in that it was perfectly reflective, like a mirror. That came in handy for moments like, for example, needing to steel himself to board a shipwreck. The face looking back at him nodded confidently, confirming that he was ready for this. He wished he was as confident as his reflection.

Auron surveyed the ship, looking for the easiest point to board. 'Let's have a look around.'

'Are you sure that's wise?' Nicolas cast his own eye over the worn wood and the way the ship listed. 'It doesn't look structurally sound to me.'

'Find your courage, kid,' was the sum of Auron's sage-like wisdom on the matter.

Carefully, the group boarded the ship. He tried not to wince at every creak of wood underfoot and was probably successful at least half the time. Finding footing on the angled deck was tricky, but not impossible, and leaning into the ascent made it easier to walk. Spreading out, the group began to search the deck for...anything, really.

'Over here.' Garaz caught the group's attention after several minutes of searching.

An errant slip would likely end up with him in the water, so he moved carefully and was the last of the party to reach Garaz. In his large green hand was the tattered remnants of a flag, with what had once been an orange griffin sewn onto it in intricate stitches.

'Is that not the heraldry of the Kingdom of Sarus?' Silva asked.

Garaz nodded in response before appearing to mull something over for a moment. 'I believe this may be King Ragus's ship.' The orc's tone was as grim as his words.

King Ragus had been ruler of the Kingdom of Sarus before Silus the Unwilling. They'd met the latter after he'd been turned into a chicken by a disgruntled gangster as part of plot by his own High Chancellor and parties unknown to assassinate him. Silus had been a reluctant king—hence the moniker—forced into power after Ragus and his family had been lost at sea in a storm while on a diplomatic mission. Looked like they weren't lost anymore.

'They must've been looting the ship.' Shift looked more disgusted than he'd ever seen them. 'I heard there's a special room in the Underworld where graverobbers are tortured by the spirits of those they've stolen from.'

Nicolas suppressed a slight gulp as he looked at the sword in his hand. It'd belonged to someone who was dead. Did that make him a graverobber?

No, it can't count when the dead person actually says you can have it.

Or maybe that was the reason Auron was haunting him? Was the spirit's unfinished business—which was less clear cut than any of them had first believed—to retrieve the sword from Nicolas's dead hands one day? That sounded preposterous. And yet, he carefully slid the sword back into its sheath, wiping his hand on his jacket as if that would remove any stain from his soul. If it were as easy as that, Silva wouldn't be following them around to atone for past misdeeds.

'Reminds me of the time I fought the *Ghoul of Nareth*,' Auron began, breaking into one of the tales of his exploits he so liked to tell. 'So this one time, I was hired by the local priesthood because something was murdering people in a four-village radius. Judging by the way it'd messed up the victims, it was clearly some kind of monster, which was why no one else wanted to touch it. I guessed it was a ghoul. The problem was that there was a lot of territory to cover and no real clue where this thing came from.' Pause for dramatic effect. 'Lesser heroes might've wandered the countryside for weeks and found nothing. Not me. Once I heard of another murder I made haste to the village, hid in the victim's coffin and waited. The look on the stupid thing's face when it opened the coffin expecting to see some half-eaten old lady only for me to jump out screaming *'surprise'* and stabbing my sword into it's gut was priceless.'

'How did you know to wait in a coffin?' Shift asked, looking a little disgusted.

'Little known fact about ghouls is that decayed bone marrow is an exquisite delicacy to them,' the spirit replied.

Shift looked sorry they'd asked.

Nicolas thought about that story for a moment. 'Hang on.' He wasn't sure he wanted the answer, but curiosity got the better of him. 'If you got in the coffin, what did you do with the body that was already in there?' The spirit replied with a look that suggested Nicolas didn't want to know.

'And what if one of the victim's family members opened it to pay their respects?' he continued. 'Poor Uncle Galbert gets stabbed by mistake?'

'It's all about reflexes.' Auron smiled.

'I think maybe we ought to search belowdecks.' Garaz obviously wanted to get back to more immediate concerns.

****

Being inside the ship was far worse than being on deck. Instead of the rickety wood being underfoot it was now all around them, threatening to collapse at any second, and it was dark enough that they couldn't see far in front of them, save for the odd, fortuitous beam of light from between the broken hull planks. Each creak seemed to echo down every corridor of the ship, promising to wake the dead crew laid throughout them at any moment. There was, however, something worse than the idea of the ground collapsing underfoot or the claustrophobia. It was the smell. Damp rotten wood had combined with the reek of decay, creating a combined stench that couldn't be held back by putting his hand over his mouth.

As much as he tried not to look at the rotting bodies he was stepping over and around, occasionally he had to. Empty eye sockets stared back at him from melted-looking green flesh with flashes of exposed bone. Debris littered the corridors, old crates and broken furniture impeding their progress. It would've been treacherous without the light from Auron's aura. Still, there were too many shadows, many of which were occupied by creatures that had chosen to make this place their habitat. Nicolas had no experience with crabs, but he really wanted to avoid offending anything with pincers that big.

'The storm really did a number on this ship.' Auron ran his hand along the interior of the ship, though he was unable to physically touch the wood itself.

Why the sceptical tone? It had to have been a storm, right?

'And the poor souls upon it,' Garaz added sombrely.

The orc had mouthed a prayer for each of the departed bodies they passed. Judging by the limbs at wrong angles and skulls caved in by heavy blows, their end must've been violent. Hopefully, it had at least been quick. Lying broken on the floor of a wrecked ship, dying slowly, was no way to go. He also began to murmur small prayers for them, wishing their souls peace in the afterlife.

Reaching the aft of the ship, the group came to a pair of thick wooden doors, covered in an overabundance of gold trimming and the heraldry of the Kingdom of Sarus. One of the doors was closed while the other hung limply on its final hinge. Beyond it appeared to be a large stateroom.

'If we're looking for a king, that'd be the place.' Shift's face, illuminated by what light was available, looked as sombre as the rest of them. This was no place for jests.

He'd expected to find the same chaos in the stateroom as in the rest of the ship, but the tables and chairs were in the same place he assumed they'd always been. An ornate table dominated the room, with other items strewn around it, thanks to the storm. Seeing it stand firm amidst the chaos was strangely disconcerting.

'They must've invested in better screws for the king's room,' he muttered, more for the sake of hearing something in the deathly quiet room than his need to share his opinion on the fixtures and fittings.

Around the table sat six chairs, four of which were occupied by rotted, skeletal figures shrouded in the tattered remnants of what once had been fine clothing.

'How are they still upright?' Shift asked.

Auron strode up to the corpses and began to examine them. His mouth curled into a grimace. 'They didn't have a choice.'

The others approached the corpses, but Nicolas hung back; this was as close as he was happy to get to anything dead, given the choice. In his short time adventuring, albeit against his will, he'd seen far too many dead bodies. It wasn't something he wanted to ever get used to.

'They were tied down,' Garaz noted as he inspected the chairs in which the figures sat. 'How odd.'

'Maybe to stop them being thrown around in the storm?' Silva suggested.

That sounded reasonable enough; it may have been the only way to ensure their safety as the sea tossed the ship here and there. Yet Nicolas knew it wasn't right.

'That doesn't explain the knife wounds in their chests,' Garaz added ominously.

'Kid, come over here,' Auron called, drawing everyone's attention to the fact that he was hanging back beside the door.

'I'm okay, thanks,' he replied awkwardly.

Auron huffed and rubbed the bridge of his nose with his spectral fingertips. 'Seriously, kid.' The spirit exhaled in the manner a frustrated father trying not to raise his voice might. 'All you've seen and you're still squeamish. You've killed people.'

'I most certainly have not,' Nicolas protested.

'What?' Shift exclaimed. 'I've seen you kill, like, twenty guys at once.'

'That wasn't me,' he retorted. 'Auron was possessing me at the time.'

When the mercenaries under the command of the necromancer attacked, Auron had taken the reins and used his skill to best them. So, Nicolas hadn't killed anyone. He'd been complicit in Silva's death, but she hadn't actually died. He'd beheaded a vampire once, but since, technically, it was already dead, that, too, didn't count.

I don't care how bad any of them were, I'm no killer. I can't be. It's not in my nature. I'm just not capable.

Breathing deeply, he knew he didn't have to justify himself. He was still the same Nicolas who'd left Hablock to deliver a message. These adventures weren't changing him, he wouldn't allow it.

'Fine, whatever.' Shift made a big show of rolling their eyes.

'Just get over here,' Auron repeated sternly, and Nicolas dredged his dubious reserve of courage to get closer to the bodies.

Eyeing the corpses warily, he inched towards them. The one at the head of the table was clearly the king, though his crown was gone, leaving only an imprint in the dead flesh. The king's clothes had been grand and regal, no amount of rotting or tearing could completely disguise that. To his right sat a woman in what had once been an ornate gown—presumably the queen. The other two, who Nicolas struggled to look at more than the adults, were children. The eyes of each hollow skull still somehow appeared to look pleadingly at him, begging for salvation.

How can someone so young die so suddenly and violently?

'So why do you stab someone who's already died in a shipwreck?' Shift asked leadingly.

'You don't,' Silva replied simply.

Shift rolled their eyes again but seemed to decide against explaining themselves to the warrior.

'These wounds were most certainly what killed them all.' Garaz stood, his examination finished. 'The royal family was murdered then the ship wrecked to make it appear as if they were lost at sea.'

'Where have we heard that before?' Auron's jaw was set, his white eyes blazing.

'It would appear we are stumbling into a far-reaching conspiracy here.' Garaz's yellow eyes were troubled.

There was an undeniable pattern to recent events. A necromancer makes a deal with vampires that leads to the death of the entire Yarringsburg royal family. A dwarf gangster attempts to assassinate the king on the orders of the High Chancellor. Something bigger was brewing, and Nicolas had no wish to meet whoever the brewer was.

How did the assassin even get to the king? He must've had bodyguards?

'But who? Why?' he asked.

'I think the who is pretty clear.' Shift was staring at the bodies of the children. Nicolas thought he caught a glint of light from a tear on their cheek. 'We met him leaving the island.'

Auron had been right; the faun was a bad guy. Nicolas had known he was an jackass of the highest quality, but this was something else. Yet the evidence was clear. You don't just turn up at a random island and accidentally find a ship wrecked to cover an assassination. Actually, that was exactly what they'd done...but that wasn't the point. The faun was behind this. Remembering the guy's smug smile made Nicolas's blood boil.

'But they were only just here, and these bodies are months old,' Nicolas said.

'There must be a reason for their return,' Garaz suggested. 'Though I cannot fathom it now.'

'I'm sure the king had a crown on his head just recently,' Shift said, noting the same thing Nicolas had.

'But to come back just to take a crown...'

'Who knows the motivations of villains,' Auron added bitterly. 'I'm more concerned with who's behind them. Neither the faun nor that giant with him seem the master planning types. I assume whoever it was that wanted the High Chancellor in charge arranged this. But then why let Silus take power to kill him anyway?'

'You don't think the High Chancellor was behind it all?' Silva asked.

'Maybe,' Auron replied, still glaring slightly at the warrior who'd killed him but keeping his revenge urges in check. 'But my hero instincts don't like it, and they're rarely wrong.'

Lack of modesty aside, Nicolas was happy to bow to Auron's wisdom on such matters.

'Are there any, you know, ghosts around that we could ask?' Nicolas nodded toward the corpses.

Auron bristled slightly at the use of the g-word before replying. 'That would be bloody handy, but no. Sorry, kid.'

'The best person to question would be the faun,' Garaz said.

'Which does us no good at all because we're stuck on this island.' In all the exploring of the ship he'd forgotten that terrible truth. 'We can't do anything with the information, as much as I'd like to bring that scum to justice.'

'Maybe kick him a few times for good measure,' Shift added, which he totally supported.

'So what do we do?' Nicolas asked.

'For now, we just survive and hope for some good luck.' Auron shrugged.

'Better luck than these guys anyway.' Shift patted the king on his dead shoulder.

The king's head lolled drunkenly to the side before falling off completely, hitting the deck with a hollow thud.

Shift looked shocked and more than a little embarrassed.

Nicolas threw up.

'We must be on another adventure.' Auron shook his head in bemusement. 'The kid's been sick again.'

It was true. Losing the contents of his stomach during an adventure was becoming a habit for him.

CHAPTER 3

Nicolas was rubbing his burning throat to try to somehow alleviate the pain when the hairs on his arms stood on end. Something was very wrong, and he didn't know what. His companions were looking around warily, so it wasn't just him who sensed it. It was as if, despite the light, the shadows were closing in on them. The darkness was getting…darker, if that made any sense.

Well, that's something to worry about.

The doors trembled suddenly as a gust of foul-smelling air blew through them, making Nicolas jump back and sending a shiver up his spine. Quickly, he drew his sword.

'There was no wind outside.' Garaz's words made his stomach knot.

It hadn't seemed like wind at all; more like an outraged gasp that had swept through the ship. He prayed to every Deity individually that it had nothing to do with Shift knocking the king's head off.

At his side, Silva eyed the door cautiously. 'I think we might be in trouble.'

Suddenly, Nicolas became aware of movement inside the room. There was a rubbing sound, and it was coming from the table behind him. Slowly, he turned. The wrists of one of the things that used to be a child ground against the ropes that bound them. With a cricking of bones that hadn't moved for some time, the head rose and let out an anguished moan.

Fear paralysed him as the creature examined the bonds that held it before renewing its struggle against them. The wrists gave out first, the mushy skin sawn through by the rope, cutting both the creature's hands from its arms as it moaned again. By now, the others at the table had begun to move. Even the king's head, discarded on the floor, opened its black-toothed mouth and cried out.

'We need to leave, now!' Silva, thankfully, put herself between the group and the animated corpses.

Keeping his eyes on the creatures as they rose from their chairs and shambled in their general direction, Nicolas used his hands to feel his way past the door and out of the room. Once out his eyes drifted down one of the dark corridors. All of them were filled with the dead. As if on cue, a low groaning sound emanated from the shadows. Soon others joined it. Each groan made his heart rate jump another notch.

Frantically, he looked around. 'We have to get out of here.'

'And here was the rest of us wanting to stay with the zombies,' Shift muttered in annoyance.

Zombies. The word alone was bad enough. First ghosts, then vampires, now zombies.

Am I cursed to meet every single form of undead creature that roams Etherius? When did things just stop staying dead? When was that decision made?

He briefly considered going to the shrine of Sha'then to suggest that the Lord of the Underworld learn to keep his dead where they belonged. Respectfully, of course.

But they had more immediate concerns.

Silva and Garaz hauled the heavy door to the king's chamber back into place, securing a barrel in front of it. By now, the groaning had become the sound of shuffling movement, which echoed down the ship's halls, making it impossible to pinpoint. They could've been at the other end of the ship or right on top of them.

Nicolas's intuition gave him a split-second warning to turn. As he did, he thankfully brought the sword up, the tip of the blade piercing the skin of the advancing zombie. The creature kept coming, dragging its ruined body forward, further onto the blade, like it didn't even notice the sword in its stomach. The creature's rotten jaw opened in anticipation.

'Duck.'

Nicolas dropped, and Silva's blade sailed over him, taking the zombie's head clean from the neck. The creature fell but stubbornly kept hold of Nicolas's sword. He tugged, but the blade seemed intertwined with some rotting organs. Putting his foot to the corpse, Nicolas gave a last heave and the sword wrenched free with a wet shucking sound and blast of decay that sent him reeling. Fighting back the nausea, his eyes widened as he saw, to his horror, that the creature still wasn't dead. Its body turned and crawled to its removed head. Gracelessly, Nicolas hacked the remaining four limbs from it. Still, the creature twitched.

'They are not dying easily,' Garaz remarked.

'Hence them being here at all,' Shift replied, taking the head from their own attacker and cutting it in two before kicking the body away.

'If we don't move, they'll overwhelm us.' Auron was peering down the corridor, excellent night vision seeming to be one of the few boons of being a spirit. Thankfully, he wasn't putting an exact number to what he saw. Nicolas would rather not know precisely how much peril he was in. Just knowing he was in peril was enough.

'Everybody look away.'

Nicolas turned just in time to avoid the flash from Garaz's staff. As he looked back, the fireball shot down the corridor, casting light in the darkness. Deities, there were a lot of them, looking more terrible as the yellow light of the fire picked out the details of their gross, decaying bodies. Where the fireball touched zombie flesh, it set them alight. Apparently, zombies were as flammable as vampires. The difference between the two species was that the zombies kept coming, immune to the pain of their burning forms as they moved toward their prey.

With scratching on the far side of the door to the king's chamber, the group moved quickly down a side corridor, Garaz in the lead and Silva bringing up the rear.

'I am going to apologise for this now.' Shift kept their sword in front of them, looking towards the shadows. 'I'll probably forget later when we're all exhausted on the riverbank after escaping the ship.'

'I wish some of your optimism would rub off on me,' Nicolas muttered.

Shift turned and gave him that twinkle-eyed expression Nicolas had come to expect just before some jest at his expense. 'Attacked by zombies, and all you can think about is rubbing on me. I do declare, Mr Carnegie, you have a one-track mind.'

At least they'd used his proper last name and not *Carnage* as everyone seemed intent on doing. Still, he found himself flushing slightly at the...image...their words conjured.

'This is neither the time nor place,' Silva scolded harshly. She wasn't wrong.

Traversing the oppressive darkness was difficult even with the light they had. The zombies were everywhere and nowhere at the same time. Every so often, one would emerge from the darkness only to be quickly sent back there by Silva or Garaz. As it turned out, Garaz's new staff, a gift from T'goth designed to help channel his magic, also made a handy club.

One of the worst things about the creatures, despite the obvious rotting bodies, were their expressionless faces. Empty eyes stared directly ahead as jaws opened and closed slowly at the promise of food to come, though there was no emotion behind them, no life. They were empty carcasses looking to feed. Thinking of himself as zombie food made an icy claw of fear run its fingers down his back.

'Ahhh.' Nicolas flinched at Shift's sudden cry.

Just in front of him, a decayed hand had grabbed Shift's wrist from an unseen opening in the corridor, already pulling his companion's arm toward the waiting hungry maw. With speed that impressed even him, Nicolas flashed forward with his blade, taking the zombie's own hand off at the wrist. As Nicolas kicked the creature backwards and secured the door to the room it had appeared from, Shift picked the clenched fingers from their wrist, looking in any direction other than at the dead hand.

Finally, it fell to the floor, and Shift kicked it away in disgust. 'I am not being zombie food.'

'You won't have to be.' Auron's tone gave Nicolas hope. 'I see light ahead.'

Emerging into a large cargo hold, there was a hatch at the top of a set of stairs, through the cracks of which shafts of light emerged. However, several of the crew were waiting, cutting off their hope of escape. Silva, Garaz, and Shift spread out to dispatch the creatures. Nicolas was about to join them when a hand grabbed his shoulder. The grip was surprisingly fierce for something so lifeless.

'It's okay, kid,' Auron cried as he charged past Nicolas, 'I've got it.'

The spirit's punch sailed toward, and then through, the zombie's head. Auron looked at his returning fist in confusion and then shame. Apparently, even he sometimes forgot he was dead. That did not, however, solve the immediate problem.

As the zombie pulled Nicolas toward him, he was at the wrong angle to bring his sword to bear. Instead, he took Auron's cue and threw a punch at the zombie, which sailed toward, and then through, the zombie's head. Nicolas retched as his fist was engulfed in wet...stuff, his wrist seeming to end where the zombie's head began.

'Let go!' he cried as he frantically attempted to pull his hand back. But it was stuck in what was left of the zombie's brain, making a disgusting sucking noise with every attempt to pull it out. The creature fell to its knees, threatening to pull Nicolas with it. That would be very bad, considering he could hear more shuffling nearby.

Using his foot to brace against the creature, he both pushed and pulled. For a few seconds, the hand didn't budge...then it came away suddenly, making him stumble backward. Flailing, Nicolas managed to bump into a heavy barrel, the only thing that stopped him from falling to the floor completely.

'Nick, this way.'

Looking at Shift, Nicolas found himself alone. Not only had the others cleared the zombies, but they were also all nearly up the stairs. Following them quickly but carefully, more walking corpses on his heels, he climbed the stairs towards the light and safety, keeping his fist as far away from himself as possible until he could wash the decayed goo from it.

It took several of them to close the large hatch over the opening. Silva would've been handy for that, but she was busy dispatching the zombies on the deck. The heavy thud when it did close was very reassuring. But Nicolas wasn't about to give into relief completely until they were off this cursed boat.

Gathering momentum, Nicolas ran down the sloping deck until he reached the edge then threw himself from it onto the bank. The ground came up quickly toward him and his roll was poor, winding him slightly. Still better than being eaten.

'We're alive!' Nicolas cried as he rose triumphantly after taking a few moments to recover. Urgently, he checked himself over, running his hands over his face and body to ensure he was correct. He only remembered that one hand was covered in zombie remnants after he'd slimed his face with the goo. Quickly, he ran to the river and submerged his face in the cool water, determined not to bring it out again until he was sure he was clean. When he did, Auron was watching him in amusement.

A groan to their left suggested that they maybe weren't as safe as he'd hoped. Several of the damned crew that had been thrown clear when the ship struck the bank were advancing on them hungrily.

'Let us finish this.' Silva advanced on the creatures with a lot more relish than Nicolas had for it.

But they could hardly just leave them wandering around out here.

CHAPTER 4

E xhausted, Nicolas sat with his companions and watched the ship burn. The spike of adrenaline had receded, leaving only the pains of the effort expended to survive. Luckily, none of them had been hurt. Once the zombies wandering the bank had been dealt with, Garaz had used his magic to set the wrecked ship ablaze, turning it into a giant funeral pyre that billowed black smoke into the sky and gave off an almost oppressive heat. Though the zombies could initially shrug off being set aflame, fire consumed their dead bodies as much as it did anything else. Whilst the inferno raged, they said a few words for the fallen—it seemed only fitting.

Those poor souls. Not only had they suffered a violent death, but they'd been doomed to rise again. They didn't deserve it. Were there glimmers of their former selves in those shuffling carcasses? Had the men they'd once been known what they were doing without being able to stop themselves? Nicolas had experienced that once, when Auron had possessed him to dispatch a group of mercenaries. He hadn't cared for it, effective though the strategy had proven. But to be completely trapped in your own rotting body...What a terrible fate to suffer. Hopefully they had peace now.

Auron stood beside him, looking toward the burning ship, his face sad. 'Are you okay?'

The spirit took a second to respond. 'Warrior funerals bring back some bad memories.'

Of course. Why hadn't he thought of that? He'd been the one to put Auron's physical remains atop a pyre and set it alight. He had no clue what to say, so he simply offered his companion a sympathetic smile.

'That escalated quickly.' Auron shook his head in disbelief as he watched the vessel burn, opting to change the subject. 'You guys are lucky to be alive.'

Nicolas looked to the single reason for their luck, Silva. 'It would've been a lot different without her.' Catching sight of Garaz in his peripheral vision he hastily added, 'And without some amazing fire magic, of course.'

Silva looked at him from the corner of her eye but didn't respond. He hadn't expected her to. When he looked back at Auron, the spirit's mouth was a thin line.

'I know I've already apologised.' Shift seemed uncomfortable as they spoke. 'But I feel like I ought to again. That was kind of my fault.'

Interesting use of the term *'kind of.'*

'Don't worry about it.' Nicolas smiled warmly at his companion. 'I've done some daft things. You've been there for most of them.'

Shift laughed and shook their head. 'You're such a gentleman, Nick. I would not be letting you live it down so easily.'

'Lucky for me, none of them have ever been as stupid as raising a zombie army.'

Shift looked at him wide-eyed. 'Perhaps I *am* rubbing off on you, after all.'

'Oh, you wish you—'

'Will you two behave.'

Nicolas wasn't sure what was more surprising, the interruption or the fact that both Auron and Silva had said it at the same moment. The spirit looked at the warrior irritably, but Silva looked away. She clearly still carried plenty of guilt for what she'd done, as she ought to.

Auron instead turned his attention to their orc companion. 'Garaz. Zombies rose. Explain.'

The orc, who'd been thoughtfully studying the ship until now, seemed slightly irked by the curt tone but didn't mention it. 'It is very interesting.' Garaz's face took on the frustrated expression it often did when he didn't know the exact answer to a question or riddle. 'The most obvious answer would be a curse. I saw no evidence of one, but it is not something I am vastly experienced in. Maybe they...' Garaz seemed hesitant to continue. '...just didn't want to move on. Or couldn't.'

Couldn't? Was he suggesting there was some kind of problem with the afterlife? Nicolas immediately dispelled the thought. It wasn't something he even wanted to consider. Besides, a curse seemed a much better explanation.

'Whether it was or not, we have more important concerns.' It seemed Silva had found her voice again. 'Namely, survival.'

They were stranded on an island. Why did he keep forgetting that? Of course, there'd been some...distractions, but it seemed he didn't want to admit the truth to himself. If he faced that reality, he would have to question his ability to survive on an island. And he wouldn't like the answer to that question.

'We need to build a shelter before nightfall and source our food and water,' Silva continued.

Sourcing water was simple, as they were right next to a river. However, the idea of drinking from something zombies had been possibly wading in wasn't one he relished. But if it was between that and dying of thirst, his reluctance could go hang.

'Food won't be a problem,' Shift reassured the group. 'I can fish.'

'I didn't know you were a skilled fisherman,' Nicolas said.

'I'm not.' Shift smiled. 'But I can turn myself into something that has a knack for catching fish.'

Their ability continued to amaze him. He wished he had some kind of power to help the group. Or any kind of skill. His lot was having the others point to things that needed moving or setting up, but at least he'd be pitching in.

****

By nightfall, they had created a serviceable camp from what nature had provided. Though it probably wouldn't stand up to even the slightest of breezes, Nicolas was privately quite impressed with the lean-to he'd built. Fortunately, the night sky was calm as he sat beneath it, enjoying the warmth of the fire. His attempts to start it had been less impressive, and only grew worse as he realised that the others had stopped their tasks to watch him with varying degrees of bemusement and disbelief. Finally, Garaz had blocked their view and used a small fireball to get things going. Had he really saved face? No. But it was nice to pretend he had.

And the fire was now being used to cook the fish Shift had provided, as well as warm them in the cold night. He lifted the skewer to his mouth and took another bite. If this was to be their home now then he'd better get used to fish making up the majority of his diet, as well as the ground being his bed.

The king's ship must've been laden with supplies.

If only they'd had time to scavenge *before* the dead rose and tried to consume them. Quickly, he stopped thinking about zombies. Picturing decaying flesh while eating did not make for good digestion.

He looked instead at his companions around the campfire. Praise the Deities that he wasn't alone. He would've probably been in a ditch right now, half-dead and waiting for the other half to catch up. But now he had companionship and...oh crap, Auron was about to tell a story.

'So this one time, there was this witch,' the spirit began with gusto, standing before the group and beginning with the dramatic hand gestures he liked to use when engaging in his tales, the fire light illuminating him as stage lighting would an actor in a theatre. 'She'd kidnapped a virgin to sacrifice, and I stumbled upon them. Who in their right mind tries to do a sacrifice in the middle of a forest just off the main track? Come, on. She hadn't even gagged the virgin, and the poor girl was screaming her head off. It was like the witch wanted to be caught. When I stepped in, the old hag lobbed some spells at me, but I was too quick. I got in close, broke her wand then, if you believe it, she drew a knife on me and went, *'Youuuuu are an honnnnourable man, Auron of Tellllllmark. Youuuuu woulllllld neverrrrrr hit a womannnnn.'* The heck I wouldn't. I punched her right in the face, *bam.*' He mimed the punch. 'Now, as a general rule, I won't hit a woman, true enough, but you draw a blade on me I don't care what gender you are. You're fair game.'

'Why did she stop using spells when you took her wand?' From Nicolas's limited understanding, magic came from within and didn't require such tools, except to focus the power.

Auron shrugged. 'Sometimes people get so used to using tools they forget how to do anything without them. Do you know how many fights I've won simply because my opponents forget you can still use your fists when holding a sword? Saved my neck a time or two, I can tell you.'

Nicolas was sure he would, eventually.

'What happened to the witch?' Garaz asked between mouthfuls of the fruit he'd foraged for earlier. There was a slight edge to his voice, suggesting the orc didn't care for witches.

'Ah, I handed her over to the witch hunters,' Auron replied, thinking back. 'I imagine they burned her or something. Now *there's* a humourless group of people. Try and start a conversation with them about anything other than burning witches and you might as well be trying to talk to an orc about anything other than *crushing humies.*'

Garaz looked up at the spirit, frozen for a moment before taking another bite from his fruit.

Auron looked wide-eyed then very sheepish. 'No offence.'

The orc weighed this for a moment. 'None taken,' he replied finally. 'Unfortunately, the stereotype of my people exists for a reason.'

Though Garaz seemed fine, an air of awkwardness suddenly descended on the camp. Even Silva appeared to feel it.

'And the girl?' Shift asked, thankfully breaking the silence.

'Let's just say I ensured she was never *suitable* for virgin sacrifices again.' Auron smiled smugly.

Nicolas screwed up his face. 'Charming.' He'd known the answer to that without asking and was sure Shift had too. He had to hear about Auron's sex life as much as his hero work. To be fair, for him, they seemed to go hand in hand. Though how Auron hadn't been riddled with the pox was anyone's guess.

The spirit shrugged with self-satisfaction.

'What about you?' Shift turned to Nicolas suddenly, looking at him intently. 'You must have a story. I don't buy this *humble village boy* bit.'

'Why don't you ask someone more interesting?' *Deities, don't make me the centre of attention*. It never seemed to end well.

'What, like Silva?' Shift snorted. 'Even if she could remember much of anything that happened before you drowned her, I don't think I'd want to hear it.' Nicolas couldn't argue with that.

If Silva had been offended by that remark she made no sign of it. She obviously had very thick skin. Surely a requirement to do the things she'd done in service of the necromancer, though she hadn't worked directly for Avus Arex, but for whatever mysterious party had backed him. He'd asked her about it once, but that was one of the blank spots. That came in very handy for said bad guys.

'I really am just a village boy.' Apparently, the question wasn't about to go away. 'I work at my family's bakery and do...village stuff.' Wow, he'd just summed his whole life up in a single sentence. Was he the most boring man in all Etherius?

What have I been doing all this time? Am I just wasting my life in my precious daily routine?

The idea humbled him.

'Okay.' Shift was evidently intent on their line of enquiry. 'But how does a village boy end up saving me from a vampire nest?' Shift was being kind. Really, they'd saved themselves and they knew it; Nicolas had just happened to be there when it happened.

'It's just because I was chosen to be a *Word Bearer*.'

Shift looked at him quizzically, as did Silva, and he realised he'd never shared this story with them. Auron and Garaz knew, but not them.

'My village—well, one guy in my village, the Oracle—receives messages from the Deities to pass on to heroes to aid in their quests...'

'I wondered what T'goth meant when he talked about giving obtuse messages to us,' Shift exclaimed. 'So much for non-interference in mortal affairs.'

'Anyway, the Oracle then picks someone to deliver the message. I got chosen to deliver a message to Auron. He didn't show because...well...'

'I was dead,' Auron cut in simply. Cue a glare at Silva.

'So I ended up waiting for him and got attacked. I fell off a bridge and was washed downriver, where I met Auron. After that I kind of got...swept up in events. The rest you know.'

'Why doesn't this *Oracle* go himself?' Garaz asked thoughtfully.

Because he's a cantankerous old ass. 'He needs to stay where he is to receive messages.'

'So you were chosen to be a hero?' Shift asked.

He didn't like where this was going. 'No,' Nicolas corrected. 'I was chosen to deliver a message.'

'Still, you *were* chosen.'

'It was a stupid ceremony.' His voice was rising in pitch, but for some reason he needed to defend himself from these accusations of being a chosen hero of some sort. 'The Oracle threw a stick in the air until it pointed to someone. It was ridiculous. It could've landed on any of us.'

'Or was it the will of the Deities?' Auron interrupted.

'What?'

'Did they influence the stick to choose you?' the spirit asked. 'You have been pretty useful, for the most part, since it happened. And you just happened to be of the right age at the right time...'

'It was a fluke.' *No way some grand plan would choose me.* It'd at least pick someone enthusiastic about being part of it.

'Was it?'

'Stop it,' he protested. The ceremony had been a silly, random thing, and he wouldn't give any credence to the idea that his choosing had been anything else.

Shift and Auron seemed frustratingly unconvinced.

'What about you, Garaz?' he asked, hoping to deflect from himself. 'Why did you become a healer?'

'To heal people.' Something about the orc's face suggested there was much more to it than that, but also that any further line of enquiry would be unwelcome. Unlike Shift, he could take a cue when someone didn't want to speak about something. Sometimes.

It seemed the rest of the group respected the orc's privacy much more than Nicolas's. Auron turned his attention to Shift. 'I know your past is a blur, but you've got to have some stories from your life as a thief.'

Shift mulled this over for a moment. 'Okay.' They were attempting a little of Auron's dramatic flair but were a mere shadow of the master storyteller himself. 'So I'd disguised myself as this tavern barmaid. Very innocent, naïve-about-the-world type. Like Nick.'

That was unnecessary.

'But pretty buxom at the same time. This tavern was a bit of a travel hub, so someone worth robbing would eventually show up. It didn't take long. This silk merchant bragged about his worth before he even opened his mouth. The sheer number of rings he wore, I'm surprised his wrists didn't ache from the weight of them. So I serve him and play my demure, chaste bit perfectly, ensuring my buxomness is clearly on display. We go upstairs, and he thinks he's in for a good old time. I close the door and turn away, *'But, sir, I'm just an unplucked flower. To do anything would be improper.'* He wanted to be *very* improper, so he turns me around to find an old hag cackling in his face. By the time he came to, I was long gone, with several very full purses of gold and pockets full of garish jewellery.'

'So you seduced this guy, scared him nearly to death, and left him broke?' How could anyone do that to another person?

Shift visibly bristled at his response, frowning at Nicolas as if he'd just compared their hair style to that of an unwashed troll. 'He was an arrogant ass and needed taking down a peg or two.'

'That'd be very noble if you didn't profit off it.'

Shift's face darkened despite the firelight on it. 'You want stories of my past...I stole from people. Those are my stories.' For a moment, they looked towards the campfire seriously, losing themselves in the flames.

Have I actually offended them? He hadn't thought that was possible.

'Do you want to know the greatest thing I ever stole, though?' Their words were quiet and full of feeling as they stared sombrely into some far off land concealed in the fire.

'Go on?' Auron asked, obviously intrigued by the seriousness of their tone. Admittedly, he was too.

'Nick's heart.'

As Shift burst out laughing, Nicolas threw a stick at them. Around him, the rest of his companions joined in the laughter. It may have been terrible being stranded on an island, but Deities, he didn't want this moment to end.

CHAPTER 5

W hen he woke, in that blissful moment between the dream state and reality, Nicolas stretched and all was good with the world.

You're still stranded on an island, you know?

Panic began its tedious dance in his mind.

No, you aren't giving in to anxiety...get up and do something practical.

It was difficult, but he forced himself up. The sun was bright and the air refreshing, which certainly helped.

Deities, I hope breakfast is soon.

'Morning, Nick.' *How does Shift look so bright?* 'I'd ask if you slept well on the ground, but considering the state of you—'

'I look that bad?' Nicolas cried.

Shift's eyes widened as they sucked their teeth, before breaking into a broad grin. 'Well, I suppose it isn't as bad as the time you woke up in a jail next to me, but it isn't far off. At least if you start whining I can walk away this time.'

He'd only been up a few minutes, and he was getting teased already. It was going to be a long day.

'There's some breakfast there if you want it.'

Well, he was famished so that was an easy question to answer. Though the mixture of fruit hardly qualified as a hearty breakfast, it'd do. As he bit into a juicy apple, he had to admit that its freshness was invigorating. The day was already improving.

'Where are the others?' he asked between mouthfuls.

'Garaz is off meditating on the beach,' Shift replied. 'The other two are over there.'

Auron and Silva stood by a tree in deep discussion. Considering they generally only spared a couple of words for each other, and on Auron's part, most of those were unkind, what did they have to talk about? At least the spirit wasn't going crazy as he once had in the presence of his killer. Whatever resentment he still had towards his murderer, which was surely plenty, he seemed to be keeping a lid on it. Which was good, since that festering anger had almost killed the entire group after the spirit got them captured by a dwarf gangster to exact his revenge on Silva.

As if they knew he was watching them, the pair turned to him as one, looking at him in a way that sent a chill up his spine. It wasn't just that they were looking at him, it was the *way* they were doing it, with a common purpose.

What do they want?

Whatever it was, awkwardness grabbed his head and made him look away.

What did I do wrong?

No, he couldn't have done anything wrong. He'd just woken, for Deities' sake.

As they approached him, he began to pray to those Deities.

'Uh oh, someone's in trouble.' Shift smirked.

Auron and Silva only stopped when they were looming directly over Nicolas. Not intimidating at all.

Haven't they heard of personal space? Or claustrophobia?

'Finish your meal then get up.' Silva's tone made him concerned it would be his last meal.

'What did I do?' Nicolas asked sheepishly, wracking his brains for a reason they might be mad at him.

'It's not what you did,' Auron answered. 'It's what you're going to do, kid.'

This was becoming more concerning by the second. 'And what's that?'

'Time for you to learn to fight.' Auron smiled.

He nearly choked on the piece of apple in his mouth. 'Beg pardon?'

'Auron and I are going to school you in the art of combat.' Silva seemed unnervingly excited about the idea.

'No thanks.'

Both seemed surprised by this response.

'What do you mean *no thanks*?' Auron asked incredulously.

Nicolas shrugged. 'I'm not interested.' Hopefully this time *'I'm not inter-ested'* served him better than when he'd tried it on the Oracle.

For him, *'the art of combat'* meant violence, and he wasn't a violent person. He barely used bad language and would prefer to keep it that way. Besides, he'd knocked out a famous hunter and wrestled a dwarf; surely, he had some basics down by now?

The spirit crouched in front of Nicolas.

'We're going after a faun who murdered a royal family.' Auron's white eyes looked at him fiercely, a *'looking directly into your soul'* type gaze. 'Up until this point, you've gotten lucky in your fights. It's time to make sure you know your stuff. When we first met, I promised to train you. And I intend to redeem that vow. Between Silva and me, we will.'

Going after the faun? Did they know something he didn't? 'But we're stuck here.'

'Details.' Apparently to Silva, it was as easy as that. Was she expecting a random ship to appear at any moment?

Good luck with that.

'But I've no intention of fighting again. You guys can go chase the faun *if* we're rescued. I intend to go home. Besides, Silva can pretty much handle an army by herself.'

'Said the boy who defeated me in two-on-one combat.'

Okay, she had him there. But that had been one of the biggest flukes in the history of Etherius.

Second only to the Choosing Stick picking me.

'Let me ask you this, kid,' Auron began. 'Did you intend on being on this island in the first place?'

'Well, no.'

'So do you think the universe bends to your intentions?'

He saw where this was going. 'That's not the point. I'm not a violent person. It's not in my nature. Sorry, guys.' He tried to sound as firm as he could, but he was dealing with wills stronger than his, so maybe the universe wouldn't bend to his intentions again?

Auron got to his feet, which didn't quite connect to the ground, and looked at Silva.

'I suppose I could always possess him next time there's a battle? Fight for him. It worked well enough last time.'

The spirit's words brought up the vivid memory of the one and only time Auron had possessed him. He imagined it was what a horse would feel like being ridden, if the rider was inside you and made of ice. If standing on the beach learning to throw a punch prevented that ever happening again, then it'd be worth it.

'Okay, okay,' he relented. 'If it makes you two happy, you can show me a thing or two.' What he really meant was *'if it gets you off my back.'*

'Oh, this should be entertaining.' Shift smirked.

Silva looked over at them with a raised eyebrow. 'I'm sure it will be, until it's your turn.'

'My turn?' Shift repeated uncertainly. 'But I know how to fight. I'm good.'

'I have seen you fight, and you're far from *good*. Passable, at best,' Silva retorted. 'Without me, you both would've been consumed by zombies yesterday. We need better than that from you as I won't always be around to hold your hands.' *That was harsh.* 'Both of you follow me to the training ground we have prepared.'

The *now* part of the sentence was unspoken, but it was still loud and clear.

Nicolas couldn't help but take some satisfaction in Shift's aghast look. *At least I won't have to go through this alone.*

****

How is it that sand is soft when you touch it gently, but when you land on it at speed, it's hard as rock?

At least this time, he'd learned to roll slightly with his landing, though all he'd really accomplished was covering his entire body and coughing out a cloud of the stuff. His coughing was followed by a loud groan that emanated from the multiple points of pain in his body.

'What was that?' At least Auron was shouting at Silva and not him. Justifiably so, in Nicolas's opinion.

'He must know how to take a punch.' Silva acted like there was no problem. Nicolas's jaw disagreed.

'That was several, followed by an overhead throw!' the spirit protested. 'I thought we agreed he needed to learn to throw a punch *first*?'

'You agreed that.' Silva nodded. 'I still believe he must learn to take one first. He is more than likely to be struck before he strikes someone because of his gentle nature.'

Nicolas chose to take that as a compliment. 'I know how to take a punch,' he protested weakly. 'I have taken a few in my time, you know?' That fact brought back some unpleasant memories.

'And yet you are still on the floor pretending it didn't hurt as much as it clearly did.' Silva stood over him, blotting out a portion of the blue sky and clearly seeing right through him. 'If I were an enemy, I would be atop you now disembowelling you.'

'I'm sure Nick's thought about Silva being atop him many a time.' Shift declared from beneath the shade of the nearest tree. 'Though I doubt you were disembowelling him.'

Nice try. Jest all you want, I see the nervousness in your smile. When Silva's finished with me we both know you're next.

'You're not helping,' Auron chided.

Shift shrugged playfully, again poorly hiding their unease. Or maybe they were hiding it well, but Nicolas was just learning to read his companion better?

'Well, it's going to be your turn in a minute.' The spirit smiled evilly. 'So I'd think twice before annoying the instructor.'

Shift looked at Nicolas lying on the floor then at the person who'd put him there. The thought of what may come had a marked effect on their willingness to make smart ass remarks, judging by how quiet they suddenly became.

Taking Silva's proffered hand, Nicolas half rose and was half pulled up, his body protesting the motion in the strongest possible terms. He tried his best to dust himself off, but most of the sand refused to budge. Really, he was just hoping to put off more training for as long as possible. The annoyed cough from Silva suggested that she knew this too.

'Let's try something different.' Silva backed away from him a couple of steps. 'Draw your sword.' What did he need the sword for? They were just training. Silva gestured impatiently toward the tree beside which it rested.

He walked over to where the *Dawn Blade* lay in its sheath and drew it. The perfectly reflective blade caught the light of the sun, and for a moment, he was blinded by it. After blinking and rubbing his eyes until the spots in them dissipated, he held the sword up again. The bruises on his face that Silva had gifted him were mirrored there. If he could just get one strike on her, he would be happy. He almost certainly wouldn't know that satisfaction today. Though if they weren't rescued soon, he'd have plenty of chance to practice.

I could become the greatest warrior in Etherius on this beach, and no one would ever know but us.

Walking back to their training ground, Nicolas took a couple of test swings with the sword. After his first adventure, he'd practiced swinging it in the woods. Knowing first hand by then the dangers the outside world contained, learning to be at least comfortable holding a sword seemed sensible, as was the urge to never leave home again. He might not have a refined technique, but at least the weight of the blade no longer hurt his wrists.

Silva lowered her stance. 'Come at me.'

Nicolas looked at the warrior incredulously. She couldn't be serious. 'What?'

Silva reinforced her command by waving him towards her with her fingers.

'But I could hurt you,' he declared, pointing to the sharp weapon in his hand. He could do a lot worse than just hurt her.

Silva's face did something that could almost have been deemed a smirk. She didn't relent, so after a few moments, Nicolas approached her slowly and cut at her with a downward swing. Having no wish to hurt her, even accidentally, he swung wide so the sword would have no chance of hitting her if she stayed still. Silva let out a frustrated huff as the sword cut limply down at her side.

'What was that?' the warrior demanded.

'I came at you like you said.' What was the issue?

'Is that where I was standing?' Silva barked, pointing at the ground where his swing had been.

'Well…'

'Well nothing! Come at me again and do so properly or I shall make you regret it.'

From her tone, Nicolas believed it.

Okay, she is asking me to attack her. She knows what she's doing, and I have no idea what she might do to me if I don't obey. If she gets hurt then it's her own fault.

Again, he swung at her, this time with a little more effort and ensuring his aim was true.

As the sword started its downward arc, Silva fluidly stepped inside his attack, lashing out with a fist. Though the blow was too fast to track, there was a sudden stabbing pain under the bicep of his sword arm. His hand opened, and the sword slipped from his grip. Before he could even try to grab it, a boot kicked him in the side of the knee, collapsing his body and then a hard slap caught him across the face, sending him spinning to the sand again. As he groggily looked up, the *Dawn Blade* was sticking out of the ground directly beside him.

'*Silva,*' Auron barked as Nicolas collected himself.

'There is a point to this,' the warrior protested. 'Nicolas does not know how to root himself. Without strong stance and footwork as a basis, teaching him anything else is pointless. If he falls down every time he is punched, he will lose every time.'

'Actually, you aren't wrong.' The spirit huffed, evidently disliking having to agree with Silva.

As Nicolas tried to get up, his arm throbbed where Silva had hit it. Was this just an excuse for Silva to beat him up? What had he done to warrant that? Was it vengeance for the near-drowning at his hands? Whatever it was, he was keen to apologise.

A hand appeared in front of his face. Taking it, Nicolas allowed Silva to pull him up, wincing as his arm throbbed again. Most of the arm was numb, and Nicolas opened and closed his hand several times until the feeling came back.

Silva regarded his injured arm. 'The body is covered in pressure points,' the warrior explained. 'Very effective if you know where they are and how to hit them properly, but that's a future lesson. Now, let's go again.'

Obeying for no reason he could fathom, Nicolas limped over to the sword and pulled it from the ground. His instructor waited for him, arms folded.

Just one hit would be nice. Just one. Not with the sword though.

'One other thing you need to learn, kid.' Auron watched him sternly. 'Stop dishonouring my sword by dropping it all the time.'

Nicolas couldn't argue with that. He'd probably dropped it more times than he'd swung it.

'Again,' Silva commanded.

Resigning himself to the fact that he couldn't duck out of this, Nicolas knew that the only thing to do now was get through it. Wincing slightly as he prepared for the inevitable pain to follow, he raised his sword and charged.

CHAPTER 6

*S*urvival Log, Day 3.

After our second night on the island, spirits are still high. We've settled amiably into a routine of camp life. Though I confess trepidation of what's to come. Since the first ship, there have been no signs of anyone, and as bountiful as this island has turned out to be, surely it cannot support us forever. How many weeks, months or years before the hope of rescue fades and we become despondent about our fate: to be forever stuck on this cursed island? Maybe I won't even make it that far anyway? Silva's training regime is punishing, to the point I've started groaning every time I rise. Who knows if my body will just give up? If the worst should happen to me and you find this journal, please give my remains the—

'What're you writing?' Nicolas jumped out of his skin as Shift suddenly appeared in front of him.

'Nothing.' Making that sound less defensive would've been nice, but he hadn't. Inevitably, the piece of wood he was now making a poor attempt to cover with his arm would intrigue Shift no end.

It did. Without a word, Shift snatched the piece of bark he'd been writing on—or carving on, more accurately. It took no thief skill; the wood slipped from his hand before he had time to react and grip it, leaving him with just the sharpened rock he'd been using as a makeshift pen.

Shift frowned at the piece of wood in their hand. '*Survival log...*' Their expression when they looked back at him was somewhere between surprise and amusement. 'You've got to be kidding me, Nick. It's day three, and you're writing your obituary? You're wetter than the sea.'

Hearing it said aloud, it did sound a little silly. Though after yesterday, it would take more to convince him death *wasn't* imminent. His whole body ached from Silva and Auron's lessons, and he wasn't even sure he'd learnt anything. The only thing he remembered clearly was where to hit someone to make their arm go numb because he'd been subjected to it.

Repeatedly. Even this morning, it still felt as if he had a stone under his skin when he moved his arm.

'I'm just being prepared.' There was that defensive tone again. Why should he be defensive? Writing a note for someone to find when you were stranded on an island seemed sensible.

Shift slowly shook their head and tutted. 'What you're being is pessimistic.' Before Nicolas could protest, they threw the piece of bark into the undergrowth with a rustling of leaves. 'You need to calm down. Probably more of an epic task than restoring a Deity's stolen power in your case, but let's try anyway.'

Before he could ask what they meant, they grabbed his hand and hauled him to his feet with surprising ease. Once he was up, they turned his body in the direction of the beach and marched him forward. As annoying as Shift could be, and was being, he appreciated the sentiment. They weren't wrong. Despite the nice evenings around the campfire, he was increasingly disturbed by the idea they might never be found.

Upon the beach, Garaz sat cross-legged facing the sea, much as he'd done most of the day before.

'Hey, Garaz,' Shift shouted, not caring that they were interrupting his meditation. 'I have a new student for you.'

Slowly, the orc turned his head and chuckled. 'You certainly need to learn to be calmer.'

'Not me, big guy,' Shift replied dryly. 'Him.' With a shove, they pushed Nicolas several steps closer to the seated orc.

'Ah, a greater challenge.' One Garaz didn't seem keen to take on. 'Though I would have thought you had had enough learning yesterday.' Garaz was well-versed on Nicolas's lessons with Silva, because Nicolas had complained at great length about them while the orc had healed the worst of his bruises.

'Ha, ha.' Nicolas sat beside the red-cloaked orc, who was twice the width of him.

'Are you okay?' Garaz asked.

Honestly, he was still in a lot of pain, which Garaz could've helped with his healing magic, again, but something stopped him admitting it. Was it a wish not to see the orc's reaction to more of his whining? Or maybe it was a pride thing—a stupid pride thing, to be sure, but when was pride sensible?

Shift answered for him as they sat across from Nicolas. 'He's being pessimistic and needs to learn to loosen up.'

Nicolas didn't bother pointing out the difference between pessimism and preparedness. Arguing with Shift was a waste of energy. Instead, he got comfortable as the trio formed a triangle of sorts on the beach.

'Shift speaks the truth. You are most certainly someone who needs to *'loosen up,'* as they put it.'

So now even Garaz is against me?

But was *'loosening up'* the right phrase? They were stranded on an island, he didn't exactly want to get comfortable here. It was a tense situation, and now it was being made all the worse because his companions were being annoying.

And why is that?

...because they're right.

Dammit, maybe I do need to calm down.

As much as he didn't want to accept their situation, it wasn't going to change any time soon. So the least he could do, for everyone's sake, was learn to handle it better. 'Can you show me, please?' he asked, roughly copying the orc's cross-legged pose.

'So the first thing to do is close your eyes and attempt to empty your mind.' Garaz's voice was soothing. 'That does not mean go blank. Thoughts will come, but pay them no mind. Let them float away again like clouds on the breeze. Observe them dispassionately as they pass if you must, but they are not important. Only the moment and your breathing are important. That is the way to find true peace.'

Going to close his eyes, he couldn't help but ask one last question. 'Why do you need to do this?' he asked Garaz. 'You seem generally pretty peaceful. Why do you need more peace?'

The orc smiled absentmindedly, as if he was mentally somewhere other than the beach. 'We all need a little more peace on occasion, young Nicolas. Even me.' he answered finally.

Nicolas closed his eyes and immediately saw an image of his skeleton lying on the beach being picked at by gulls. How was that a thought he could casually observe and allow to pass him by? Opening his eyes, he began to fidget uncomfortably.

Whose bright idea was it to sit on sand?

'That lasted long.' Shift smiled sympathetically.

Instead of feeling calmer, he was more frustrated than before he'd closed his eyes. 'I don't get how you guys can be so calm about all of this,' Nicolas cried, before pointing to Garaz. 'Especially you. We are *stranded* on an island with no hint of rescue, and you're just taking it all in your stride. How do you do it? What's your secret?'

'I believe,' Garaz replied simply.

Nicolas gestured at him to continue.

'Like it or not, we were sent here by T'goth,' the orc explained. 'The fact that he sent us to an island that just happened to contain the wrecked ship of the former king of Sarus was no coincidence. There was a reason for it, a reason we are here. I do not believe T'goth would have sent us here with a purpose and no hope of leaving the island again. All we need to do is wait and be patient.'

Nicolas was sure that last word was directed at him specifically.

'What if our one way off was the faun's ship?' Despair crept over him. He didn't have the imagination to picture a rescue. Their grizzly deaths he could picture for infinity, but anything positive, no. 'Because I doubt he's coming back, except maybe to laugh at our corpses in a month or two.'

'That is a possibility.' *How does Garaz keep his voice so level?* 'But I do not believe it to be true. Either way, we have supplies and a good camp. We can make do here until we are found.'

Nicolas needed to know more, for Garaz to make him believe as he did. However, before that could happen, Auron interrupted.

'Hey, kid,' the spirit shouted from the edge of the beach, looking at a familiar piece of wood Silva was holding. 'I don't even need to ask who wrote this. From the content, it's clearly your work. Anyone ever told you that you need to calm down?'

'It's been mentioned,' he muttered

Survival Log, Day 3...It's national Get On Nicolas's Back day on our new island home.

Sighing, he turned his attention back to Garaz, only to find the orc looking past him as if he weren't there. That wasn't going to help him achieve inner peace. Instead it caused him to fold his arms indignantly.

'So when do you expect this miraculous rescue to be?' he asked insistently. 'Can you give me a date and time on that? Because that would be helpful before I *really* start to panic.'

The orc smiled broadly. 'I would say about another hour.'

It took a moment for Nicolas to register the implication of Garaz's words, but when he did he instantly followed the orc's gaze out to sea. On the horizon was a large black dot that could only be a ship.

****

Garaz's guess of an hour had been pretty much spot on. Though they were more wary this time around, none of them could ignore the exciting prospect of being saved. Garaz and Silva had lit a signal fire, while Nicolas and Shift packed up their camp.

Thank the Deities' they didn't ask me to start the fire, or we may never get rescued.

As great plumes of smoke rose into the sky, the ship dropped anchor off the coast of their sandy prison. It looked different to the faun's vessel—much larger, with multiple masts and a beautiful figurehead. In fact, it looked exactly as Nicolas had imagined a seafaring vessel would—but could it be the faun returning on a different ship to laugh at them? That would be in keeping with what he knew of the idiot's character. His hope spiked as a rowboat descended from the side of the ship before slowly making its way through the water toward them, increasing further when the men rowing it came into proper view and were a lot more savoury than the group who'd abandoned them.

'If these people leave us here too, I swear to the Deities I'm going to...' Actually, he didn't know what he would do. He imagined it would involve a lot of cursing. And maybe the shedding of a few tears.

Auron looked from the rowboat back to the ship it had come from. 'Purple sails are a little gaudy, don't you think?'

In truth, he did. But he wouldn't care what colour the ship's sails were if it took them from this Deities-forsaken place. The prominent ballistae on the deck were slightly more concerning than the sails, but every ship must need to defend itself. What was really disturbing was the unnecessarily large cleavage on the figurehead, complete with prominent nipples that poked from beneath its sculpted dress.

Yes, I'm looking to have a figurehead carved on my ship. My specifications? Giant breasts. That is all thanks.

'Indeed,' Garaz confirmed, showing the streak of snobbery that poked its head out every so often.

'You don't think it's some kind of...pleasure vessel, do you?' Shift eyed the ship warily.

'What's a pl... Never mind.' He didn't need to know. He could undoubtedly guess if he gave it some thought. His innocence was dwindling fast of late.

Auron shrugged. 'As long as it gets us off the island, I don't care.'

Silva looked a little perturbed as she stared out to the sea. Not the most verbose of people, she was most likely on guard, just as she always was.

The rowboat, like the faun's, stopped a little way off the beach, treading the surf so it didn't get pulled to shore. On her prow stood a woman in a red bandana from which a long, black, plaited ponytail emerged. If Nicolas had to describe her with a single word, *grizzled* would be his first choice. Yet *personable* would be the second. He hoped he was right. Though he was surprised a woman could be a salty sailor.

But then, what do I know about sailors...? Or women?

'Be ye friend or foe?' she called to the group in a thick accent.

'Friend,' Nicolas called back. *Daft question*. He'd hardly have admitted to being a foe, even if he was.

'A foe might say that,' the woman shouted back after a moment's thought. 'What're ye doin' on that thar island?'

'We were stranded...in a shipwreck,' Shift replied.

It wasn't totally a lie. The island did have a shipwreck on it. *Just a pile of ash now, really.* But trying to explain the circumstances that had brought them here...well, the sailors might think them crazy. It was an option Nicolas considered every now and then.

'Have ye seen a faun at all? Or a black ship?' the woman shouted through cupped hands.

'Yes, we've seen a faun,' Nicolas called back, before impulsively adding, 'And he's a giant goblin turd.'

'Hope she isn't friends with the faun, kid.' Auron smirked despite the seriousness of his words.

He hadn't thought of that. Just his luck if his big mouth got them stranded again.

'So yer no friend o' the creature?' The woman's tone was suspicious. There was obviously a right and wrong answer to her question.

As his companions looked at each other to decide the right one, Shift just went with their gut. As usual. 'If the faun were drowning, I'd be more likely to put my foot on his head than offer him a hand ashore.'

Well, that's that then.

Whichever way this went, they were committed now.

The woman seemed to be weighing up their response, taking far longer about it than Nicolas cared for.

'Ye comin' then or not?' she called finally.

Obviously not a friend of the faun then.

Well done, Shift. Not that he'd say that aloud. They looked smug enough about it as it was. Not needing a second invitation, the group quickly made towards the water as the boat rowed ashore. Nicolas and Shift were so pleased to be rescued that they waded out to meet it. Garaz and Auron soon joined them. Only Silva remained on the beach as the others, save the spirit, helped pull the vessel ashore.

As Nicolas climbed aboard, relief engulfed him. They were saved. Closing his eyes, he took a quick moment to simply enjoy the rush. When he opened them, the red-bandanaed woman was looking at him, bemused. Her smile was sweet for someone so rough looking.

Quickly, Nicolas rose and smoothed down his wet clothes. Best to make a good impression on their saviours. 'Thank you.' *Even a rowboat at sea is a place for good manners.* 'My name is Nicolas Percival Carnegie. And you are Captain...?' He offered his hand. The hand that gripped and shook it was attached to a heavily tattooed arm.

The woman chuckled heartily. 'Nah, I ain't captain o' the *Irrevocable Amora*. I'm the first mate. Name's Hayley Clarkey, but *Hay Sharkbait*'s how I'm known hereabouts.'

'*Irrevocable Amora?*' Auron repeated.

'*Hay Sharkbait?*' Shift asked.

The sailor grinned at them knowingly. 'Got my name cause o' this.'

Nicolas instinctively put his hands in front of his eyes as the sailor suddenly lifted her shirt. What was she trying to show them? Peripherally, he could see slack-jawed expressions from Auron and Shift, and that made him curious. Tentatively, he peeked, his hand falling away completely as his mouth fell open too.

The sailor's sun-kissed torso was interrupted by an angry-looking, large, semi-circular red scar, running from just under her armpit down to her hip. Nicolas was no expert but judging by the unevenly spaced indents in the scar, it was a bite mark. Her nickname made it simple to guess what had done the biting.

How did she survive that?

'I bet she has a brilliant story about how she got that.' Auron sounded awestruck as the sailor lowered her shirt.

'Well, thank you for saving us, madam.' Garaz offered a small bow.

Hay Sharkbait chuckled. 'No *madam*s here, green fella. Yer almost as formal as this 'un.' Okay, Nicolas was formal, so what? 'It's just *Hay Sharkbait*. The *Sharkbait* is obvious, and the *Hay*...well, sailors love a good pun, don't ye, lads?'

The men in the rowboat cheered raucously in agreement.

'And as fer the savin', think nothin' o' it. Not gonna just let ye die stranded on an island now, are we?'

Hay Sharkbait was certainly a jovial lady. Had she always been like this, or had whatever caused that terrible scar given her a renewed lust for life? Either way, the formal part of him wasn't entirely comfortable with calling her *Hay Sharkbait*. He had a strange thing about nicknames ever since *Nick Carnage* started dogging him.

'What about your captain?' he asked as the sailors heaved on the oars, turning the boat around before heading back towards the ship.

Hay Sharkbait chuckled at the question. 'He'll want te introduce himself.' The sailor smiled.

If he was as amiable as his first mate, Nicolas looked forward to meeting him.

****

The rowboat pulled itself alongside its parent ship, the bobbing of the waves causing it to continually bump against the bigger ship's hull in an almost rhythmical beat. There was a ladder waiting for them as they arrived, a flimsy looking rope thing that looked neither secure nor able to hold his weight.

It's fine, it must've been used countless times in the past.

But surely that just means it's worn and likely to snap at any moment?

Silva was the first to test it. She went up quickly, not even waiting for him to be gentlemanly about it. Keeping a watchful eye on the ladder, to see how it fared with use, it took him an uncomfortably long time to realise he could see right up Silva's armoured skirt. His attempt to look away subtly backfired, and Shift shook their head at him in a bemused way.

Garaz went next.

That will be a true test of the ladder.

Nicolas was glad he didn't voice that aloud. It didn't sound particularly kind, but Garaz was the largest of the group. Nicolas took a deep breath. He should've been elated at being saved, and instead he was obsessing over a ladder.

'You going or not?' Shift's tone seemed almost accusatory, so he steeled himself and gripped the rope.

Carefully, he ascended the side of the ship. *Very carefully*. The ladder moved much more than he cared for, and he found himself praying not to fall. He wasn't sure what would be worse, the pain of it or the embarrassment.

He chanced a look up, and happily, a gloved hand awaited him. Though the hand was right beside him, the gap between it and the ladder he was clinging to seemed miles. With a deep breath that he attempted to hide, Nicolas let go of the ladder, and took hold of the hand, allowing it's owner to help him up onto the deck.

When he reached the lip of the deck, he breathed a sigh of relief, before noting the fancy metal tipped boot that was right beside his head. Disliking the idea of being this close to someone's feet, he quickly hauled himself up onto the deck proper. His palms stung from how tightly he'd gripped the rope, and he took a second to blow on them. The soothing effect was minimal.

The fluttering of a cape nearby distracted him from the pain. The cape belonged to a figure who cut a silhouette that could only be described as dashing. He stood with one boot on the edge of the deck, the sun at his back. At a glance, it was everything he'd imagined when he'd read that one seafaring adventure as a child. From the wide-brimmed hat with a feather in it to the sword hung prominently on the hip to ensure it was seen. It was all...dramatic.

The figure took a single step forward, something on his boot jingling as he did. 'Welcome aboard the *Irrevocable Amora*,' the man said, smoothing along the ridge line of his hat with two fingers before removing it and bowing low, flourishing his cape as he did.

Wow, he's talking to me.

Something about the sheer *confidence* of the man was intoxicating, as if he were blessed that the—he guessed—captain had deigned to speak to him. He found himself standing a little straighter, puffing his chest out a little more. He didn't need to impress this man. And yet the chest was pushed out just those few millimetres extra.

'I am Captain Roberto Ramirez.' The man winked, then gave him a roguish smile that revealed the single gold tooth he clearly liked to show off. 'At your service.'

He's at my service. Why do I feel like I'm flushing?

'He knows how to put on a show.' Auron had ascended the ladder and stood beside him, seemingly less impressed by the captain's pageantry.

Nicolas stepped forward and offered his hand. 'Nicolas Percival Carnegie.'

The captain took his hand and shook it. The firmness of the captain's grip made Nicolas go *ooh* inwardly. Why had he done that?

'I appreciate a man who knows how to properly introduce himself.' Ramirez's accent was thick and rolling, almost like a constantly purring kitten.

'Don't get too used to it, kid,' Auron whispered in his ear. 'You'll be *Nick Carnage* sooner or later. It's inevitable.'

That damnable name.

Why was it that everywhere he went people insisted on trying to adopt that frankly daft moniker? Carnegie was easy enough to pronounce, as was Nicolas.

'But we all call him Nick Carnage.'

Nicolas turned with an audible huff.

Shift's head peeped out beyond the edge of the deck, grinning with self-satisfaction, most of which he assumed was due to the reaction they'd gotten from him. They knew the captain couldn't hear Auron and hadn't wanted him to miss that stupid name.

How kind of them.

'Ah, Nick Carnage.' Captain Ramirez seemed impressed as he stepped past Nicolas to offer his hand to Shift. 'A strong hero name if ever I heard one.'

'So I've been told,' he muttered, glaring at his companion as they were pulled aboard.

'But I think Nicolas will do.' Ramirez winked at him, giving Nicolas another *ooh* moment.

As the captain pulled Shift aboard, he held their hand up for a moment and planted a small, tender kiss on it, not taking his eyes from theirs. 'Forgive my forwardness, but I am not used to saving stranded people who are so...beautiful.'

Did Shift just...giggle? Why's their face going pink like that?

Nicolas's nose wrinkled as the captain studied Shift much more intently than he cared for. *And why is Shift suddenly messing with their hair like that? Why are they standing like a demure maiden? What is going on?*

As he watched the captain flash his wink and grin combination at his companion, Nicolas began to notice the worn edges of Ramirez's bravado. Crow's feet lined the smiling eyes. Tinges of grey peppered the pointed beard and moustache. The removed hat revealed a receding hairline as a middle aged gut fought against a leather tunic that it had fit into perfectly...once. Yet the sheer confidence of the man made him want to ignore all of it.

Tough, I see you now..

'I'm...um...uh...I'm Shift.'

Oh, so now they're stammering. Where did that come from?

'Thank you for gracing my ship with your beauty.' Ramirez threw out a second wink, and as Shift put their hand to their mouth and coughed, Nicolas got the sneaking suspicion that it was done to suppress another giggle.

I'm still on the island, aren't I? This is all a hallucination due to heatstroke. Right?

Not breaking that ridiculously intent eye contact, Ramirez passed one gloved hand over the other, and a rose appeared in his previously empty hand. When he handed the rose to Shift, they giggled openly again.

Suddenly Shift's smile dropped and their face hardened. Nicolas almost giggled himself as he saw Silva scowling at Shift, holding a single red rose.

Perhaps they won't be so enamoured with the captain and his flower magic now?

The two continued to stare at each other like animals trying to mark their territory. What was going on? Could they not see what he saw? It was just some middle-aged man in a fancy outfit on a boat.

Beside him, Auron was smirking. 'Perhaps if you ask him nicely, he'll show you how to do that trick? Or maybe you find him dashing and just want one yourself?'

'Can you not use every opportunity I give you to jest at my expense?'

'Nope.' Auron smiled. 'It builds character.'

And annoyance.

On the bright side, at least they were all safe now. His sudden dislike of the captain aside, Nicolas sensed no danger here, and they were all still together. Not a bad result after being dropped on an island by a Deity and then stranded by a faun.

Deities, my life has gotten strange of late.

'What an eclectic group you are,' Ramirez mused, looking them over.

'True enough.' Garaz smiled. 'And we must thank you for saving us. Had you not happened by, who knows how long we may have been stranded?'

'Think nothing of it.' Ramirez gave a dismissive wave of his hand. 'I would not turn my back on travellers in need. My hospitality and that of my ship is yours.'

'Very...hospitable.' So now the usually talkative Shift was stumbling over their words? *Great*.

'Are you okay?' Nicolas whispered to them.

'Yes,' they replied tartly.

'I must, however, admit that we are not passing this very lovely island by chance,' Ramirez continued. 'In that regard, I have a question to ask you.'

Oh, here we go. Of course, there had to be a catch somewhere.

'We are in pursuit of a ship. Have you seen any others pass by?' The question seemed casual enough, but Ramirez's eyes betrayed his eagerness for the answer.

'Just one.' Wow, Nicolas hadn't known he could growl like that. 'There was a faun on it.'

That had been the right answer; the captain's curiosity was piqued. 'A faun, you say?'

'He was at the island when we...arrived,' Nicolas continued. 'He actually refused to pick us up. He laughed at us as he left. Can you believe that? That was a few days ago.' Thinking about it made his blood boil again.

Ramirez looked out to sea and stroked his beard thoughtfully. 'Then we are gaining on him. Soon, we will have the key to rescuing the princess...and possibly my vengeance.'

'Princess?' Shift asked.

Was there a jealous tinge to their voice?

'Hmm?' It seemed Ramirez had forgotten they were there. *Probably an age thing*. 'Yes, the Princess of the Tidal Kingdom has been taken by my nemesis, who is in league with this faun. We have been tracking the faun for several days now with no success. Every time we seem to get close, they slip away.'

'Janessa?' Auron whispered, aghast.

A memory flashed in his mind, but not one of his. Since Auron possessed him, he had the occasional flash of one of the spirit's memories. Just when he thought they'd all faded away, some trigger would cause another one to appear. Usually, the trigger was one of Auron's stories, and normally the memories were of heroic deeds. The memory this name triggered was of more...adult deeds that made Nicolas screw up his face.

'So this nemesis and the faun are not currently together?' Garaz asked.

'No...' Ramirez was hesitant to respond. 'My nemesis's vessel has vanished somehow. So we have been tracking the faun in the hope he can lead us to him, and the princess. That is how we came across you.'

'Why did the faun and his ally take her?' Silva held the rose in her hand more tenderly than Nicolas had ever seen her do anything.

'That I do not know,' Ramirez admitted. 'A few days ago, we came across an emissary ship from the Tidal Kingdom. She had been ambushed. We searched for survivors, but found only one. He was confused and rambling about something attacking the ship.' *Something?* 'What he did remember clearly was that the ship was boarded. He described someone who could only have been my nemesis and in his company was a faun. He saw them make off with the princess after finishing off the crew. He was lucky, but not lucky enough to survive the wounds he had sustained.'

'I knew that faun was a bad guy,' Nicolas muttered. Again, that smug expression flashed through his mind.

Ramirez nodded slowly, his eyes hard for a moment. 'If I may ask, do you know what the faun was doing on the island?'

Briefly, they gave him a rundown of finding the Sarus flagship and the murdered royal family. They left out the part with the zombies and how they'd reached the island. It seemed beside the point.

Ramirez considered their story then slammed his fist on a nearby railing. 'The fiend. He shall be brought to justice for these heinous crimes. I mean to hang him from the rigging by his neck.'

Nicolas kind of liked the idea but didn't want to see it in person.

'It would appear that terrible things are afoot.' Garaz looked thoughtful but determined. 'Captain, if you will accept, we would like to aid you in this endeavour. And then, once it is done, maybe you can see your way to taking us home?'

The captain beamed at them then gave an open-armed gesture. 'My friends,' he declared, 'I would be honoured and appreciate any help you can give.'

That...sounds suspiciously like us going on another adventure.

'We're going to help save the princess?' Nicolas asked quietly.

Auron seemed equally determined. 'You'll love it, kid. Saving princesses is the meat and potatoes of hero work.'

'*That* many princesses get kidnapped?' *Surely these women have guards and castles to protect them?*

'Well, not always princesses, per se,' the spirit admitted. 'But damsels, priestesses, virgins, maids...it's all the same kind of thing. Sometimes people kidnap the same one multiple times. I heard of this orange-haired guy who kept nabbing the same princess, like the outcome was going to be any different the fifteenth—'

'Uh, forgive me,' Ramirez interrupted. 'But are you talking to someone?'

'A ghost accompanies us,' Nicolas replied. Calling him a ghost was bound to annoy Auron, but the spirit was never shy about annoying him, so it was fair play. Still, Auron looked thoroughly unimpressed.

'Oh, okay,' Ramirez replied, taking it in his stride. 'I have seen many stranger things at sea. Whoever your companion is, he is as welcome aboard as you.'

'Auron of Tellmark,' Garaz offered helpfully, since Auron couldn't introduce himself.

Ramirez seemed taken aback. 'The legendary *Dawnblade*?' He gasped. 'If anyone knows anything about saving princesses, it is him. Truly our quest must be blessed to have such experience with us. How can we fail?'

Auron's grin was almost too much to look at directly as the spirit enjoyed the captain's praise. Hardly surprising for such a shameless self-promoter.

'So the plan isn't just to go straight home then?' Somehow, he wasn't even surprised. Why would fate make it easy for him to go home and be with his parents when watching Nicolas stumble from one life threatening situation to another would be far more entertaining?

'And just walk away from a kidnapped princess?' Shift asked leadingly.

Nicolas looked around. Ramirez had a ship, a crew, and the rest of his companions. What would they need him for? 'There's plenty of experience here without me.'

'Captain,' Garaz asked. 'Which way are we heading?'

'East,' Ramirez replied.

'And which way is Yarringsburg?'

'East.'

'See, kid, it's even on the way.' Auron smiled in a faux-charming way. 'It was meant to be.'

'But you don't need me for this,' he protested.

'How many times have you made a difference?' Garaz asked him.

Oh no. He knew the way this was going, but it was like being trapped in a corridor with only a spiked wall behind you. The only way was forward.

'A couple of times, arguably,' he answered finally, knowing any open disagreement he made would be disproved instantly.

'And maybe you can make a difference this time too,' the orc continued. 'Maybe not. But do you want to leave this young woman's fate to chance when you could be the one who tips the scales of victory in our favour?'

Damn you and your logic Garaz.

'I suppose not.'

'If there is one thing I have learned about you, young Nicolas,' the orc smiled. 'It's that you would never truly walk away from someone in need, not really. It is one of your best qualities.'

The mental image he had of being home, sat at the dinner table with his parents began to evaporate. It didn't vanish completely, why would it? This was a detour, nothing more. And once it was done, he could finally return to Hablock.

I've fought vampires, a necromancer, a minotaur and gangsters. How much worse could a faun be than any of them?

'Okay, I'm with you.' He sounded more determined than he felt.

His companions smiled at his declaration. Except Silva, but even she seemed happy in her way.

'That's the spirit,' Ramirez cried gleefully, before turning to issue commands to his crew to get the ship underway.

Garaz put his hand on Nicolas's shoulder. 'I am glad you are with us.'

This was going to be dangerous, he wasn't a fool. But his companions pleasure at him joining them gave him a pride that he was unaccustomed to and didn't know what to do with.

Save a princess and takedown a nefarious villain or two, then home.

Auron smiled at him like a proud father. 'Adventure time.'

Nicolas blinked a couple of times as he tried to get his head around something. Those two words, *adventure time*. He'd heard Auron say them before. But this time they caused an emotion in him that he hadn't expected. It had come and gone briefly, but he'd felt it.

Excitement.

CHAPTER 7

With all the usual trepidation that came with being on another adventure, and pretending the pang of excitement had never occurred, he'd completely failed to factor in how jarring it would be to travel by ship. The constant moving was most unsettling—the feeling that he was never on stable ground as the ship rose and fell with the currents around it. Then there was the creaking. With each groan of the ship's wooden frame, he worried it might fall apart.

How is something so large even floating in the first place?

His mind reeled with images of drowning as the ship sank around him.

How are all these sailors walking so confidently around the deck? He couldn't keep himself from holding on to the ship for dear life.

Shift, as usual, seemed amused by his discomfort. 'You're going as green as him.' Garaz offered a slight chuckle as Shift pointed to him. 'And we've only just weighed anchor.'

'Alas, we are not all born with nautical blood.' Ramirez grinned, being generally dashing as he manoeuvred the wheel of the ship as if dancing with a lover. 'He will become accustomed to it. Do not be too hard on him.'

'That'd make a nice change.' He was loath to speak much, as opening his mouth when he felt so sick seemed like tempting fate, yet he couldn't let Shift get away with *all* of them.

'Alas, my friend, I fear this beautiful young rose has a thorny tongue.' Ramirez smirked, causing Shift to flush again.

Yup, definitely going to be sick.

'You'll get your sea legs in a bit.' Auron smiled reassuringly for someone whose legs were unaffected by anything.

Allowing the wind to waft his cape behind and raising his chin to breathe in the salty sea air, Ramirez began to rhythmically tap the ships wheel, the beat getting progressively louder. It took Nicolas a second to realise that the sound was getting louder only because the crew on the deck below were all joining in. Soon the tune reverberated across the ship.

How nice of them to make the ship shake more.

To Nicolas's surprise, Ramirez sang in a deep bass voice, his crew soon picking up the tune and joining him as the rhythmic beat continued.

'With wind in our sails and courage in our hearts,
We put to sea and adventure starts,
Weigh, ho, ho, weigh, ho, ho.
Though we may suffer storm and gale,
Deities ensure we ne'er run out o' ale,
Weigh, ho, ho, weigh, ho, ho.
It's our fortunes we go to seek,
Even if the outlook is bleak,
Weigh ho, ho, weigh, ho, ho.
We beseech thee, mistress o' the sea,
Ensure there's a pretty girl waitin' for me.
Weigh, ho, ho, weigh, ho, ho.'

Nicolas looked around in confusion. Was this normal? His companions seemed to be enjoying it well enough. Garaz was even tapping his foot along with the sailors. And who would've guessed Hayley would have such a melodious voice?

'First time people have spontaneously broken into song around you?' Auron asked at his side.

'Yeah. You?'

The spirit rolled his eyes and exhaled sharply. 'I wish.'

Despite himself, Nicolas found the song strangely cheering. He imagined it would be easy to get depressed when surrounded in every direction by an endless blue-green mass, and what could be more uplifting than a good song? He wanted to join in, but that would've meant opening his mouth more than he cared to.

A nautical adventure that starts with a song. I kind of...

He stopped himself. Home was his focus. This was just...the scenic route, with added peril.

'Where are we exactly?' Silva asked thoughtfully once the song had ceased, absentmindedly playing with the rose in her hand.

'Look on every horizon and you will see the spread of the Kingdom of Merida,' Ramirez replied as the sun glinted off one of his large-hooped earrings.

Nicolas actually knew Merida, as it shared a border with Yarringsburg. This wouldn't be one of those times when his lack of world knowledge made him look a fool. The kingdom, one of the Nine Kingdoms of Man, looked tiny on the map, no more than a strip of land to the northwest of

Yarringsburg. However, that strip was only a small part of the kingdom itself, the majority of its landmass being made up of the chain of islands that dotted the sea it claimed as its territory. The Meriduns were known as hardy seafarers and pretty tough to boot. Nicolas supposed you had to be when the only way to get anywhere was by boat.

So T'goth didn't send us to the other side of Etherius.

That was good news. Once they'd completed this quest, the journey home should be a formality. And the quest would probably be done pretty quickly. Sea legs or not, they knew what they were doing. And it was just a faun.

'Ask him why he's chasing the faun,' Auron said.

For a moment, Nicolas didn't realise Auron was talking to him. He was getting so used to everyone being able to see and hear the spirit he'd forgotten he needed to be his mouthpiece sometimes. It was only when Auron raised his eyebrows and jerked his head towards Ramirez that he realised his mistake.

'It seems a bit out of character for pirates to go chasing a kidnapped princess without some angle,' the spirit added, ensuring he kept giving Nicolas the '*evil eye*'.

These are pirates?

Nervously, he looked at the crew. They all seemed like nice enough people—nicer than the faun and his crew, anyhow. But weren't pirates all thieves and brigands, or was that just another fact about Etherius that he had gotten wrong? He didn't feel that he was in any danger, and none of his companions, who must know already, showed signs of concern.

Auron coughed abruptly. Another prompt. Finally Nicolas posed the spirit's question to the captain.

'Ah yes.' Captain Ramirez appeared almost sheepish for a moment. 'Well, firstly, my friend, I will be frank with you. I am not always what you would call a *legitimate* seaman. We do not say the '*P*' word here, but it is not entirely inaccurate. Normally, I would not interfere in the affairs of other seafarers who share my...*profession*, nor those of the Tidal Kingdom. However, I happen to have sworn an oath to hunt down and kill my nemesis, who is in league with this faun. Rescuing the princess is just a by-product of that.'

How noble.

'Even if it takes until I am old and infirm, I shall corner my nemesis, run him through, and be avenged.' Ramirez's words were delivered with gusto, but there was an almost-false quality to them Nicolas couldn't put his finger on.

'Yeah, you mentioned a nemesis before.' Shift kept their eyes closed as they spoke, seeming to enjoy the sea breeze. 'What's that about?'

'Captain Killgore.' Ramirez spat on the deck. 'My mortal enemy, and a mangy, tick-ridden, dog if ever there was one. He took something precious from me, and I am sworn to make him pay for it with his life.'

'Killgore?' Shift laughed. 'He had to have given himself that name. Who would name their child Killgore?'

'Someone who wanted a pirate for a son?' Nicolas suggested.

'Definitely a bad guy name,' Auron added.

'That cannot be his full name,' Garaz chuckled. 'I'm sure it is a family name.'.

'Says the orc with the single name.' Shift smiled ironically.

'Firstly, I have a second name. You have just never asked.' Garaz sniffed haughtily. 'Secondly, you are one to talk.'

Nicolas was taken aback and more than a little embarrassed that he'd never asked either. Everything they'd been through together, and he didn't even know his companion's second name. That made him a bad friend, even though Garaz wasn't always the most open of people. Better than Silva, though.

'His first name is Ezekiel. And yes, his second name is a moniker he gave himself,' Ramirez explained. 'He is a filthy, honourless cur. Do I rob ships? Yes, it is what my folk do. But I always leave the crew unharmed and the ship intact. He burns ships and murders the crew. He gives pir...professionals like ourselves a bad name.'

'He gives seafaring thieves a bad name?' Nicolas asked.

'Indeed,' Ramirez replied, oblivious to the sarcasm.

'What did he take from you?' Garaz asked.

For a moment, Ramirez's face hardened. At his side, Hay Sharkbait looked a little sheepish. 'It is not to be discussed.' The captain's tone was firm. 'Suffice to say, the dog will pay. When the sole survivor of the attack on the princess's ship described someone that could only be him, I knew fate had put him in my path so that I may take my final revenge on him.'

'Fate seems to be putting a lot of people where they need to be.' Garaz gave Nicolas a sidelong glance.

Nicolas didn't care for it. To him, being here was a random set of events that he'd become caught up in. It wasn't his choice and certainly not some divine plan that had chosen him. The stick had fallen randomly on him. There was no way anyone, anywhere, would've chosen him for this. And if some higher power *had* picked him, it either had a warped sense of humour or they all needed to weep for the state of the world.

'Do you know much of the partnership between Killgore and this faun?' Garaz asked.

'Alas, little,' Ramirez admitted. 'Just that they are working together. Though it is strange, as my nemesis is not the type for partnerships. I had initially assumed they were both aboard his ship, the *Black Death*. But you have confirmed that the faun is on a smaller vessel and the *Death* is nowhere to be found. Strange for a ship so large and...so prominent. But this is good. It shall be easier to commandeer the smaller ship once we catch them. Then this faun and I shall have a long talk about Killgore's whereabouts.'

'How will you be sure the faun will give you the information?' Silva asked.

Ramirez shrugged. 'I shall beat it out of him.'

'Simple and effective,' Silva noted in an impressed, slightly dreamy tone.

Of course she'd like that.

'I save the grand ideas for the romancing of beautiful women,' the captain replied with a sly wink to Silva.

The warrior looked back out to sea. Had her face reddened slightly? How was he doing this? How did Silva and Shift not see an overweight, middle-aged man with a receding hairline? Were they blind? Maybe Ramirez had some kind of seduction magic?

Am I just going to pretend that I wasn't struck by the dashing persona when I boarded? I wonder what broke the illusion for me?

'I don't like it,' Auron grumbled to himself, passing his hands thoughtfully through some thick rope that connected something Nicolas couldn't name to something else he couldn't name.

'Why not?' Nicolas asked.

'If you go to the trouble of helping a notorious pirate kidnap a princess, you don't just wander off visiting shipwrecks for a spot of graverobbing afterwards. You stay with the pirate and your captive, because you don't trust him any more that he probably trusts you. Everything I know tells me Killgore and the faun should be together.'

'Not everything has to fit into your rules of hero work.' Garaz chuckled.

'Pfft.' Auron snorted. 'Listen to the voice of experience, people. Something is off with this.'

****

The rolling and pitching of the ship was almost relaxing once he finally found his sea legs, yet he still stood close to a rail at all times. Just in case. The sea sickness had been the worst, his stomach constantly churning in time with the ship, causing repeated spasms in his throat that he fought back. Hard. He already had a reputation for being sick on an adventure, and he wanted to break that stereotype. Plus, throwing up on the ship of someone who'd saved you just seemed rude. His attempts to save face were, as usual, for naught as Shift had taken to *mistakenly* referring to him as Garaz.

'Ye need te focus on the horizon, laddie,' Hayley told him as she casually wound a rope around her forearm at his side. 'The horizon's the only stationary thing. Look at it long enough and ye'll reset yer equilibrium. After that, ye'll be well away.'

Ignoring the advice of a seasoned sailor would be stupid.

And so, he looked at the horizon, the point where the endless ocean met an endless sky. Slowly, his body began to right itself again, the nausea fading.

May it never return again.

'Thank you, Hayley,' he said sincerely, still keeping one hand on the rail.

'*Hay Sharkbait,*' the sailor corrected him. 'And think nothin' o' it.' With a wink, she discarded the rope and walked away to other duties.

She'd probably just been messing with the rope as an excuse to help him discreetly.

Deities bless her for that.

Now all he had to do was overcome his anxiety about the boat capsizing or otherwise randomly sinking, and he'd be all good.

Standing at the edge of the deck and looking out to sea, he watched the ebb and flow of the water, the salty air caressing his face. It was easy for someone's mind to drift amongst the blue-green currents. Focusing on it made him feel almost peaceful. Was this what it was like for Garaz when he meditated? A couple of times, the waves broke beside the ship as large fish jumped from the water. He'd never seen such creatures before, but they looked so...at home in the sea as they rose and sank and swished through the water. He was even getting used to the smell of old, wet wood. Thank the Deities for that, too. It was hardly avoidable on the ship.

Look at us, crashing through the waves on our way to fight pirates and rescue a princess.

He looked down at his chest, wondering why his heart was racing. He wasn't scared of anything and it couldn't be anything else. Surely.

'Feeling better, Seaman Carnegie?' Shift asked, appearing at his side.

'I don't think they'll make a sailor out of me.' Nicolas shrugged. 'But at least they won't have to clean up after me.'

Shift laughed. 'This sea air is quite invigorating.' They stretched their arms wide, as if preparing to be carried off in the same breeze that bulged the sails. Though their auburn hair was short, it still caught the breeze and danced playfully. Nicolas imagined his own shaggy mane was doing the same. It was actually a nice moment, one his brain decided to sour for reasons unfathomable to him.

'Maybe it's not the sea air that's invigorating you?' He spoke quietly, wanting to say the words but half hoping Shift wouldn't hear him.

They heard. 'What do you mean by that?'

He'd set himself on a path, he might as well walk it. 'Well, what was that back there? That whole *blushing, giggling* thing you were doing around the captain.'

Judging by the look on his companion's face, this path was fraught with danger. 'It's called having charm, Nicolas.'

Oh no, they actually used my first name properly.

Funny, this was the first time he'd really noticed that they called him *Nick* all the time. How strange.

Never mind that, you may be in trouble.

'But he's just a middle-aged guy.' Despite the warnings in his mind, he persisted. 'Just look at him. Definitely past his prime. I mean, yeah, he has some showmanship, but beyond that, what?'

They both looked to the bridge, where Ramirez was stretching his back as if he'd somehow tweaked it. Not the dashing image he usually cut.

'You're not wrong.' Shift seemed put out by that fact. 'But he has a certain confidence that's...endearing. And it more than makes up for a little wear and tear.'

Well, bully for Ramirez.

'You know jealousy isn't attractive, right Nick?' Shift continued dryly.

Jealousy? What?

He wasn't jealous. He was just...concerned. Maybe the captain had glamoured them or something? 'I'm just worried about you getting...I don't know...used or something. He's a sailor, and they have reputations.'

Did they?

He didn't know for sure; he was just saying words now.

Shift pursed their lips and looked past him, their face suggesting they were looking at a pile of cow dung. 'I wouldn't worry,' they said finally. 'My competition is edging in, anyway.'

Silva hadn't moved from the bridge since boarding the ship. She stood in her set position, holding the rigging to steady herself as she stared towards the deck. The warrior looked really awkward. It was strange to see from someone usually so confident and... Emotionless seemed harsh.

Guarded. That's better.

Every so often, Ramirez would turn to Silva and speak, and she'd nod and...smile. Occasionally she even *played* with her shoulder length blonde hair as he talked.

Silva smiling. Weird.

'Maybe the captain has a preference for women who could murder him in his sleep,' Shift noted tartly as they observed the interaction.

'Now who's jealous?' His tone was petulant, but he couldn't take it back. Maybe lightening the mood would be a better choice right now. 'Besides, she isn't that person anymore. Also, she's perfectly capable of murdering him when he's awake.'

Despite themselves, Shift let out a laugh, smiling at him and shaking their head.

'I like funny stuff,' Auron said as he approached. 'What's the joke?'

'Silva and the good captain,' Nicolas informed him with a suggestive eyebrow raise.

The spirit looked back at the bridge. 'Well, she does like older men. Good luck to him. She's a handful.'

That's odd. Surely the pair hadn't...

The spirit looked almost uncomfortable for a second before changing the tone. 'Does she seem a little...*tense*...to you?'

Sometimes, with all the glares, and cutting remarks, and murder, he forgot that Silva and Auron had worked together at one point. How had that come about? How had she changed so much? At some point, Auron would surely tell the story, for if anything was true in the universe, it was that Auron liked telling a story.

As for Silva, she always seemed a little off, so Nicolas shrugged. 'It's hard to tell. I don't really know her that well.'

'Probably nothing,' Auron muttered before looking pointedly at him. 'Speaking of tense. Another adventure. How are you doing with that?'

Nicolas gestured to the sea around them. 'It seems as if I'm in whether I like it or not.' He laughed. 'I am as much a prisoner here as the princess is on the other ship.'

'C'mon, kid,' the spirit scoffed. 'You've seen and done enough by now to be getting used to this. You aren't a natural, but you're learning and better than half the posers I've met.' Auron leaned in close and whispered, 'I know you're secretly loving this.'

His insides clenched as if some terrible secret had been discovered. Though he couldn't understand why he reacted like that.

'I'm kidding,' Auron said, shaking his head. 'I see the anxiousness is already making you jumpy, and we aren't even in sight of any pirates yet.'

Yes, anxiousness. That's all it was.

'I've said I'm in,' he confirmed once he'd composed himself mentally. 'You know I don't care for this stuff, but a princess needs rescuing, so...'

Why does it feel as if I'm lying? What's going on with me?

Auron beamed. 'Great stuff, kid.'

'Good news?' Garaz asked as he approached, evidently having raided the ship's larder.

'The best,' Shift said with their teasing grin. 'Nick isn't going to whine all through this adventure.'

'Those are glad tidings indeed.' The orc chuckled.

'The way I see it,' Nicolas said, 'if we're chasing a faun and a pirate around the sea, at least they don't have some ridiculous underground lair or tunnel. After our last two *outings*, I've had my fill of underground villain's lairs and going through dark tunnels.'

There were murmurs of agreement from the others.

'How about you?' Nicolas asked Auron. 'I suppose nautical adventures are pretty standard for you.'

The spirit shrugged. 'Actually, this is my first one.'

'Really?' That meant no related stories for a while. *Praise the Deities.*

Auron casually looked out to sea. 'The closest I've ever come is when I saw Janessa off when we parted.'

Nicolas scrunched his face up. 'Hang on,' he said. 'If you've never had a nautical adventure, how did you even meet a princess of the Tidal Kingdom?'

Slowly, the ethereal face turned to him, and from the growing grin Nicolas understood the trap he'd just walked merrily into 'So this one time,' the spirit began slowly, 'I was summoned to a peace conference. Apparently, there were rumours of an assassination attempt, and they wanted to show they weren't messing when it came to security.'

'Well done, Nick,' Shift muttered to him through a closed mouth.

'Now to catch an assassin, you have to think like an assassin,' Auron continued, breaking into his storytelling flair. 'What I didn't know at the time was that there were actually three assassins. Turned out one of the assassins had been hired to kill the original assassin. The party that hired assassin number one, some minister with a grudge, wanted to cancel the job and couldn't get in touch with the assassin, so he hired another assassin to take him out instead. The best bit...after he'd sent assassin number two out, he realised that he needed the first assassin to do the job after all, so hired a third assassin to take out assassin number two, because he couldn't get in touch with him to cancel that job either. Now this is where it gets complicated...'

'If he says *assassin* one more time, I will never heal another of your wounds again,' Garaz muttered from behind closed lips.

Well, that's crap.

If Nicolas was good at picking up one thing on his adventures, it was wounds.

Fortunately, Auron never got the chance to repeat the word, because just then they were interrupted by a shout from the crow's nest high above that land had been sighted.

CHAPTER 8

On the bridge of the *Irrevocable Amora*, Nicolas watched the shape on the horizon gradually growing larger. As it did, more details became clear: the crags and jags of the rocks, the green foliage, and the distinctions of the rising hills. It was strange to think that something so tiny would soon be big enough for him to walk on, let alone contain forests and maybe villages. The world was an amazing place indeed.

'Which island is that?' he asked Ramirez, who was standing by the helmsman, ensuring that the ship stayed on course, and looking as flamboyant as possible doing it.

'Who knows?' The captain shrugged. 'There are so many named islands around here that I do not bother committing them all to memory.'

'What? Then how do you ever know where you're going?'

'The sea guides me,' Ramirez replied with a wink that wrinkled his face. 'I do not have to know the names of the places to know which way I am going, my friend.'

He sighed. Of course he was on a ship piloted by the one captain in all Etherius who didn't know the names of the islands he was navigating around. He kicked himself slightly for even being surprised at the information.

'Hopefully, the faun has passed here recently and there will be someone who can point us in the right direction,' Auron suggested hopefully.

Nicolas conveyed his thoughts to the captain.

'If they kept their course true, they would have passed by,' Ramirez said firmly. 'If not then no matter. There is no cove or dock where they can hide that shall stop me from finding them and quenching the thirst for vengeance in my heart.'

'That Killgore must have *really* done something terrible,' Shift commented in a low voice.

'Indeed,' Hay Sharkbait confirmed, obviously overhearing them. 'We been hunting that dog fer nigh on six months now. We get close,' the first mate gave the captain a sideways glance, 'but somehow Killgore always manages te slip through our grasp. Ne'er fear, though. Captain's gonna send him straight te the underworld when we do catch 'em.'

Six months of dogged pursuit? This was quite the grudge. The air the captain gave off suggested an easy-going man with few cares in the world. Certainly not the type to swear an oath of blood vengeance or try to follow it through. Maybe Killgore killed his parents? That seemed like a thing to require vengeance. Or maybe they'd fallen out over some woman? That sounded more legitimate for a passionate seafarer such as Ramirez. Intrigue scratched at Nicolas's brain, urging him to find out more.

'Do you have someone special on any of the islands around here?' he enquired casually.

Instantly, both Silva and Shift glared at him. Maybe this line of enquiry would break whatever hold he had over them.

Good.

'Beg pardon?' the captain asked.

'Well, sailing around, you must meet a lot of women?'

'Ah.' Ramirez smiled. 'You mean the old adage about a captain having a girl in every port?'

'Yes, that.'

'I will give you the same answer I give any who ask that question.' Ramirez leaned in close, dropping his voice to a conspiratorial whisper. 'Only one per port?' As the captain winked at him, Shift and Silva's glares intensified.

It wasn't Nicolas's fault they were enamoured with what appeared to be a very loose gentleman, and they shouldn't get upset at him for uncovering it.

'So we're on a quest to save a princess, and you want to know how much *pleasurable company* the captain gets?' Auron asked distastefully. 'Thinking of becoming a pirate captain when this is done, are we?'

'Nothing like that. I was just curious,' he replied awkwardly.

'Far too curious,' Silva rebuked, as she scowled at him.

'If you are trying to make a point about the captain's relations for Silva and Shift's sake, I would avoid it. You are seldom thanked for interfering in affairs of the heart,' Garaz said.

'What he said,' Shift added huffily.

'I wasn't,' Nicolas protested.

Beside him, Auron was chuckling to himself.

'What about *your* love life then?' he asked the spirit. 'We are chasing one of your ex-bed partners, aren't we? Is she going to remember you fondly or did you slip away like a thief in the night?'

'Leave it.' The spirit's cold tone shocked Nicolas.

He did as he was asked. If he'd known it was such a touchy subject, he wouldn't have mentioned it at all. Was he bound to upset Garaz in a few moments too, as the orc was the only one left not annoyed with him?

Before he could, Nicolas decided to focus on the island, which was getting ever clearer. Now he could make out people at the top of one of the cliffs that was constantly battered by the sea's relentless waves.

'What are they doing?' Garaz asked, using his hand to shield his eyes from the sun's glare just as the rest of them were.

The individuals were concentrated around something, some kind of structure maybe. There was a sudden flash of movement followed by a deep splash. Nicolas rubbed his eyes for a moment, just to check they were still working properly. Because what he'd just witnessed made no sense.

'What *are* they doing?' he asked. If the figures were doing what he thought they were doing, then why they were doing it was a matter of great concern to him.

As it turned out, he *was* seeing correctly, and what he was seeing was pretty darned weird. Having ridden a cow-dragon hybrid creature and seen a talking chicken, Nicolas didn't think he'd ever find anything weird again. Yet here he was.

Huh.

As the *Irrevocable Amora* floated lazily in the tide parallel to the coast of the island, the strange scene repeated itself again. Two men hefted a large stone into the bucket of the catapult, walking away from their charge stooping like men who'd lifted too many large stones that day. Once they'd stood clear, one of them signalled to the man at the contraption's lever, before returning to rubbing and stretching his back. With a nod of confirmation, the man pulled the catapult's lever, dramatically releasing the tension of the rope and causing the arm, with its payload, to swing up, launching the stone into the air, the whole machine bucking nosily as it did.

The stone arced through the air then crashed into the sea just like the others had, throwing up a great spray of water. Back on the ridge, the catapult's crew cheered, as did the archers around the base of the machine. Looking back to where the stone had struck and now sunk, Nicolas could see no obvious target. There certainly seemed nothing worth the men's enthusiasm.

'Ahoy, there,' Ramirez called out, putting some kind of speaking horn to his lips that amplified his voice.

One of the men broke from the group and walked to the very edge of the cliff. 'Ahoy Captain,' he shouted back in a deep bass voice through his own contraption. These speaking horns must be quite common In

Merida. They were certainly handy. It was like the man was right in front of him.

'May I ask what you are doing?' Ramirez asked.

'Protecting our own,' the man answered fiercely. Though it was hard to tell properly at this distance, he, like the rest, seemed to be village folk. No soldiers amongst them.

Nicolas had so many questions but thought it best to stay out of the conversation between Ramirez and the islander for now.

'From whom?' the captain enquired.

'Damned merpeople,' the man replied. Nicolas watched him rear back and jerk forwards aggressively. Judging by the tone of the man when he answered, the motion was most likely spitting.

Charming.

Nicolas looked out to sea again, but there was nothing in sight. Maybe these people were mad? Could they have been isolated for too long? Suddenly, he imagined himself and his companions still stuck on the island, hurling makeshift spears into the sea at phantoms.

'Saw some of the filthy creatures swimming around this morning just off the coast there. Trying to intimidate us,' the man continued in a thick accent that made it difficult to follow his words. 'If they think they're going to do to us what they did to the other islands, they're making a big mistake. They won't find us wanting, no sir. We're giving them a few warning shots, just to remind them what's what. If they can't take a hint and want more than that, they can come and get it. We'll hook 'em, and it'll be fish supper all round.'

Hopefully, that was just big talk, and the man didn't intend on actually eating merpeople, because, well...people.

'And what if you hit one?' Ramirez asked. 'You could start a war.'

The man shrugged nonchalantly. 'One less cursed merperson,' the islander replied as if it were a small thing. 'After what they've been doing, the truce is over. They want a war, we'll gladly give 'em one. And if they're stupid enough to swim in the way of our rocks, well, that there is just natural selection, yes sir.'

'He is really riled up,' Shift muttered beside Nicolas.

'They're shooting rocks into the ocean. I don't think they're completely right in the head.' Auron was most likely correct in his analysis. It didn't seem like the kind of thing sane folk did.

'All we've got to do is hold out for a few more days,' the islander declared gleefully. 'The fleet's gathering, you see. When it does, we'll give those scaley dogs the drubbing of a lifetime. They won't ever want to come back to the surface again after our navy's done with them, no sir. And good riddance, says I. They can go and sleep with their fishes.'

'If they wish to hold out more than a day, I suggest they stop wasting their stones in such a manner,' Silva commented with a raised eyebrow.

'I wouldn't tell them that,' Shift said, their tone to the warrior slightly frosty. 'They seem pretty invested in their task.'

'I was not going to, but thank you for the advice,' Silva replied, equally frostily.

Nicolas already wished the pair would give up on this stupid feud over who gets Ramirez's attention. Shift should just let Silva have it.

'Look, Captain,' the islander said as one of his fellows called him back to the catapult. 'I've got to get back. Two more to go. If you follow the coastline around, you'll come to the dock and the township. Just make sure when you dock, that *that* behaves itself.'

The *that* the man had referred to, as if talking about a cow pat in a field, was Garaz, who looked less than impressed by the comment. 'Charming,' the orc huffed, his face stern.

'Thank you, kind sir,' Ramirez shouted back. 'Good luck with your...endeavour.'

'Don't need luck, no sir.' The islander smiled. 'Just need a proper target, is all. Need to show those...fin-havers...who's in charge around here.'

Fin-havers. What sort of insult was that? If you are going to create devices that make conversation between ship and shore at distance so easy, then using them to fling ridiculous insults just seemed wrong. Hopefully, people at the township would be more sensible, as this group weren't the best ambassadors for the island. He doubted it, though. Chances were everyone on this island just as equally insane.

'Racist idiot,' the captain muttered as he waved and smiled at the islander then gave orders to get the ship underway.

Following the line of the coast, the *Irrevocable Amora* soon found itself entering an atoll, the opening bordered by pincers of rocky coast. Judging by the archers and ballistae arrayed near the entrance, the township was taking no chances with its security. This didn't feel like a safe place.

Beyond the shore appeared to be a thriving fishing town which ran the length of the coastline. From it extended multiple docks, capable of mooring ships of various sizes. Most of these were occupied by smaller vessels that were fishing boats, judging by all the nets he could see.

He could also see that word travelled fast across the island, as a welcoming committee was already awaiting them at the largest dock. Though the closer they got, the less welcoming the party appeared. Being met by armed guards didn't give the impression of hospitality.

Perhaps I should just stay on the boat?

As the mighty ship came to rest at the dock, Nicolas marvelled at the efficiency of the crew as they threw out and secured lines and brought down the sails. It was all quite beyond him, and he didn't think he could learn it if he sailed for a hundred days. *No.* He stopped himself there. He *could* learn these things given enough time. He had to stop selling himself short. Had he not already proven himself capable of many things he'd never believed possible? Nicolas's internal monologue was cut short by a wooden thud as the ship's gangplank landed on the edge of the dock.

'Shall we?' Ramirez stood on the edge of the walkway, gesturing for Nicolas and his companions to accompany him.

'Maybe I ought to stay aboard,' Garaz suggested, not very enthusiastically. 'Judging by what the other islander said, I doubt I will be welcome.'

Ramirez scrutinised the orc for a second. 'Screw them,' the captain said finally. 'You are good people, so you are coming with us.'

Hopefully, the captain's diplomacy would be better when they were on the dock. Telling the islanders to screw themselves was unlikely to be taken well. Garaz didn't argue; in fact, he seemed pleased with the vote of confidence as he smiled and bowed his head to the captain.

Silva insisted on going first for...whatever reason the inscrutable warrior had. As she stood on the edge of the gangplank, she hesitated for a second. In that moment, Ramirez took her hand and brushed it lightly against his lips. Shift didn't look impressed.

Good, they don't need the amorous affections of some old captain anyway.

'Your concern for our safety is appreciated,' Ramirez spoke softly as he returned Silva's hand.

The warrior coughed awkwardly and turned away. After a deep breath, Silva proceeded carefully down the ramp.

'Like we aren't all concerned for each other's safety,' Shift grumbled quietly behind him.

'Captain Ramirez,' the leader of the welcoming party, a well-to-do gentleman in a long robe of office, greeted him with open arms. 'Always a welcome visitor to our little community.'

'Mayor Mendos.' Ramirez smiled warmly, embracing the robed man before releasing his grip and patting him on both arms. 'It is always a pleasure to visit your little slice of paradise.'

The mayor chuckled heartily, his spectacles and the tufts of white hair on either side of his head bobbing up and down as he did. 'Oh, I don't know about that. We do our best.'

'How are Elora and the children?'

The mayor seemed hesitant to respond for a second. 'They are well,' he replied finally. 'They are off to the mainland at the moment, visiting relatives.'

Ramirez nodded sympathetically. 'It is always a shame to be parted from family.'

'Alas, I'm needed here. With everything that's going on we have harsh times ahead, methinks.' The mayor appeared reluctant to elaborate further but gave his guards a wary glance.

This friendly discourse was strange to Nicolas. The pair seemed to know each other well, though how were a pirate and an elected official so close? Also, why did the rest of the mayor's party look like they were ready to beat them all right back onto the ship?

'Be careful,' Auron counselled quietly, even though most couldn't hear him. 'Watch what you say and how you act. I imagine it won't take much for this to turn nasty. Especially you, big guy.'

Nicolas wouldn't have called himself the most observant person, but even he was picking up on the glares and animosity directed at Garaz...though they were pretty blatant, to be fair. The orc was keeping a neutral face, but there was a hint of sadness in his yellow eyes. They had nothing to fear from Garaz. The orc was a gentle soul, and it was offensive the way the welcoming party's hands were resting on their swords.

'What brings you here, old friend?' Mendos asked genially. 'More wares to sell that conveniently jumped off cargo ships?'

The people of this island had no qualms about buying stolen goods, then. With all his dashing and bravado, it was difficult to remember that Ramirez was essentially a thief. But then, the captain wouldn't be the first thief he'd travelled with. He glanced at Shift, who caught his look and mouthed an enquiry. He shrugged awkwardly and looked away.

'I am not about that kind of business today,' Ramirez replied coyly. 'Today, my business is chasing pirates.'

'Find your reflection, and you'll have caught one, you old dog.' Mendos chuckled jovially, clapping his hands in glee at his own jest.

Ramirez feigned offence. 'I am naught but a humble seafarer,' the captain said with a knowing wink. 'But I think you know who I am after.'

'Oh, *him*,' the mayor replied with a distaste. 'Still chasing Killgore down, eh? Well, you won't find him here. We don't parlay with that ilk.'

'I know this, of course.' Ramirez laughed. 'But you do hear things. Sometimes very interesting things. Also, my crew could do with some firm ground beneath their feet for an hour or two, so let us...'

Ramirez took a step forward, toward the island itself, only to find his motion arrested by a raised hand. Suddenly, Mayor Mendos's face became very serious. Grave, even. Nicolas found his hand slipping towards his sword, noting that his companions were doing the same. Beside him, he felt a slight build up of energy, suggesting that Garaz was summoning his power.

'I know we normally have such good relations,' Mayor Mendos began diplomatically after a slightly awkward cough. 'And believe me, I wouldn't do this under normal circumstances. But circumstances are not at all normal of late. Before I allow you ashore, there is a matter to discuss.'

The mayor looked pointedly at Garaz, who was keeping his temper admirably. When he looked at his companion, the sun must've caught the orc strangely for a moment, as he could've sworn there was a hint of red in those yellow eyes.

'Jasper,' Ramirez protested, genuinely aggrieved. 'We have been friends for years. We have done each other many favours, and now you treat a friend of mine like this? Where is your hospitality?'

Mayor Mendos seemed to bristle at the insult to his honour. 'The hospitality of my community is never found wanting,' he huffed. 'However, in these turbulent times, certain assurances are needed when dealing with...outsiders.'

'Assurances?' Shift interrupted, and the mayor glared at them, seemingly offended that they'd inserted themselves into the conversation.

'I shall need you to vouch for the orc,' Mendos continued, his men ready to back him up. 'I need your word of honour that his conduct in our community is your responsibility during your stay and that he will keep to the utmost good behaviour.'

'What in the Underworld?' Shift cried. 'How dare you treat a person like this? You listen here, you little...' Shift was about to engage in a full-on rant—which, thanks to his companion's lack of tact, could lead to swords being drawn—but they stopped when a large green hand rested on their shoulder.

Garaz had a mixture of sadness and pride in his yellow eyes. 'It is okay, my friend,' the orc said simply. 'Whatever makes them feel most comfortable. This is their home, after all.'

'They can—' Shift's sentence was cut off by a firm look from Garaz, and they backed down.

Ramirez looked at Garaz, and they exchanged heavy nods. 'You have my word.' The captain was clearly as unhappy with this as anyone else but would play along.

'He will be accompanied by one of your party and two of my men at all times,' Mendos continued. 'He is to keep to designated areas of the island and is forbidden to interact with the townsfolk. Should his conduct be unbecoming of a guest...action will be taken.'

Nicolas kept his face neutral as anger churned in his gut. He'd heard Garaz tell of his general treatment in the world of humans, he'd even seen a little of it first-hand, but this was ridiculous. Garaz was no threat to anyone.

He's a healer, for Deities sake.

Though Nicolas had seen him burn a vampire's face off and behead another, in reality Garaz was naught more than a gentle giant. It offended him that others would see him any differently.

Ramirez looked to Garaz for acknowledgment. When he received it, he looked back at the mayor. 'Very well.'

'Excellent.' Mendos didn't conceal his sigh of relief very well at all, nor did his guards. 'In that case, I welcome you all to Kohot Island. I am Jasper Mendos, magistrate and mayor of this fine community. Please avail yourself of our hospitality.'

Hospitality? Yeah, provided you weren't green.

Apparently, Ramirez was similarly disturbed by the islanders' behaviour—he whispered to Hay Sharkbait to keep the crew aboard the *Amora*.

Now that the mayor was satisfied, he gestured them toward the island proper, their escort moving in step with them, two of whom clung very closely to Garaz. Nicolas hung toward the back with Auron.

'That was tense,' he whispered, unclenching things he hadn't even realised were clenched.

'Wrong, is what that was,' Auron said grimly. 'Very wrong.'

****

Walking the cobbled streets between the wooden houses that made up the township on Kohot Island, all of the homes had a quaint, rustic look to them, which added to the picturesque nature of the place. Though it was clear the smell of fish was destined to follow them wherever they went, but what else would you expect from a fishing community.

It'd be a nice place to explore properly, if we were allowed.

Indeed, with the escort flanking them as they were led through the streets, it seemed more as if they were being marched to jail, rather than being treated as welcome guests.

That certainly seemed the opinion of the island folk, as they eyed the newcomers suspiciously. Not surprising given the spectacle being made. At a glance, the hardy, tanned folk would've seemed good-natured enough, but for the glances and whispers Garaz's presence invoked. Had it not been for their escort, the people might've started hurling vegetables at any moment. Maybe the escort was there to protect them as much as keep them in line? Whatever the case, Nicolas wanted to be away from this island as soon as possible. He couldn't imagine how Garaz felt. There was no way to tell, either; the orc's face was completely neutral.

Mayor Mendos led the party through the winding, ascending streets towards a large manor house atop a hill overlooking the community. It was certainly a fanciful dwelling that spoke of opulent, if dubious, taste judging by the garishness of the statues in its gardens—a series of gyrating stone figures more befitting a brothel than a quaint garden. As they passed through the archway into the manor's gardens, the smell of fish gave way to sweet floral aromas. That must've been no easy task. By the door to the manor house, servants in white wigs with immaculate suits awaited their approach. The doors were opened for them as the servants bowed, greeting the master of the house upon his return.

Nicolas had little time to dwell on the grandness of the reception hall as they entered and were quickly herded toward a side study. The room had so many books in it, he found it hard to believe that one person could've read them all. Either being mayor of this island was a very easy job or this was a poser's library. Judging by the rich, smoky aroma, Mendos enjoyed a pipe when he read. He also enjoyed his alcohol, with a wide variety of beverages displayed on a nearby drinks' cabinet of the same dark oak that made up the rest of the furniture. Sitting on a large leather chair that creaked beneath his weight, the mayor gestured for them all to sit. Only Garaz stayed standing, a single act of defiance toward their *host*. The intent seemed to be noted by Mendos, but not mentioned, the mayor apparently happy enough to overlook it. Probably a good thing—Nicolas wouldn't put it past the man to have any chair Garaz sat in burned once they'd left.

As they made themselves comfortable, Nicolas couldn't help but chuckle inwardly at how uncomfortable the two men escorting Garaz seemed. He wasn't surprised, the orc being considerably broader and taller than both men. Having seen Garaz fight, he had no doubt that he'd make short work of those pair, an idea that didn't seem lost on either of them. Not that it'd come to that, of course.

'Jasper.' Ramirez leant forward in his chair and spoke earnestly. 'What is going on? The catapult firing into the ocean and then that business at the dock. This is not like you, old friend.'

The mayor rubbed his chin nervously. 'Dark times.' His voice was as grim as his expression. 'Dark times indeed. We need to be careful. Now more than ever.'

Any further conversation was delayed by a servant carrying a tray of drinks, which were offered around and accepted, with one notable exception. As welcome as refreshment was, the servant was frustratingly slow when there was such an ambiguous statement to clarify.

'So about the dark times?' Shift prompted as the servant left the room.

'I take it you have heard about the princess of the Tidal Kingdom being kidnapped?' the mayor asked, before taking a long sip of his drink.

'That is part of the reason for our visit,' Ramirez answered seriously.

'Her people think *we* did it. By that, I mean our kingdom. Can you believe that? To openly accuse us of such dishonourable behaviour.'

Mendos scoffed, his jowls shaking. 'They approached our government and demanded her back. Let me ask you, how do you give back someone you haven't taken? You cannot. Well, those scaley curs didn't accept that, so there have been...reprisals.'

'Reprisals?' Ramirez asked.

'They have taken children.' Mendos's jaw was clenched in outrage. 'The filthy creatures have raided several islands, coming in at night after all are asleep. Parents tuck their children into bed, kiss them goodnight, and when they go to them in the morning, they have vanished. Can you fathom the kind of low mind to come up with such a devious counter?'

'How can you be so sure it was them?' Nicolas asked.

Conspiratorially, the mayor leaned forward, his voice a whisper. 'It is common knowledge, young sir. Personally, and I don't mind saying that I'm not alone in this, I believe they took their own damned princess as an excuse to have at us.' Mendos nodded with certainty. 'It's been brewing long enough. Let them try, says I. The good people of this island fear nothing the sea has to offer, least of all a bunch of half-fish upstarts.'

'So it'll be war then?' Ramirez asked thoughtfully.

The mayor nodded solemnly. 'The Nautical Accords will be torn asunder, and we shall show them who the real masters of these waters are.'

'Nautical Accords?' Nicolas asked.

'You do not know your history, young sir?' Mendos replied, slightly aghast.

'He knows nothing about anything.' Auron chuckled.

Nicolas spared him a contemptuous sideways glance but didn't respond. Now was not the time to start talking to someone most of the room couldn't see.

'I'm sorry, but I am unfamiliar with them.' Ignorance was always a hard thing to admit, but this was important information so pride would have to suck it up.

'As you know, the Kingdom of Merida extends far across these seas,' Ramirez began. 'Yet the Tidal Kingdom claims dominion over all waters in Etherius. It goes without saying that they didn't take kindly to us humans sailing through their waters, never mind claiming parts of it. There was a...scuffle that lasted several years until cooler heads prevailed and the accords were drawn up. It provided a compromise. That Meriduns are masters of the surface of the water and the islands situated in it, while under the ocean is the realm of the merpeople. They don't like living on land and we can't live under the sea, so it seemed ideal. There have been...*skirmishes* since, but it never fell to open war.' Ramirez sat back with a little sigh. 'However, the bad feeling has always been there on both sides.'

'And now it's all in chaos,' Mendos interjected with gusto. 'War is coming again. We have seen activity below the surface on the west side of the island. We know those merpeople have a forward post there to spy on us Deity-fearing folk. Exactly the kind of sneaky behaviour they favour. We're just making sure they keep their distance. They shall not have the children of this island. By the Deities, they will not.'

'And you don't think firing large stones into the water may...provoke them?' Shift was being pretty diplomatic, for them.

'Provoking them is not my concern, madam.' Shift's mouth became a thin line at being referred to as *madam,* but they kept any thoughts about it to themselves as the flustered mayor continued. 'The safety of this community is. If they do not get the message to stay clear, then that is up to them. Besides, the ships defending the island have been called away. An armada gathers, a grand armada, at Merida Minor. Once it puts forth, the merpeople will give us back our children or the seas will be littered with their floating corpses, yes indeed.'

'Have you seen any other ships pass by recently?' Nicolas asked, hoping for some kind of lead so they could move on quickly.

Now there was a potential war at stake, it didn't do to be hanging round sipping tea in a fancy manor. They needed to find the princess as soon as possible, and a number of children too, apparently. This was getting more complicated by the second. He didn't know what a war at sea would look like but was damn sure he didn't want to be sailing around in the middle of one. But they had stopped a vampire apocalypse, so he was confident they would get the job done.

'Young sir, we see all sorts of ships all the time.' The mayor laughed, seeming to relax slightly when not talking about war. 'You'll have to be more specific.'

'It would be a small ship. They had a faun aboard,' Shift added.

Mendos thought for a moment. 'Nothing like that,' he declared finally. 'We would have remembered. We are careful about whom we let land here nowadays.' The sentence was finished with a sly glance at Garaz that made Nicolas's disgust towards the old bigot increase.

'This has proven to be a big waste of time.' Auron huffed, pacing the room, examining anything that half took his interest.

After necking his drink, Ramirez stood and offered the mayor a bow. 'I thank you for your time, good sir. But we must now take our leave.'

The guards beside Garaz looked visibly relieved, as did the mayor. 'Shame you cannot stay longer, but I understand that seafaring business waits for no man.' For a politician, Mayor Mendos couldn't fake sincerity very well at all.

Auron was eyeing Ramirez suspiciously. 'Maybe it hasn't been such a waste of time, after all.'

It seemed the spirit knew something he didn't.

CHAPTER 9

Ramirez stomped across the deck of the *Amora* towards the bridge with purpose.

Okay, so when the man is motivated, he does look pretty dashing.

Maybe he did see a little of what Shift and Silva were so aflutter about. Not that he was fluttering. At all.

'We head south,' the captain declared. 'And with all haste. I want this island as far from us as possible.'

'Why south?' Nicolas followed in Ramirez's wake like a man in a chariot being pulled along by its speeding horses.

'Because the faun's ship did not pass here.' The captain climbed the small ladder to the bridge of the ship with practised ease, and Nicolas fumbled after him up the steep steps that were neither stair nor ladder, really. 'There will be naval patrols to the north of us, and as we have not passed him already...he went south.'

'You know where the naval patrols are off the top of your head?' Shift asked, seeming slightly impressed.

Ramirez turned and offered Shift a sly smile. 'It pays a man in my *business* to know where the authorities are at all times.'

Nicolas's companion's cheeks seemed to brighten again. He was going to have to try to learn this magic. Any attempt he made to be charming usually led to haunting embarrassment.

Ramirez shouted orders to his crew, who obeyed in earnest, running about their business. Watching them, Nicolas found himself itching to get involved, his fingers flexing as he looked for something to do.

Finally, we have their trail. I cannot wait to...stop it!

Where were these random bursts coming from? He didn't need a job to do, he needed a distraction. Looking out over the deck, he saw there was something he *could* perhaps help with. Garaz sat out of the way to one side of the deck, engrossed in something. Maybe he needed to talk about what had just happened? He didn't really want to pry when Garaz seemed busy, but it might be worse to leave it. Taking a deep breath, he descended the stairs and approached the orc.

'Are you okay?' he asked once he was in easy earshot.

It was only when he was stood directly beside Garaz that he realised the orc had been reading. He was wrong to have disturbed him.

Maybe not, though.

The orc looked up at him with a furrowed brow. Whatever he was reading, Garaz held it as if it might bite him at any moment. 'I am well, thank you for asking.' At least Garaz wasn't upset about being interrupted. 'That was not pleasant, but it is sadly not something I am unaccustomed to. I fear it shall only get worse with this kind of...literature.' There was an edge to that last word.

Garaz held the book out to Nicolas, who took it inquisitively. It wasn't a book at all; it was a pamphlet.

'*Treatise on the Inhuman Problem.*' Reading the title aloud caused him to scrunch his face. It didn't sound like a nice document. The picture of a shield on which was painted a gauntlet closed into a fist seemed to reinforce the idea that this was not a fun read.

Slowly, Nicolas leafed through the pamphlet, amazed at the hate that spewed from each page. Though it was admittedly well-presented, whoever wrote this had obviously intended it as a provocative piece. Surely no one could find either logic or truth in these words?

One must remember the devious nature of those creatures that do not share our human ancestry and blood. Though I would not call them intelligent by any means, they do possess a low cunning that can be detrimental to our safety and security. Knowing they are outmatched should they attempt to take what we have by force of arms, they use much more devious, subversive methods to tear down and overthrow that which good, honest, hardworking humans have built. Yet in these acts, we are not found wanting. Indeed, we as a race, stand up and strike down these attempts as simply as one may swat a fly. Was it not in Yarringsburg that a horde of vampires attempted to lay waste to the city? Was it not in Sarus where a dwarf unleashed a monstrous creature of annihilation? And where were our so called 'champions' from the Hall of Guardians when these events occurred? Drinking and fornicating. No matter. In each case, brave human soldiery brought these villains to heel, though not before regrettable loss of human life. It is time for us to pull together as a race as never before. We are not Nine Kingdoms of Man, we are one race of man. A race under siege.

Look at those inhuman creatures that live amongst us. Are they neighbours, true of heart? Or are they spies and saboteurs ready to unleash all manner of mischief upon us? Their minds and natures may be alien to us, but I can tell you in no uncertain terms that each smile hides a dagger behind its back. The moment you turn your back...

He couldn't read another disgusting word, so he dropped the pamphlet to the deck and rubbed his hand on his jacket, in case any of the document's venom lingered on his fingertips. Who could write such things? Nicolas eyed the pamphlet suspiciously, lest it start spewing its hatred at him from the floor. 'By the Deities, what is this trash?'

'Vile rhetoric, written by small-minded bigots.' Nicolas started. Obviously, Auron had been reading over his shoulder. 'Sadly, they are everywhere.'

'Yeah, I understand that, but who's started publishing them?' he asked.

Garaz picked up the pamphlet with two fingers, checking its cover for an answer. 'This was written by a *Tobias Helstrum*. He is apparently leader of an organisation called *The Custodians of Humanity*. Sounds charming.'

'Never heard of him or them.' Auron seemed aggrieved. Maybe it was the aspersions cast on his fraternity, though there was a lot to dislike about this work.

Garaz gave a derisive chuckle. 'I would take that as a blessing.'

'Where did you even get it?' Nicolas asked.

'The mayor's study,' the orc replied. 'It was on his coffee table.'

'Hang on,' Nicolas said after a moment. 'You had guards watching you the whole time. How could you have taken it without them seeing?'

'Magic,' Garaz replied with a knowing grin. 'Or maybe a certain companion of ours showed me a thing or two.'

Shift hasn't taught me anything. Where was I when this lesson occurred?

'If that crap is what that stuffy mayor's reading, no wonder he has certain opinions regarding orcs and others.' The idea that anyone in power was reading things like this unnerved him greatly. Where would it lead?

'I'm sure having the local merpeople stealing their children only fans those flames.' Auron pointed to the pamphlet. 'I'd bet every cloud of smoke that makes up my body that you can find those things on every island around here.'

'It is concerning.' Garaz thumbed the pages again. Why was he even entertaining another readthrough? 'Disgusting though it is, items like this can be persuasive to those open to such ideas.'

'Who would be persuaded by *this*?' Nicolas cried.

'People who survived a vampire apocalypse. People who saw a giant lizard creature tear part of their city asunder,' Garaz began. 'People who have had their children taken?'

Those were all fair points.

'But I saw all those things,' he protested. 'And I don't think like that.'

'Because you have perspective, young Nicolas.' Garaz smiled. 'You have seen these things internally, as they occurred. For those outside, the view can be somewhat different, especially when others point their eyes in a certain direction.'

'I know, big guy,' Auron sounded sympathetic. 'But right now, we need to focus on our goal. If we can find that faun and rescue the princess, we can calm this whole situation before it goes too far. That should take the wind out of the sails of this *Helstrum* guy.'

That was good, because by the sound of it, *too far* would be pretty bloody.

'I think stealing children in response is already going too far.' How could someone do something so terrible? This squabble was between grown men, why bring innocent children into it? What must those poor children be going through? 'You don't think the merpeople might, you know, eat them or something?'

Auron looked at him like he was a fool, which was pretty standard for their relationship. 'You obviously don't understand the finer points of hostage exchange,' the spirit explained testily. 'One cannot exchange hostages if one has already eaten said hostages...if the merpeople took them at all.'

'You believe the faun to blame?' Garaz asked, seeming to have already come to that conclusion himself.

'My hero instincts don't like the merpeople for it,' Auron replied. 'They can be proud and pretty fierce if provoked, but it just doesn't sit right. I'm betting the faun's behind it, yeah. Too much of a coincidence for me.'

'Why in the Underworld would a faun want to start a war?' Nicolas asked. 'The guys a jackass for sure, but stealing kids is...well...bad. Terrible, even.'

'Obviously.' Auron chuckled. 'But then why would a necromancer unleash a vampire massacre on a city to make himself famous? Why would a dwarf gangster try to assassinate a king for his own high chancellor? In fact, how would the writer of that little piece of hatred in Garaz's hand even know that'd happened? We were only in Sarus a few days ago. That's not long to find out about it, write it up, print it, and distribute it to a chain of islands.'

Like it or not, the parallels were clear. 'You believe this is all connected?'

'I think someone is stirring a big pot,' Auron said grimly. 'And that pamphlet is just another ingredient in their stew.'

'To what end?' Garaz asked. 'How does one benefit from such destruction?'

'Someone always benefits,' Auron said sardonically. 'The arms dealers who provide the weapons, the men who get paid to rebuild afterwards, the kings and lords who extend their influence, the sad little men who want to push forward their agendas of hate. There is always a beneficiary, but it's never the day-to-day folk or the soldiers on the battlefields.'

'Then we stop this before it starts.' Nicolas was already committed to this, of course, but the stakes kept getting higher. Garaz was right, he had perspective, and the document was wrong in one very fundamental sense. Both of those tragedies had occurred due to humans and non-humans working *together*. The same was true here, with the faun and Killgore. 'We find the faun, subdue him and his associates, rescue the princess and the children, and stop a war. And to the Underworld with anyone who stands in our way.' With each word his anticipation of what was to come increased. As much as he tried to chide himself that getting home should be what he anticipated more, there was a stirring in him that just would not be quiet.

Both Garaz and Auron were looking at him wide-eyed.

'Kid.' Auron smiled broadly. 'I do believe I'm a bad influence on you.'

That's what I'm afraid of.

****

As the sun lowered in the sky, casting a final golden glow over the horizon, highlighting nearby clouds before it disappeared completely, the deck of the *Amora* was a hub of activity. Captain Ramirez had insisted on holding an impromptu welcoming party for his new guests, though Nicolas believed the captain needed little excuse to throw a celebration. Tables had been brought up from the galley and set up under the glow of lanterns, which now hung from the masts. The lanterns also illuminated the fine feast laid out for them, created by a proud chef who insisted on standing in the corner of the ship to watch people enjoy his delicacies. Nicolas didn't particularly love someone watching him eat, but the enticing smell of the food could only be fended off for so long. And the chef was right to be proud. Everything was delicious, with music and chatter adding to the atmosphere. When the music had begun, Nicolas had winced at the first whiny tones of the accordion, but the merriment with which it was played and the infectious jigs emanating from it soon overcame his initial reaction. As the cool night air set in, so did a mood of fun and camaraderie.

'C'mon.' Shift sat next to Nicolas, leaning eagerly across the table to talk to Hay Sharkbait. 'You gotta tell me.'

She shook her head firmly.

'But I've got to know.'

The first mate laughed and took another swig from her tankard. 'Sorry, but I don't tell that tale te just anyone.' Hay Sharkbait smiled, and several of the crew around them chuckled as if they were in on a private joke. 'I need te know yer *man* enough first.'

Odd choice of phrase, coming from a woman.

They sat back, an offended look on their face. 'Oh, I am man enough.' Shift rose to the bait. 'I can change into any man you fancy...and even when I don't, I've got more balls than most men I've met.'

The crew around them laughed, as did Nicolas.

True enough.

'It's not about the size o' yer balls,' Hay Sharkbait said coyly. 'It's about fortitude.'

'They've got fortitude...*all* the fortitude,' Auron cried, standing beside the group but only heard by a couple. The spirit, for some reason, was desperate to know the tale of how Hay Sharkbait got her scar. To do this, he'd press-ganged Shift into asking the jovial first mate. However, when it became clear that she was unwilling to share her story, Shift had become as engrossed in finding out as Auron. Hence, the dance they'd been doing for a good few minutes now. Despite himself, Nicolas was interested too.

'My fortitude says I can drink you under the table.' Shift presented their tankard to a chorus of *'oooooh's'* from the crew.

The first mate laughed again, a harsh cackling sound but full of fun. 'It'll take more than a drinking challenge te prise that nugget from my lips.' Hay Sharkbait laughed before leaning forward and whispering intently. 'But it's not about the drinking. Yer fine folk, I'll give ye that. But not one o' ye have ever tried te lower the mainsail as Mother Sea tosses yer ship from side te side, the rain pourin' down on ye', lashing yer back like a thousand small whips.' If that happened to her then she looked good for it. 'I need te see something else that proves yer ready fer me tale, that ye've earnt it.'

'Like what?' Shift asked.

The first mate shrugged. 'I'll know it when I see it.'

Behind them, Auron tutted loudly.

'Seems as if I have no luck at all today.' Shift swigged their drink. There was something in their tone, a disappointed edge, that made Nicolas curious.

'What do you mean?' he asked.

'What?' Shift looked at him enquiringly before understanding what he meant. 'Oh, nothing really.'

It's something then.

He kept looking at them until they relented and opened up. 'I just seem to be losing out a lot at the moment.' Shift smiled. 'For example...'

They drew his eyes over to Ramirez, who sat close to Silva, telling some tale of seafaring adventure, judging by his exaggerated hand gestures. It was like Auron of the Ocean. The warrior beside him looked enthralled.

'It appears the good captain likes his companions a bit more muscular and emotionless. I tried talking to him earlier, but I don't think he was interested beyond some blatant flirting.'

'Well, why not?' Nicolas asked, aware his voice had risen in pitch slightly.

'What?' Shift asked, frowning, tankard stopping half way to their mouth.

'What doesn't he like about you?' he continued. 'You're great to be around. And you look...well...what's the matter with him?' It didn't make any sense...and that was pretty damned annoying.

'I don't...'

'So you're okay with this?' he cried, aware of the bemused looks he was getting from those around him but not caring.

'Well, no one likes to be rejected but—'

'So you're upset?'

'Well, kind of, I suppose.' Shift was looking at him strangely.

'So the captain's upset you?'

'Nick, what're you—'

For Nicolas, the most likely explanation of what happened next was that it was the product of drinking too many ales coupled with a low tolerance for alcohol. Before he knew it, he was stomping over to Ramirez's table. Nicolas was vaguely aware of Shift calling after him, but he was outraged and intended to do something about it.

'*You!*' he shouted, slapping his palms onto the wooden table in front of Ramirez, which hurt more than he cared to let on.

'Are you okay, my friend?' The captain seemed both curious and bemused.

'No, I am not,' he replied, having to concentrate on every word to ensure his slurring didn't garble what he was trying to say. 'You flirted with Shift, built their hopes up then just dropped them without so much as a sorry.'

'Nicolas...' Silva's tone and facial expression was in full warning mode.

He was having none of it, though. 'No, no *Nicolas*,' he retorted before pointing at Ramirez. 'You have offended my companion, sir...' Acting purely on impulse, Nicolas snatched up Ramirez's discarded glove and slapped the captain across the face with it. '...and I demand satisfaction.'

The glove slap seemed to echo across the deck, across the very ocean itself. Privately, Nicolas had an image of the faun hearing it on his ship, wherever that was. That wasn't the only effect it had. Not only did all the revelry come to a sudden and abrupt halt but Nicolas sobered up very quickly. There was a deathly hush across the deck, and he realised he was the focal point of everyone's attention, for all the wrong reasons.

Ramirez looked at the glove as the surprise finally melted from his face. 'I will give you a second to think about your challenge and maybe revoke it,' the captain said softly as he rubbed his cheek.

Ha, maybe he's afraid.

No, that's most likely you.

Oh. Right.

Listen, he's giving you a way out. You need to take it.

But...

But nothing. You just challenged the man to a duel. Are you insane?

Oh Deities...

Instead of answering, he stood still, glove in hand and no idea how to proceed but very sure he didn't want to duel. Though he was surprised. He'd assumed Ramirez would've jumped at a duel.

He let out a yelp as a hand grabbed him and turned him around roughly.

'What are you *doing*?' Shift cried, practically snarling at him in rage.

'I...I...'

'*You...you...*' they mocked harshly. '*You* don't need to defend my honour because I'm bloody well capable of doing it myself!' They were livid, their green eyes blazing.

He'd just been trying to... He didn't know what he'd been trying to do. 'But...'

'*But* nothing,' Shift shouted. 'You really are as dumb as a rock some-times, aren't you?'

Shift looked past him to Ramirez. 'He rescinds his challenge,' they said firmly.

'Understood,' Ramirez said calmly. 'For my part, I apologise if I caused any offence. I am a natural flirt and sometimes forget myself.'

'We're good,' Shift said to the captain before looking at Nicolas again. 'We are *not* good,' they snarled, jabbing him in the chest with their finger.

Well, at least he'd only been humiliated in front of the entire crew. Why had he even done that? *Stupid pirate ale.* 'Sorry,' he muttered sheepishly as Shift stormed off.

Part of him wanted to follow them, but the other part, his survival instinct, told him not to. Best let them cool down first lest they toss him overboard. Around him, gradually the festivities resumed to amused muttering from their audience.

'It is noble of you to defend your companion's honour.' Ramirez stood and put a reassuring arm around him. 'They will see that in time.'

How long, exactly? The idea of being the object of Shift's ire wasn't a pleasant one.

'My question is,' the captain continued, 'how well you can defend your friends should you need to again. You carry a sword, but can you use it as well as you slap with a glove?'

'I can...unsheathe it.' The damned ale was making him too honest, especially when he had a large audience around to chuckle at him. 'Anything after that is anyone's guess.'

Captain Ramirez waved his finger in the air with a tutting sound. 'I cannot have a man on my ship carry a blade who does not know how to use it.'

Rising, Ramirez took off his cape with a grand sweep then laid it on his seat. He walked to the centre of the deck, a space clearing for him. The captain gestured for Nicolas to join him, drawing some cheers and *uh-ohs* from his attentive audience. Feeling the pressure of the crowd's expectation, Nicolas slowly walked to the centre of the deck.

'Let us see what you are made of, shall we?' the captain asked, playing to the crowd, who began to stomp their feet rhythmically in anticipation.

Had he been sober, every inch of Nicolas's anxiety and common sense would've told him that swords weren't playthings and begun calculating the possibilities of getting hurt, hurting someone, or the most likely outcome, making an ass of himself. However, he wasn't sober, so he drew the *Dawn Blade* from its sheath.

'A magnificent blade.' Ramirez seemed genuinely impressed as he looked at the perfectly reflective sword in Nicolas's hand.

Nicolas's reflection looked back from the blade as if asking what he thought he was doing. He ignored it.

With an excessive amount of showmanship, Ramirez drew his own, thinner, curved blade, swiping it through the air several times with sharp whistles. Finally, he raised the blade to his face and saluted with it. Nicolas copied the gesture, and they both bowed to each other.

'Come at me.'

As simple as that?

Take the tool made for killing people and just come at me.

Ramirez didn't appear concerned about the consequences, which somehow gave Nicolas the confidence to accept the invitation.

After taking a second to steel himself, he took a step forward and swung his sword. One moment later, his buttocks thumped against the hard wood of the deck as he fell on his ass with no clue how he'd gotten from point A to point B. But it'd happened. The laughter of the crew was worse than the pain of the fall.

From the side line, Silva gave Nicolas an icy stare. 'I have taught you better than that.'

Okay, she had. But in his defence, she hadn't taught him how to do those things when he wasn't intoxicated and on a moving surface.

Rising, Nicolas brushed himself off and, at the captain's invitation, took another swing at him. As he did, Ramirez stepped to the side, tripping Nicolas as he overreached, and playfully smacking his bottom with his own sword as Nicolas staggered past him. Stumbling forwards, he fell against some rigging, holding on to it but then swinging around as it gave under his weight. Onto the floor he went again, much to the continued amusement of the crew.

Ramirez held out his hand for Nicolas, smiling. 'You need some pointers, my friend.' As Nicolas took the hand, he was hauled back to his feet. 'Especially if you want to go around challenging people to duels.'

'Care to share some tips?' he asked as the captain readied himself again.

'Of course,' Ramirez replied with a cheeky smile. 'You may not have heard the bell ring, but school has begun for you, my friend.'

For the next hour, the pair did their dance. Nicolas would swing at Ramirez, who would promptly put him on his ass before picking him back up and making a comment on his form or footwork. Slowly but surely, it began to take longer for the captain to knock him down, though the fact that he would was a certainty. The crowd around them were rapt and, toward the end, they were chanting for Nicolas. Apparently, sailors loved an underdog.

Standing again after the captain had drawn him in and used his belly to knock him to the floor, Nicolas readied himself, lowering his stance and gripping his blade just as the captain had taught him. He cleared his mind, mostly, and focused on his opponent.

'Whenever you are ready.' Ramirez smiled.

With a grin, Nicolas stepped in with a downward swing. Ramirez parried it to the side easily, but Nicolas followed the momentum, spinning around into a horizontal strike. As the captain stepped back from the swipe, Nicolas changed the direction of his sword again, stabbing forwards. Once again, the blow was parried then Ramirez became the aggressor. The man was going easy on him, but Nicolas successfully parried each strike until the swords locked, and he found himself face-to-face with the grinning buccaneer.

'You are learning, my friend.' Ramirez said proudly.

'Good teacher.' He smiled back.

Hoping his opponent was distracted, Nicolas attempted to hook his foot around Ramirez's boot and pull it towards him, as the captain had done to him several times. However, when he came to make the move, the boot wasn't there. Instead, it stepped down on Nicolas's foot, pinning him to the deck as the captain pushed him away with his not inconsiderable weight. Nicolas hit the deck again and cursed.

'You have promise, Young Master Carnegie.' Ramirez laughed as he picked Nicolas up.

Despite his aching rump and general embarrassment, he did feel like he'd learnt something. It felt...*good*.

Maybe I did judge Ramirez too harshly earlier. He is pretty dashing, and decent, despite the worn edges.

Why did I react to him like that? I'm sure it was just concern for my companion...companions.

'If you have finished playing then maybe you are ready for a real challenge?'

There was a mock gasp from the crowd as Silva stepped forwards, sword in hand. The world around him shrank until he realised she'd been addressing Ramirez. Every single one of his muscles suddenly released the tension that had gripped them, and gratefully, he stepped aside and allowed Silva to take his place.

'Who am I to deny a lady who wishes my attention?' The captain smiled, stroking his beard.

'You will find me no lady on the battlefield.' Silva half-smiled as she saluted with her blade.

'Even better,' Ramirez purred, returning the salute.

Silva, unsurprisingly, did a much better job matching Ramirez than Nicolas had. It took only moments for the two to get into a rhythm of clashing blades that seemed more like a dance than anything else. Every-one was engrossed in the sparring pair, a couple of the crew members placing bets on the outcome of the spirited exchange. As far as he could see, though, they were evenly matched and completely fixated on each other. Eventually, they locked blades, just as Ramirez and Nicolas had, coming face-to-face, but much closer and sweatier. The pair looked into each other's eyes as they panted hard from the exertion, until the captain dropped his sword and broke away.

'I am matched,' Ramirez declared, to a chorus of cheers and jeers from the crowd. It was pretty obvious who had won and lost their wagers.

Silva, for her part, looked confused by the whole affair.

'We have taken up the dancefloor with our swordplay for long enough. It is time to dance,' the captain declared with raised arms, returning his blade to its sheath as if it had never been drawn in the first place. 'Musicians, play.'

The music fired up with gusto, and soon sailors were dancing all across the deck.

Nicolas walked up to Auron, who stood with his arms folded away from the revelry. 'Did you see that?' Nicolas couldn't believe he'd shown an improvement in such a short time. He was ready for this adventure. 'I think I'm actually getting better.'

'Nice one, kid.' Auron turned and wandered off.

'What was that about?' He'd expected a little more than that from his companion.

At a tap on his shoulder, Nicolas turned, Shift was looking at him with folded arms, expression inscrutable. He desperately tried to assemble words in his head to adequately explain himself, but before he could say anything, Shift held up a silencing hand, which was probably for the best.

'Objectively, what you did just then, as stupid and senseless as it was, was also quite sweet,' they said levelly.

Nicolas's jaw fell open.

'So it appears I can't stay mad at you about it,' Shift continued. 'Though I have no clue what you were thinking and why, I'm prepared to let it go, on the understanding that I have no real interest in Ramirez, it's just nice to get some flattery once in a while, and that I do not, under any circumstances, require you to defend my honour. *Ever*.' The last word was said slowly and carefully.

Assuming that anything he said right now could only sully the moment, he simply nodded.

The moment was instead interrupted by a splashing in the water near them. What appeared to be several large fish were shadowing the boat, occasionally jumping out of the water playfully or expelling gouts of water from the holes in their heads.

He'd never seen anything like it. 'What are those?'

Shift laughed, their frosty exterior cracking as they shook their head in bemusement. 'Those are dolphins. You really are just a boy from the village, aren't you?'

'Did you seriously not believe that?' Nicolas chuckled. 'I've given you plenty of evidence to prove it.'

'Very true.' Shift looked up at the moon, and he followed their gaze. It was a single white orb dangling in the sky above them, surrounded by the stars, which out at sea seemed brighter than anywhere else. They smiled, enchanted. 'It's so beautiful.'

It's not the only thing.

With a sudden slap against the guard rail of the ship that made Nicolas jump, Shift turned to him, eyes twinkling with excitement. 'I want to dance. Fancy it?'

Nicolas flushed slightly. He'd never really danced before. All around him, men were moving to the music. It didn't seem that hard. But what if he tripped or stood on Shift's foot? And so, he found himself saying exactly what he didn't want to say. 'I'm okay, thanks,' he replied awkwardly.

'Your loss.' The twinkle diminished, before Shift shrugged indifferently to turn and shout across the deck, 'Hey, Garaz. Dance?'

For the entirety of the party, Garaz had been on the far side of the deck, still engrossed in his pamphlet. The orc seemed almost obsessed with it, as if continued reading might yield some hitherto unseen information. Or maybe the orc was just torturing himself? Upon hearing his name, Garaz looked up, considered Shift's request, then rose with a nod. Shift walked off to join their new dance partner, leaving Nicolas to lean against the side of the deck regretfully.

'You should have said yes.' Silva leant on the railing beside him, watching the festivities. 'You can still go after them.'

'I think I missed my moment.' Nicolas half-smiled. There would be plenty of opportunities to dance with his companions, not that he fancied ever dancing with Auron and Garaz.

'You men are strange creatures,' Silva muttered disgruntledly.

'What've I done now?' he asked with a sigh.

'Not you, fool. Ramirez,' the warrior snapped. 'He plays, and he flirts, and he gives me signals of his desire, but when I step forwards, he steps back. Why? It is...frustrating.'

'How should I know?' he replied.

'Surely you have experience in such matters?' Silva turned to look at him and read the expression on his face. 'Oh,' she said. There was a moment of awkward silence. 'Well, you do sometimes have the odd decent insight, regardless of experience,' the warrior added finally.

'Thanks.' Nicolas laughed. 'But I'm out of my element on that.'

Silva seemed disappointed as she looked down at the deck soberly.

Feeling bad, he decided to try to give her *something* to work with, at least. 'Look, I don't know much. But I think if he's right for you, he'll realise it soon enough. If he isn't then he's an idiot. You're very attractive—'

'I know, I catch you looking sometimes,' Silva interrupted. Apparently, Nicolas was destined to be embarrassed multiple times at this shindig.

'...And any man that deserves you will prove it. Don't waste your time on those who won't,' he continued, trying to let Silva's comment roll past him.

Silva seemed to consider for a moment. 'Those words did not make me feel better, but the gesture is appreciated.' The warrior nodded. 'I shall repay it with some advice of my own. Next time someone asks you to dance, *do so*.'

Looking around, merriment covered the lantern lit deck, against the backdrop of a beautiful starlit sky. Why in the Underworld had he said no? No matter, the party was still going, which meant he hadn't missed his chance. If he could only find Shift. Somehow, they'd disappeared in the crowd, so he looked for Garaz instead, who should've been much easier to spot.

Nicolas's search came to an abrupt halt when he saw Ramirez across the dancefloor, exchanging urgent words with a member of his crew. Moments later, the captain was calling for the music to cease and the lights to be doused. It seemed he'd missed his chance, after all.

Something was going on.

CHAPTER 10

E ye pressed to the view-glass he'd borrowed, which—once he'd been assured it wasn't magic—was an amazing piece of technology, Nicolas could make out the silhouette of a ship sitting off the coast of the nearby island. The ship radiated menace. Even in the darkness, it looked like something straight from the seas of the Underworld itself. If he was seeing it right, its figurehead was a skeleton, screaming in its death throes due to the large sword sticking out from between its ribs. Nicolas much preferred the *Amora*'s buxom beauty. The bone motif was continued with skeletons hanging from the side that Nicolas just knew weren't carved from wood. Even from this distance, he could tell that the ship outsized the *Amora* considerably, and it wasn't messing around in the armament department. This vessel was made for one thing: terrorising the ocean and sending any who crossed its path straight to its depths.

'That is her, the *Black Death*,' Ramirez snarled, spitting at the name of the vessel.

Of course Killgore's ship would have a name like the *Black Death*. Why not give it the scariest, most intimidating name possible? Though by the look of it, he would've found it just as intimidating were it called the *Bunch of Flowers*.

'The ship of the thieving bottom feeder who shall taste the edge of my blade.' To reinforce his point, the captain drew his sword.

Given the distance between the ships, what exactly did Ramriez intend to do, beyond waving the blade around dramatically?

On the deck of the *Death* were several lit torches, the crew evidently unconcerned about being spotted. All the torches on the *Amora* had been doused to ensure the ship was as invisible as possible in the night. That gave them an advantage. With a ship that big, they'd need it.

Shame we've come across Killgore's ship, and not the faun's.

His day of reckoning with the creature would just have to wait. That was okay, though. As impatient as he was to get some payback, he wasn't about to go around declaring blood oaths like certain people he was stood beside right now.

'So what now?' As unlikely as it was the pirates across the way would hear him, Nicolas whispered anyway. You could never be too careful when dealing with murderous kidnapping pirates.

With a thoughtful sigh, Ramirez sheathed his sword.

'Caution must be our path right now, my friend,' the captain said.

Really? Ramirez didn't seem like the *caution* type. In fact, Nicolas would've put gold on them charging over there and putting the ship to the sword. That sounded more like the kind of fantastic and bloody thing that would be right up Ramirez's alley.

Auron was apparently even more surprised about it. 'What does he mean *caution*?' Nicolas hadn't often seen the spirit so animated. 'She's right there with no idea we're here. We could take the ship before they've even raised the alarm. Caution be damned. Let's go kick their heads in and rescue a princess.'

'So we are not going to attack when we have the advantage?' Silva asked, obviously as confused as the others, but acting more diplomatically than Auron.

Normally, Nicolas didn't agree with Silva, being the first for a bit of caution, but this time he did. Most of the *Death*'s crew were probably asleep. It seemed like a waste of an opportunity.

Besides, charging aboard a pirate ship at night, swords swinging, and—

These random bursts of excitement were starting to make Nicolas worry he was possessed, somehow, as he mentally reigned himself in. It must be something to do with the sea air, or all Ramirez's swashbuckling was infectious, just like his charm.

'And what of the hostages when the fighting starts?' Ramirez asked. 'We need to first ascertain who is aboard before taking any action. *Then* we make our move and litter the sea with the bodies of our enemies.'

'Don't want innocents gettin' hurt.' Hay Sharkbait nodded solemnly, backing her captain as a good first mate should. 'At least we have the ideal person to sneak aboard without getting caught.' Nicolas smiled as he turned to the railing beside which Auron stood.

'I remember a time when my usefulness went beyond just walking around places and looking at stuff.' The spirit sighed.

'That was my initial idea.' Ramirez nodded. 'But I think your ghost will need support. There may be an opportune moment to spirit away the princess and any kidnapped children you find aboard, and we cannot waste it.'

'*What* did he just call me?' Auron raged as his aura reddened. He stared at the captain as if he intended to melt Ramirez with his gaze.

Hang on, did he just say 'you'?

'You want *me* to go?' he cried.

The captain turned to him with a knowing twinkle in his eye. 'Of course, my friend. Who better than you and your companions?'

'Well, speaking for myself, literally anyone else really. You have a ship full of experienced crew, any of whom would blend in much more easily then me on a ship full of pir...professional seamen,' he quickly corrected.

'My crew are all inebriated,' the captain stated flatly. 'Besides, as great seafarers as they are, none of them are known for their subtlety. I think being around me too long is responsible for that.'

'*I've* been drinking,' Nicolas protested.

'I think we all saw how quickly you sobered up after the glove-slapping incident.' Apparently, Shift was still a little aggrieved that it had occurred at all.

With no better way to respond, he offered his companion a sheepish and apologetic smile.

'I'm obviously in,' Shift said to the captain. 'I think it's safe to bet that Killgore has any hostages locked up, so the party will need probably the best lockpick in Etherius.' They offered a faux curtesy to put an exclamation point on their claim.

Nicolas looked at his companion then back at the *Black Death*. As much as he didn't want to go, there was no way he could let Shift risk themselves and not be there to offer what help he could.

I am pretty slight, so it'll be easy for me to hide behind barrels and beams. So why wouldn't I make a good scout?

'Okay, I'll go,' he said finally, nodding as he stared at the skeleton-laden vessel he intended to sneak around.

Shift frowned slightly as they studied him. They probably thought he was trying to protect them again. Of course it wasn't that, he just...

'At least if we get into trouble, Garaz can...I don't know, set a sail on fire or something, so we can escape,' he declared, distracting himself from his own thoughts.

'I am not coming.'

His head whipped around so hard that, for a second, Nicolas thought it might fly off his neck completely. 'You're *not*?'

Garaz gestured to his large form. 'Do I look built for sneaking?'

Of course he isn't. Why do I miss such obvious things?

Nicolas shook his head as if waking from a dream. 'Yeah, of course, sorry. It's fine. Silva can take care of any trouble an—'

'I am not going.'

'I beg your pardon?' Nicolas laughed aloud, assuming this was the warrior's poor idea of a joke.

'I am not going,' Silva repeated.

'The Underworld you aren't,' he scoffed.

Judging by the folded arms and level stare, the warrior was set on her course. 'I am a warrior, not a spy. I am unsuitable for this mission.'

'And I *am*?'

'You have snuck around a necromancer's fort and a gangster's lair before.' Silva shrugged.

'And got caught, *both times*,' he reminded her.

He looked at Silva and waited for a reply; none came.

Oh, so that's that then? Thanks, Silva.

There had to be a reason behind her refusal. But judging by past experience, it would be quicker for him to learn to sail the *Amora* single handed than try to prise it from her.

He had one last gambit to try. 'You're sworn to protect me.'

Silva raised a quizzical eyebrow. 'I do not recall ever taking the knee before you and *swearing to protect you*,' she replied cooly. 'I am here to learn from you. Protecting you is a by-product of that. And teaching you is a much better way to protect you than following you around everywhere. Just keep your head down and stay out of trouble.'

When, in the last few months, have I ever managed to 'stay out of trouble'?

But there was no more argument to be had. It was him, Shift, and Auron then.

He looked back at the ominous dark shape resting in the sea near the island. Death walked it's decks like a member of the crew. And he was about to go over there. A young man of dubious adventuring experience, a shapeshifting thief and a ghost, against whatever the ship had to offer. Who knew what lurked...

Stop it. You're sneaking aboard, having a look around, freeing any hostages and then fleeing like a mouse at a cat festival.

He reminded himself of everything he'd been through to get to this point. They could do this, *he* could do this. And he would. By the time the sun rose, the princess and the children will be safe aboard the *Amora*.

I wish I could be there in the morning to see Killgore's face when he finds that all his hostages have vanished in the night. Assuming Ramirez hasn't stuck a sword in his gut by then.

He barely noticed the half smile creeping across his face as he stared at the dark ship ahead of them.

****

As the current forced the rowboat toward the *Black Death*, Nicolas and Shift put their hands onto the pirate vessel's hull to ease the boats together and prevent the fateful thud that would end their mission before it had even begun. The idea of touching anything called *Death* wasn't an appealing one, but the alternative was worse. Bending his arms in time with Shift, Nicolas helped slowly edge the two boats closer until they touched with the gentlest tap. That was the first hurdle, and he was already sweating profusely.

Actually, that was incorrect; the first hurdle had been making the trip between the *Amora* and the *Death*. Even though it was the dead of night, all it would've taken was one eagle-eyed scout to spot them in the open water and raise the alarm. Nicolas was surprised it hadn't happened. He was about to praise the Deities for his fortune so far, until he remembered that one of them had gotten him into this mess.

'I'll keep her here waitin' fer ye,' Hay Sharkbait whispered, seemingly still full of energy despite rowing a boat with two passengers all this way. Three, technically, but one of them didn't contribute to the weight. Either way, her arm strength was impressive.

The tap on his shoulder made him turn. Shift pointed towards the thick anchor chain running down the side of the ship, keeping the *Death* from floating off wherever the sea fancied taking it. The metal loops, even in the dark, looked wet and slippery. But the chain provided natural foot and handholds, so he was confident he could climb it. In reality, maybe *hoped* was a better term? His gaze fell to the surface of the water. What would be waiting beneath it if he fell in?

'I'll check it out first,' Auron said flatly, before beginning to ascend the mighty chain without even touching it.

It was unsettling how his form followed the curve of the chain so fluidly. Their normally talkative companion had been in an unusually quiet mood the passage over. The spirit seemed almost melancholy, but this wasn't the time to ask why.

After a few tense moments, the spectral figure drifted back down to them. 'Just a couple of watchmen on the deck. Nothing you shouldn't be able to handle.'

Maybe Auron was giving him too much credit? Considering how much the deck of *Amora* creaked underfoot, he doubted creeping around the pirate ship would be easy, especially without any background noise to hide their mistakes. Still, hanging around on a rowboat wasn't getting any less dangerous. And there were people in need of rescue.

I hope. How disappointing would it be to sneak aboard, only to find that none of the hostages are here?

'Now or never, Nick.' Shift nodded at the anchor chain with confidence. 'You didn't fancy dancing with me, but how do you feel about shimmying up a chain with me?'

Was that a simple jest or were they legitimately upset about his refusal to dance?

'Oh, and just so we're clear, I saw you watching Silva climb the ladder when we boarded the *Amora*. None of that here,' Shift warned with a grin. 'Don't want you to slip and fall now.'

'What?' he whispered. 'I wasn't *watching* Silva.'

Great, now they'd said that, he was bound to look. He would also rather not have heard the words *slip* and *fall*. If there was a worse way to jinx what he was about to do, he didn't want to know about it.

Jumping in an almost graceful fashion, Shift leapt from the boat and grabbed the chain, clinging on to the metal and making their way up it with almost as little effort as Auron had. Nicolas imagined this wasn't the first time the master thief had done something like this. But it was his. After a couple of moments of self-encouragement, Nicolas made the jump himself and grabbed the cold metal loops. The chain was slimier than it looked, and it took a couple of fearful seconds to get a decent grip, but when he had, he began his own ascent, after a hefty sigh of relief.

Only once did he risk a glance up to see how much further he had to climb. It was, naturally, the exact moment that Shift glanced back down. It was difficult to tell in the dark, but he was sure they were shaking their head. The rest of the climb he spent concerned his shoulders may pop from their sockets. He wasn't used to trying to lift his own bodyweight. Sure he'd carried heavy bags of flour around the mill for his father, but this was much different, and the muscles he never really used before burned in protest.

Slowly but surely, he made his way up the chain until it disappeared back into the ship itself. From there, he copied Shift and used a nearby piece of rigging to haul himself up onto the deck. For a second, his strength wavered as he hung out in the open, legs dangling in the air above the sea, but he reminded himself of what was at stake: the kidnapped princess and the stolen children.

And the damned faun.

With painful effort, he pulled himself up over the side of the *Death* and onto her deck.

Ensuring that his feet touched the wooden deck as lightly as possible, toes then heels, Nicolas crouched to keep himself and his outline low. As a hand covered his mouth and pulled him back into the shadows, Nicolas nearly cried out, but Auron was looking at him levelly, which suggested he'd been abducted by Shift. He had to hope someone else grabbing him would cause more alarm. In the cramped confine of the space under the stairs where he'd been dragged, the hand was slowly removed from his mouth, and he turned, finding himself practically nose to nose with Shift. The closeness was...oddly comfortable.

'I saw you look,' they whispered, a mischievous twinkle in their green eyes.

Thankfully, the dark concealed the reddening of his face.

Beside them, Auron stood in the open, not a care in the world. Hopefully, no one on the ship obeyed whatever random set of universal rules allowed people to see the spirit, or they'd be instantly doomed.

No doom came. Instead, Auron gestured toward the centre of the deck.

Looking out from their hiding place, between the steps of the stairway that concealed them, Nicolas could see the two watchmen, who seemed relaxed as they patrolled the deck. One of the men laughed at something the other said. Judging by the laugh, it had been dirty.

Only two, for a ship this big?

The fact that the crew didn't feel the need to seriously guard their ship at night suggested they believed their reputation alone would keep away intruders. What had they done to earn a reputation like that? Thankfully, he didn't know, or that ember of excitement that was intermingled with the fear may be doused completely. And right now, it was the only thing keeping him going. Or maybe it was just his constant, and annoying, drive to do the right thing?

As the two watchmen had their backs to the pair, thoroughly engrossed in their conversation, it seemed it'd be simple to sneak up on them and knock them out. Shift got his attention with a light tap, and mimed striking the guards on the back of the head, so that was the plan. Good, because he wasn't sure he could do anything worse to them if he had to. He wasn't a killer, and he wasn't about to start now.

Before they could move, Auron held up a hand to stay their advance. 'Wait.'

What the spirit had seen, or sensed, were the four other men walking up to the deck. They'd evidently been patrolling below and were here at the perfect moment to make things more difficult for their scouting mission. The two watchmen called to the newcomers and summoned them over. In a group, they shared some pirate camaraderie, which, judging by the dirty laughter, was telling raunchy jokes.

With another tap to get his attention Shift motioned toward a nearby door. Keeping to the shadows as much as possible, Nicolas followed his companion as they slid toward it. Shift reached it first and gently turned the handle. The door didn't open. Carefully, they tried it a second time. Nothing.

That's...concerning.

The guards weren't going to talk forever.

Slowly, as if it were a mighty weight, Shift pulled at a piece of rope hanging around their neck. On the end was the key-shaped object given to them by T'goth for their part in his restoration, which the Deity claimed would open any lock. They looked at it sourly for a second, before pressing the edge of the key to the lock. There was a faint click. This time, when they turned the handle, the door opened.

Okay, so I guess I owe a certain Deity a little *thanks now.*

Shift looked less thankful. 'It really does take the fun out of it,' they whispered sourly as they slipped through the door. 'But there's a time and a place I suppose.'

Nicolas would take speed over enjoyment in a dangerous situation every time.

Keeping one eye on the guards, he pushed the door closed carefully, shutting it again with the barest whisper of a click, before turning to examine his surroundings. From the general look of the place, they appeared to be in the captain's cabin. Office. Throne room. Whatever they called it on a ship. It *did* have a throne, of sorts: a large chair with skull-headed armrests and more skulls bordering the chairs back. The skulls clearly hadn't been part of the original design either—added at various times, too, judging by how some looked older than others. The fresh ones unnerved him more. This wasn't helped by the plinth beside the throne on which a skeletal hand rested upon a cushion in a glass case. The way it was placed...there was almost a reverence or tenderness to it.

The throne/chair was situated before a thick table which was covered in everything Nicolas, in his limited experience, may have expected from a pirates table. There were charts, a compass, some randomly strewn gold coins and jewels, a couple plates of half eaten food and a knife which protruded proudly from the wood. Nicolas fought his initial urge to tidy up. If Killgore came in to find the room suddenly clean, he might guess that they'd had visitors.

Still, he lives like a pig.

Then there were the walls of the cabin. One was horrifically adorned with skulls on spikes, some of them cracked and holed by what he guessed were the wounds that killed those the skulls had previously belonged to. Despite his urge not to, his eyes drifted to every single one, and he couldn't help but picture his skull added to the collection.

The opposite wall looked more cluttered, a large cabinet running along it's length with the most random assortment of items Nicolas had ever seen. There was a set of teeth, a dagger, a broken viewing glass, a dented tankard and other miscellaneous objects. Most of it looked like junk, save the jewelled crown that caught the torchlight in the room. Nicolas's eyes widened, remembering a corpses head with an indent where that crown must've once sat. When he noticed the tags beside each item the real horror of the room became apparent.

Killgore doesn't just take the skulls of those he kills. He takes trophies. He collects keepsakes of his victories and victims.

Or maybe these were just the most auspicious victories and the pirate captain had killed thousands more who didn't rate display?

'She's not here.' Auron's tone was bitter, his jaw set, drawing Nicolas's attention to the only thing that *wasn't* in the room, hostages.

'This isn't the only room. We haven't searched the whole ship yet.' Nicolas was trying to be reassuring, but the spirit didn't appear to want reassurance.

'Before we go below, I'll check the charts. Maybe they have a base of some kind, or we can pinpoint the faun's ship.' Shift was already leafing through the pages on the desk. 'You guys root around and see what you can find.'

Opting to search the opposite side of the cabin to the skull wall, Nicolas walked over to the cabinet and began to examine the trinkets. One thing caught his attention, a single item at the cabinet's centre, given pride of place. It was a glass cylinder, surrounded by a wooden frame decorated with gold filigree, so it was obviously something Killgore prized. Inside the cylinder was a liquid that cast an eerie green glow, containing...

Are those pearls?

At the bottom of the wooden frame was a small golden plate with two letters carved into it that he couldn't quite make out. His curiosity piqued, he grabbed the frame and lifted it down from the shelf. The container was much heavier than he expected, the weight catching him by surprise and his unprepared arms failing him. The cylinder dropped instantly, wrenching itself from his hands as it fell.

The thud when the container hit the floor echoed throughout the cabin like a thunderclap, though, somehow, it hadn't shattered. The floor was certainly dented. When he turned slowly, Shift and Auron were staring at him aghast, still in the middle of what they'd been doing before he'd dropped the container.

'What in the Underworld, kid?' Auron shouted finally.

Unfortunately, he wasn't the only one. 'What in the Underworld was that?' yelled a nasally voice beyond the door of the cabin. This was followed by the sound of multiple boots clomping upon wood, coming closer.

'Move, idiot,' Auron cried, pointing towards a door at the back of the room.

Shift was already halfway there.

He wanted to put the container back on the shelf—it was evidence they'd been here—but the urgency of the approaching boots told him there was no time. Making all haste, he followed Shift and Auron through the door and down the steep set of steps seafaring vessels seemed to favour.

What's wrong with a gentle decline?

"Ello?' he heard one of the watchmen holler. They were in the cabin.

'Someone's been 'ere,' another shouted sharply, probably seeing the cylinder on the floor. Nicolas might've wondered how he could've been so stupid, but it happened quite often. Still, he cursed himself as he followed Shift down the steps. All he'd had to do was be quiet and he'd ended up making the most amount of noise possible other than actually shouting, *'Hey, everyone! We're sneaking around your ship.'*

At the bottom of the steps, they entered the bowels of the *Death* itself. Just like the other ships he'd been inside recently, this one featured a maze of tight walkways and blind corners. Auron took point to ensure they had plenty of warning of people coming in the other direction. Nicolas's claustrophobia intensified in the knowledge that they would be pursued soon enough. It wouldn't take an academic to work out that the intruders had left through the only other door in the cabin.

Potential pursuers became definite pursuers as Nicolas heard the unmistakable sound of a door opening and multiple heavy footsteps on the stairs behind them.

'You had to drop something,' Shift muttered as they looked behind him. 'And the heaviest thing in the room, no less. Well done.'

'Sorry,' he whispered back feebly.

The footsteps closed on them, and the trio were forced to pick up their pace.

'This isn't good,' Shift lamented, looking behind them again.

'Maybe you can change into a pirate and tell them you caught me, and we can slip away somehow?' Nicolas suggested hopefully.

'I think the pirates might raise an eyebrow or at least question one of their own strutting around in women's clothes.' Shift huffed, indicating their tunic, which had clearly been designed with breasts in mind.

'I don't know what they get up to belowdecks,' he ventured. 'It might be a normal occurrence.'

The glare from Shift shut down his line of thought quite quickly. There wouldn't be any way out of Shift's bad books for a good while after this. Unless they were killed by pirates, of course. Then it'd all be academic.

Weaving through the tight corridors, they were eventually stopped by a door blocking their path.

'I'm going to—' Auron began, before Shift cut him off by simply barging through the door.

The pirate on the other side of the door spun round, his face registering an instant of surprise before Shift cracked him right in the jaw, dropping him with a single blow. Had they channelled their annoyance at him into the punch?

'And Silva says I can't fight.' Shift snorted, looking at the unconscious pirate as they shook their hand.

'Now who's not being stealthy?' Nicolas muttered, entering the room behind them.

Shift turned slowly and their wide eyes made him regret speaking aloud. 'I'm sorry,' they said, voice dripping with sarcasm. 'But I thought that since you were lobbing heavy objects around, stealth was out the window. If I'm incorrect then I'm truly sorry and beg your most humble forgiveness.'

'Okay, sorry,' he mumbled.

'Guys.' Auron clicked his smoky fingers between them. How did they even make a clicking sound? 'If you could please keep your attention on what's going on around you.'

A wave of fear ran up Nicolas's spine as both he and Shift slowly turned around. Numerous surprised and confused eyes looked back at them. The room they were in was long and open, with rows of benches on either side with unkempt men sat upon them, manning the oars. The slaves sat chained to their posts, and though their long scraggly hair and beards spoke of a lack of care on the part of their masters, their muscular arms and torsos spoke of men who spent their days working hard to move the large vessel across the seas. Nicolas felt scrawny by comparison. Nicolas *was* scrawny by comparison.

These poor wretches.

How could anyone do that to their fellow man, chain them and force their labour? Looking down at the pirate on the floor, the man had held a whip, which looked well used. He was sure the backs of the slaves would tell the same story.

As much as he wanted to free them, they had no time. Pirates were on their heels and every second counted. Though the guilt of leaving them hit him like a punch in the stomach. That guilt became intermingled with the awkwardness at being the centre of the massed slaves attention.

Coughing to both clear his throat and give him a moment to collect himself, Nicolas stepped forward with an open-handed gesture. 'Don't mind us, gentlemen. We're just passing through.' The slaves stared at them blankly. 'If you could not tell anyone we were here, that'd be great.'

'They're going to know as soon as that guy wakes up.' Auron pointed to the body on the deck, shaking his head in exasperation and disbelief.

Nicolas could barely believe how badly this was going himself. 'Oh, yeah,' he replied sheepishly.

'Whose idea was it for you to come?' Shift rolled their eyes as they shoved past him, stomping irritably down the narrow pathway between the gangs of slaves. They stopped suddenly, their eyes drawn to the chains running along the floor that secured the slaves to their benches. Shift's fingers flexed as if they wanted to grab the chains and snap them.

I know the feeling.

'There's no time,' Auron told them both. 'I get that you don't want to leave them, nor do I. But we need to get off this ship before the deck is swarming with pirates. Once we get back to Ramirez, we will right this wrong.'

Damn right we will. As soon as Ramirez takes this ship I'll be the first one down here.

He tried not to look directly at any of the men as he followed Shift, lest he give in to his urge to attempt to free them, reminding himself that their pursuers were close and that they'd help no one by being dead.

All three of them were nearly at the far door of the galley when the door they'd entered from opened abruptly.

'Ha,' the pirate exclaimed in triumph with a brown-toothed smile, sword ready. 'Got you, poppit.'

Shift wheeled around, heckles apparently up. 'Are you calling me poppit or him?' Shift snapped, pointing to Nicolas.

Charming.

'Oh, we have a feisty poppit here, fellas. Don't worry, poppit,' the pirate grinned as he and his five companions stalked into the galley, 'we won't hurt you...much.'

As Shift went to lunge forward, Nicolas quickly grabbed them, doing his best to restrain his freakishly strong companion as they kicked and told the bemused pirates in the strongest possible terms what they thought of being called *poppit*, in between making crude remarks about their ancestors' fondness for livestock.

Nicolas looked between the door and the pirates.

What do we do? Run or fight?

If they fought, then they may buy themselves some time to free the slaves, but the battle may also wake the rest of the ship. But the longer he was in the room, the harder he was finding it to leave and abandon these poor people, no matter how much he intended to come back.

His gaze was drawn to the back of the nearest slave, it was criss-crossed in scars, both old and new. Nicolas drew his sword.

I'm not leaving them.

The pirates charged.

But they didn't make it far. Within moments the surprised attackers found two thick wooden oar handles blocking their way.

'Hey,' the leader cried. 'What is this?'

Soon more of the handles were pulled across the walkway, cutting Nicolas and his companions off from their pursuers.

'We'll flay you alive for this,' the leader snarled.

One of the slaves, an old man with a scraggly grey beard, turned to them. 'Go,' he said firmly.

Nicolas looked at the door again. 'But we can't just…'

'*Go,*' the old man insisted.

At the end of the walkway, the pirates were doing their best to circumvent the barriers placed in their way, shouting and screaming to alert any of their fellows nearby.

Dammit.

'We'll come back, I swear it.'

The old man gave a dry chuckle. 'I pray that you do.'

It took sheer force of will, and necessity, for Nicolas to tear himself from the room and follow Shift out the door, sheathing his sword. Both his companions looked as sorry as he did that they were leaving, the curses of the pirates following in their wake.

Giving up all thoughts of stealth, Nicolas and Shift bolted from corridor to corridor until they found another set of steps back up to the deck.

Ascending quickly into the cold night air, Nicolas and Shift dropped the hatch over the stairway to prevent pursuit, placing a heavy barrel over it, just to be sure.

'Uh guys,' said Auron, once again the bearer of bad tidings.

Nicolas and Shift both turned to find another fifteen smug and heavily armed pirates behind them.

'Dam—' Nicolas's curse ended in a strangled, choking sound as Shift abruptly grabbed him by the collar, yanking him behind them as they threw themselves over the side of the ship.

Shock drove the air from his lungs as he hit the freezing water, his testicles abruptly stopped being an external appendage, and his body tensed as he began to sink. He had to will his limbs to move again. If he didn't, he would sink to the bottom of the sea to be a night-time snack for some fortunate sea dweller. Gasping for breath, the air bubbles from his own mouth blinded him as he flailed in panic. The last time he'd been in water was when a crazy mercenary with a bear fetish had knocked him off a bridge.

This time, though, he had the benefit of being conscious and fought away the panic, regaining control of his body to coordinate the movement of his limbs. Pushing through the water, Nicolas moved in the direction he assumed was up.

With a mighty gasp of air, he broke the surface. Cold and disorientated, limbs aching and lungs burning, he still managed to make the short swim, before clawing his way onto the beach, the sand coming away under the pressure of his fingertips and the waves smacking his behind with every movement.

Finally out of the water, he hacked and coughed, spitting out the sea water he'd swallowed in his panic. He needed to rest. Just for a moment.

'No time to rest,' Shift cried beside him, soaked through. 'They'll be after us soon.'

Good point.

Driving himself up through sheer force of will, Nicolas got unsteadily to his feet, fighting the weight of his soaking clothes. Quickly, he followed Shift as they ran from the small cove and up the grass hill beyond. The incline was steep, and his already drained legs protested every movement, but they had to push on. The pirates could already be on rowboats headed after them. For a moment, Nicolas thought he could hear music but put it down to the sound of the sea still crashing in his ears.

No wait. That *was* music.

Where's that coming from?

Once the pair crested the rise, the music stopped abruptly, as did Nicolas and Shift.

The faun looked at them in disbelief, dropping the pipes from his mouth. 'Where did you soggy-looking peasants come from?'

CHAPTER 11

Having no clue how to react, Nicolas defaulted to staying still and quiet. Actually, that wasn't entirely true; he knew exactly how he *wanted* to react. He wanted to march across the grass and punch the oh-so-smug little gnome-dick right in the face. His hand closed into a fist. However, doing that would be suicide.

The faun was just one of a larger party. Of course, he had his little toad-butler thing with him, looking at them inscrutably, as well as a group of pirates. The most prominent of these was the giant brute of a man from the rowboat. The skulls on his shoulder pads made it simple to work out who the menacing monster was. Captain Killgore. What surprised him, more than the size of the man, was the fact that he had only one hand. The other forearm ended in a stump halfway up, with some kind of metal plate fastened to it, which had runes engraved around it.

'Oh, hey…hey, I remember you guys.' The faun laughed finally. 'You're those castaways I left stranded on that island.' He put his hands on his hips and shook his head. 'Well, fancy seeing you here. Midnight dip, was it?'

Oh, he's so punchable.

'You remember the chumps from the island with the poor king's ship, right?' The faun chuckled heartily, turning to Killgore, who dwarfed him easily. Nicolas couldn't believe the faun wasn't even slightly intimidated by the captain, who glared at them with murderous rage.

'What're they doing here?' Killgore asked with a voice like rolling thunder.

'That's an excellent question.' The faun clicked his fingers and wagged his finger towards them in the most patronising fashion possible. 'How about it then? Care to enlighten us?'

Nicolas found himself stammering and looking at Shift, who looked equally stunned by the whole thing. With the pirates in front of them and the sea behind them, they were in more than a little mortal peril.

Killgore looked past Nicolas, back toward the *Death*. 'Were you snooping aboard my ship?'

Nicolas risked a brief glance. Lights bobbed urgently on the deck, and the shouts of the crew readying boats carried across to them. He didn't intend to answer, but apparently his face gave it away completely.

Killgore snarled like a charging animal and took a menacing step forward, but the faun's hand on his chest stopped him. For a second, the captain looked as if he wanted to rip the faun's hand off and feed it to him. Nicolas could relate.

The faun seemed unconcerned. 'Before you go gutting them and whatnot,' he began, 'I would like to know how they got here. You can't tell me this is a coincidence.'

Nicolas had a couple of choices here. The first was to stay tight-lipped and wait for them to beat it out of him; the second was a bit of a gamble. 'We're here with Captain Ramirez,' he declared, puffing his chest out slightly to appear a lot more confident than he felt. 'We're only one of several parties coming ashore. The others will be surrounding you as we speak, so I suggest you either flee or surrender.'

Beside him, Shift palmed their face and groaned as the pirates burst into laughter. From Killgore, laughter was an ugly cackling sound.

'That bilge rat still hunting me down, is he?' Killgore roared. 'He keeps getting close but can't finish the job. I wonder why? I don't think he has the *balls* to face me himself.' The pirates with him laughed raucously. 'If old Ramirez is so desperate for me to take another piece of him, he's welcome to challenge me. Yet he doesn't come himself, or send his precious *crew*. Instead he leaves it to a couple o' sea urchins he picks up to prowl around my boat.'

More laughter from the pirates.

'You know, *boy*,' the faun said after scrutinising Nicolas for a moment. 'I think half of that is true. Ramirez brought you here, but you two were just sent to snoop, maybe free some captives? There aren't any other parties ashore or whatever fantastical army you were going to try to sell us. Poor try, boy. Poor try.'

He really wanted to kill that faun.

'Then we gut them,' Killgore declared, practically drooling as his men grunted their agreement.

Briefly, he pictured his skull ending up as part of Killgore's décor. He wanted to keep it on his neck, where it belonged.

'Hold up, hold up.' The faun stared at Nicolas, pursing his lips. 'Just because he isn't here doesn't mean Ramirez isn't nearby. If he's made it this far, he may take the final step and actually do something. We need to get the ship underway, or we'll be vulnerable.'

'You don't tell me how to sail *my* ship, faun,' Killgore snarled.

Loving partners, these two.

Slowly, the faun turned to the captain and levelled a gaze at him that seemed to make it very clear to Nicolas which of them was in charge.

With a grunt, the captain relented. 'What about them?' Killgore's tone was now more pouty child than terrifying captain.

'Some of our new passengers can deal with them.' The faun smiled. 'And I can have some fun whilst you get the *Death* ready to sail.'

Nicolas and Shift looked at each other in confusion.

Stepping to the side, the faun revealed a line of children behind them. That was why they were on the island. They'd been stealing more children, taking them from their homes in the night. It was despicable. It was disgusting.

Nicolas's hand grabbed the hilt of his sword.

'Oh, feisty one here,' the faun chuckled.

Ready to draw the blade and have at the vile abductors, something occurred to him. Why were none of the children crying or screaming? He certainly would've been if a group of pirates stole him from his home at night. Yet they were eerily silent. It was hard to tell in the dark, but there was something off about them. Their eyes appeared to be glazed over and they swayed slightly on the spot as if they were in a trance.

'Yeah, this'll be funny.' The faun chuckled to himself as he put his pipes to his mouth.

Blowing into the instrument, he played a tune very different to the one Nicolas had heard as they climbed the hill. This tune had more of a low thumping beat to it, which seemed to resonate all around them. It made his ears itch. The faun smiled from behind his instrument.

Slowly, the children's limp heads rose. Blank, entranced expressions contorted into nearly inhuman, feral snarls, their glassy eyes becoming blood-red and enraged. They snarled and hissed, and Nicolas nearly soiled himself. Watching something so innocent become so...corrupted was worse than many of the things he'd seen on his adventures so far.

'By the Deities,' Shift whispered beside him, as shocked as he was.

'Kill,' the faun commanded offhandedly with a slight wave in the direction of Nicolas and Shift.

As the pair broke to the side in an all-out sprint, the children began to pursue. Nicolas didn't need to see it, he could hear it, the kids howling and snarling like rabid animals.

The way was dark and the wet grass treacherous underfoot, but they couldn't slow down. Behind them, almost inhuman growls signalled their continued pursuit. If he hadn't seen the children himself, Nicolas might've believed them chased by a pack of wild dogs. Maybe he could turn and fight, but numbers were against them, and he was loath to hurt a child under whatever hold the faun had over them. Besides, who knew what the children were capable of in their current state. All he could do was flee, praying with each step that his footing wouldn't betray him, causing him to slip and stumble. His breath came out in ragged pants; half exertion, half fear. But he needed that air, he needed to fuel his legs and keep them going. Speed was his only saviour now.

Following Shift, they abruptly moved from the open grass to the foliage. He guessed that Shift hoped they could lose their pursuers if they weren't in plain sight. But the amount of noise they were making as they dashed through branches and bushes negated that. Twigs cut at his skin and thorns dug into his legs as they pressed on, frantically slapping aside any obstacle nature put in their way. Adrenaline from fear dulled the outward pain, as if it were happening to someone else. But the pain from his burning lungs and aching legs couldn't be so easily ignored. It didn't matter though. What would come if they stopped or slowed would be so much worse.

Behind them fierce rustling agitated the bushes as the children doggedly chased them down. Nicolas used it to drive himself onward.

For a fateful second he slipped on a wet leaf. Continuing forwards in a stumbling manner, he directed himself towards the nearest tree, striking the trunk heavily. But it did the job, giving him something to grab to stop him falling completely. Behind him was a triumphant howl, as if the children knew their prey had faltered.

No. Please Deities no.

The rough bark scraped his sweat drenched hands as he pushed himself off and continued his flight. His legs took a few moments to get up to speed again, muscles thinking they had the opportunity to rest. There was no rest now, only survival.

His vision tunnelled as he focused on Shift, not wanting to lose sight of his companion, knowing he couldn't survive this alone.

Pushing through the next bush, his arms found air as they were out in the open again.

Keep going. Keep going. Keep going.

Making it over the next rise, Shift changed direction dramatically. Nicolas, following, nearly slipped at the sudden swerve but just managed to keep his footing. The pair angled down back towards the beach. He guessed Shift intended to use the natural rise of the coastline to conceal them. That was a good thing, as fatigue was threatening to overwhelm him. Fear of death or not, he couldn't keep this up for much longer.

Finding a natural indent in the rocky outcrop before them, Shift pulled him into it with them. It was small, and they were pressed closely together. They were both struggling to control their breathing, their chests rising and falling rapidly against each other. But by the Deities, he wasn't about to let an errant gasp give them away. At some point, he would feel awkward about being pressed this close to his companion's body, but right now, they had bigger issues.

Looking up after a few moments, Shift put their finger to their lips. Nicolas could hear it, too: the scuffling along the edge of the rise beneath which they hid. The children were no longer making loud, animalistic noises, but still moving and hunting, sniffing like pack hounds looking for a scent. Mentally he prayed for salvation. Pleaded, actually. Being mauled to death by possessed children sounded like a terrible way to go.

Several tense seconds that felt like hours passed then the scuttling sounds diminished.

'This is crazy,' Nicolas whispered quietly.

'So the faun has magic pipes then.' Shift looked exhausted.

He knew the feeling. 'And he's been using them to kidnap children.' Deities, he hated that guy. How long before their pursuers came back and found them? He looked out toward the sea. He could just make out the waves as they caressed the edge of the beach. They sounded a lot fiercer than they looked in the dark. But beyond the waves that was all there was: dark. 'We need to get back to the ship.'

There was no sign of the *Amora* and salvation. He wasn't even sure what side of the island they were on right now. Maybe they could just stay put? The sun would rise eventually, and search parties would most certainly come looking for the stolen young ones.

'Hang on.' Shift's lips curved into a slight smile as they looked out to sea. 'There.'

It started as a faint bobbing light in the dark, hazy and unfocused. Then the light seemed to grow, getting closer to them and becoming clearer. Soon, Nicolas recognised the ethereal glow.

'Auron.' Rescue was here. Nicolas would've breathed a sigh of relief, except it might attract the feral children, so he would save it for later.

Within minutes, the sloshing of oars reached his ears and the glow from their companion marked out the edges of the rowboat and the vague features of Hay Sharkbait heaving the boat toward them. Nicolas grinned, filled with a whole new affection for the scarred sailor.

The only problem was that Nicolas and Shift weren't the only ones who'd spied the rowboat. With the promise of salvation came noise on the ridge above them as the possessed children returned, knowing that their prey must be close.

'Do we make a run for it?' he asked, looking at the sand and thinking that the lighter children may have the speed advantage, given his last few experiences travelling across the stuff. And his legs were numb. He wasn't sure how much his body had left to give.

Hopefully just enough to get me to that boat.

'We can't exactly stand and fight,' Shift whispered. 'They're only children.'

'Obviously.' Nicolas huffed, offended Shift had felt the need to say it aloud.

The boat neared the shore, and the sound of movement near them intensified. The children were just waiting for them to break cover so they could pounce.

Auron seemed to spy them in their hiding spot and waved.

'I think we're running out of options.' Nicolas looked upwards nervously.

Shift looked up at the ridge, too, their screwed-up face suggesting how much they rated their chance of escape...then a thought seemed to occur to them. 'I have an idea.' From their expression, Nicolas assumed it was a long shot. 'It may only buy us a few seconds, but I think it's the best we have.'

With that, Shift's face shimmered, the features moulding and changing until they were a replica of a certain faun. He had to remind himself that it was Shift, his urge to strike the face almost overwhelming.

'Get ready to move like the wind.' Shift's voice was spot on, down to the self-satisfied edge.

He didn't know if he could. The distance between them and the boat might as well be a thousand miles for the state his body was in right now.

No. I can do this. Hayley is just there. We can make it.

Shift moved away from the earthen bank they were concealed behind.

'Over there, idiots.' Shift waved their arms in the air, pointing to the left as they cried in the faun's voice. 'They're over there. Go, go.'

There was an animalistic bark above him, then movement. Shift spared him a brief glance, the light in their eyes telling him that the plan was working.

Thank the Deities.

'Now,' Shift shouted to Nicolas, turning back into themselves and heading for the boat at speed.

Nicolas wasted no time, pushing off from the cold rock and running toward the rowboat. Each footstep kicked up a tuft of sand in his wake as the beach once again fought every movement. After a second or two, there was a howl of alarm and frustration behind him, soon echoed by many other voices.

They're coming.

Hay Sharkbait waved the pair on with enthusiasm, as did Auron. Though judging by the concerned look on the spirit's face, the children were closing.

Shift made it to the boat first, wading into the water and throwing themselves onto the small wooden vessel. Nicolas crashed into the surf, doing his best to ignore both the incoming waves and the splashing behind him. Driving himself on, Nicolas finally grabbed the side of the boat, ready to haul himself in. Relief crashed over him like one of the waves that was trying to push him back to shore.

I made it.

He turned abruptly, feeling something other than the sea grab his leg. The child crawled up his leg like a giant insect, grabbing his collar and snapping at him with eyes of an animal focused on the kill.

Using his forearm to hold the child back, he was surprised at how strong the boy was, despite the size difference between him. Right now it wasn't a child, it had been warped into a cannibalistic creature, it's desperation to bite into his flesh giving it almost inhuman strength.

He strained against the weight being pressed on his forearm as the child's head tried to reach him, to fulfil it's command. To kill him.

'Nooooo,' he cried, putting all of his energy into forcing it back. He wasn't winning.

As the gap between his face and those gnashing teeth became just inches the only way to survive became to do something he'd hate himself for.

With one sharp movement, he headbutted his attacker. Instantly the child reeled back, the grip on his collar slackening. Nicolas used his moment, grabbing the child and throwing him back into the sea and clambering aboard the boat.

Before he could take solace in his success, he looked out over. The relief to see that the child was still alive, albeit thrashing through the water to get to him again, was almost better than the euphoria at having survived.

Or have we.

Beyond his attacker, another twelve fought the current to reach them.

'Go,' he cried as Hay Sharkbait began to row, the oars working hard against the current.

The boat moved away from shore, the distance between them and their pursuers becoming greater. But the children weren't stopping. Would they keep going until they drowned?

There was a melody in the air.

Suddenly the children stopped, their feral faces dropping and snarling ceasing as they turned back toward the island. Slowly, as if sleepwalking, they returned to shore.

Atop the rise that had shielded them, stood the faun, pipes to his lips as the melody continued, summoning the children back to him. The melody only broke when the faun realised Nicolas was looking at him, then the creature lowered his pipes and smiled. Bringing his free hand up to his neck, the faun drew a single finger across it, before pointing to him.

Digging his hands into the side of the boat until there were splinters beneath his fingertips, Nicolas shook. He had been angry before, but this was worse, a pure rage that would've scared him, had he not been so focused on the cause of it.

'Not if I get to you first,' he snarled as the coastline became ever more distant.

I will get you. And when I do, you're going to pay for everything you've done. And the children will be safe, the slaves will be safe and the princess will be safe. Enjoy your final days, scumbag.

****

'She's getting away,' Nicolas cried, pointing towards the *Black Death*, already underway thanks to the efforts of their rowing slaves. The slaves' backs had surely suffered for their poor mutiny, and part of that was on him. He couldn't imagine what it would be like to be whipped, but he knew he couldn't just abandon them to their fate. He'd promised to free them. And those children...

Beside him, Ramirez stroked his beard thoughtfully. 'We need to be careful,' the captain said finally. 'We cannot see the faun's ship. If we engage now, we may be outnumbered. It would be a disaster.'

'Ridiculous.' Auron stood aside from everyone, arms folded and jaw set. 'You don't just let an enemy escape with kidnapped children when they're right there.'

Nicolas was inclined to agree.

'Plus, the faun has magic on his side,' Shift added, looking pointedly at Auron, blanket wrapped around them to stave off the cold of their wet clothes, just like Nicolas had. 'Who knows what he can do?'

True, but we have magic too.

'What about you, Garaz?' Nicolas cried. 'Can't you throw a fireball at it or something?'

'You wish me to throw a fireball at a wooden ship on which there are child hostages?' Garaz's voice was calm, but he looked at Nicolas as if he were insane.

Okay, admittedly, that wasn't the best plan, but he really didn't want the faun to get away. Especially with those children. They had to do something, so why was no one doing anything? It was a bad day, indeed, when he was the one suggesting they charge in. His body may be a wreck right now, but he would get one more fight out of it. He could rest when everyone was safe and the villains vanquished.

And yet we still aren't moving?

'But we can't just let them go,' Nicolas pleaded, sagging slightly from exhaustion and frustration. 'We must do *something*.'

'We will, my friend.' Ramirez put his hand on Nicolas's shoulder. If the gesture was supposed to reassure him, it didn't. 'We will. But now caution is called for. Especially when we do not know where the princess is. When we do, those fiends will pay, you have my word.'

There was a certainty to Ramirez's words that he allowed himself to accept, even though it ate at him to do so. But he couldn't ignore the advice of more seasoned adventurers. His nod of acceptance seemed to draw the ire of Auron, who glared at him. Nicolas shrugged apologetically, and the spirit rose and stormed off.

Like I feel any happier about it than you.

Looking back at the escaping ship, he tried to reassure himself that this was a minor setback. At some point in the very near future, he'd give the faun the comeuppance he so richly deserved and save all those he'd taken.

By the Deities, I will.

CHAPTER 12

Minimal sleep hadn't dissipated his frustration, instead giving it time to take root in his mind as a deep melancholy. He couldn't reconcile the idea that he'd let those children be taken, no matter how many rational arguments he came at himself with. The slaves only added to the weight he bore.

You were outnumbered and couldn't do anything.

It was Ramirez's decision not to pursue them.

Nothing shook the foundation of his disappointment.

Maybe everything would've turned out differently if I hadn't gone throwing ornaments around Killgore's cabin?

There was no *maybe* about it, and that was on him. The only way to make it right was to find those children, rescue them, free the slaves, and bring the evildoers to justice. And rescue the princess too, of course.

On a side note, how did the crew manage to get any sleep in these hammock things? He wanted a word or two with the genius who'd decided that the best type of bed on a constantly moving ship was a bit of net fastened between two pieces of wood. At least he'd given his companions and the crew plenty of entertainment trying to get into the bloody thing. They'd repaid him by snoring loudly, keeping him awake most of the night. The only benefit of that was that no one had been up to see him nearly fall out of the thing. Several times.

'Are you okay?' Garaz asked as he approached Nicolas in the ship's mess.

He'd made a very obvious effort to sit away from anyone and wished the orc would respect that. Still, he couldn't be rude, even if he wanted to, and gestured for Garaz to sit, which he did, sweeping his thick red cloak aside as he lowered himself onto the bench.

'I believe my earlier question was a formality, as I already know the answer.' Garaz examined his bowl of stew—identical to Nicolas's own meal, which thankfully tasted much better than it looked. 'So I shall rephrase it,' the orc continued. 'What is wrong?'.'

For a moment, he didn't want to answer, but looking into the orc's genial yellow eyes, he couldn't help talking. Garaz only wanted to help. 'I...let the mission down.' He breathed heavily as the words left his mouth, as if the information had been held prisoner. 'I let those children down. I should've saved them. Instead, I messed up and let them get taken. I didn't help anyone, and nearly got myself and Shift killed.'

Garaz considered this for a moment before replying. 'And knowing you as I do, you have already gone over every rationale as to why you could not have helped them or what you may have done differently?'

Nicolas laughed, part of him hating being so obvious.

'Then my advice is simple.' Garaz smiled. 'Take that energy and put it into getting them back.'

'As simple as that?' he asked incredulously.

'As simple as it need be.' Garaz shrugged. 'You want to kick yourself for letting them get away? Pointless. Learn from your mistake and make sure it doesn't happen again'

Looking at his companion, he let the sense of his words sink in. With an idea in mind, Nicolas wolfed down the last of his stew and rose from the table. Going to take his plate away and enact his idea, he found himself stopped by a large green hand around his wrist.

'You have a good heart, young Nicolas,' Garaz said with feeling. 'It is one of your best qualities. Do not let your overthinking and anxiety bury it.'

There was something in the orc's tone. 'Are you okay?' it was his turn to ask.

For a moment, he wasn't sure Garaz would reply. 'That pamphlet we found has disturbed me greatly,' the orc admitted. 'I believed myself accustomed to being the outcast all this time, but when I see documents like that, I realise that some people can yet sink lower. It is perplexing, and frustrating. Yet you remind me that not all are like that. Do not lose that.'

'For what it's worth,' he replied, 'I wish everyone could know you like I do. You taught me that you can't judge a race based on rumour and legend. There aren't many I'd rather have at my side when doing crazy stuff like this. You're a good and true friend, and I'm honoured to call you so.'

Garaz gave a hearty laugh. 'I am also honoured to have you as my friend.' The orc smiled. 'We have done some real good together, young Nicolas. Once I have finished my meal, I shall meet you on deck to continue our work.'

****

The sun was high in a cloudless sky, the air warm, making him feel as if he glowed. All around Nicolas was the bustle of everyday ship life, about which he was still none the wiser. However, seafaring wasn't what he'd come on the deck to learn. He looked around.

Captain Ramirez stood on the edge of the deck, one foot on the rail, looking outwards as he held the rigging, his cape flapping around him. How did the man manage to tread the line between looking dashing and over the hill? Beside him was Silva, standing a few steps back from the side of the vessel. The pair were deep in conversation.

Finding it handy that they were both together, he approached the pair, stopping only when Silva let out a slight giggle. The sound wasn't as surprising as who it had come from, but he had business with them both, so he pressed on. Just as he reached them, Silva went to touch Ramirez's hand, only for the captain to move it, sweeping it around to dramatize whatever tale he was telling her. Had the captain done that on purpose or simply not noticed the hand?

'Ah, Nicolas.' Ramirez smiled as he reached them. 'Glad to see you up and about. The pursuit goes well. We are following the course of the *Death* and the head wind is good. Hopefully, we can catch up to her later today, and maybe the faun, too.'

'Great, but I'm not here about that,' Nicolas replied, focused on his task. 'I need a favour.' The tone in Nicolas's voice got their attention. Silva inclined her head slightly in curiosity as Ramirez gestured for him to make his request. 'I want you two to continue training me.' He shoved aside the painful memories of his last training session with Silva.

'You did not seem so enthusiastic last time,' Silva noted as she scrutinised him carefully.

'That was before I let a group of children get kidnapped,' he admitted, his passion rising. 'I keep wandering around on these adventures with no real clue how to handle myself, and that isn't good enough. Not anymore. I will not let my inadequacy give the bad guys chances to win. Not again. I need to do better, and I'll only learn that from people with more experience than me.' He pointed to Silva, then to Ramirez, just to be sure he was completely clear.

Silva seemed impressed and Ramirez was beaming and nodding. 'Good attitude, my boy.' The captain chuckled, slapping him on the back. 'I can, of course, teach you more of the sword, and I am sure Silva has many deadly skills to impart. Just let us know when, and we are at your service.'

Nicolas looked around the ship and out to sea. 'I'm not doing anything now.'

****

'At least you are pulling your punches less.' Silva remarked as he looked up at the sky, sprawled across the deck, again. It'd been...he was unsure how many times it had been. Enough that he missed doing this on sand.

Sitting up and catching his breath, Nicolas tried to ignore the aches and pains crying out for attention. The warrior was right, of course; he'd been pulling his punches to avoid accidentally hurting her. It was taking him some very painful lessons to teach him that there was no room for courtesy in a fight, but it was starting to sink in. Being thrown onto a wooden deck repeatedly was an effective learning tool, as it turned out.

'Do you need me to heal those bruises?' Garaz asked cheerfully from the side lines, snacks in hand.

Nice someone's enjoying the show.

It wasn't just the orc either. Any of the crew not currently busy with day-to-day ship duties had taken the opportunity to enjoy the entertainments.

'Let's wait until she's finished giving me the bruises first.' He smiled in return.

In reality, he wanted to crawl over to the orc on hands and knees to beg for some healing magic. Instead, he carefully picked himself up and brushed himself off, taking a moment to stretch out some of the limbs that were currently a mix of stinging and burning.

'At least you keep getting back up.' Shift sounded almost impressed.

Pride flashed through him.

That was true. No matter how many times Silva knocked him down, he kept getting back up. But it was only because he had to learn to handle himself in a fight. Flukes, and timely interventions, and jumping from the sides of ships weren't going to save him forever. He wanted to start doing this right, and unfortunately there was no magic way for him to instantly learn everything he needed.

It'd be great if there was though.

The realisation of what he was doing sunk in. He wasn't whining to go home or longing for it. Instead he was working on becoming better at something contrary to everything he used to believe he was.

Am I changing? If I am, what are the consequences of that?

Should this be something he was excited about? Wasn't his place still at home with his parents? So many conflicting thoughts and emotions were yapping for his attention that he could've kissed Silva when she impatiently snapped her fingers and awoke him from his frustrating introspection.

'Again,' Silva demanded, annoyingly fresh while Nicolas's clothes were damp with sweat.

Remembering the stance she'd shown him, Nicolas planted his feet, keeping his weight loose to enable quick movement. Raising his guard, he advanced towards the frustratingly nonchalant warrior. He decided halfway to her that he was going to fake the warrior with a left hook but then come through on an uppercut. This time, Silva was going to be the one on her ass. The small audience would cheer him, and Silva would give him an impressed nod, looking—

Focus on the fight.

Closing the gap, Nicolas launched his left hook. However, Silva didn't block him as he'd anticipated. Instead, she stepped under his punch and to the outside of it, putting her out of range of his uppercut. Expecting the left swing to be stopped, Nicolas had thrown too much weight behind it and was now overbalanced. Silva gripped his punching arm, pulling it forwards and then around in a large circle, taking Nicolas with it as an unwilling passenger. One flick of the wrist later, and his back and the deck had a short, sharp meeting.

'I could see in your eyes exactly what you were planning.' The warrior stood over him, arms folded. 'You need to take your mind out of the equation.'

'How do you not think when you fight?' Nicolas asked, a slight groan escaping his lips before the words did.

The concept seemed insane...and yet it was something he'd done before. Sometimes, like when Grimmark had been keen to beat him to death with a hammer on a bridge, he would let go and give into his instincts. One of those moments had ended up with Silva being knocked from a bridge by that same hammer. He just had no idea how to do it on purpose. Knowing that he was capable of it but unable to do it at will was maddening.

'It is like a dance,' Ramirez offered from the side lines. 'You let the music take you then you find that your body knows what to do.'

'I don't think he can dance either.' Shift grinned.

Quickly, he turned the comment over for signs they'd been upset by his refusal to dance. He...wasn't sure.

Taking Silva's hand, Nicolas allowed himself to be pulled back to his feet. As he straightened his back, there was a flare of pain. Garaz would have his work cut out for him later. 'I won't be dancing for a while after this.' He tried to make the words light, but he was serious.

As he stood again, hoping to last a little longer on his feet this time, Auron was standing to the side of their makeshift training area, scowling. When he saw Nicolas looking, he walked off, disappearing literally through one of the ship's doors.

'Speaking of dancing.' Garaz sat up, cocking his head to the side, his green face lined with concentration. 'Can anyone else hear music?'

For a moment, it seemed the orc was going mad as there was nothing but the splashing of the sea against the ship's creaking hull. Then he heard it: the edge of a melody, faint but somehow alluring. It sounded like someone singing a single resonating harmony that left him dazed and light-headed. From the looks on the faces around him, they could all hear it too.

We should go towards it.

Beside him, Ramirez gave himself a brief shake, as if waking himself up. 'It is a siren.'

'Siren?' he asked dreamily.

'Vile creatures,' the captain continued offhandedly. 'They use their song to lure ships onto the rocks. Once the vessel is grounded, they eat the crew.'

His eyes drifted to the edge of the deck. He wanted to walk off the side of the ship and swim toward the sound. He could tell that Shift, Silva, and Garaz did, too, and the song was barely audible. Yet somehow, the crew of the *Irrevocable Amora* seemed relatively unconcerned, noting it as a passing fancy but nothing more. While he...He wanted...He had to...

Ramirez slapped him hard across the face.

'Ow,' he cried, rubbing his stinging cheek.

Ramirez rolled his eyes, muttered, *'Landlubbers,'* and slapped his companions. 'Back on board now?' the captain asked with a broad grin once his work was done.

And yes, now that Nicolas was focused on the pain on his cheek, he wasn't really paying attention to the background music.

Ramirez glanced disdainfully in the direction from which the melody came. 'Stupid things are supposed to be extinct.'

'How are you lot not affected?' he asked, keen to learn this skill as well.

'We are professional seamen,' Ramirez replied as if it were obvious. 'Save such tricks for landlubbers and children. No hardy man of the sea falls prey to a siren. It would be...embarrassing.'

I suppose if it eats you then you won't have to live with the embarrassment for long.

'Is that why they are meant to be extinct?' Garaz asked.

'Indeed,' the captain replied. 'They all starved or were hunted down, as far as I knew. Until today.'

'Um, I don't want to sound like I'm still glamoured, or whatever a siren does,' Shift said, 'but maybe this siren saw certain other ships pass by here?'

Ramirez considered this for a moment, which involved a lot of beard stroking. 'I suppose it is worth an ask,' the captain said finally. 'But if any of you tourists get eaten, it is not my responsibility.'

CHAPTER 13

Rocky outcrops in the middle of the ocean were strange things. They weren't islands, they were just...there, in defiance of the mass of water around them. The one they approached looked like a large hump protruding from the water, but the hump itself was covered in rises and dips of wet grey stone. The strangest thing about it was the lone figure on one of those dips, shaded from the sun by the peaks behind its back.

As soon as the ship sighted the outcrop, the siren had stopped singing. It must've decided it was a pointless exercise to continue as the ship was already heading for it. Was the creature lazy or cocksure? Either answer was concerning.

Ramirez was taking no chances with the siren, keeping the ship at a distance from the jagged spikes of rock surrounding the outcrop and ensuring he had archers on deck, bows nocked and ready.

When the ship drew parallel to the siren, Nicolas stood on the side of the deck with his friends so he could get a clear look. The siren lay casually on the rock, plucking aimlessly at a harp. The human half of the body was female, if a frumpy, emaciated one, looking as if she needed a good meal.

It won't be me.

The lower portion of the body was feathered like a giant chicken, with wings lying at rest at the creature's sides. If that was what all sirens looked like, no wonder they were going extinct. If his ship had been lured this far, upon seeing the siren, he would've promptly turned back in the other direction, song or no song.

'Hello there.' The siren nodded in the direction of the vessel that had pulled alongside it as if only just noticing it. The creature's voice carried across the air without the need for it to shout. That was eerie.

'You are not even going to glamour yourself into a beautiful woman to entice us?' Ramirez called back from beside Nicolas, his lips pursed in a way that indicated his distaste for the creature. 'I am insulted.'

'Would it have worked?' the siren asked with a tilted head. The question seemed rhetorical.

Ramirez gave a scoffing laugh and puffed his chest out with pride. 'Not on my crew,' he declared.

'Well, then I would just be wasting time.' The siren shrugged. 'If it was these four alone, I would have, but I've heard of you and doubted your crew would fall for it.' The siren smiled wanly and sighed. 'There was a time whole crews would butcher each other in fits of passion to get to me. Those days are gone. But maybe they'll return, if promises are kept.'

Promises? Something about this bothered Nicolas, but he couldn't put his finger on it. 'You ever dealt with these creatures before?' he asked Auron, who stood to his other side.

For a long moment, the spirit didn't reply. Instead Auron just stared at him, his eyes wide in mock surprise. Why? Because Nicolas had asked him a question? 'Like I said before, kid, I was never one for nautical adventures.' The annoyance in his voice matched his body language perfectly. 'I prefer to keep my business on dry land, where the *real* action is.'

There was no need to be so petulant. He'd only asked. Besides, Nicolas had only been at sea a day or two and had seen plenty of *real* action. It'd been sandwiched between a lot of travelling, which was a little tedious, but it seemed to him now that most of adventuring was just wandering around looking for stuff then having a fight when you found it.

Ignoring his companion's attitude, he turned his attention back to the conversation, which was still stuck on Ramirez bragging about how able a seaman he was and that he would never fall for the cheap illusions of a siren. He suppressed an eye roll, especially when he saw the reaction it was getting from Silva. Her dreamy-eyed look was disturbing and not at all in keeping with the woman he knew. Ramirez was better at glamouring than the siren.

'...it would stain my reputation as a captain,' Ramirez continued.

'Ha,' the siren scoffed bitterly. 'It is a sad day for my kind when we cannot even work our magic on a womaniser like yourself. Though I'm not surprised.'

Silva actually snarled slightly when the siren pointed out Ramirez's reputation with the opposite sex.

'Yet you knew we would come?' Garaz interrupted, evidently tiring of the boasting too.

'I gave you a little tease and hoped for the best.' The siren fluttered its eyelashes at Garaz in a very unflattering way, which did not go down well considering the look of distaste on the orc's face. 'Well, I gave you passengers a little tease.'

'Wait a minute.' Shift appraised the creature through narrowed eyes. 'You sound like you knew we were aboard.'

The siren sniggered slightly, an ugly sound. 'I was told you were aboard,' it replied smugly.

That feeling that something was off suddenly jabbed at Nicolas again, and it wasn't his usual anxiety either. Something about this was very wrong. The only people who could've given the siren that information were the faun, or Killgore. If that was true, that meant this was a trap. Judging by the drawing of swords, Ramirez, Silva, Shift, and Garaz had come to the same conclusion.

But where is the danger? It's just one siren.

Though he had to admit, for a creature that had multiple arrows trained on it, the siren seemed way too calm. He scanned the rocks around her to look for any signs of attack. What he needed to do was keep this conversation going until he figured out what the trap was.

'Who told you?' he asked.

The siren finally noticed Nicolas properly and craned her neck to get a better look at him. 'A little on the scrawny side,' the siren mused, licking her dry lips slightly. 'But not bad. I would eat you, but I wouldn't necessarily seduce you first.'

'*Hey*!' he snapped, looking down at himself. Why *wouldn't* the creature go all out to eat him? He was hardly a shining specimen of manhood, but he deserved a bit of effort. And these creatures were supposedly starving, so wouldn't that make him a prime piece of meat in her eyes?

What am I thinking?

The opinion of a sea creature that ate folk wasn't important. And neither was his bruised pride.

'Hey, bird girl,' Shift shouted, clicking their fingers to attract the siren's attention. 'His question is still good. Who told you?'

'Ro,' the siren said.

Nicolas and Shift looked at each other in confusion. Was that even a word? 'Is that a name?' Shift asked.

The siren leant its head back and let out a huff. 'You're chasing some-one, and you don't even know his name. Ro is the faun,' she replied finally, looking back at them again. 'He told me he was being followed. Asked me to take care of it.'

'But your silly song didn't work on us because of the captain.' Shift smiled as they pointed to Ramirez.

The siren laughed again. 'And yet you are here,' she said, indicating the rocks on which she sat.

That was a fair point. Regardless of the poor effect of the siren's song, they'd still come. But if it was on their own terms then surely the trap was moot? If only he could believe that.

'Enough of this!' Silva cried. 'You will talk plain, creature, or feel my steel.'

That was more like the Silva he knew. It was kind of comforting, even though she stayed a good several paces away from the side of the ship. She'd need to get much closer to make good her threat.

Rubbing her temples, the siren muttered to herself before addressing the group again. 'It's like none of you have ever heard of an ambush.' The siren smiled, showing rows of razor-sharp teeth set in a cruel grin.

And the trap was sprung. Opening her mouth unfeasibly wide, the siren let out a scream that seemed to shake the air itself. His eardrums threatened to burst even as he clapped his hands to his ears. Then the vibrations of the scream plucked his feet from the floor like a leaf in a hurricane and flung him across the deck. Hitting the hard wood and sliding, he struck the other side of the ship—fortunately, the raised side prevented him from shooting right over into the sea. As Nicolas lay on the deck, watching it sway and move, his temples throbbing, he heard another shrill call from the siren, one which was answered by the rustling of multiple feathers.

From the far side of the rocky outcrop emerged a group of six shadows with large wings. Whereas the siren was more woman than bird, these were more bird than woman, with razor-sharp beaks and talons, which looked massively at odds with the bare breasts that bounced with every flap of their wings. The creatures shrieked as one and dove towards the ship.

'*Harpies!*' He knew Ramirez was shouting, but it sounded like a far-off whisper as he watched the captain scuttling across the deck on all fours until he had a sturdy barrel between him and danger.

Nicolas didn't need the name of the creatures to know they were dangerous and that he should take cover. However, the siren's scream had left him too disorientated to find it, the ringing in his ears distracting him further. Fortunately, he had enough wherewithal to roll aside as one of the creatures bore down on him with its talons extended, gouging deeply into the wooden deck where he'd been, before flying off with a shriek of frustration. Screams from around him suggested others hadn't been so quick off the mark. Also that his hearing was coming back.

Using the side of the deck to pull himself to his feet, Nicolas saw an area behind some stairs that would provide partial cover, at least until he came to his senses and could do something useful. Walking towards it proved more difficult than expected as he stumbled along, listing from side to side as if he'd drunk a whole tavern's worth of ale. Though he could hardly complain when a fortuitous stumble to the side put him out of line of another set of talons that swept down on him. He really was better when he wasn't thinking about it.

He rubbed his eyes furiously to try to get them to focus. Maybe he ought to sit down and wait it out? Except...

Harpies, remember?

To his left, a sailor with a bow was firing arrows into the air. He gave the man a wave. Seemed like the thing to do. The man didn't return the gesture nor pay attention to it. He was too busy screaming as his arm was torn open after a flash of feathered wings passed him.

The talons gripping his shoulders brought him back to reality with a spike of pain. The harpies claws dug into him and yanked upwards. Suddenly the ground was no longer beneath his feet. Flailing, he desperately tried to reach a deck that was no longer there, until the harpies talons finally penetrated the skin. Then all he could do was scream.

Control yourself. You can't let it take you.

What would it do if it did? Would he be tossed into the sea to be eaten by the creatures that dwelt there? Maybe the harpy would eat him herself? Or maybe she just planned to lift him up high and drop him back to the deck, shattering every bone in his body?

The options passed through his mind in a flash, but it was enough to force him to act through the pain. Desperately, he reached out and grabbed a nearby line.

Finding it's motion arrested, the harpy shrieked in fury, beating it's wings frantically to try and break his grip. The rope burned his hands, but he held tight. The harpy's talons pushed against the wounds they'd created, threatening to tear right through his shoulders. But he couldn't let go.

'*Let go,*' he cried through gritted teeth as his arms shook against the force pulling against them and the pain weakening them.

He looked down. His panicked state of mind couldn't judge how high up they were. Maybe a couple of feet, maybe a couple of hundred. It was hard to focus when pain and fear screamed for his attention.

I don't know how long I can hold on, or take this pain.

Something was going to give, and he was certain it wouldn't be the harpy.

Suddenly the grip holding him vanished, the harpy howling in pain. Gravity took Nicolas's body, dropping it back toward the deck. Acting in almost slow motion, he looked up and saw a harpoon protruding from the back of the creature as it fought to stay aloft.

The rope he held snapped taught as it took his full body weight. The sudden jarring motion was enough to finally break his hold, and he fell, the deck getting larger fast as he plummeted toward it.

Pain shot up his legs as he landed. The height hadn't been as great as his panicked mind had made out. It wasn't enough to break any bones, but damage had been done, and he blacked out for a second.

Lying there bleeding and broken like a tasting platter in full view of the harpies wasn't an option whilst the battle still raged. Blinking, he managed to turn himself onto his stomach and push himself from the floor enough to reach the edge of the deck and use it to pull himself up again. He wasn't sure if it was the blood loss or the impact of the fall that was making him dizzy, but he knew he needed to be on his feet.

His left ankle refused to take his weight and he found himself clinging to the side of the deck to stay upright. That was when the harpy hit him.

Flying erratically in it's death throes, the creature that had grabbed him smashed into him, causing him to topple over the edge of the deck.

Scrabbling frantically again, he somehow managed to hold on to the side of the ship. His already torn shoulders yanked furiously against their sockets as they suddenly took his weight, and he screamed in pain. Fighting through the agony, he pulled himself up until he was resting against the rail on crossed arms, but that was as far as he got. Could get. Blood loss was making him lightheaded. Any second now, he'd be taking an involuntary dip in the sea.

On the deck of the *Irrevocable Amora,* the fight continued in earnest. Shift was holding a harpy at bay with a harpoon they'd found somewhere. Garaz was launching his fireballs, flinging them into the sky with passion. One struck home, the harpy blackening and screaming as it fell from the sky, feathers ablaze. To his immediate right, Silva, after discouraging a harpy's attack with her sword, finally noticed him hanging on for dear life.

'Help!' he croaked. His arms were weakening as blood poured from the puncture wounds in his shoulders.

To his surprise and then dismay, Silva didn't rush to his aid. For a moment, it looked as if she might, but after hesitating, she began to look around.

Any time now.

Everyone else still on the deck was either wounded or currently engaged with a crazed bird creature, so Silva eventually, tentatively stepped towards Nicolas, though it was much too slow for his liking.

'*Come on!*' he cried, the exertion of shouting sapping more of his strength. He only had seconds before another long drop.

Shaking herself, Silva closed the gap between them and grabbed his hand. She was still a little far from the edge of the ship, but it didn't matter when she had muscles to spare. Silva's arms bulged as she took his weight, pulling him back onto the safety of the deck. Relative safety. Judging by the feathers raining down, the harpies were still a threat.

How are the creatures staying aloft when they moult so badly?

'Thanks.' He didn't sound too thankful, but his gratitude had been dented by his companion's apparent reluctance to save him.

Not that Silva appeared bothered about his tone. The warrior had more immediate concerns, such as the harpy slashing at her with it's talons.

Pain flaring in his shoulders, Nicolas drew the *Dawn Blade*. It was better to hold a sword, than hold illusions that he'd make it to safety any time soon. In his lessons, Ramirez hadn't covered fighting flying monsters while bleeding profusely, but he was sure the principles were the same. Swing, stab, repeat. He was almost in the frame of mind to fight when he was knocked from his feet and promptly executed his trademark move: dropping his sword.

'I know there's a battle on, but maybe just a quick bite,' the siren purred as she straddled him, grinding on him in a way that made him feel a little used and sick.

Trails of fluid ran from the siren's lips as she salivated at the idea of eating him. All he could do was stare wide eyed at the creature atop him as blind panic bound him to the deck.

Lowering her head, the siren licked one of the wounds on Nicolas's shoulder. He retched at the sight of the creature's tongue, covered in *his* blood, retracting into her mouth as she savoured what she'd tasted.

'That'll do nicely,' she purred, that cruel smile reappearing before she opened her mouth impossibly wide.

Staring into a black, razor-toothed maw and quite set on not getting eaten, he reached around him in desperation. His hand found the hilt of his sword. This time he hadn't dropped it too far from him. Maybe he was getting better? Using his fingertips to inch the hilt close enough as he tried to hold the siren back, he grabbed it and swung the blade. But his body was too weak and beaten to completely obey his commands, and instead of a swing that took the siren's head from it's shoulders, he somehow managed to smack it in the temple with the hilt instead.

Deities damn it.

He was still pleased with the effect. Crumpling, the creature fell to the side and off him. A win in his book.

When he got back to his feet, his shoulders were now so weak he could barely lift the sword. Doing anything practical with it was out of the question. Beneath him, the siren stirred. Unable to use the *Dawn Blade*, he settled for booting the creature in the side of the head with his good foot as hard as possible. The stirring stopped. The movement nearly cost him another trip to the floor, as his weak ankle took his full weight for a moment, but the result was worth it.

Taking stock of the situation, he could clearly see that the battle had turned in their favour. The last two harpies were taking tentative swipes at the crew, more a last gasp before fleeing, than a committed attack. Several of the harpies lay dead on the deck, but so were several of the crew. As the creatures hovered indecisively in the sky, Shift decided to encourage them by lobbing their harpoon in their direction. Their aim was good, but the weapon fell just below the harpies before returning to the ship and embedding itself in the deck. It was, however, enough for the bird monsters to make up their minds to flee, screaming and squawking. He didn't care if they were shrieking curses at them or be-moaning their fallen sisters as long as they buggered off and didn't come back.

Finally giving in, he slumped to the deck. At least his friends were well. Shift shouted curses at the fleeing harpies while Garaz tended to the wounded. Silva stood off to the side, pointedly avoiding eye contact with him. Auron was walking, or floating, towards him with an impressed smile.

'My boy, you did it,' Ramirez cried, looming over him. For a second it looked like the captain was going to grip his shoulders in delight, but he took one look at the state of Nicolas and thought better of it, instead crouching down and patting him on the leg. 'You captured the siren and helped save the ship. Bless you.' The captain kissed Nicolas on either cheek—an unwelcome gesture, but apparently Ramirez didn't need permission.

Auron stopped, before turning and walking away again.

'Victory, my noble crew! *Victory*!' Ramirez cried, raising his bloodless sword aloft.

The crew stopped clearing the deck to cheer with their captain, the wounded sailors letting out some weak groans in honour of their victory. A bit rich considering Ramirez had almost certainly been behind the barrel the whole time.

Not where I'd expect him to be at all. Where did all the dashing and bravado suddenly go?

But he wasn't about to sully the moment. He had more pressing concerns, such as not dying.

Flourishing his cape, the captain turned to the siren and used his boot to disdainfully flip the creature onto her back, pressing his sword tip into her flabby throat. 'You have dared to besmirch my vessel. You have harmed my crew,' Ramirez snarled as the siren alternated between looking at him and the sword at her throat. 'You will tell me which way this faun went, and I shall reward you for this service by dispatching you quickly. If not, it will be...shall we say *unpleasant* for you.'

'He went that way.' The siren pointed frantically. 'There's an island with a volcano that he's using as a base. Follow that course, and you'll get to him.' Evidently, the siren didn't care for whatever *unpleasant* might have entailed.

Nicolas had at least expected some curses first, maybe a bit of pleading. At the very least, he'd thought the creature would hold out for more than a second.

As it turned out, he needn't give the siren any more thought. Without further hesitation, Ramirez drove his sword into her throat. Nicolas wasn't sure which was worse: the wet sound of the blade cutting into flesh or the slight *thunk* as it came out the other side and hit the deck. The death gurgle of the creature as her eyes bulged wide was also pretty bad. On reflection, they were all equally gross.

Raising his bloody sword again, the captain instigated another round of cheering before shouting orders for his men to clear up and set course.

Please don't hang around and try to help me stop bleeding.

From where he was he could see Garaz, getting to him was a different matter. His throat was too raw to even call out. He wasn't sure if the deck was lolling in the sea, or if it was him.

'You okay?' It was difficult to tell Shift's expression as their face kept going in and out of focus, but they probably looked concerned.

How to answer that question?

'I've had worse.' He smiled thinly. 'Or have I? I'm not sure.'

'You're talking nonsense, so I think you'll be fine.' Shift chuckled. Was there relief there?

Of course there is. That's only natural. Don't read into it.

'Good for you then, because you obviously care.' He laughed as the world bounced in and out of focus. It was strange. Hazy, clear, hazy, clear. It really needed to make its mind up.

What's that look on their face?

'Garaz,' Shift called. 'Nick needs some help, big guy.'

CHAPTER 14

Nicolas found himself back in the ship's mess, which was appropriate as he was a bloody mess himself. Being attacked by bird-women creatures had worked up an appetite, plus he needed to sit a while so his body could heal and restore his blood supply. He was still slightly lightheaded, but at least he was properly aware again. Right now, he was just happy to be alive, riding the wave of euphoria he was starting to notice after surviving a fight, once the adrenaline had calmed down and he'd had time to process what had happened. He'd made it through another one, albeit barely.

Garaz had tended to his wounds, sealing and healing them before giving him a herb for the pain, which was very effective. There was a lingering ache, but considering how bad it could've been, he put it aside. His only niggle was his ruined shirt, caked in his now-drying blood. He'd complained to Garaz after the orc healed his wounds.

'I am a healer. Take up laundry matters with a laundress,' the orc had snapped before moving on to the next patient. Nicolas had forgotten how much using magic could drain the orc. Probably not the right time to bemoan his attire.

Opening the holes in his shirt, Nicolas looked at one of the still-red talon wounds in his shoulder. Hopefully, they wouldn't scar. His mother would have a fit if he came home sporting a multitude of scars.

My parents.

He wanted to be guilty about his lack of drive to return home, but he couldn't. They still had work to do here. When it was done, he would earn the right to go home. Until then...he just couldn't dwell on it.

—Mind you, there are no harpies at home. And good food, and my bed, and...

'That was intense.' Shift slumped down on the bench across from him, looking exhausted and perfectly interrupting his train of thought. 'I could quite happily never see a harpy again.'

'Mmm-hmm,' he replied absentmindedly with a nod.

His companion looked at him strangely for a second. 'Stop it,' they chided him finally.

'Stop what?'

'You're thinking of how much better being home would be. Don't try to deny it. You might as well be screaming it with that hangdog expression and drooping shoulders.'

He sat upright with some fidgeting. 'I don't like how well you can read me.' He huffed.

Shift let out a single laugh. 'Like it's hard.'

He suppressed the smile, just not quickly enough.

'What are we talking about?' Auron asked as he appeared beside Nicolas, making him jump.

'About how easy Nicolas is to read,' Shift answered.

'Oh that.' The spirit nodded. 'Yeah, you aren't subtle, kid. You scare easily too. Don't think I didn't notice the flinch when I appeared.'

'Well, I'm sorry I'm not all guarded like Silva.'

'You're definitely her complete opposite.' Shift sniggered.

'I don't know.' Now, Auron's voice was cool. 'You both seem overly fond of Ramirez. Actually, let me correct myself. You seem overly fond of him when he's showing you how to prance around with a sword.' *Where did that come from.*

Even Shift eyed Auron in disbelief.

'What do you mean by that?'

Do I need to defend myself right now?

Auron scoffed. 'You three make quite the team.' The spirit made a big show of rolling his eyes. 'They get to be the honourable teachers and you the willing student. All very cosy.'

'That's a bit uncalled for, don't you think?' he said tartly.

Auron shrugged so Nicolas looked to Shift for support, but his companion seemed to be as confused by this as he was. Awkwardness wrapped itself around him like a thick cloak. What had he done to earn Auron's displeasure? It was a positive relief when Hay Sharkbait entered the mess.

Instantly, Auron's mood changed to that of a giddy child. 'Ask her again.' The spirit was almost bouncing on his heels.

Shift didn't seem impressed with Auron's attitude but turned anyway to watch the first mate approach. 'What about it then?' Shift asked. 'I just helped fight off some harpies. You ready to tell me how you got your name?'

Standing beside them, the sailor laughed heartily. 'Ye handled yerselves well up thar, 'tis true.' From what he could remember from the few actual images he'd picked out of the melee, she'd handled herself well too. The blood covering her tunic certainly suggested there was at least one less harpy in the world because of her. The first mate leaned in close to Shift, her voice becoming a mere whisper. 'But I don't think ye'll ever be ready te hear my tale.'

Standing again as if it had never happened, Hay Sharkbait changed back to a conversational tone. 'Captain wants ye on deck,' the first mate declared then wheeled around and headed in that direction herself.

'Oh, I have to know her story,' Shift and Auron said in unison.

****

When he emerged from the lantern-lit depths of the ship into the sun once again he instantly saw Silva, stood by the mast looking ruefully towards the aft of the ship. He hung back and let Shift and Auron go on ahead before approaching the warrior.

'So what's up with you then?' he asked. Nearly killing each other had earned them a certain forthrightness in his opinion.

'What do you mean?' the warrior asked, bristling instantly.

Normally, he would've found the stern gaze off-putting, but not today. 'I nearly fell overboard, and you hesitated.' He didn't see the need to add *and I nearly died,* as that part was obvious.

'I was merely assessing the situation to ensure the best course of action,' Silva replied smartly. 'It was the middle of a battle.'

'You hesitated,' he repeated, staring hard at the warrior. If she wanted to play some kind of stare-down game, he wouldn't be found wanting.

'And yet here you are, moaning like an ass instead of thanking me,' the warrior snapped.

'Maybe you're too lovestruck to keep your mind on the important stuff.'

Oh no. Too far.

The minute the words left his mouth, he knew they'd been a mistake

Silva grabbed him by his ruined shirt and pulled him in close. Her face was the very definition of rage. 'Let us assume I know more about fighting battles than you, boy.' Silva sounded a lot like the old Silva right now. The murdering mercenary he'd first met. Although *boy* was a bit rich; she was only a few years older than he. 'You would do well not to—'

'What?' Garaz stood beside them. 'What would he do well not to do?' the orc continued, expression neutral.

After a moment, Silva huffed and let him go. The warrior hesitated, as if there was something she wanted to say. 'Nothing,' she said finally, before stomping toward the bridge.

'Complicated woman,' Garaz observed.

'Scary woman,' Nicolas added.

'That too.' The orc chuckled.

He stared after Silva in bewilderment. What exactly was going on with her? It seemed like more than simple romantic entanglement.

Turning back toward the bridge of the ship, Nicolas looked briefly at Garaz and stopped suddenly. The orc's green skin was paler than usual, which only served to accentuate the bright strip of orange hair atop his head. His yellow eyes were similarly drained. 'Are you okay?' he asked with concern.

'I am well,' Garaz said with a smile. 'Healing so many of the crew has taken it out of me I fear. I will return to normal soon enough.'

From his companion, Nicolas had learned that magic wasn't the all-encompassing power he'd believed it to be. Indeed, magic was linked to its user's life force and could be depleted if overused, which was why most wizards only specialised in certain schools of magic. Thinking of nothing soothing to say, he simply patted Garaz on the back, but the orc seemed pleased at the show of affection.

On the bridge of the ship, Captain Ramirez was talking to Hay Sharkbait in earnest, eye pressed to his looking glass. The object of his attention was a tall, thin island off their portside. That had to be the pirate's lair. Generally, it seemed like every other island he'd seen on his travels so far, save for the prominent volcano emerging from its centre, which he really hoped was dormant. It had to be; no sane person would make their base on an island with an active volcano...right?

'I believe this is the island the siren directed us to, my friends.' Ramirez didn't take his eyes from it as he retracted his scope. 'The faun and that dastardly scumbag Killgore are hidden here. I can feel it.'

First Auron's 'hero instincts' and now Ramirez's 'captain instincts.' When do I evolve this kind of sixth sense?

'So what do we do?' Shift asked. 'Do we storm in with the element of surprise and take the hostages back?'

Nicolas glanced at the island again. Where would they storm into? There were no obvious buildings or signs of life.

'No,' Ramirez replied a little too quickly. 'A gentle touch is required. Firstly, we must know the enemy's location and disposition. I propose a scouting party. Once we find their base, we shall wet our blades with the blood of our enemies.'

Looking at the island, he knew exactly what he had to do.

'Shift, Auron and I will go,' he declared without thought.

'Are you sure, my friends?' Ramirez asked.

'I am.' And he was. There were wrongs that he needed to right, and he wasn't going to do any of that hanging around the ship. Besides, he had half an idea that Ramirez would suggest him again anyway. The captain had an allergy to risking his crew. Why that was so was an interesting question. Every now and then Nicolas thought he was close to the answer, yet he couldn't quite grasp it. It was there, but not, like if he tried to hug Auron.

'Scouting means stealth, Nick.' Apparently, he wasn't destined to live the accident on the *Death* down for a while as Shift looked at him distastefully. 'That means keeping quiet. Can you handle that?'

'Yes, I won't make the same mistake again.' He probably should've been more apologetic, but it was infuriating to have his nose rubbed in his cockup.

'And I will be there to support you,' Garaz said, patting his shoulder.

He looked at Garaz's dull skin. 'Are you sure you're up to it?'

'I am,' the orc nodded firmly. 'I should have been there to back you up last time. I will not make that mistake again.'

'I thought you didn't do sneaking and stealth?' Shift asked with a half smile.

'I will manage,' Garaz replied firmly.

'You're coming this time, right?' he asked Silva, changing the subject.

From the corner of her eye, Silva glared at him as if annoyed to be put on the spot. As far as Nicolas was concerned, they could've used her last time, so she wasn't worming her way out of it again. 'We need your skill,' he continued. 'We don't know what's out there and if we run into trouble, you're the best chance we've got.'

Silva didn't answer but continued to glare at him.

'You can't atone for past sins sitting on a boat and letting us get killed.' It was a cheap shot, but it was all he had left.

Nicolas had thought Silva had been glaring at him before. How wrong he was. *Now*, she was glaring at him. But he wasn't about to let her play love ship with Ramirez while they risked their lives again, so despite every natural urge he had, he held her stare.

'Very well.' The words came through gritted teeth. 'I shall accompany you to ensure you don't die.'

It was reluctant and insincere, but he'd take it.

'I'm also coming,' Auron muttered off to the side. 'If you're interested.'
****

As Hay Sharkbait rowed towards the island, Nicolas wondered what awaited them. He couldn't help but feel a sense of déjà vu. Hopefully, this mission would fare much better. This time, at least, he wouldn't be the one to give them away. Okay, he would *try* not to be the one to give them away. In fact, he hoped they would be in and out without anyone even knowing they were there. Then they could come back in force finish this once and for all. That would be much easier with a crew of pirates backing them up.

If Ramirez finds his courage.

On the plus side, they had Garaz and Silva with them. The former still looked weak but had insisted, presumably feeling guilty that they'd nearly died last time. The latter had been more reticent but was currently in the centre of the little boat with her eyes closed, likely doing some form of pre-mission warrior meditation. Auron sat sullenly at the aft of the rowboat. Something was definitely up with the spirit. Usually, he would've been regaling them with tales of his past deeds, as he was wont to do any time there was a lull in the conversation. Instead, Hay Sharkbait was filling the empty air with her local knowledge and impressing him with her ability to single-handedly row a boat with four passengers. He'd never challenge her to an arm-wrestling match.

'Funnily enough, the main feature of this island is the dormant volcano you can all see,' the first mate continued, like some overenthusiastic tour guide. 'They say the island's never been settled due to some superstition about ghosts that haunt the volcano, maybe from an age-old settlement claimed when the volcano erupted previously. But I reckon it's got more to do with the chance of it reawakening. I wouldn't like to live somewhere that could be covered in hot lava at any moment.'

Bad enough they were about to land on a pirate island, but now it might also be haunted? After vampires and zombies, he really wanted to limit his contact with the undead to Auron. Maybe he could ask Auron to have a friendly chat with any local undead spirits and ask them to give the group a wide berth? But looking at his companion, Nicolas didn't think he was in the mood to talk to anyone.

How bad can the ghosts be when the pirates are obviously unafraid of them?

Finally, the first mate stopped rowing. 'If ye lot need me just signal and I'll come rowin' in.' Hay Sharkbait's genial tone wasn't suited to the task of landing people on an island to search for a pirate lair.

'You aren't staying here, Hayley?' He tried not to let uncertainty creep into his voice.

'Deities, no.' Sharkbait chuckled. 'Ghosts can't swim so I'll keep my distance 'til ye call. Pirates are one thing, undead a whole other.' He didn't want to spoil the first mate's illusion by reminding her that Auron had gotten from the *Death* to her rowboat perfectly fine, regardless of his deceased statues. 'Also, it's *Hay Sharkbait*. Not everyone wants te be as formal as ye, young 'un.'

Perhaps it was his aversion to being called *Nick Carnage* that made him not want to indulge other nicknames? But if that was really what she preferred to be called, he shouldn't argue.

Shift snorted derisively. 'How bad can the ghosts be? We have one of our own.' Instantly Shift had to look away as they took the full force of Auron's unimpressed stare at being referred to as a common ghost.

In any case, it was clear Hay Sharkbait intended to get no closer to the island, and she wasn't exactly known to be persuadable. Bracing himself for the cold and wet, he stepped over the side of the rowboat into the sloshing water. The cold and wet were awaiting him with open arms.

Trudging to the shore, Shift's sniggering still in his ears from the noise he'd made when coming into contact with the freezing water, Nicolas looked back toward the rowboat—Hay Sharkbait wasn't wasting time putting distance between her and the island—and then the *Amora* beyond. Why, with a ship full of crew, did Ramirez keep throwing them in the way of danger? He knew he'd volunteered this time around, but the captain hadn't even offered an alternative. Surely there was some seafarers' code about it being impolite to keep shoving one's guests towards your pirate nemesis?

And yet I think I'd be disappointed if I wasn't here right now. Warmer water would be nice, mind you.

CHAPTER 15

Dense undergrowth surrounded the dormant volcano, making it look as if it were rising from some kind of giant green nest. It wasn't at all suitable for travel, which was very unfortunate for their group, who had to travel through it. Simply muscling through the leaves and branches hadn't worked, so they'd resorted to hacking their way through. The trees around them held in the heat, turning the place into a veritable oven. Beads of sweat irritated Nicolas's skin as they rolled from his temples down his cheeks. Maybe some of those beads were due to the fear of discovery? The dizzy spells were definitely due to the heat, and he tried to temper really needing to drink with rationing his water supply. His companions seemed to be struggling just as much, except one. There was also the issue of readjusting to walking on a surface that didn't bob and heave underfoot.

Cutting their way through the jungle was noisy work. Leaves simply couldn't be hacked quietly. If there were any pirates close by, they'd definitely hear the intruders. But if there were, they would've known about it by now.

Unless the enemy's waiting in ambush?

In the hot, cramped jungle, it was easy to be paranoid, so Nicolas changed his train of thought. Besides, ghosts were his main worry.

Are the ones that haunt this island pirate ghosts? Would that be worse than regular ghosts?

It took him a few seconds to realise he'd just leapt from one paranoid thought straight to another. Still, he found himself keeping close to Auron. His companion could give them early warning of any of his kind.

As the group went deeper into the jungle, the light became progressively more muted due to the thick canopy above them, but at least it was oppressively hot as well! Nicolas would've hated not being completely uncomfortable doing this. His arms already ached from the hacking. He looked at the sword in his hand. It seemed wrong to use such a fine weapon to clear a path, but he lacked any better tool.

Focusing back on the task at hand, Nicolas looked up to find the large leaf Shift had just pushed aside swinging back to hit him in the face. 'Ahhhh.'

That was embarrassing.

His companions had stopped to look back at him, their expressions ranging from surprised to annoyed. Crying out in the middle of the jungle wasn't going to change his reputation as the guy most likely to give them away.

'Sorry.' He looked anywhere but directly at them.

Why are they still staring?

'You're not going to give us away this time, are you?' Shift's voice had the tone of an annoyed teacher.

It made him squirm slightly. 'No.'

'Are you?'

'No, I am not.' There was no need for them all to be so salty with him. Okay, he'd screwed up once, but... Nicolas sighed. They were right to be worried about him. He'd said he wouldn't give them away, but was it a promise he could keep?

Shift shrugged, apparently taking this at face value, but Silva seemed less convinced. Auron, for his part, looked like he wasn't paying attention to the conversation, and Garaz smiled at him sympathetically.

Twice my size, and manages to make less noise than I do when passing through a jungle. How is that even possible?

'This is difficult terrain under stressful conditions.' As much as he knew the orc was trying to be sympathetic, it did underline the fact that he'd made a mistake. Again.

'Thanks,' he replied anyway.

With every onward step, the claustrophobia of their enclosed surroundings increased. One of the things that bothered him most was that there were no animals, no signs of wildlife at all. What sort of island jungle didn't have at least a bird of some kind? Nicolas had no experience with this kind of ecosystem, but surely there should be life here?

Nicolas stopped suddenly, his ears pricking. 'What was that?'

Silva was alert instantly, scanning the area for signs of danger. 'What?'

'I heard something.' He strained to listen and pick out the noise again.

'You're edgy and you're hearing things.' Shift's remark was slightly discourteous. Maybe hoping he was wrong more than believing it?

'Yes, I'm hearing things,' he confirmed testily. 'As in, *I heard something*. I'm trying to listen for it again, but all I can hear are your snarky remarks.'

Shift bristled, but any potential argument was interrupted by a strange sound.

Vindication.

But what was it?

The sound itself was hard to describe. It was a harmonic, high-pitched note that seemed to whistle past them then disappear, only to return moments later. Every time the sound passed, it sent a chill up Nicolas's spine, though he assumed that was his usual fear reaction rather than the sound's doing. Still, it must've unnerved his companions, too, because they formed a rough circle where they stood. The sound seemed everywhere, but nowhere at the same time.

Nicolas eyed the foliage around them with unease. 'Auron, go check it out.'

'Why me?' Auron protested.

'Well, because—'

'Because I'm already dead and therefore can't get hurt?' The spirit's sarcasm was more tangible than his cloudlike body.

'Um...well, yeah.' The honest answer probably wouldn't improve the conversation any, but what good would it do to lie or sugar-coat it?

Auron stared hard at Nicolas for a moment before turning and stomping off through the foliage, muttering angrily to himself, which was more audible than his stomping.

'I think our companion has a problem,' Garaz whispered as the light aura faded between the leaves, just a few wisps of cloud marking where their companion had gone.

'Yeah, he does,' Shift added as they kept their sword ready. 'But now is neither the time nor the place for it. We can discuss his emotional issues later.'

The sound came again, this time at a much higher pitch, high enough to make Nicolas start. Without meaning to, he slowly backed away from the direction of the sound and out of the protective circle his companions had formed. He stopped suddenly when his back connected with something hard just beyond the nearest leaves.

Nicolas turned, screamed, and swung his sword. Letting out a continuous scream that was half battle cry, half terrified yelp, he cut and slashed with his sword until he was exhausted, crumpling into a panting heap on the jungle floor.

Finally letting out one last big breath, he opened his eyes and looked at his handiwork. Before him, the floor was covered in straw and pieces of torn cloth. To his side, half the remnants of a carved wooden face glared at him evilly.

Garaz leant over his shoulder and inspected the carnage he'd wrought. 'I believe the scarecrow is dead.' As Nicolas looked up, the orc had the face of someone very obviously trying not to laugh.

'Your form was poor but results adequate,' Silva commented as she moved to his side and kicked the half-cut head back into the foliage.

'Is it a scarecrow or a scareidiot?' Shift laughed.

Nicolas barely heard their conversation. Shock thrummed through him, making their voices tinny and far away, as he stared in horror at what he'd done. At the violence he'd unleashed. He hadn't known himself capable of such destruction, and he looked at the sword in his hand as if really seeing it for the first time. Maybe all this adventuring and danger was having a more profound effect on him than he'd first realised? He hoped it was a one-off; he didn't like the idea of doing that to a person one day.

First the pangs of excitement, and now this?

'Wind chimes.' Auron strode back through the leaves. 'They're set up all over here. There are scarecrows as well...but I see that you know that already.'

'It would seem someone has gone to quite a bit of effort to make people believe this place is haunted.' Garaz picked up and examined some of the scarecrow's torn clothing; several pieces of straw still attached to it fell to the floor.

Auron gave the first smile Nicolas had seen in a while. 'Scarecrows to keep snoopers away. That just means we're in the right place.' For a second, it looked like the spirit was going to break into one of his characteristic stories, but Auron seemed to think better of it.

****

Proceeding through the other side of the jungle with renewed purpose, the group found the going getting easier as the foliage thinned until it became sporadic, giving way to the rocky terrain that led up to the dormant volcano. The island itself being small, it seemed the only thing to do was keep walking until they found something. If there was something here to find.

'Are we sure they're even here?' Nicolas looked at the bleak stone landscape ahead of them. 'I mean, the siren wasn't exactly a reliable source.'

'You are not wrong,' Garaz noted. 'But someone is trying to hide something on this island. Why else go to such effort to dissuade visitors? As Auron said earlier, we are most likely in the right place.'

He supposed that the orc, and by extension Auron, was correct, but the lack of any other visible sign of life unnerved him. The whole mission unnerved him, but by now that had become nothing more than background noise in his head, instead of the insistent distraction it once was.

Just another sign I'm changing.

'I agree.' Silva scanned the horizon. 'Something is here. We need to keep to cover as much as possible, just in case whoever placed the scarecrows did not rely on them entirely for their security.'

Nicolas wasn't about to argue with Silva's analysis any more than he would've argued with Garaz about magic. Though there were no visible lookouts, that didn't mean they weren't there. There were so many outcrops around just perfect to conceal a lookout or two. So the group concealed themselves as much as possible, moving from one cover to the next to avoid any eyes that might be watching. Which worked well until they ran out of ground.

Before them, the rock parted into a deep ravine that led to a sheer drop down the side of the volcanic mountain. He instantly regretted the peek he took over the edge, his stomach dropping at just a glimpse of how high they'd come without him even realising. He'd been too busy looking up for sentries to notice the increasing sprawl of the jungle around them.

From somewhere above, water exploded, cascading down the mountainside in a mighty waterfall that fed the river below. It rumbled past them like the charging of ten thousand knights. It was almost too deafening to think. To one side of them, there was a sheer drop. To the other the steep rise of the volcano. The opening was too wide to jump. It seemed they were stuck.

'It would seem we are stuck.' Garaz looked over the edge of the crack, his yellow eyes widening at the sheer drop.

'Maybe we should go back?' Nicolas suggested.

'I'm sure you mean double back around the volcano and not back to the boat, right?' Shift asked with a cheeky smile.

'I'm not going back to the boat until our mission here is complete,' he replied flatly.

Shift rolled their eyes, but kept any additional comments to themselves.

'I think there's a route behind the waterfall,' Auron shouted, inspecting the edge of the water.

'Of course there is,' he muttered as he looked at the raging example of nature's ferocity. He had no idea how long it had taken to cut its path through the rock, but it would cut him down in a second, and he was about to try to slip behind it.

When he got to Auron, Nicolas was even less impressed. This *route* of his was little more than a ledge.

Auron looked at him and seemed to read his thoughts. 'It's fine.'

'I think another way would be better.' Judging from the look on everyone else's faces, they were as shocked that it was Silva who'd spoken as he was. She never went back. Only forwards. That was where the fighting would be.

'Well, this is a direct route,' Auron protested, seeming to take offence at his idea being challenged. 'And we have seen no other obvious route.'

'Then we go back,' the warrior replied simply.

What was going on? Why was Silva talking more like him?

Shift tested the ledge tentatively. 'This is fine.' Someone needed to tell their face it was fine. 'Keep your back to the rock and shuffle carefully, and it'll be no problem. You can fit two of Garaz down here, I reckon.'

'So I am the judge of space as I am the biggest?' the orc asked with a raised eyebrow.

'Yeah, but it's all muscle.' Shift grinned.

'Indeed it is.' Garaz smiled back.

'It's probably quite slippery, though,' Nicolas added. If a hardened warrior like Silva didn't think it was a good idea, it was time to be extra cautious.

Shift rolled their eyes again and let out a long, elaborate sigh then, before Nicolas could stop them, they pressed themselves to the ledge and began to shimmy across the gap. With every movement of their feet, he prayed they wouldn't slip and be taken by the water. Whether it was due to his prayers, or skill, or luck, Shift made it to the other side and waved at the group in a very smug manner.

Auron went next, walking across the ledge and paying no mind to the waterfall as the fierce current passed right through him...or he passed through it. Garaz was equally confident and made it to the other side. That left Nicolas and Silva.

'You may go first.' Silva's tone suggested the end of a conversation.

Well, that is mighty gentlemanly of me.

Dubiously, he approached the edge of the ledge. Carefully, he put his toes down and tested the rock; it was slippery. Stepping back, he took a few moments to steel himself, trying to encourage the belief that it would be fine. He was not succeeding.

This isn't going to get any saner with me standing here dwelling on it.

Pressing himself to the rock, he started to edge out. The crashing water was less than a metre from his face and the spray soaked his skin and clothes, but it wasn't as bad as he'd thought. For a second, his right foot slipped slightly, but it was nothing. Then a hand grabbed his roughly.

'Nicolas, stop!' Silva cried, yanking him back towards her.

Nearly toppling forwards with the force of the grab, Nicolas had to catch himself and pull back with greater ferocity before he fell over the edge. Fortunately, where Silva stood was more slippery and the warrior was thrown towards him. The pair collided and fell back against the rocks, which gave way under their combined weight.

Nicolas cried out as he and Silva tumbled backwards down a short slope. With each roll, a new part of his body was introduced to the hard stone floor and a new tender spot was presented for Silva's minimal armour to dig into. As the slope came to an end, the pair continued to roll for a moment, ending in a heap on the floor. Letting out an involuntary groan he tried to ignore the cuts, scrapes, bruises and general pains screaming for his attention. Behind him the waterfall continued to rumble, but it's sound was now muted slightly.

'Are you okay?' Shift shouted, appearing in the hole through which they'd fallen before sliding carefully down the slope to them.

Nicolas quickly checked himself over. 'I don't think I broke anything, but that wasn't pleasant.'

He let out another groan as the weight atop him shifted, Silva standing and brushing herself off. Even from this angle he could see how rapidly her chest was rising and falling. He watched her blink several times until her eyes weren't as wide as they had been and her chest began to settle back into a regular rhythm. There were several cuts and scrapes on her exposed skin as well, but he had a more pressing issue with the warrior. 'What in the Underworld was that?' he snapped. 'We could've both been killed.'

Silva didn't answer; she simply looked down at Nicolas.

'Well?' he pressed, not about to let this go a second time.

'Uh, guys,' Shift called. They were looking out over the edge of the wide ledge they'd landed on, urgently gesturing with their hand that the others should approach..

Pushing himself up, he looked at the far wall of the cavern they were in. And far was exactly the right term. They must be in an enormous cave. Following the curve of the rock upwards, the cavern got smaller the higher it went, even though he couldn't make out where it ended.

We're inside the volcano. It's hollow.

At least he could remove *'death from exploding volcano'* from his list of concerns. There was no heat. In fact the cavern was quite cool.

Approaching Shift, he crouched beside them at the edge of the ledge, looking over. His jaw dropped.

Auron gave a semi-impressed snort. 'Looks like you don't get your wish, kid. A hollowed-out volcano is still technically an underground lair.'

Ignoring the frustrating fact that the spirit was right, he instead tried to take in what he was seeing. Across from them, at sea level, the rock wall split into a large opening, allowing the water to enter and creating a vast sea cave, which was occupied. A system of docks extended from the rocks below, connecting the water to the large settlement attached to the inclining cave wall. The town, if that was what it should be called, consisted of numerous levels of wooden buildings, held up by vast supports dug into the rock itself. There was a great deal of activity on both walkways between the levels and the docks below.

One of the docks harboured a very familiar black ship. Beside the *Black Death*, a large system of pulleys was lowering some sort of device onto the ship's deck. It was like a giant looking glass, but stripped down. The metal framework contained various sized lenses which ended with the smallest pointing from her bow.

'That looks somehow familiar,' Garaz muttered, the orc's brow furrowed as he studied the contraption.

In the docks around the *Death*, four ships were under construction, their skeletal structures surrounded by scaffolding. The sound of hammering and sawing echoed through the cavern.

On the scaffolding, swarms of small figures moved about.

Small? Not small. Young.

Nicolas let out an involuntary gasp as the horror of what he was witnessing became apparent. Gangs of children swarmed across the scaffolding, hammering and sawing as large pirates bearing whips oversaw the work. Though he couldn't fathom why the whips were needed, beyond pure sadism. The children went about their tasks like automatons, clearly under the faun's spell.

'Someone's building themselves a fleet,' Auron commented.

'And using child labour,' Shift added. 'Very cost effective.' Nicolas looked at them aghast. 'Kidding.' Shift hadn't even looked at him to see his expression.

'If they can successfully provoke a war, in the aftermath, they will be the power in these waters with even such a small fleet,' Garaz added soberly.

'Surely that won't be the case,' Nicolas replied. 'It's only a handful of ships.'

'I don't know much about it, kid,' Auron answered, 'but from what I've heard, a war between the Meriduns and the merpeople would be mutually assured destruction.'

'And after that,' Silva added, 'even a handful of ships will be enough to shift the balance of power.'

So that was the plan. Steal a princess and children to provoke a devastating war so they could take power in the void that was left. Even the idea disgusted him. All that destruction and terror. All the lives that would be lost.

'Then we take the slaves.' He was resolute as he looked at the dazed looking children being put to work. 'Without them, they can't build their fleet.'

His companions looked at him wide eyed.

'What?' he asked.

'Well, it's just a daring plan...' Shift looked at him awkwardly and their sentence trailed off.

'For me?' he finished with a raised eyebrow.

'Well, yeah.' Auron shrugged. 'Although it's not a *plan* yet exactly, just an idea. A daring idea, to be sure.'

Nicolas looked back at the scene beneath them. 'Something about seeing those kids put to work makes me pretty daring. I will not abandon them again. This time, they all come with us,' he declared resolutely. 'Plus, I really want to stick it to that faun.' The mind behind all of this. That creature was going to pay.

Auron nodded at him with a proud half smile, which made him feel quite good, despite being sat on a ledge in a pirate's lair. 'So what's the actual plan then?' the spirit asked.

In coming up with his idea, the hope had been that someone else would come up with a way to enact it. But he wasn't about to shy away from his responsibility now. Briefly he assessed what they were up against, and what they had to work with. 'Okay,' he began after a moment. 'Shift and I will wait here while Silva and Garaz go back to the ship and tell Ramirez what we're doing. Also, some food would be nice, please. Then we wait until nightfall, sneak down, liberate the slaves, and escape in some of those row boats by the dock.'

The others mulled this over for a minute.

'One slight change,' Shift said. 'I'd take the slaves just before sunrise instead of nightfall. I've had some experience with pirates, and they aren't the early-night type of folk. By sunup, we can guarantee that those who aren't already asleep will have passed out drunk.'

Part of him wanted to ask about their history with pirates, but a larger part of him didn't want the answer. 'Fair enough.'

'Another addition,' Silva added. 'I will stay here with you.'

Nicolas looked at the warrior, hoping for an explanation. There was none, just her fixed expression that brooked no argument, and this was neither the time nor the place for one.

'Fine.' He was reluctant to let Silva stay because she'd been so unpredictable of late, but he couldn't force her to go.

'So me and Garaz to the boat then.' Shift smiled, before patting Nicolas sympathetically on the shoulder. 'Sorry, Nick, looks like you don't get me to yourself.'

'What? I...no...I mean....' He looked at his companion's self satisfied grin and stopped talking.

'Whatever you were planning with Shift, you know I'd still be here, right?' Auron asked, before seeming to realise something. 'Oh, I see, kid. The others go then you send the spirit off to scout so you can get some quality time with Shift.'

He didn't reply, instead giving the chuckling spirit an unimpressed look.

'Must you always play some kind of lewd angle?' Garaz smirked.

Oh please, everyone continue to make fun of me. We're only inside a volcano surrounded by pirates. What better time?

'Before you adjust your *plan* because I am staying instead of Shift, realise that I am too much for you,' Silva added, in a shocking moment of contribution to the banter. 'I would break you.'

He believed it too. 'You guys are all jackasses.'

CHAPTER 16

Even though he continually reminded himself there was no way the pirates below could see him, the openness of the ledge made him uneasy. Or maybe it was the mission to come? There was so much at stake now. Kidnapped children, slaves, a princess to rescue and a war to avert. It all seemed just too...big. It threatened to overwhelm him, but he refused to let it. The need to make all this right burned fiercely, enough to consume the doubts as they manifested. In his craziest moments, he was even half tempted to storm down there right now, fight his way through who knew how many pirates and rescue everyone. But intense though Silva's training was, he was nowhere near ready for that.

One day though.

Tentatively, he peeked over the edge again. The *Death* was still there, the work on her and the other ships continuing earnestly – along with plenty of carousing, judging by the sounds coming from the town. There was no sign of the ship he'd first met the faun on, and the question of whether the creature was here or not tantalised him.

It's all just a waiting game now.

He kept telling himself this, but the waiting was interminable.

Maybe a conversation would take his mind away from how slow time seemed to be crawling? 'I wonder where they'll find the crew for all these ships?'

'They must have an idea of some kind,' Auron replied. 'You don't just build a fleet of ships with no one to crew them.'

'Maybe they'll use the children for that too?' he suggested absentmind-edly.

'I'm sure that'll work well, kid.' The spirit laughed. 'I doubt most of them could reach the wheel, never mind trying to hoist those heavy sails, or fighting.'

Auron might've been underestimating them in a fight. Just thinking about those feral childlike faces made his stomach knot. It was somehow worse than the childlike vampire he'd faced once. Evil was part of that thing's nature; these innocent children had been forced to it against their will, corrupted.

Deities, the faun will pay. Now, or later.

'War attracts bad people and profiteers. Those who believe they can make a fortune in the chaos,' Silva stated bluntly. 'What better type of crew for your pirate fleet?'

Nicolas had no experience of war, and no wish to have any—or know about Silva's—but it did make some sense. It was also the first time she'd spoken in an hour, and even now she didn't look at them, instead keeping watch on the pirates as diligently as he would've expected from the warrior. He needed to try talk to her again, to discern what was really wrong with her, but doubted that would be possible with Auron around.

'Auron.' He really hoped he sounded casual. 'Perhaps while we wait, you should go and look around? Find out where the slave pens are and maybe where the princess is so we're ready when the time comes?'

The spirit narrowed his eyes at him. 'I suppose I could do that,' he said suspiciously.

'It'd save us having to run around searching for them.' He made several head gestures that he hoped indicated he should go so Nicolas could talk to Silva.

'Okay then.' Auron had a lewd smile on his face. 'I shall go and...*scout.* While you two...*wait.*'

Nicolas mouthed the word *jackass* to Auron, shaking his head as the spirit made his way down the side of the cavern to the pirate's den. It was strange how casually he walked down the steep slope. If you could call what he did walking.

If only I could move down the rock face so gracefully.

Now they were alone, he looked at Silva.

'Did I not warn you what would happen if you tried anything?' The warrior didn't even look at him. How did everyone know he was about to speak without looking? Did he give off some signal?

'No, it's not that.' He flushed slightly at the suggestion. 'I just wanted to talk to you and didn't think you would with others around.' That statement seemed to pique the warrior's interest, and she turned to him. 'Are you okay?'

The warrior looked confused by the question. 'I am well,' she answered hesitantly.

'Yes,' he pressed. 'But are you okay?'

Silva huffed. 'I do not understand what you mean? Speak plain.'

'Something's off with you.' He was on treacherous ground, but at least Silva was less likely to shout at him with a horde of pirates in potential earshot. 'Beyond the Ramirez thing. You seem...tweaky, lately.'

'Tweaky?' The warrior scrunched her face up in distaste, as if Nicolas had called her smelly.

'Yeah.' This was hard work. 'Tweaky. Off. Not yourself.'

'I can assure you I am not *tweaky*,' Silva said flatly.

'Yes, but—' His words were cut off by a wide-eyed expression from the warrior, a warning not to continue. She couldn't shout at him, but that was worse.

'Okay then,' he muttered as Silva returned to her watch.

That had not gone the way he'd intended, even slightly, and he'd prepared himself for it to go pretty badly. Something was clearly wrong, and he wished she'd open up to him. If not for her sake, then for his, to dispel the worry that she might be reverting back to her old self, the amoral mercenary who would do anything for gold. Silva had technically died—for a while, anyway—which had affected her mind. Maybe that damage was healing, and the old Silva was returning? Despite not really believing it, he backed away slightly.

'I am not going back to my old ways.'

He looked up in surprise.

How did she know what I was thinking? Had he spoken it aloud and not known?

'I—' he began.

'Your concern for my wellbeing is appreciated.' Silva obviously found the words difficult. 'But I will never be that person again. I would throw myself off this ledge before I allowed that to happen. I am doing better, and that is thanks to you. I apologise for being sharp with you.'

'You realise it's endangering us, well me, right?' he said. 'You hesitated to save me from the ship, then you try and yank me off the ledge. Have I done something to upset you, or...' He didn't have another option to give.

Silva's eyes softened a little. 'I am sorry. It's just...travelling with all of you and getting used to the way you are with each other, and to looking out for others, and trying to be a better person isn't easy for me. It's a difficult road, especially with the constant guilt of being around Auron. I find myself confused, torn, making the wrong choices. But I need you to believe that I am fighting to do better. I will do better.'

'What about Ramirez?'

'Another reminder of how difficult my journey is. I have feelings for him, but he is a happiness that I don't deserve. Maybe I will one day, but that day is far away. There is a lot of work to do between now and then and it...weighs heavily on me. But I will not be deterred in my goal.'

The obvious tension in the warrior's body told him how difficult it was for her to tell him all of this, but that wasn't all of it. There was something else. But she had already opened up more than he thought she was able, and he got the impression that digging further right now would be fruitless. All he could do was take her at her word that she'd do better.

****

An hour later, Auron returned.

'You guys still have your clothes on then?' he asked with a big grin.

Even Nicolas quailed under the glare Silva gave Auron.

'What's up with her?' Auron whispered to Nicolas, leaning in close.

'I asked her if she was okay.' Nicolas shrugged in reply.

'You monster,' Auron said with a raised eyebrow.

'What did you find?' He really wanted to get away from this topic of conversation.

Auron gave a knowing smile, suggesting he'd achieved a lot on his little stroll around the lair. As much as he was getting used to the spirit's theatrics, sometimes he wished he would just get on with it.

'Luckily,' Auron began, 'the slave pen is right by the docks. Obviously, they don't want their workers to have a long commute. So breaking them out and getting them to the boats should be easy, provided you can get them to follow you. They all seemed pretty out of it. Whatever magic the faun uses, it's a powerful trance.'

'Unluckily?' He sensed there was bad news as well.

'Janessa will be harder to get to,' the spirit replied sombrely. 'She's in a cage in the captain's lodge. She's unguarded, but the building is at the highest peak of the town, so we'll have to go right through it to get to her, and to get her out.'

'Great.' Of course it wouldn't be as easy as he'd thought. 'What was it like seeing her again?' Nicolas winced at how ham-fisted he'd just been. All this time he hadn't really asked Auron how he felt about Janessa, someone he'd been intimate with, had been taken. And now here he was just wading into it. Getting Silva to open up a little had made him cocky.

'Strange.' Auron's smile was thin, and he seemed to be struggling through some tough emotions, until he shook himself and returned to form. 'I mean, she had clothes on. That was strange.'

Fantastic. I'm stuck on a ledge in a pirate's lair with one person who refuses to talk unless it's dragged out of her, and another who turns everything into a joke.

Not long after Auron's return, Shift and Garaz also returned, with much-welcomed provisions. Keeping watch was hungry work, and he enjoyed every morsel of food they'd brought back. The only thing they seemed to have missed was blankets. They'd be camping here for a while, and the rock ledge wasn't at all comfortable. He cursed himself for not thinking of it before and asking them to bring back something to lie on. But if he *had* asked, there may have been some judgment. Maybe Auron would think him a less macho adventurer? Still better than sleeping on bare rock.

'So we briefed Ramirez,' Shift explained, not eating. Probably had their fill on the way back. 'He seems to think the pirates are unlikely to venture out now, so he's going to bring the ship closer to the opening. Once we've freed the children and loaded them onto boats, we send the signal and he'll meet us halfway. We should be away before the pirates wake.'

'Signal?' Nicolas asked.

'I am going to throw a fireball into the sky,' Garaz answered. 'Simple but effective.'

Simple. Right. Granted, his experience of adventuring was limited, but in that experience, nothing ever turned out simple. He had a bad feeling about it. Unfortunately, he had bad feelings about everything, and no way to discern between general anxiety and actual premonitions for the most part.

'Ramirez isn't going to come charging in with his crew for his vengeance then?' Nicolas asked as a sidenote.

'He thinks it's best to get the hostages away first and come back later to finish things.' Garaz's answer didn't surprise Nicolas. Ramirez's reluctance to actually face his nemesis was becoming pretty standard by this point. Briefly his mind wandered back to the jar in Killgore's cabin, but he didn't know why.

Either way, they had more pressing concerns right now. Nicolas looked back over the edge at the activity below, checking the distance between the dock and where Auron had said the princess was held. 'I think it's best if Silva and Garaz go and free the children and secure the dock, which will be guarded. And that way when Shift, Auron and I rescue the princess, we'll have somewhere strong to fall back to. Just in case something goes awry.'

As so often happens.

Feeling a set of eyes burning into him, Nicolas turned to see Auron looking at him with an unimpressed expression. 'I mean...' he stammered, 'if you think that's a sound plan?'

The spirit said nothing, just continued to stare.

Suddenly, he needed to fill the silence. 'I thought that you, Shift, and I would be good for sneaking around,' he said awkwardly. 'Obviously, Garaz isn't a natural for sneaking into rooms, and Silva will need to take out the guards that are bound to be on the docks.'

'So I can neither fight nor sneak then?' Garaz asked with a raised eyebrow. 'Why do you not believe me a natural sneaker, young Nicolas?'

Oh, troll crap. 'Well...I...just...your size, you know?'

'And what of my size?' The orc's face was fixed in a neutral expression.

'You're...big.' Every word he said seemed to dig him deeper into the hole.

'I see,' Garaz said simply.

'I mean...not *big*, big...just, large...not fat...just tall...'

'And once again I am body shamed by my companions.' Garaz seemed to mull this over for a moment. 'Interesting.'

'Look,' Shift interrupted. 'I'm all for making Nick squirm, but an important factor in deciding who's on the stealth team is that you, Nick, are a dropper.'

'I'm a what?'

'On the pirate ship, you dropped something and gave us away.' They shrugged. 'Therefore, you are a dropper.'

'That's unfair,' he protested. 'I didn't do it on purpose.'

'Yet it happened,' Auron said with an unsympathetic shrug.

'And it won't again. I won't touch anything. Okay?'

'Well, you can be on my team.' Shift was obviously loving the moment. 'But you're demoted to look out. Think you can handle that?'

'Yes,' he muttered.

'And I shall go and free the children,' Garaz declared. 'Unless young Nicolas has concerns about me falling through the dock because I am too...big.'

'Sorry.'

The orc seemed unconvinced whether to accept the apology or not but said no more about it. Suddenly, their rocky outcrop felt much smaller than it had a few minutes ago.

****

Having a hand clamped over your mouth wasn't the most pleasant wake-up call. The surprise of it made him start, preparing himself to struggle free from some attacker. Instead, he sighed with relief when he realised it was Silva sitting over him, finger on her lips for a moment before she took the hand away. Would his pounding heart ever recover from the shock? It was also quite a shock that he'd managed to sleep at all, between lying on a rock and being in the middle of a pirate lair. Another sign he was getting used to this adventuring malarky.

'It's time,' the warrior said softly before moving away from him.

Funny, Silva waking him was something he'd had nightmares about. How times had changed. Being the last to be woken, he stretched and made his way over to the others.

'We ready?' Peeking over the ledge, the shanty town below was quiet with no visible lights save the odd weak lantern along the walkways.

'I have heard nothing for over an hour,' Silva reported. 'Judging by the merriment I heard below I wasn't sure they'd ever go to sleep. These pirates certainly make the most of their evenings.'

Good. That meant they would be passed out drunk, which would make it easier to slip amongst them and complete their mission.

'Let's go then.' He blinked as his heart pounded in excitement in time with his exclamation.

One by one, the group descended from the ledge. Though the gradient wasn't too steep, the rock wall was wet and therefore treacherous if not approached with the proper respect. As Nicolas moved carefully down, a couple of guards walked the dock far below them. Fortunately their attention was focused solely on the mouth of the cavern and dock itself, or their plan may have come to an abrupt end.

After some careful manoeuvring and one near slip, he made it to the walkway at the topmost tier of the shanty town, alongside Shift and Auron.

'Good luck,' he whispered to Silva and Garaz, as the pair slid past them to the base of the cavern and the captive children.

Shift and Nicolas followed Auron through the maze of walkways towards the captain's lodge. All around them was quiet, which was worrying, because each step he took on the old wooden walkway caused a creak that sounded as loud as a battle horn. There was also the question of the construction, which looked very suspect. Each tier of the shanty town was held up by a scaffolding of thick logs that didn't seem secured to anything.

What if the whole place collapses?

No. This must have been here for many years. It was unlikely to collapse just because he'd set foot on it.

Unlikely, not impossible.

Auron was pretty lucky not having to worry about making a sound when he walked, or about the walkway collapsing beneath his feet.

Am I envying a spirit?

The poor man was dead.

I'm an ass.

After a few tense minutes, they reached what was obviously Killgore's lodge. It was easy to tell simply because it was way grander than any of the other crappy huts dotted around. Plus, his fetish for trophies extended to his home. The walls outside were adorned with various swords and skulls, all of which he assumed had been taken from defeated enemies, as well as some more exotic trophies, giving the lodge a terrible patchwork quality. It also made the place look seriously foreboding. This wasn't the home of someone you called upon for tea, cake, and a nice chat.

'Could you check the room?' he asked Auron.

For a moment, the spirit looked disgruntled, but he nodded and disappeared through the door. Seemed strange he bothered to use the door when he could've gone through any part of the wall, but maybe that was just a reflex?

'You're on lookout,' Shift reminded him as they waited. 'That means you are looking, and out. If someone comes along, get our attention in a discreet way. No shouting or trying to do bird calls or any nonsense. Got it?'

'I know what a lookout does,' he whispered back testily.

Where's the trust?

Auron appeared again. 'Everyone's asleep.' The spirit didn't bother whispering.

'Everyone?' Nicolas asked.

'Well, Janessa's in her cage and Killgore is asleep with several...wenches, I suppose is the best word.' The spirit shrugged.

Several? He was suddenly quite happy he wasn't going in there. Bloody horny pirates.

After fiddling in their hair, Shift produced a small hair clip. Kneeling carefully, they inserted it into the lock and wiggled it carefully.

'Why don't you just use the magic key T'goth gave you?' he whispered.

'Because I don't want to lose the skill,' Shift whispered back. 'Now shut up, I'm concentrating.'

Brilliant.

Of all the times to train in picking locks. If they were that passionate about it, the *Amora* had plenty of locks. On a mission in the middle of the pirate lair wasn't the time. Also not the time for arguing, so he put up with it.

After a few seconds, there was a soft click, followed by a very pleased grin from Shift. Carefully, they turned the handle, opening the door just enough to slip into the room. Disappearing into the dark beyond, Auron followed his companion, leaving Nicolas to keep watch.

It was one of those moments he hated, where seconds seemed to stretch to hours. Waiting always seemed worse when there was danger of discovery. Pressing himself into the shadows cast by the overhanging porch of the lodge, he carefully dodged the hanging blades, watching and waiting. This time, he wouldn't mess up.

As it turned out, he was right.

'*What goes on here?*' a voice roared from inside the lodge. He winced and let out a big sigh, disbelieving that they'd been caught out again, but strangely pleased it hadn't been because of him.

Seconds later, Shift burst through the door, pulling with her a woman whose skin almost seemed to shimmer, even in the dark. Behind them, Auron emerged, shaking his head. Dumbfounded, he watched the trio run away from the lodge at speed.

Shouldn't I be following them?

The heavy footsteps behind him made him turn slowly. The open doorway of the lodge was filled by the large form of Captain Killgore, who looked very bright for someone who'd just been asleep. No, bright wasn't the word. Furious. That was it. In his hand, the captain held a thick club. At first, the captain's eyes followed his retreating companions then they settled on him.

'What 'ave we here?' Killgore's voice was a threatening purr.

Not entirely sure what he thought he was doing, Nicolas drew the *Dawn Blade* and held it defiantly before him. Okay, Killgore was bigger and much angrier, but he also only had one hand and a club. And he was barely dressed. Even with the size difference, Nicolas fancied his chances against a half-naked disabled man when he was better armed. At the very least, he could hold him off and give his companions a good head start.

'If you don't step back, you'll lose the one hand you have left.' He couldn't allow himself a moment to be impressed with his own tough talk, there was a dangerous pirate right in front of him.

Killgore looked at the sword held toward him and snorted derisively. How did the captain seem so confident against a better-armed opponent? Killgore dropped his club and slowly raised the stump of his missing hand, presenting the metal plate that had been fastened around it. With the unpleasant smile of someone who knew something you didn't, Killgore whispered to the plate. The runes surrounding it glowed green.

Oh no.

Smoke emerged from the plate, rising and taking shape until it solidified into the biggest sword he'd ever seen. Which explained the captain's apparent overconfidence. Killgore gave him a gap-toothed sneer.

'Shit.'

Looking at the massive magical blade, he wanted none of it. But at the same time, he didn't really want to turn his back on his opponent and just run. Killgore looked slow, but then a few seconds ago, he'd looked disabled, and Nicolas wasn't about to take the chance that the captain was a poor runner when his life depended on the gamble. Coming up with a third option, Nicolas grabbed a spiked helm hanging from one of the many trophy hooks on the wall of the lodge.

Using all his might, he threw the helm right at the pirate captain's leg. The helm was heavy and hard to aim properly, but Killgore was a big target and it struck the pirate captain on the shin, hobbling him instantly. As Killgore roared in pain, rubbing his injured leg, Nicolas turned and ran for his life.

'*Intruders! Thieves! Sound the alarm!*' Killgore's voice boomed in his wake.

As he passed one of the houses at speed, the door ahead of him opened. Lazily, a pirate poked his half-asleep head out to see what the commotion was. Without breaking stride, Nicolas punched the pirate across the jaw, sending him spinning back into his dwelling.

Stealth out the window, again. He charged down the maze of timber walkways, each thudding footstep announcing his presence to the world. Around him there were sleepy and confused exclamations, as well as shouts for him to '*keep the damn noise down.*' The pirates were taking their time waking or shaking off their drunkenness. That was good. Every second counted. As long as nothing brought them around faster they'd be alright.

The alarm bell rang.

'Shit.'

On some watchtower at the peak of the town, the ringing bell echoed throughout the cavern. Confused exclamations became the angry shouts of people preparing for a fight. Deities, he hoped he could avoid giving it to them.

By the time Nicolas reached the docks themselves, there was the sound of organised pursuit behind them. Angry, organised pursuit. That was not a shock. What was a shock was that the children weren't in the boats and ready to go.

'Why are they still in the cages?' he cried to Garaz and Silva.

'They won't come,' Silva replied, obviously frustrated.

'What do you mean *they won't come*?'

'The children will not move.' Garaz gestured for him to try himself if he liked.

He did like. Sheathing his sword, he stepped into the cage. 'Come on, kids. Let's go,' Nicolas demanded, clapping his hands.

The mass of children stared blankly into some middle distance.

'Now. Come on,' he pressed.

Nothing.

When he looked back at Garaz, the orc shrugged as if to say '*see?*'

Bootsteps were getting closer, so he grabbed one of the children and tried to lift him. The boy was a dead weight, even when he put his back into it. How was that even possible? Determined not to leave these kids again, he tried once more, and the boy began to lazily push him away.

'They're coming,' Silva called from behind him.

They certainly were. When he peered out of the cage, a mass of half-dressed, but well-armed, pirates were running at them.

Levelling his staff towards the docks, Garaz muttered something, and a fireball shot from the staff. The fireball looked more impressive than the ones he'd thrown from his hands before. Obviously, T'goth's gift was doing a good job of enhancing Garaz's natural abilities. The flaming sphere struck the docks ahead of the oncoming pirates, creating a wall of fire between the pirates and Nicolas and his companions. Unsurprisingly, the pirates came to a sudden stop, and several were knocked into the water as their fellows behind bumped into them.

'That will not hold them for long,' Garaz cautioned.

The orc was right. They needed to go, fast, but he wasn't about to just leave the children. He refused. Looking around for inspiration, he saw one of the unconscious guards by the cage door. Or was he dead? Silva wasn't known for her light touch. Either way, he had an idea. He wasn't proud of it, but it may be their only option.

Even so, his hand hesitated before picking up the guard's whip.

It's just a prop, that's all. A necessity. I'm not whipping anyone. I'm not a monster.

Looping the thong of the whip in his hand, so no accidents could happen, he coughed to ready himself for the performance to come.

'Get on them boats, ye no good little maggots,' he shouted in his best approximation of a pirate voice, waving the looped whip overhead. Hay Sharkbait sounded more manly.

Though he felt an idiot doing it, strangely, the children complied, believing the commands were coming from one of their captors. Slowly, they filed from the cage and made their way to the boats, where Shift and Auron were waiting with the princess. Garaz and Silva looked at him in surprise. He shrugged at them before running for one of the boats himself.

With the mass of children, they filled three row boats. In his, Nicolas was happy to let Silva row since they wanted to get out of this cave today. As she powered the oars and the boat made its way from the cavern, he looked back. Pirates were attempting to board the other rowboats around the dock, only to discover that Silva and Garaz had scuppered them. The small vessels began to sink instantly when weight was placed on them, and confused pirates howled in fury as their peers fell into the water.

As they left the mouth of the cavern, the sun began to rise, framing the sea ahead of them in a rich tapestry of golden yellows as behind them, the pirates on the dock spat curses in their wake. Several made some unpleasant remarks about Nicolas's parentage. In a rare moment of showmanship, Nicolas stood and gave the pirates an exaggerated bow. Sitting again, he spied the faun, sitting casually on the roof of one of the nearby houses, hooved feet swinging from the edge. So, he was here, after all. That was a missed opportunity.

Catching his eye, the faun gave him a wave, jiggling his fingers. Judging by the faun's smug expression, this wasn't over by any means. He really hated that guy.

CHAPTER 17

'Well done, my friends. Well done.' Ramirez beamed, grabbing Nicolas by the shoulders and shaking him heartily as he climbed back aboard the *Irresistible Amora*.

He didn't need shaking; he was already shaken from having to use the rope ladder again. Why couldn't seafarers use good old-fashioned wooden ladders? It seemed to work well enough for everyone on land.

He turned to look back at where he'd come from, at the volcanic island rising high from the sea. He could feel the broad grin lighting up his face. They'd made it. The children and the princess were safe.

Killgore still has his other slaves.

The thought dulled their accomplishment slightly, but they'd be back. Whether it was with Ramirez, the Meridun fleet or just them in a rowboat, he was coming back.

The faun and Killgore still need to be made to account for their actions.

Maybe bringing a fleet would be wise, considering the fearsome captain and his magic sword arm.

Either way, this *was* a victory. Now all they had to do was get away from the island. In that, Silva and Garaz had ensured them a good head start, disabling the wheel of the *Death* when they scuppered the rowboats. But it wouldn't be long before it was repaired and Killgore was on their heels.

Getting the children to board the ship had cost them some of that time. But his performance with the whip had worked just as well the second time, and now Hay Sharkbait was herding them into the hold of the ship. The poor kids all looked emaciated, their hands worn and blistered with hard labour. How long had that filthy faun worked them to the bone? At least now they had some distance from the island, whatever spell was affecting them was wearing off. Dazed faces were becoming worried ones as the children woke, but not at home. Shift was with them, doing their best to comfort and reassure them and doing a surprisingly great job of it, considering empathy wasn't something he normally associated with the shapeshifter. Although maybe they understood better than he'd thought. They'd just awoken one day in an unfamiliar place with no memory of home.

Nicolas looked at the whip in his hand; a vile, pain inducing implement. In disgust, he threw it over the side of the ship.

'Shouldn't we be going?' he asked, looking toward the cavern opening, sure the *Death* would emerge from it sooner rather than later.

'You worry too much, my friend,' Ramirez replied confidently. 'The only ship they have fast enough to catch us from here is that little sloop the faun runs around in, and I do not fear that.'

The ship hadn't been at the dock anyway. Yet the faun had been.

Nicolas looked to Auron, hoping for some words of wisdom he could use to urge Ramirez to action. The spirit scoffed at his look. 'You asked him, not me.'

As Ramirez strolled around giving orders to his crew like he had all the time in the world, he wanted to scream at the captain to hurry up. Nicolas and his companions had done the hard work, the actual rescue, all Ramirez needed to do was spirit them away, fast.

It's Ramirez's ship and he knows his business.

That wasn't convincing, but it wasn't Nicolas's ship to command. Maybe to distract himself, he walked over to Princess Janessa, who was wrapped in a blanket talking to Garaz.

The merprincess was beautiful, with human-like features that were slightly off in a way he couldn't pinpoint exactly. The princess's light-green skin shimmered and her hair was long and golden, glistening just as her skin did. Her eyes were of a slightly more oval shape, spaced a little further apart than humans. Maybe her face was longer than it ought to be?

No, her face was probably normal for her people, and it was wrong to judge her by his standards. If Garaz heard him judging others by human standards, he'd be displeased. He was pretty displeased with himself.

Janessa regarded him curiously as he approached.

'Princess.' Knowing he was in the presence of royalty, he gave the best bow he could, but leaned forward a little further than was comfortable. The only royalty he'd been in the company of before had been a chicken.

I hope Silus is okay after his transformation back. We didn't even get a chance to say goodbye.

'Another of my saviours,' Janessa replied with a polite nod, the strain of her captivity evident in her eyes. 'You have the thanks of me and my people.'

'You're too kind.' He smiled, hoping he was hiding his beaming pride. His modesty prevented him from making a list of his accomplishments since he'd begun adventuring. But if he did, *rescuing a princess* would definitely be on it.

The floor lurched underfoot. Happily, they were finally underway.

'The princess here was just telling me some troubling news.' Whatever it was, Garaz seemed pretty damn troubled about it.

Nicolas looked to the princess for clarification.

'When you passed the dock, did you see a multi-lensed device being mounted onto the *Black Death*?' she asked.

He nodded.

'It's a weapon,' Janessa continued sombrely. 'I don't know the specifics, but I know they intend to use it to start a war between our peoples.'

'They're doing enough of that without some special weapon,' he remarked, thinking of her kidnapping and the poor stolen children.

Curse that faun.

'All they've done so far is pull back the bow and nock the arrow.' It seemed the idea of war weighed as heavily on Janessa as the rest of them. 'They've stirred up much enmity between our peoples. There will be a standoff between our forces, but in the end, cooler heads will prevail, as they always have. We understand as much as you the mutual devastation of a war. I believe this weapon will be the final nudge to release the arrow from the bow, and after that...'

'How do you know all of this?' Garaz asked.

'The faun.' Janessa's beautiful features contorted with distaste. 'He enjoyed coming around every so often to tell me things. I believe he enjoyed hearing the sound of his own voice as much as he did watching my despair at his tidings.'

'Is that why he kept you alive?' Nicolas asked.

Janessa's face hardened. 'Partially. He said he wanted to see the look on my face when he showed me my burnt kingdom. He said it'd be *'hilarious'*.'

Nicolas could see the princess fighting back the tears.

'We have you now.' Nicolas smiled. 'When we return you to your people and you tell your story, this war will be averted, weapon or no weapon.' And then the faun would pay.

Janessa didn't seem to share his confidence. 'Provided we get to my people.'

'We will get you to safety,' he countered. 'Captain Ramirez won't steer us wrong.'

The princess appeared less than enthused at the captain's name. 'Yes, I have heard of his...reputation.'

He had no idea what to say to that.

'All will be well,' Garaz interjected, thankfully.

If Janessa disagreed or had doubts, she didn't voice them, and Garaz left to check on the wellbeing of the children. Nicolas was about to follow him—having a large orc suddenly appear might unnerve the children more than they already were—when a soft hand grabbed his.

'You know Auron.' It wasn't a question. 'Your orc companion told me he travels with you. His...spirit, anyhow.' Janessa's eyes searched his, the sadness in her voice catching him off-guard. She played with a piece of black ribbon on the arm of her dress.

'That he does,' he replied, looking across the deck at the spirit, who seemed intent on keeping as far from Janessa as possible. Though he looked like he wanted to be exactly where Nicolas was right now. The pair had just had a fling, right? When he looked back, Janessa was smiling dreamily. Her face flushed when she focused on him again.

Was it more than I thought it was?

'We were lovers once,' she spoke coyly, as if not wanting to admit the truth aloud. 'More than that, in truth, though we could never admit it to each other. As princess of the Tidal Kingdom, I could not legitimately consort with human...vagabonds.' She laughed slightly, as if remembering some private joke. 'I would've been outcast and he put to death. Being the only heir to my line gives me more responsibilities than I care for. And in the end, he died anyway. I wish...' After a moment, Janessa stood up straighter and seemed to shake herself. 'I'm sorry. I don't know why I told you that.'

He was shocked by the admission himself. Auron bragged so much about his conquests in the bedroom that he'd assumed this was just another of those. To think the pair had feelings for each other, feelings they could never act on...did he know Auron as well as he'd thought? It'd certainly explain why he'd been acting so off lately, disappearing by himself and generally being sour.

'Don't be.' Saying it couldn't have been easy. He couldn't imagine trying to repress your feelings for someone because of protocol. 'I have no idea how difficult any of that is, but I can still listen.'

The princess smiled thankfully.

'I have a bit of an inkling how he feels, though. Or felt, for you,' he added, a memory coming to mind.

'How so?' Janessa's eyes betrayed her hopefulness.

'Auron possessed me once, and I shared his memories. None of that stuff really stuck with me after, except I remembered you, so you must've been important to him.' It hadn't occurred to him until now, but it sounded right.

Janessa turned away, looking out towards the sea for a moment. Nicolas didn't need to be told she was taking a moment to compose herself. He'd done it himself on occasion. 'Thank you,' she said as she turned back, voice filled with emotion.

Suddenly, something occurred to him, and his mouth worked before his brain could stop it. 'Your legs?'

'What of them?' Janessa asked quizzically.

'You have them,' he remarked. 'I thought merpeople had fish tails?'

'My people can switch between the two to allow us to move on land or through water. It's a trait we evolved.'

'But in Auron's memories of you, you always had the fish tail.'

Janessa looked awkward for a moment, her mouth working as her skin became a darker shade of green. Finally, she found the words. 'He preferred it that way.'

And that right there was much more than he'd ever wanted to know. Quickly, he excused himself and went to check on...anything else.

The thing he ended up checking on was Auron.

He approached the spirit sheepishly. 'I owe you an apology.'

The spirit's brow furrowed in confusion.

'I didn't realise the connection between you and Janessa,' he elaborated. He didn't know why it was important that Auron knew this, but Nicolas had misjudged him and wanted to make it right. 'I thought it was just a physical thing. If I'd known it was deeper than that, I would've...talked to you about it.'

The spirit looked slightly bemused at his fumbled words. 'Is that what she said?' Auron asked casually.

'Yes.'

'She wishes,' was all he said before walking away.

Nicolas stood there for a moment, unsure where to go next. That hadn't worked out at all like he'd expected, though it was more in line with his view of the deceased hero. The fact that she'd been a conquest to him when he'd been blatantly more to her heavily dented his respect for Auron, which the spirit was good at doing from time to time.

****

An hour later, Nicolas stood with his companions, having been summoned by Ramirez, who was looking out to sea, viewing glass to his eye. 'We have company,' the captain remarked quietly.

Nicolas didn't need a glass to make out the ominous speck on the horizon.

'It's the faun's sloop,' Ramirez informed them.

All Nicolas could see was the speck. Thank the Deities it wasn't the *Death.*

That was odd. That ship hadn't been in the cavern, he was certain of it. How had it caught up to them so quickly if it hadn't even been on the island...in the island...whatever? As a matter of fact, the faun had been on the island without his ship. That didn't really make sense to him, but he couldn't put his finger on why.

'They are certainly on our tail quickly,' Garaz remarked.

'It wasn't exactly a clean getaway, was it?' Auron pointedly looked at Shift.

'Okay, so I sneezed,' Shift cried defensively. 'That place was filthy and covered in dust. Would it kill them to get some of their slave kids to dust between the ship building?'

'You've got to stop making jokes about the slave kids,' Nicolas said.

'You need to stop being so sensitive about it.' Shift smiled annoyingly. 'Besides, who said I was joking?'

They were always one sentence ahead of him. It was frustrating trying to keep up. At least they could no longer ride him about getting them discovered. They were on an even field in that respect now.

Shift's head shook a little, then they dropped their voice low. 'We have seen some horrible things, and taking children as slaves is very near the top of that list. I make bad and inappropriate jokes so I don't focus on how terrible it all is. It just, helps. Okay?'

Nicolas didn't know why he was suddenly blinking so much. Maybe the honesty had physically stunned him? 'Um, yeah,' he replied finally.

'We will take them.' Ramirez declared, returning his spyglass to his belt, his face stern but tinged with anticipation.

'We will what?' Nicolas asked, sure he'd misheard.

'Bring us about!' Ramirez animatedly yelled to the helmsman, who began spinning the wheel rapidly, the ship lolling to the side as it turned to face their pursuer. 'We can take that ship,' the captain continued. 'We outweigh her, and based on her size, she won't have a large crew. We can take them.'

Something about this concerned Nicolas. 'Surely if they're chasing us then they're under the impression they can take *us*?' It didn't make sense to chase down a ship you knew you couldn't overcome. Mind you, Ramirez's behaviour didn't make sense either. All these times the captain probably should've fought, and he waited until they were supposed to be fleeing for safety to pick a fight?

Why did the glass cylinder in Killgore's cabinet keep popping into his mind?

'No, my friend.' Ramirez stared at the oncoming ship with absolute confidence in his eyes, as well as a little bloodlust. 'We have the advantage here, and I mean to use it. We may get valuable intelligence from the crew. We might even catch the faun. Either way, it's a victory. I...we, need a victory.'

We have one. We are literally sailing away from a victory. Is he mad?

'Nicolas saw the faun in the cavern,' Garaz interjected, seemingly equally concerned. 'And his ship was not there, so it is unlikely we will find him aboard.'

'Still,' Ramirez continued, not taking his eyes from the sloop, 'it is an easy victory. We can take them.' There was something in his tone that made Nicolas think he was trying to convince himself as much as anyone else. Beneath the bravado, there was a hint of uncertainty. Maybe fear. Yet he seemed committed to this, and again, it was his ship. They were passengers at best, cargo at worst.

Slowly, the ship came about until it was facing the oncoming sloop. Ramirez gave commands about sails and other things to make the ship go faster, most of which Nicolas didn't catch and wouldn't have understood if he had. Sails bulged as the wind filled them, and they sped toward the enemy. Nicolas took a deep breath. It was only a small sloop. How much trouble could it be?

As the two ships converged on each other, time became a measure of seconds until battle. On the side of the *Amora*'s deck that would end up parallel with the sloop, a boarding party was prepared—armed men waiting with grappling hooks to throw out when the ships crossed to ensure the enemy vessel couldn't escape while she was boarded and taken. Nicolas looked at the preparing men, with Hay Sharkbait at their fore, then at the steps leading from the bridge to the main deck.

Should I join them? I'm as much a part of this as the crew. But I'm not exactly experienced in naval warfare.

'Leave them to it, kid,' was Auron's sage advice when Nicolas asked him what he should do. 'They know their stuff about warfare at sea, and I don't fancy trying to fish you out of the water if you get involved.' The spirit's faith in him was less than impressive. Though he was slightly relieved not to have to fight this time.

Beside him, Silva still stood armed and ready. He was quite surprised she wasn't down on the deck already, waiting to be the first one aboard. But then, she'd doubtless find her way to the thick of it when the fighting started. Nicolas watched in fascination as the ships came ever closer, until something in his peripheral vision distracted him.

Beside him, Garaz was rubbing his temple tenderly.

'You okay?'

'I think so,' Garaz replied. 'I have this buzzing in my head, as if strong magic were nearby. I cannot tell where it is coming from, though.'

Though Nicolas knew little about magic, something in Garaz's words gave him a moment of clarity. How did the sloop and the *Death* keep switching places? The sloop was at the island they were stranded upon, but the pursuit had led them to the *Death*. The *Death* was at the island base, yet it was the sloop that chased them. The sloop. That small ship made a very tempting target to a vessel that outclassed it...

'Oh Deities...' he whispered.

'What?' Shift asked, curiosity piqued by his tone.

The two ships began to pass each other.

'It's a—'

Before the word *trap* left Nicolas's lips, the features of the sloop blurred, becoming unfocused as they warped and changed. Beyond the haze, the ship grew in size, considerably. Multiple masts appeared as did gangs of howling pirates where before there'd been but a couple of deckhands. The featureless prow of the ship now bore a familiar skeletal figurehead.

'Trap.' Shift finished his sentence for him.

Ramirez was staring dumbfounded at the oncoming vessel. Beads of sweat covered his forehead, and his jaw was slack in a very unhandsome fashion that matched his rapidly paling skin.

'Captain?' he shouted. 'Ramirez? We need to turn. Ramirez? Turn the ship. *Now*!'

Nothing. Ramirez stood transfixed by the much larger vessel now pulling alongside them as the *Death*'s crew hollered in glee. Under his breath, he was muttering something Nicolas couldn't make out and didn't care to try.

'Turn the ship!' he shouted at the helmsman. 'Turn her now!'

But it was too late. There was no time to manoeuvre or flee; this was happening. A wave of grappling hooks launched from the side of the *Black Death*, soaring through the air to strike the deck, scattering the crew, before pulling back, cutting deep gouges in the wood until they found purchase and held firm. Slowly, the *Amora* was pulled in close to the *Death*.

Again, he looked to Ramirez, but the captain seemed locked in some personal Underworld. Nicolas was starting to have a good idea what was there awaiting him, but this really wasn't the time for it. Considering the number of times he'd frozen, he sympathised with the captain, whilst understanding his companions previous frustrations with him to the fullest.

Either way, now was not the time for sympathy or awkward memories. He had to do something. Drawing his sword, he ran toward the main deck, ready to defend the ship. But when he reached the steps to the deck, he'd forgotten how steep they were. He didn't fancy climbing down them one-handed, nor making the jump, so he sheepishly sheathed the

Dawn Blade and climbed down. Planting his feet on the deck, he redrew the sword and charged into the fray.

Except there was no fray to charge into, just the crew of the *Amora* with their hands raised. Still holding his sword aloft, he slowed, his battle cry petering out into an embarrassed gulp as the crew looked at him in shock. Across from him, on the deck of the *Death*, archers aimed their flame-tipped arrows in his direction and several armed ballistae pointed directly onto the *Amora*'s deck. Coughing awkwardly, he sheathed his sword again and put his hands up. Nicolas glanced behind him in the hope that some of his companions had followed him and he hadn't been singular in his embarrassment. He was.

From the railing of the *Death*, Killgore looked at him with a wide smile as he leant casually on the side of his ship. Beside him stood the faun, amused and smug as ever.

****

Hooves clopped on the deck as the faun walked around his companions and the crew of the *Amora*, all of whom knelt on the hard wood in neat rows. The clopping stopped just in front of Nicolas, just as he'd somehow known it would. The faun crouched to come eye to eye with him as his little toad servant stood by dutifully.

'It was a nice try,' the faun began. 'Truly. Sneaking into a pirate camp, stealing our workers and hostage, and making a run for it. And you were soooo close...' The faun raised his hand and created a small gap between his finger and thumb to emphasise his point. 'And then it all got spoilt because you got cocky,' the faun continued. 'Old Ramirez thought he had us outmatched. The old captain got a bit too *ballsy*, didn't he?'

The assembled pirates from the *Death* chuckled. He got the joke, but he didn't find it funny.

The faun stroked a single finger down Nicolas's cheek, pouting his lip in faux sympathy. 'And now look at you.' He shook off the faun's finger and glared at him defiantly. 'Oh, *look* at you.' The faun got closer, studying his face. 'Getting all angry, are we? What are you going to do?' The faun pinched his cheek, jiggling it several times before releasing his grip and smacking it twice, hard. 'Nothing, that's what,' the faun whispered, before standing.

The urge to act coursed through him, itching in his bloodstream, curling his fists. But his enemy was correct. He was going to do nothing, because there was nothing he could do. It wasn't just his safety. If it were down to that, he would've been happy to take a chance swing at the smug git. But the safety of his companions—along with Ramirez and his crew—also hung in the balance. They were destined for a grim fate, maybe even death. Yet somehow, he still couldn't act, as if his inaction would somehow stave off the inevitable.

'So it seems old Killgore here has a score to settle with you,' the faun declared aloud, gesturing to the seething captain. 'Something about throwing a helmet at his leg? Well, I do have a punishment for all of you, a pretty ironic one for the newcomers, but it wouldn't do not to let the good captain get his licks in first. Plus, who here doesn't like a good show?'

The crew of the *Death* cheered in agreement as Nicolas was roughly grabbed and hauled to his feet. The two pirates holding him dragged him toward the nearest mast. In his peripheral vision, he saw his companions make to rise, only to be held down by the pirates, using the points of their swords to reinforce their message. As they struggled, he caught their eyes and shook his head slightly. He wouldn't have them dying for him. Reluctantly, they knelt back down. Panning around, he caught a glimpse of a robed figure standing by Killgore. He looked younger than his greying hair suggested, and he was glaring flaming daggers at Garaz. The look was returned with interest.

'That was cute, telling your friends to stand down,' the faun remarked in his ear. 'Remember, boy, whatever happens next, Killgore wanted to kill you quick. It took some convincing to get him to spare your life, but I think it'll be worth it.' The faun was about to walk away but stopped suddenly, turning and leaning back in close. 'I hope you appreciate the irony of this punishment. I saw your little theatrics with the whip to get those filthy human spawn to follow you, and it gave me an idea. Let's see how much you like whips after this, shall we.'

Rope burnt his wrists as his hands were bound together in front of him but on the far side of the mast, holding him in place. Two of the pirates tore at his shirt, ripping it open and exposing his bare back. Craning his neck, Nicolas saw Killgore step forward, smiling eagerly. Again, the captain whispered to his metal stump and again, green smoke emerged from it, this time forming a long whip. His stump could make different weapons? Fantastic.

Auron appeared before him, his white eyes full of sadness. 'I'm so sorry for what's about to happen.' He didn't need the expression on the spirit's face to tell him this was going to be bad. 'I'm here. I wish...I wish I could do more, take this for you. But I'm here. This is going to hurt, kid. Try to breathe out when it hits.'

When it hits.

Deities. The realisation finally sank in. He was about to be whipped. Instantly his mind went back to the slave galley of the *Death* and the poor wretches held prisoner within. Their backs had been criss-crossed with fierce looking lash marks.

And now that's going to happen to…me.

He let out a choked cry as his fate became apparent. At least Auron was here with him. Tears welled as he fixed his gaze on his companion. When the pirates stomped their feet on the deck rhythmically in anticipation, the tears escaped his eyes.

Abruptly, the stomping ceased, Nicolas took a deep breath in and waited. Would the anticipation of the strike be worse than the strike itself? His body shook at the sound of the whip being worked behind him, loosening it up for what was to come.

The strike was worse. The lash burned his back, pulling down as it struck, tearing the skin in it's wake. For a moment he was too stunned by the sudden pain to cry, he just opened his mouth, letting out a wordless scream. With each successive lash, the scream became more and more audible, interspersed with sobs and cries. His body shook as pain caused him to lose control of himself, the ropes cutting into his wrists as he convulsed with every strike. He became caught in a terrible rhythm; the whip would crack, he would scream, the pirates would cheer. He was desperate to pass out, but adrenaline from the pain kept him conscious. By the fifth lash, he would've told the faun anything he wanted to know. By the eighth, he prayed for death.

Auron stood before him, trying to hold his gaze with trembling lips. But each time the whip struck, his ethereal form blurred out of focus, until Nicolas's strength failed and his head lolled limply beside his shoulder.

Dizzy, and pained, and sweating profusely, as the tenth lash receded, his legs finally gave out and he slid down the mast. He was vaguely aware of Auron talking to him, but pain dulled his every sense. In a heap on the floor, spent, he sobbed. His back was aflame, his entire body shaking with agony and shock.

Why won't I just die?

'That tough, was it?' the faun asked, smirking as his shadow loomed over Nicolas. With great effort, he looked up at his captor.

'I'll kill you,' Nicolas spat, froth spilling from his mouth. 'I'll kill you.'

'You most certainly will not.' The faun brought his fist down on him, and Nicolas floated into nothingness.

CHAPTER 18

Waking suddenly, he raised his head, gasping in air. As he blew out, sand spat from his lips. Sand again? Why was he facedown in sand? He tried to get to his knees, and the long lash lines down his back snatched his attention away from that question. Following the route of his pain, he could map each one. He prayed he would never see them; the mental images were bad enough. Thinking back to the deck of the *Amora*, which he was clearly no longer on, he remembered Killgore, and the whip, and the pain.

I'm still in danger.

Pushing against the sand, he tried to rise again, the skin of his back pulling taught with the motion and stirring the wounds on his back to produce fresh agony. Gritting his teeth, his arms shook, trying to keep him aloft the inch he'd managed to rise.

Killgore. The faun. My companions. Danger.

He couldn't form a coherent thought. Words and images appeared, only to vanish again instantly as the throbbing of his injuries consumed his mind and banished them. But some subconscious drive knew exactly what he needed to do, and he pushed again. The pain was like a weight, trying to hold him to the floor. Did he have enough will power to fight it off?

Shift. Auron. Garaz. Silva.

With each name he rose a little more, until with a final internal cry that shook his very bones, he forced himself to his knees.

Sweating and panting, he swayed on the spot as he tried to collect himself for the next stage. He looked down at the sandy floor.

Why is there sand?

Confused, he half turned and saw the beach sprawl before him. On the sea, two shadows grew smaller as they became further away.

The Death and the Amora?

Even in his addled mind, the implication was clear. The sound that came from his mouth was half laugh, half cry. 'No,' he said, his voice coming out in a slur. 'No. *No, no, no, no, no.*'

Jumping to his feet, pushing through the pain which threatened to drag him back down to the floor, he shambled towards the water. Voices tried to get his attention, he ignored them. Hands grabbed at him, but he swatted them away. He moved faster, each stumbling step potentially being the last before he fell. Was he trying to catch the ship, or outrun the pain? He knew he was making noises as he moved, but he didn't know what. He was too busy trying to keep the ship in the centre of his vision as it swayed from side to side. Or maybe he was the one swaying?

Seeing a rock on the floor, he didn't break stride as he scooped it up. Suddenly, the shifting sand beneath his feet became the wet sea, his progress impeded as waves crashed against his shins. Yet he waded further, the ship was seemingly no closer than before.

'Come back and fight,' he screamed, launching the rock from his hand. His wounds made him pay for the sudden, sharp motion, and his body spasmed in pain. But his rage wouldn't be denied. 'Come back and fight me!' His projectile fell ridiculously short. 'I'll fight you.' He clenched his fists, raising them in a futile gesture. 'I'll fight you all!'

The focus of his vision changed abruptly. Hands held his head gently but firmly and turned it toward a familiar face. Who was that? He fought a reflex to throw a punch. The figure, whoever they were, was speaking to him. What were they saying? Their green eyes were watery and filled with empathy and sadness. He tried to struggle free of the grip, but the hands wrapped around his neck and pulled him in tight. He felt a head next to his, another heartbeat thumping like a drum. A familiar presence.

'It's okay,' Shift soothed. 'It's okay.'

'They won't fight,' he mumbled.

'It's okay.'

'C...cowards,' he stuttered. He began to sob—harsh, choked sounds that caused the arms to hold him tighter. 'It hurts so bad.'

'I know.' The voice didn't know. *How can they?* 'I'm here. Come back with me.'

His legs failed, and his body slid down to the water, Shift sliding down with him. As the ocean touched his back, it turned to fire, burning his skin in writhing lines of agony. He cried out.

Shift held his head again, pulling his face close, touching his forehead to theirs. There were tears in his companion's eyes. Their thumb stroked his cheek. 'Let's get to shore.'

'It hurts.' He'd said that already, but the pain wasn't going away. Could it not just...*vanish?*

'I know,' Shift whispered, guiding him slowly back toward the sand.

As he reached the shore, other hands took him, large green ones and hard female ones. Half walking, half carried, he was taken to grass and laid carefully on his front. There he lay, panting hard in between choked sobs. He felt a presence above him, hands held slightly away from his skin. He was aware of light and then a warmth covered him, soothing him down into the dark.

****

The next time he came to was much less traumatic. Waking as if from a terrible dream, he blearily opened his eyes. There were quiet voices around him. His back was so sore. Turning his head slightly, he squinted at the familiar glow beside him.

'Are you okay, kid?' Auron looked like a concerned parent as he knelt beside him.

'No, I am not,' he groaned weakly.

The spirit didn't seem to know what to say to this.

'How's my back?' he asked.

Again, the spirit seemed at a loss, opening and closing his mouth a couple of times before finding the words. 'Garaz did good work, kid,' he began. 'But some of those lashes were...deep. And the whip was magic-made. There'll be some scars.'

He'd guessed that for himself. Between those and the puncture wounds from the harpy, he wouldn't be running around shirtless again for a good long while.

'Thank you.' His voice was hoarse, a side effect of all the sobbing. 'You stayed with me when they did it. You...' He didn't know what he wanted to say as a look of frustration creased Auron's features.

'I wish I could've done more, kid.' The spirit's voice broke slightly. 'So much more. My only real use seems to be as a nightlight or for checking rooms. I'm no good for anything else.'

'Is that why you've been so off lately?' he asked weakly.

Auron's face said it all. 'Well, you've got Silva and Ramirez teaching you.' The spirit chuckled dryly. 'You don't need me anymore. No one does. Someone I loved...love is in danger, and all I can do is watch and touch stuff sometimes. And I can't even move on because I don't know what my unfinished business is anymore. I'm stuck in this terrible limbo where I can't help but I can't leave. I've always been the useful one, and now I'm a glorified lantern.'

Nicolas ripped a clump of grass from the floor and threw it at Auron, who blinked in surprise even though it passed through him. 'You utter ass,' he snapped. 'You think you're useless? I'm here because of you.'

Auron looked at his back and winced slightly.

'No,' he continued, 'I don't mean like that. I mean here, helping. The only reason I've been able to do any of this is because of you. I would've run straight home after being knocked off that bridge. But I didn't. Instead, I ended up taking on a necromancer and an army of vampires. And why was that? Because *you* were there. *You* prodded me on. *You* gave me an example to follow. You still do.' He sighed, not believing that they were having this conversation when he was lying on an island recovering from being whipped. 'Not a very good one right now, mind. Wallowing in self-pity after I've been whipped to an inch of my life isn't your best self. But I couldn't have done any of this without your guidance, never mind who's showing me how to throw what punch or parry a sword. You've made me better.'

For a moment, the spirit stared at him, unblinking. 'You mean that?' Auron asked slowly.

'Yes,' he snapped. 'I'm in no fit state to even try lying.'

Auron looked away, clearly trying to hide the beaming smile crossing his cloudy face.

The ego on this guy. He sighed to himself. 'Bloody ghost.'

Auron opened his mouth, but clearly thought better of it and closed it again. Good. He deserved it.

And there's someone else who deserves it too.

With a grunt that was half pain, half determination, Nicolas forced himself from the floor. Fighting against his wounds insistence that he stayed down, he got to his feet, taking a moment to recover from the dizziness that met him when he did.

'You should be resting,' Garaz protested as he approached.

'In a minute.' He waved the orc off. 'I have to put someone else in their place.'

'Why exactly did I bother becoming a healer? None of my patients ever listen to me,' Garaz grumbled in his wake.

Scanning the beach and the figures milling aimlessly around it, Nicolas soon found who he had an issue with, pointing an accusing finger directly at them. '*You!*'

'Me?' Ramirez asked in confusion, standing from the circle of his crew he sat amongst.

'Yes, *you*,' he shouted, drawing the attention of everyone in the vicinity. 'I need a word with you.'

'I do not care for your tone—' Ramirez began.

'And I don't care for a captain who doesn't defend his ship.'

There was a collective gasp. He'd offended Ramirez's honour. For a moment, the captain's hand went to a sword that was no longer there, though Nicolas doubted he would've drawn it even if it had been.

'I do not know what you mean,' the captain said defensively.

'You could've done something. Anything. But you didn't, and I know why.'

'Yes, we were out matched and—'

'*I. Know. Why.*'

Through the Amora *being taken and the pain he'd endured from the whipping there had been a moment of clarity about that bloody jar and Ramirez's reluctance to get into a fight.*

Ramirez looked at him wide-eyed, understanding the implication of his words. Slowly, the captain shook his head, begging him not to continue.

'It's the same reason you won't ravish this beautiful, crazy, deadly woman here.' He pointed to Silva, who didn't look at all pleased about being brought into whatever was going on. 'The same reason you've shadowed the *Death* for so long without closing on her and finishing your little feud with Killgore. The same reason you sent us out multiple times to fight battles you won't.' Nicolas took a breath, the exertion of his frustration requiring him to stop and collect himself. 'I saw. In Killgore's cabin.'

'He kept them?' Ramirez exclaimed.

'You know he did.'

'I...suspected,' the captain confirmed. 'But I hoped not.'

'Nick, what's going on?' Shift asked.

'Tell them,' he said to Ramirez.

The captain seemed to shrink, shaking his head and looking away.

'S'okay, Captain,' Hay Sharkbait said at his side. 'We already know the reason fer ye grudge. The *real* reason.'

'You do?' Ramirez's voice was weak, the fight and theatrics gone from him.

'Killgore wasn't quiet about it.' Hay Sharkbait looked at her captain with sympathy.

Ramirez let out a derisive laugh. 'I doubted he would be, my friend. But still I hoped.'

'What's going on?' Shift asked.

Ramirez kept his eyes on the sand as he spoke. 'Killgore and I have always been rivals due to our differing styles of piracy. I see no reason why you cannot pillage a ship and be polite about it. There is no reason to strike down the crew if they comply. That is why they call me the *Gentleman Pirate*. Killgore, well, he is more the *'decks will be washed with blood'* type, and he hates me. He sees my way as weak. In his eyes I am not a real...to call me what I really am...pirate.' Ramirez took off his hat and rubbed his neck wearily. 'There was a ship, containing fine antiquities on a shipping lane near our normal berth. I planned to take her. The treasures there would have set the crew and me up for life. It was to be my one big haul, the one that cemented my legend in these waters. We approached the ship, boarded her, and...' The captain's face hardened. 'Killgore had gotten there first. The crew's heads were lined up across the deck. The captain of the ship had a note in his mouth, a message from Killgore to let me know he had sunk the treasures to the bottom of the sea. He didn't even want them. He just wanted to embarrass me. Somehow, he was one step ahead of me, just as he always managed to be.'

'What did you do?' Silva asked.

'Killgore has his skillset, and I have mine.' Ramirez chuckled harshly but didn't meet the warrior's gaze. 'Let us just say that I...*dishonoured* his sister...and his mother...and two cousins.'

'Grandmother already dead, was she?' Shift scoffed.

Nicolas glared at them.

'They say you could hear Killgore's roar of rage across two leagues when he found out.' A small smile crept onto Ramirez's face. 'When he did, he came straight for me. I was on an island, in a tavern, drowning my sorrows when he grabbed me. His men took me to a back room where that fiend waited to dish out a punishment he thought appropriate to my crime... Let's just say that he *unmanned* me.'

'Nearly happened to me a few times,' Auron remarked sympathetically.

'Since then, I have tried to hunt him down, to take my vengeance, but every time I get close I just...can't.' Ramirez's shoulders slumped a little further. 'I cannot even commit my beloved crew, lest they end up similarly deformed, or worse. And now you know. I am no more than a seafaring eunuch.'

'He keeps them in a jar on his ship,' Nicolas told Ramirez.

'That son of a bitch,' Ramirez snarled before correcting himself. 'I should not slur his mother. She is a fine, accommodating woman. If a little rough.'

'Lovely,' Garaz noted sarcastically.

'*That's* what you dropped in the cabin?' Shift exclaimed. 'I owe you an apology, Nick. I would've dropped those too.'

Ramirez paled at the statement.

He wasn't about to admit that it'd just been too heavy. It was one less embarrassment he'd have to worry about being reminded of constantly.

'We were even the minute you went sneezing in Killgore's house.'

For a moment, his companion looked outraged then they shrugged. 'Fair enough.'

'I have failed you all,' Ramirez said grimly.

Nicolas walked over and took Ramirez by the shoulders. 'I did the same to my companions once,' he told the captain. 'But I faced my fears, worked through it, and saved the day.'

'But I am no longer a man,' Ramirez protested.

'What's in here, matters more than anything else.' He pointed to Ramirez's heart. 'At the end of the day, you could've fled to the other side of the world from Killgore, but you didn't. You shadowed him instead. You kept pursuing him. You never gave up completely. Something is still in there, Ramirez. Trust me.'

'I will,' Ramirez said solemnly.

The captain closed his eyes and breathed deeply, visibly trying to gather himself and find the truth in Nicolas's words. Finally, when he opened his eyes again, a roguish smile crossed his face.

'Thank you, my friend,' Ramirez said, patting his shoulder heartily. 'You are truly wise beyond your years.'

As much as he wanted to have faith in the captain, he still didn't see the fire in Ramirez's eyes that he was looking for. Maybe this was a good start, though.

Stepping back, Nicolas let the crew of the *Amora* surround their captain.

'We're always with ye, Captain.' Hay Sharkbait grinned, leading the crew in a cheer to their leader.

'That's two taken care of. Anyone else with emotional issues for me to deal with?' Nicolas muttered. 'I'm in my flow, so now would be a good time.'

'Who else was troubled?' Garaz asked.

Auron, somehow, was no longer anywhere in sight.

****

Nicolas looked out to sea, watching the water ebb and flow. 'We're stranded on an island again.'

'So it would appear,' Garaz answered calmly.

'I take it they took Janessa and the children with them?'

The orc nodded sadly.

'Dammit.' He ran his hands through his hair. 'We were so close to saving them.'

'I know.'

He caught himself as he wheeled around on Garaz, ready to rebuke him for just agreeing instead of giving him something positive to hold on to. But as soon as his eyes met the orc's yellow ones, the fire in him was doused. He had a lot to thank his orc companion for. Had it not been for his ministrations, he imagined he would still be in agony. Maybe he would've even died of his wounds? It could've been an infection, or maybe his body would've just given out from the pain. Once again, Garaz had saved him.

The only real problem he had now was that the sand kept getting on his wounds, making them itch and driving him insane. When he did give in and scratch the itch, he cried out in pain. He didn't even know how it was getting on him. He was being as careful as he could be. Were grains of sand jumping from the floor for the sole purpose of sticking to his back? It wasn't a theory he discounted offhand.

'Leave it.' Garaz's voice was stern as Nicolas's hand crept up his back again.

Nicolas gave him an open-palmed gesture to confirm he was obeying.

They were sitting on the edge of the grass with Ramirez, Hay Sharkbait and the rest of their companions. The captain's crew were attempting to build shelter and find food, though it was tough going. The island on which the faun had stranded them was smaller and more desolate than the last. The scum had certainly learned from his mistakes.

'Why, though?' Shift asked. 'Why strand us here? Why not just kill us? Not that I'm complaining, of course.'

'Because he's sadistic,' Nicolas said simply.

'Well, yeah,' Shift replied.

'To make us suffer,' Ramirez stated as if it were natural. 'So that we die slowly. With no food or resources, we will eventually turn on each other, giving into cannibalism until only one remains to eventually die of starvation.'

Though his initial reaction was, obviously, to be appalled by the concept, his gaze somehow wandered to Garaz's thick forearm.

How tough is *orc skin?*

Suddenly aware he was being watched, Nicolas looked up and saw the frowning yellow eyes studying him. Sheepishly, he looked away.

We need to get off this island.

'It won't come to that.' If only he could've shared Silva's confidence.

Since the admission of his...injury, Silva had stayed close to Ramirez, who seemed to appreciate the gesture. They seemed closer now than during any of Ramirez's flirtations.

'Not for me anyway,' Auron muttered to himself.

'*Really?*' he asked incredulously, looking at the spirit, who'd clearly intended to say that under his breath.

'What are our options?' Garaz asked, not sounding like he expected much.

'Poor.' Ramirez chuckled. 'There is no food nor enough wood to build a serviceable shelter, never mind any kind of craft like...the *Amora*.' Pain creased his face. Evidently Killgore had decided to take it to add to his fledgling fleet, before describing to Ramirez in great detail how he planned to remodel her. Nicolas understood the feeling of loss; his sword had also been taken. Probably on the captain's trophy wall by now.

'So we're helpless then?' he asked.

The unspoken consensus seeming to be a resounding yes.

For a moment, the group was silent, presumably contemplating their fate. The word *cannibalism* began to float through his mind again. 'Was it just me or did the pirates have a wizard with them?' he asked, hoping for a distraction.

'Oleg Hobrath.' Garaz practically snarled the name.

'You know him?' Auron asked.

Judging by Garaz's clenched fists, it wasn't a happy acquaintance. 'He was at the *Academy of Magic* when I was,' the orc explained. 'We had some classes together. His hair went grey and began to recede early in life. They used to call him *Old Hob* because of it. You know youngsters and nicknames.' He'd heard that name somewhere before, but where? 'He is a battle wizard, specialising in elemental magic. He is also a colossal ass.'

'Upset you, did he, big guy?' Shift asked.

'He was the most vocal in the movement to have me removed from the Academy. There was a...*rivalry*.' There seemed to be a bigger story there, but the orc became suddenly tight-lipped.

'What are they doing with a battle—' Nicolas began before something distracted him. 'What in the Underworld is that?'

Surely I haven't been here long enough to start hallucinating?

He must've been, because he couldn't possibly be seeing what he was looking at right now. But if he was, then why was everyone else reacting to it too?

Discounting any form of group madness, he watched the four un-manned rowboats drift lazily toward the shore.

CHAPTER 19

Quickly and hopefully, they ran into the surf and secured the boats, pulling them to land where the tide could no longer snatch them up. Nicolas did so more carefully than the rest, not wishing to aggravate his back any more than necessary. Each seemed in good working order, with the oars inside. Was this a miracle? Perhaps T'goth had intervened as another thank you for saving him? Whether it was the Deity or not, someone was intervening on their behalf. Four random rowboats don't just appear on an island that happens to have stranded people.

The initial excitement everyone held at salvation was quickly muted as reality reasserted itself. All around them was featureless ocean. Even if they used the boats, where would they go? And how long would they last when they did? There was no sign of any other ships, nor anything the boats could have appeared from.

'I've found something,' Shift called from one of the boats.

They held up a bottle with what looked like a piece of paper inside. Shift threw it to him, and he caught it, after some fumbling. Straining, he removed the stopper from the bottle with a *pop*. Using two fingers, he reached into the bottle and tried to grab the parchment but couldn't get enough purchase to pull it out. Turning the bottle upside down, he shook it fiercely. Still the note wouldn't come.

Silva snatched the bottle from him with a sigh and smashed it on the side of the nearest boat. Leafing through the broken glass, Nicolas grabbed the parchment, unfurled it, and read aloud:

'Enemies of my enemy,

I have been following your progress in impeding the plans of the faun and those he is allied with. I believe we may be able to help each other to avert a war before it begins. However, I cannot do this while you are stuck on that island. Use these boats to get to safety. I understand their appearance is troubling, but the faun has not left you unguarded and I cannot get too close to the island.

Head back in the direction they came from. If you survive, I shall seek you out.

Should you make it beyond the reef, I will contact you.

A potential ally'

'What does our *potential ally* mean about us not being *unguarded*?' Shift asked, looking out to sea nervously.

Yeah, he'd picked up on that as well, and *'if you survive.'* Looking at the calm waters ahead of him, there was no obvious sign of anything being out there, though it made sense the faun would've left something to watch them. They'd made it off the last island he'd stranded them on, after all, despite the zombies. What was it, though? A magical barrier? Some kind of sea creature? He wished the note writer had been a little more specific.

'So what options do we have?' he asked.

'Without more information, it seems our only recourse is to get into the boats and make a run for it.' Garaz appeared uneasy with the idea. But it beat cannibalism any day.

'What if it is a trap?' Silva asked.

It'd be in keeping with what he knew of the faun's character. Or lack thereof.

'True,' Shift said. 'But we'd die here slowly anyway. Why bother messing with us?'

Also a fair point. The choice seemed to be possible death on the sea by some unknown horror or staying on the island and maybe getting eaten by someone he knew.

'We go,' Nicolas said firmly.

'No,' Ramirez said firmly. 'We stay.'

This guy.

'You're kidding, right?' Shift asked.

'I will not send my crew into the unknown to die,' the captain replied.

If the captain was making any attempt to hide his fear, it was a poor one. His eyes were wide, his mouth trembled beneath his moustache, and his hands clasped and unclasped in agitation. He did, however, seem set on his path.

'You'd let your crew die slowly on an island? Maybe killing each other?' It seemed to Nicolas the best strategy was to appeal to his love of his crew rather than try to call him out again.

Instantly, the captain's resolve wavered. 'I...love my crew.'

'Then do right by them.' Garaz picked up on his lead perfectly. 'Give them the option. Do not condemn them to die here.'

As an internal struggle clearly raged within him, Ramirez turned to his crew. 'My crew,' the captain began. 'We have a chance for escape. It is a slim one, but it is there. Or we can stay here and try our luck on the island. I would stay, but I cannot speak for you all in this, so let me hear your voices now. Do you go, yay or nay?'

The unanimous shout from his crew was *yay*. That settled that. Ramirez seemed almost relieved. Maybe he just wanted the decision to be taken out of his hands? Hopefully, the captain would come with them. Worst case scenario, they'd knock him out and take him anyway.

'Psst.' Auron gestured for him to approach.

'What is it?' he asked, sidling up to the spirit.

'So this one time—'

'Is this really the time?' Auron wanted to tell a story? Now?

'So this one time,' the spirit was obviously annoyed by the interruption, but undeterred, 'I was part of a group of heroes hired by a duke to defend his lands against some marauding barbarians. I'm not usually one for group work, but the duke insisted. Sounded like a simple enough job, the money was very good, and I knew the others I'd be working with, so I said yes.' Auron looked away and shook his head. 'Turned out, Mr Duke had vastly underexaggerated the size of the barbarian horde, and we had to pull back to the keep, quickly. Ended up in a siege situation. Now, barbarians aren't your *'hang around and outwait your opponent'* types, so they were going to attack.'

Nicolas had no idea where this was going or how it was relevant. Maybe Auron just hadn't told a story in a while, and he was getting withdrawal symptoms?

'So me and my guys are on the wall surrounding the keep, either side of us are ranks of ducal guard, all ready for the big fight. Turns out, the barbarians were also more sophisticated than they'd let on. They had a fair few catapults. First thing we knew about it was when this line of giant stones appeared in the sky coming down toward us. It was a breech-wetting sight, I can tell you. The stones hit. *Bang, bang, bang.* When the dust settled, I looked around, and me and my company are stood there just fine, while the battlements either side of us are rubble. There was a five-metre piece of the battlements left around us and the worst we'd gotten was a bit of rock dust in our eyes. The ducal guard...all gone.'

'Is there a point to this?' Nicolas asked.

'Yes,' Auron confirmed testily. 'In my travels, I've found there is a certain *universal luck* that surrounds adventurers like us. If you gather that luck together, combine it, your chances of survival are increased over, let's say, some random soldiers or village folk.'

What is he going on about? It struck Nicolas as ironic that a dead person was talking to him about luck.

'Just make sure that you, me, Garaz, Silva, Shift, Ramirez, and Hay Sharkbait are all in the same boat, okay?'

As confused as Nicolas was, the spirit seemed vehement, so he nodded in agreement. As he turned to leave, Auron stopped him.

What now?

'One more thing,' the spirit said. 'We defeated the horde when I killed the leader in single combat. Can you believe that? There were probably still a few hundred of them left against six of us. But their leader was dead, so they just ran off. It was a great victory.'

'Is there a point to that?' he asked testily.

'I thought you'd want closure on that story.' Auron grinned.

****

They juddered sharply with the swell of the sea, making him queasy. Slowly, he looked toward the horizon again, the one fixed point, to calm his seasickness. Garaz and Silva, the latter looking more worried than he was, strained to keep the boat moving forwards against the tide. On either side of their boat were the others, filled with Ramirez's crew. Nicolas had insisted on arranging the boats as per Auron's suggestion. He'd received some strange looks, but nobody openly questioned it.

Tensely, he scanned the sea around them. They all knew something was out there but had no idea what or where it would come from. Lacking swords, bows, spears or anything else vaguely useful, they were all armed with sharpened sticks. Would it be effective against whatever was out there? Most likely not. Was it better than fist fighting a sea monster? Yes.

Getting beyond the surf, the boats made for open sea, following the course directed in the note. Each second was worse than the last as the prospect of attack became more and more imminent. Time slowed as it did when he was in a fight, his breathing quickening. His hands were clammy with sweat, so he was glad he wasn't rowing. It was coming. Any second now. Would their boat be the first to be attacked? The anticipation was driving him insane.

'So, Hayley...Hay Sharkbait,' he corrected himself quickly. *Damn my formality.* 'You and the captain never...you know.' In all honesty, he didn't really care; he just wanted to ease the tension.

Hay Sharkbait gave him a sideways glance. 'Ye don't go hoisting the mainsail o' someone ye sail with.'

And he was already sorry he'd asked.

Plus, it hadn't worked. The tension still weighed on him like a basket of rocks. Part of him wished whatever was going to happen would just happen so they could get it over with. The rest of him hoped it would never happen.

Someone screamed.

Large red tentacles emerged from the water, curling around the boat furthest from them as men flung themselves from it, gripping it so tightly that the splintering of wood could be heard over the rushing of the water. Once the tentacles had engulfed the boat, they pulled down sharply, smashing the wooden vessel to kindling. Orders were shouted to come about and pick up the survivors, which was the right thing to do, no matter how little he wanted to park their boat where he knew that thing was. But before they could, the crewmen in the sea disappeared under the water one by one, as if pulled down with incredible force.

'What in the Underworld?' Shift gasped.

'The faun's got a kraken,' Ramirez whispered hoarsely, looking as if he might keel over from fear. 'Great Mother Sea, we're doomed.'

Except...they were completely untouched. He now had an inkling what Auron had meant with his little story. When he looked at the spirit, Auron nodded wisely. As much as he was glad his theory had proven correct...those poor men. Looking back at the remains of the rowboat, he prayed for their souls.

He was so engrossed in scanning where the furthest boat had been for signs of the creature that he failed to keep an eye closer to home. Nicolas yelped when a slimly tentacle wrapped around his waist and yanked him into the air. As he rose, a hand grabbed his. Silva. Thank the Deities' for the reflexes on that woman. Silva's strength couldn't match whatever was attacking them, though, and she was pulled into the air with him before they were both plunged into the cold water.

Everything became dark shades of green and blue as he was dragged down, pulling the warrior with him. The grip on his waist was unforgiving, and despite himself, he let out a cry, bubbles of valuable air escaping from his mouth. Beneath him, a loud, groaning cry seemed to reverberate through the water. He looked down.

Beneath him was a giant, multi-tentacled monster. Its single large eye watched its dinner approach as a thick beak snapped open and closed in anticipation.

Wait, that wasn't an eye. *It's a target.*

He'd dropped his own stick, obviously, but Silva's was tucked into her belt. It took some desperate scrabbling to reach it, Silva fighting him every step of the way as she flailed around manically, but with the tips of his fingers, he worked it from her belt. It nearly slipped, to be lost to the depths, but he managed to get a firm grip on it. Weapon in hand, he shook Silva off and turned, moving toward the sea monster. With him now working with the pull instead of against it, the monster didn't have time to react to his sudden attack, and Nicolas drove the stick directly into the large eye. With the proportion of eye to stick, he wouldn't blind the creature or do critical damage, but eyes were soft, and this would hurt regardless. Black fluid emerged from the puncture wound, and the creature screeched in pain, the sound making the water around them vibrate. It quickly retreated into the black depths of the sea, tentacle releasing its iron grip on his waist.

It took a moment for him to get his bearings and work out which way was up again. Seeing the light, he rose toward it, even if he didn't care for the metaphor. The strategy was sound.

Something grabbed his ankle. He looked down with a bubble-releasing cry, expecting the monster to have renewed its attack. Instead, Silva was flapping her limbs around, panic evident in her eyes as she pulled him back down. What in the Underworld was she doing?

Oh Deities, she's afraid of the water.

Grabbing her arm, he pulled her up to him with some effort, taking hold of her body as she continued to kick and thrash like a wild animal. Bubbles emerged from her mouth in a constant stream. Why was she not conserving her air? She was going to get them both killed.

As she continued to cry out and fight, her eyes rolled back into her head and her movements slowed as she expended the last of her air. Silva became a dead weight in his arms. At least she wasn't fighting him anymore. Kicking for his life, for theirs, he tried to lift both his own weight and Silva's through the water. Even giving it all he had, he didn't think he would make it, despite seeing the underside of the rowboat directly ahead of him. But it didn't stop him trying, forcing his muscles beyond their limits.

Finally, he broke through. His head emerged from the water, coughing and spluttering, his lungs burning. His whole body burning, especially his back. Hands grabbed him, but he shook them away, instead lifting Silva and letting her be carried to safety first. After she disappeared over the side of the boat, the hands grabbed him and hauled him in too.

Hitting the deck of the boat with a thud, his body spasmed as he coughed out the sea water he'd swallowed and tried to breathe properly again. Beyond him, Silva was lying prone, Garaz breathing into her mouth before pressing down on her chest. On his third try, Silva spat a load of water directly into the orc's face and began to cough and spasm just as he had. Once the worst was past, Silva looked at him as they lay across from each other, a mixture of thanks and fear in her eyes.

'You're scared of water,' he said quietly, still unable to use his voice properly. 'That's what's been wrong with you.'

The warrior closed her eyes and exhaled deeply. 'I'm terrified of it,' she confirmed. 'I didn't even realise properly until we ended up on the *Amora*.

Every second we've been on the ship it was like I was in a cage. Even being near the water makes me cold with fear.' She chuckled sadly. 'As much as I have tried to fight through it, to deny that I could be scared by anything, this whole trip has been one long nightmare for me. That's...that's why I was hesitant to grab you when you hung over the side of the ship. Then, when I thought the waterfall may take you, I panicked. I'm so sorry.'

'I get it,' he said. 'I nearly drowned, too, once.' Twice now. And Silva had been there both times. 'We're on the sea.' He tried to be both sympathetic and firm. 'You don't have the luxury of giving into fear now. If a ghost can get past his jealousy and a captain can find his courage, you can handle this. You're strong enough to handle anything. Besides, I can't even comprehend the idea of you losing a fight, I don't care who it's against; a giant, a thousand angry gnomes, the sea...they're all waiting to be crushed by the mighty Silva Destrone.'

Taking a moment to process what he'd said, Silva finally nodded, obviously ashamed of her fear and that it had nearly killed them both. Slowly, she reached across the deck of the boat and held his hand. *Thank you,*' she mouthed.

'You've just been through a traumatic experience, kid.' Auron smiled like someone who was both happy and annoyed. 'So I'm going to ignore you calling me a *ghost*, this one time.'

They had much more pressing concerns than Auron's hurt feelings. 'The kraken will be back, we need to go.'

As if he'd tempted fate, the boat began to shake. Nicolas's sea sickness renewed itself with vigour. Around the boat, the sea became choppy as he hefted himself onto the side of the boat to look over. The sea bulged, a large shape emerging from beneath it. As the water fell from the shape pushing through it, the monster became visible, it's blood shot eye looking at their boat in fury as it's mighty tentacles thrashed around it. Was this the creature that had destroyed King Ragus's ship?

Probably.

As he locked eyes with the creature, Nicolas was sure that he was about to die. His skin prickled with fear.

No, wait.

It wasn't fear; it was a massive build-up of magical energy. Beside him, Garaz's arms were wide, a giant fireball rolling and burning between them, the strain creasing the orc's features as he gritted his teeth. With a mighty cry, Garaz unleashed his power. The giant fireball flew faster than Nicolas's eye could track, but he definitely saw the flash of flame as it struck the creature's giant eye, which instantly melted into a mass of smoking wet goo before pouring from the eye socket into the sea. The creature's shriek of agony pierced their ears, but it was no siren wail. The smell of cooking fish forced its way up his nostrils. Nicolas threw up.

'Over the side, landlubber,' Hay Sharkbait cried as she retracted her feet.

Nicolas wiped his mouth, looking at the first mate apologetically. Then a loud bubbling caught his attention. He looked out just in time to see the kraken sink back into the depths from whence it had come. Maybe to die, maybe not. As long as it didn't come back.

There was movement in Nicolas's peripheral vision. Without thinking, he reached out, catching Garaz in unison with Shift, before the pale orc fell to the deck. Garaz's head was hung low, his breathing heavy. Eventually, he raised his head and managed a strained smile. 'That drained me.'

'You did a lot better than our sharp sticks would've,' Shift declared, patting him on the arm.

'Truly, you people are heroes of legend.' Ramirez appeared awestruck by their efforts.

Even Hay Sharkbait seemed impressed. 'Suppose that were pretty fancy. Maybe ye deserve my story after all.' Stepping forwards, the first mate winced and looked down at what she'd stepped in. 'And maybe not.'

CHAPTER 20

The monster gone, they checked for survivors around the ruined rowboat but found none. It saddened them all. But three out of four boats surviving against a kraken was almost miraculous. Assuming the faun had left but one guardian around their island—a fair assumption considering how big the guardian was—their only option was to continue onward in the hope their mysterious benefactor would reveal themselves.

'There's nothing,' Nicolas cried, looking out around them at a sea that hadn't changed in the half hour they'd been rowing.

'The boats came from somewhere,' Garaz soothed. 'All we can do is continue in the direction from which they came and hope for the best.

The orc was right, of course, but how long would it be before they happened upon another sea monster? Or worse?

What was worse than another sea monster?

Maybe a storm that would throw us...

No, he needed to stop thinking like that. Garaz was right. Whoever it was would make contact with them eventually.

He'd put his hands on the side of the rowboat as he gave himself a talking to, but stopped abruptly as he noticed the vibrations shaking the boat. It wasn't the tide, it was something else. Slowly, the vibrations increased until they became ripples on the water to their right. A lot of ripples.

Oh no, there is another sea monster.

As the three boats came to a halt, the water bulged upward again, rocking the boat violently. Grabbing a sharpened stick, Nicolas readied himself, as did all the others. He hoped Garaz was up to another large fireball. The orc still looked drained from the last one.

I really hate being at sea.

He could've made that decision at any point on this horrible adventure, but apparently, this was the last straw.

The waters parted to reveal a huge shell, belonging to a giant sea turtle, only slightly smaller than the tentacled monster that had attacked them. Though that wasn't the most surprising thing about the creature. That had to be the structures atop its flat shell and the figures around them. At the fore of the creature were two ballistae somehow grafted directly into the shell, both their lethal projectiles pointed at the rowboats. Between and slightly behind them was a raised chair on which a figure sat, holding reins which extended to the turtle's mouth. Each of the three figures on the creature wore armour fashioned in fish scale and had the green tint to their skin that marked them as merpeople. The figure on the chair rose, securing his reins and picking up the trident that rested beside his seat. Standing and fanning out his seaweed cape, he raised his trident in salute.

'Hail, Captain Ramirez and fellows,' the figure declared in an authoritative voice.

Ramirez doffed his hat with an elaborate bow. 'Hail, merfolk,' he replied. 'May the tides be kind to you this day.'

'Hopefully kinder than they have been to you and your companions of late,' the merman replied. 'Though it is my kindness that has allowed you to sail these waters again.'

'And for that you have our gratitude,' Ramirez responded.

'I need it not, human,' the merman replied, with slight distaste. 'What I need is what you know. We must speak and at haste.'

'I do not think shouting at each other across our vessels is inducive to conversation.' Garaz had a good point.

'You speak true, orc.' The merman chuckled. 'Which is why we shall not converse here.'

Raising his trident, the merman started to chant. Nicolas's skin prickled, telling him that magic was in the air.

Is this dark magic?

It couldn't be. Why go to the trouble of sending rowboats to save them just to magic them to death? Before he could react, a large bubble encased each of the three boats, and they began to sink beneath the surface of the ocean.

'What's going on?' he cried, all his instincts telling him that going under water was a bad idea. His initial reaction was to desperately try and fill his lungs with as much air as he could, but he knew that was panic talking.

'Just trust it, kid.' Auron didn't sound completely confident despite his statement. 'If he wanted to kill you, he needn't be so elaborate. He could've just left you on the island.'

The spirit coming to the same conclusion as him gave his theory more credence and enabled him to drown out his survival instincts yelling for him to throw himself from the sinking boat. Beside him, Silva was trying to control the shaking of her body, her breathing fast and fierce. Ramirez went to her, wrapping an arm around her and whispering to her softly. While she barely seemed to calm, at least she didn't get any worse.

The boat sank below the sea. Down and down, they went. Every so often, Nicolas took a deep breath to check he could.

Shift slapped him on the arm. 'The air will last, but not if you keep doing that.'

'Fascinating.' Garaz's eyes were full of wonder. Following his companion's gaze, he saw why. Before them in the murky depths rose a structure connected directly to the seabed itself, fashioned like the tower of a grand castle. Atop it was a large open platform surrounded by a bubble similar to those encasing their boats. The platform itself contained several docks and various figures moved about. All around the tower floated luminescent jellyfish, bathing the structure in a light glow similar to Auron's aura. It was beautiful, a beacon of light in a dark sea. In fact, the entire ecosystem below them was beautiful, full of bright, strange plants and odd creatures that weaved through the water.

Ahead of them, the turtle entered the structure. Whatever force was pulling them along in its wake also brought them through the bubble and into the docks until they finally came to rest. The bubble around their boat faded away, as if it had never been there at all. Nicolas took a couple of tentative breaths until he was sure he could breathe just fine. The air around him was cool but fresh.

How?

He'd never know, so he'd write it off as simply *magic.*

'Where are we?' he asked, looking around in awe as the others secured the boats.

'Underwater,' Auron answered sarcastically.

'We are in a fortress of the Tidal Kingdom,' Ramirez replied, unable to hear Auron's snarky remark.

'Come,' the merman from the turtle beckoned as he dismounted his ride. 'We have business to discuss.'

He looked at his companions uncertainly. It seemed they had nowhere else to go. And it would be a strange way to treat someone you intended to kill. Nicolas was learning quickly exactly how strange the world was, though.

'Your crew shall be attended to, Captain Ramirez,' the merman said as he walked away, servants with trays of delicacies passing him and approaching the other boats.

Ramirez, seeming satisfied with this, stepped onto the dock with Hay Sharkbait in tow and followed the merman.

Briefly, he paused and looked back at Nicolas. 'Are you coming?'

Slowly, his companions disembarked the rowboat and followed.

****

They were led to a large dining hall that was a bright mixture of blues and greens. The glistening walls were decorated with various pearls, resting on shells placed along the wall. The table itself was adorned with various dishes containing exotic-looking delicacies, all fish-related, of course. Probably hard to keep cows down here.

Garaz regarded their host as he seated himself across from Nicolas. 'You must have been confident in our ability to pass the sea creature.'

'No. Sometimes you must play the odds.' The merman smiled amiably. 'I would not risk the lives of my people fighting that thing, so I trusted to hope. It did not let me down.'

Once they'd all been seated, their host gestured for them to eat, taking no food himself as he studied them. It was off-putting, but Nicolas was starving. One of the worst parts of going adventuring was not being able to eat three square meals a day. He'd always liked to know exactly when he was going to eat. Still, whatever he was eating now, it was delicious. Only Silva didn't eat, looking as green as the merpeople around her.

'Allow me to introduce myself formally.' The merman rose from his chair and bowed. 'I am Zal Numar, Reef Lord of this collective.'

One by one, the group introduced themselves. When it was Nicolas's turn to stand, Auron whispered in his ear. 'Please say Nick Carnage,' the spirit said pleadingly. 'Come on, own it.'

'Nicolas Percival Carnegie.' He gave Auron a sideways glance of victory as he bowed.

The spirit shook his head.

'It is good to finally meet you all,' Zal said, before sipping his drink.

'*Finally?*' Shift asked.

'I have followed your exploits from afar since the incident with the siren. The denizens of the sea have kept me apprised of your progress.'

Does Zal mean he talks to the fish?

But he obviously ate the fish too. So...

'We share a common purpose. To avert a war.'

'So you understand that humans aren't to blame for kidnapping the princess then?' Nicolas asked.

'Yes,' Zal replied heavily. 'We are a remote outpost, but it gives me the benefit of a perspective my leaders and peers lack. I have tried to impart this wisdom to my people, but my messages go unanswered. I fear the call to arms drowns out words of reason. They are outraged and demand blood as recompense.'

'So there will be war?' Ramirez asked.

'Potentially,' Zal confirmed. 'Unless we intercede. Dawn tomorrow, the forces of my people will make for Merida Minor, the largest island of the Kingdom of Merida. There, they will demand the release of the princess, or else. Already I know a human fleet assembles there in response to the kidnapped children. The two fleets shall face off, and war may be on the horizon. If it occurs, it will devastate both our peoples. There will be no victor.'

'What if cooler heads prevail on the day?' Ramirez asked. 'It has happened before. How many times have our two peoples rattled sabres at each other?'

Zal rolled his eyes. 'Numerous times,' he replied dryly.

'This'll be different.' Nicolas hadn't even realised he'd spoken until he saw all eyes upon him. 'The faun,' he continued. 'He doesn't seem the type to leave it to chance. He's trying his darndest to start a war so I doubt he'll give anyone the opportunity to talk peace.'

'You may be right,' Shift added. 'You don't go building a pirate fleet if you aren't sure of the outcome.'

'Fleet?' Zal questioned.

Briefly, they outlined what they'd seen in Killgore's lair. Zal seemed to take this all in, his face giving away nothing as he sat back with steepled fingers.

'You are correct in your guess,' Zal confirmed finally. 'The only way five ships would be a threat to anything is if our fleets destroyed each other, which would occur if a war began.'

'Six ships now,' Ramirez added bitterly.

They undoubtedly planned on building more ships than that. 'But how do they intend to ensure the war begins?' he asked. 'They can't just sail up to one fleet and say, *Those guys over there were cursing your mothers,* or something like that.'

Behind him, Auron chuckled, evidently listening to the whole thing but not contributing when some at the table couldn't see or hear him.

'What about the device we saw on Killgore's vessel?' Silva's voice betrayed her queasiness. 'That has to be something.'

Everyone at the table jumped when Garaz slammed his large palm down on the table. The few guards in the room tensed and readied their weapons, only withdrawing them at Zal's raised hand. 'Of course,' the orc exclaimed triumphantly. 'That is what it was.'

'Care to elaborate?' Shift asked beside him.

'I thought I had seen something of the like before,' Garaz began. 'It is a focusing lens. It can be used to channel magic over great distances. I saw a smaller, prototype version when I was at the Academy.'

'And they have a wizard.' His mind went back to the deck of the *Amora*, where he'd caught a glimpse of said wizard, Oleg.

'Oleg was none too scrupulous even back then.' A slight snarl crossed Garaz's lips. 'He came up with the design. He hypothesised that if he were to direct one of his elemental spells through the lens, he could fire it over a good distance without the target seeing where it came from.'

'And thus starts the war,' Auron muttered behind him.

The faces of everyone at the table reflected the gravity of the spirit's words, even those who hadn't heard them understood the seriousness of what was about to happen.

'But he would still need to be in the general area, surely?' Nicolas asked, 'And you can't exactly hide a ship as big as the *Death* in the middle of the sea.'

'Unless you can,' Garaz conjectured. 'We have already seen that they can camouflage the ship as a smaller one, so why not hide it from sight completely?'

'They could do that?'

'Oleg is pretty powerful.' The declaration seemed sour. 'Assuming he is the spell caster, which is most likely, then yes. Though I have never known him interested in illusion magic. He was always more...direct.' The orc's brow furrowed at an unspoken memory.

'So what do we do?' Shift asked.

'We strike first.' As time ran short, the most direct course of action seemed the best. 'Their base isn't far from here. We wait until nightfall and raid it, scupper the ships and retake the hostages. Then they can't do anything.'

Silva perked up at the prospect of a fight, while Ramirez took on her green pallor.

Zal seemed impressed. 'You are correct, brave young man. The time of subtleties is at an end. I have watched and waited and gathered information, but now it is time for dramatic action. Only that will win the day. I shall accompany you with a squad of my finest warriors. We shall strike down these curs before they enact their plan.'

Around the table there were murmurs of agreement.

Touching his arm gently to get his attention, Shift leaned in close. 'You don't have to do this you know,' they whispered urgently.

'What?'

'This fight,' they replied. 'You've done enough, been through enough. If you want to stay here after...what happened, then no one would blame you. There are enough of us already to succeed.'

Glancing up, he caught Auron's eye. The spirit nodded in agreement with Shift.

That's not an option.

But it was. He could just stay here, wait it out and go back to Hablock and his parents, where he belonged. Home hadn't called to him for a while now, but that didn't mean it wasn't still there, waiting.

Do I still belong there though?

As much as he did silly things, Nicolas wasn't stupid. He could see he was...growing, was that the right word? Either way his travels and the dangers he faced were changing him. He'd been whipped for Deities' sake, yet somehow the idea of walking away now disgusted him.

Being whipped should've made him less daring. But he needed something to show for his suffering. A resolution. Victory. Revenge. Something.

No. It's justice. I need to see justice done. I need to know that no more innocent people are going to be hurt and that the villains are vanquished.

He wasn't excited anymore. That had been silly, a childish emotion in such a dangerous world. No, now he was determined. Determined to see this through to the end. Everything else they could work out after.

Though he couldn't deny the anticipation of giving the faun his overdue comeuppance. Hopefully he could deliver it personally, right between the eyes.

'I'm going with you,' he said firmly.

And I'm going to make it count.

CHAPTER 21

Even with preparations proceeding as quickly as possible, it still took them a good half hour to organise to leave. Most of that time Nicolas spent pacing around impatiently. It was strange; not long ago he would've wanted to stall as long as possible for fear of what would be waiting for him. Now, he was eager to get going. He knew what they had to do and how much was against them, but by the Deities, he was going to do it. Though, of course, the fear hadn't gone away. Facing the man who'd whipped him wasn't something he looked forward to, but it needed to be done.

Who am I becoming?

Walking to the docks, he wasn't sure if he was excited or nervous about riding on one of the giant sea turtles. There was nothing to hold on to, which unnerved him, but the merpeople rode around on them all the time, so it must be a safe way to travel. The rowboats certainly weren't fit for what they had to do next. In total, six of the creatures would be setting off, carrying them and Ramirez's crew as well as twenty of Zal's best warriors. Nicolas had no measure of what made a good merwarrior—or warrior, in general—so he took Zal's word for it.

Standing beside the resting creature that would be his transport, he tentatively placed his foot on the shell, before removing it again.

'It won't bite.' Shift smiled as they made a big show of jumping on the turtle's back.

True, the creature seemed amiable enough, but he was pretty far out of his comfort zone.

'It is difficult for me too,' Silva admitted as she stood beside him. 'I have issues with the water, yet here I am, ready to ride beneath it on a giant turtle.' There was a slight hesitancy in her voice.

Nicolas would've assumed that anyone sane would be hesitant about riding beneath the sea on a giant turtle, but Shift had just proven him wrong.

Nicolas offered Silva his hand. 'Together?'

The warrior looked at the hand as if she'd been offered a wet fish, but reluctantly she took it and they stepped onto the back of the turtle together.

'Don't get any ideas, my friend.' Ramirez chuckled, passing him and slapping him on the shoulder. 'She is spoken for.'

'I have already warned him that I would break him,' Silva remarked flatly.

Ramirez turned and appraised Silva, a half-smile forming on his lips. 'Indeed you would,' the captain purred in a return to form. 'Indeed you would.'

What's the matter with these people?

He had a very strange taste in companions. Who was he kidding? He'd chosen none of them; they'd all just ended up together.

Maybe it's fate?

No, he would give no credulity to the idea that the stick had chosen him on purpose. Even if he somehow became the greatest adventurer Etherius had ever seen, he'd still deny *that*.

Everyone aboard, the pilot of the turtle took his seat and spoke a single word. A large bubble rose to encase the creature. With a pull of the reins and another word, they were away. Nicolas almost stumbled with the sudden lurch of the creature, but a sly hand from Garaz helped him stay upright, the orc winking at him when he mouthed his thanks.

It took some getting used to, but he quickly found his footing, enjoying the wonders of the sea as they cut through it. All around the bubble, exotic, colourful plants he couldn't describe danced in the water. Various sea creatures, both beautiful and horrifying, passed them by. Schools of fish jinked and turned in perfect formation. Everything was quiet and peaceful. This world beneath the waves was truly amazing, but he had no time to really appreciate it now.

The plan was straightforward enough. Their party would disembark the turtles and swim into the pirate's lair at night, which should allow them to secure it before the pirates could react. They definitely had the element of surprise; the faun would be thinking they were still stranded on the island he'd left them on. Or eaten by his pet. Once the town was secure, they could free the princess, and the children, and the slaves, and destroy the pirate fleet. Any boats that happened to make it out of the sea cave would find the turtles and their deadly ballistae waiting. Though he was no general, the strategy seemed sound.

Again, he gave in to the anticipation of seeing the faun in chains. Capturing the faun was almost as important to him as rescuing the prisoners now. If...when they caught the faun, they would make him confess his deeds and diffuse the brewing war in an instant. Though hopefully the creature wouldn't give in too easily. After he got in a couple of punches, at least. Not the most honourable thought, but he still wanted it. Really, his rage should've been toward Killgore, the one who'd actually whipped him, but there was something about the faun. He was the conductor, getting everyone around him to dance to his tune, and he needed to pay for it. Even the memory of the faun made his back sting, like the wounds were still raw.

For a moment, the bubble brought him face to face with his reflection and he was shocked. There was a determination in his eyes he hadn't expected. He knew he was committed, but to see it was something different.

Am I just tempting fate?

The number of times he'd nearly died on this adventure already, the answer was a resounding *yes*. And he'd known that well before he'd set foot on the turtles back.

Yet I'm still here, ready to fight.

His hand brushed the hilt of the blade at his side. Months ago he'd never even held a sword, but now he missed the *Dawn Blade* on his hip. Instead he had a ridged blade borrowed from the merpeople. But it wasn't his sword.

Is it my sword though?

In truth it was Auron's, he was just...borrowing it? That wasn't right. The spirit couldn't exactly ask for it back. So was it *his* now. It was strange how much he liked that idea. Once this was done he'd make finding the sword a priority. It shouldn't be hard, Killgore likely had it on display.

'If anything you look the part,' Auron said at his side.

He tapped a couple of times on the fish-scale armour he wore, again a loan from the merpeople. The armour seemed hardy enough, but he wouldn't know until he tested it. The only thing he knew was that it fit, which was always a good start.

'I'm pretty sure between you, Silva and Ramirez I'll do a little better than just *'looking the part',*' he smiled.

'I'm sure you're enemies are trembling in fear as we speak.' The spirit returned the smile. 'Trust me, it's always good to have a reputation that unnerves your opponents *before* you fight them.'

'Except they don't know we're coming,' Silva interjected.

'Maybe we *should* announce ourselves beforehand then,' he suggested. 'Then again, I want to see the look on Ro's face when we just appear.'

'That should be pretty damned satisfying,' Auron chuckled. 'He'll be flapping around, going *'ah, I stranded you on an island again, but you escape, again, ah.'* Then he'll cry because he realises his pet's dead.'

'Then I'll beat the sense out of him.' Nicolas shouldn't really relish the idea, but he couldn't help himself.

'You'll have to get to him first.' Silva again reasserted the reality of the situation. 'He has many pirates at his command.'

'There'll be no shortage of asses to kick.' Shift smiled.

'Indeed,' Garaz added. 'We shall put our boots to many buttocks.'

Shift laughed. 'Near enough.'

Nicolas was distracted by a hand on his shoulder. 'I need to speak with you,' Ramirez whispered in his ear.

He nodded, though it was hard to have a private conversation on the back of a sea turtle.

'I cannot go with you, my friend.' The shame was obvious in Ramirez's voice. 'I am too...I am a coward. I thought I could do this, but it is all I can do now not to curl up in a ball and weep. You were right. I did keep my distance from Killgore on purpose, because I fear...most things. If I were to go, I would be a burden to you all. It takes all my will not to forbid my crew to go, but...I cannot deny them their revenge, though I shy away from my own.'

He looked into Ramirez's eyes and knew that nothing he could say would ease the terror behind them. He'd felt that sort of fear himself. The captain needed to face it but was unable to. Maybe courage didn't come from the heart as he'd believed; maybe it truly did come from the...manhood? No, that was ridiculous. Women were as courageous as any man. Whatever the reason, he knew that arguing would only waste time.

'What about it, Captain?' Shift asked over Nicolas's shoulder. 'Looking forward to getting stuck in and getting your ship back?'

'I don't think that's a good idea,' Nicolas interrupted. 'If any ships get past us, we'll need an experienced captain to run the blockade and ensure they don't get far. Who better than Ramirez?'

'Fair point.' Shift shrugged. If they were suspicious of his motives, they gave no indication of it. Though they were smart enough to read between the lines.

'Thank you, my friend,' Ramirez whispered gratefully. 'I owe you. Or we are at least even for you shouting my predicament across a beach.'

He'd take that.

****

Kicking his legs rhythmically, he treaded water. Directly above him were the wooden planks that made up the docks running through the pirate cavern. The old wood creaked as boots put pressure on it, a shadow passing over them as a figure briefly blocked out the shafts of lantern light that snuck between rotting wood.

Beside him, Garaz and Shift watched the progress of the guard in earnest, both as wet as he. Auron also bobbed beside them, looking frustratingly dry and quite smug about it.

The boots stopped, the deck creaking as they idly shifted their weight from one foot to another. There was a flash of shadow and a stifled cry. Moments later, the guard was lowered carefully into the water. Two knocks sounded on the deck.

When he swam out from their hiding place, Silva was crouched on the dock, looking around warily. One at a time, she pulled them onto the dock along with those of Ramirez's crew who'd joined them. He couldn't help but admire the way she was facing her fear now. There was a tense edge to her eyes that told him how much she had to fight her natural reaction, but if you could say anything about Silva, it's that she was up for a good fight.

On the far side of the dock, Zal and his warriors ascended in the same manner. It seemed to take an eternity to get them all out of the water; every second potentially being the one they're discovered. Fortunately, it seemed the pirates were still lackadaisical in their guarding, even though their sanctum had only recently been breached.

'So far so good,' Zal whispered as the two groups came together. 'Now to split up and finish this. You, Nicolas, and your companions shall accompany me to Killgore's lodge, while Ramirez's men secure the children and ensure those ships never make it to sea.'

'Except that one.' Shift indicated the *Amora*, which was docked nearby.

'Of course,' Zal confirmed with a half-smile.

'I don't think stealth will be our strong suit,' Nicolas said, looking down at himself.

Even jumping onto the deck, his wet clothes had pulled back on him, slapping around with every movement while managing to cling to him like a second skin at the same time. Having the sodden clothes clinging to his tender back wasn't pleasant. He tried to ignore the pain but wasn't completely successful.

Zal regarded their clothes for a moment before clasping his hands together, chanting under his breath. When he opened his hands, a hot wind blew across the group, instantly drying them and their clothes.

'It comes in handy quite often.' Zal smiled. 'Stealth missions, diplomatic functions. When you live under the sea, it pays to know how to dry yourself quickly.'

Nicolas could appreciate that.

Leaving the crew to their work, Nicolas and the rest of the party made their way silently into the shanty town itself. Weaving through the buildings and walkways, Killgore's lodge soon loomed ahead of them. Instantly he picked out the *Dawn Blade,* hung prominently from the porch. It wasn't staying there long. These pirates were really rubbish when it came to the security of their own lair. Once they had Killgore, it should be easy to make the rest surrender. At least that was what Ramirez, Zal, and Auron had each assured him. Shift and Garaz, too, when it'd continued to play on his mind.

It only occurred to Nicolas that this could be a trap a second before the archers appeared on the roof.

Arrows thudded into wood, skin, and muscle. Several of Zal's warriors fell instantly. The pirates cheered as they nocked their bows for another volley. Nicolas and his party were out in the open, sitting ducks. Not waiting for the next wave of arrows, Zal waved his trident, chanting intently. Moisture pooled from the floor and walls around them, forming a solid ball of water that obscured his view of the archers. Moments later, there were multiple plinking sounds as arrows harmlessly struck the watery shield. With another wave of his trident, Zal dismissed the ball of water, and it splashed to the floor, discarded arrows littering the ground around them. Using the opposite element to Zal, Garaz threw several fireballs at the roof of Killgore's lodge, dispersing the archers in flashes of flame. At least one fell from the roof, screaming as fire consumed him.

At the very moment Nicolas thought *'there must be more of them than* that,*'* the doors to the buildings around them opened, and pirates charged them, brandishing weapons and baying at them like wild dogs. Zal's soldiers proved to be as good as their lord bragged, raising their shell-like shields and quickly forming a circle to defend against the attack. Nicolas wasn't even sure which way to face.

'Hey, kid,' Auron called to him over the sound of battle cries. 'Do you remember when T'goth told me to keep practicing with touching things?'

'Yeah,' he replied, though this wasn't exactly the best time for a conversation.

Bending down, Auron picked up a rock and threw it at the oncoming pirates. The throw struck true, one of the pirates falling to the floor as the projectile opened a nasty gash in his head. Beside him, the spirit smiled in satisfaction. 'All those times I sloped off, I wasn't *just* sulking, you know. I was practising.'

Nicolas gave him an impressed nod, but then there wasn't any more time for thinking. The two forces clashed. Zal's warriors had discipline and training on their side, the pirates had the numbers and ferocity. Within seconds, the battle had become a swirling melee of the kind he was sure he'd never get used to. Flashes of movement around him were punctuated by the unmistakable sounds of clashing blades or cries of pain. It was difficult to discern friend from foe; it was all just figures.

Though the man running directly at him with the sword was probably a foe. He raised his own blade, and the pirate's downward cut caught in the ridges of Nicolas's sword. Not wasting the opportunity, Nicolas stomped down, kicking the pirate in the knee. As his attacker began to collapse, dropping his sword, Nicolas brought the hilt of his own around in an arc, smashing into the pirate's forehead, sprawling him out on the floor.

'Stop pulling your punches,' Auron shouted from behind him, throwing a stone at another pirate. 'They won't hesitate to kill you.'

Well, that just makes me better than them, doesn't it?

He wasn't a killer and had no intention of becoming one if he could avoid it.

Someone grabbed his waist from behind, gripping him tightly before he had a chance to react. Fortunately, some of Silva's lessons had stuck and he dropped his body weight to make himself harder to lift, bringing his heel down hard on his attacker's instep. As the grip slackened, Nicolas drove his elbow back fiercely into the pirate's stomach then wheeled around with a stinging haymaker that laid the pirate out...and caused his knuckles considerable pain. He shook his hand and admired his handiwork at the same time.

There was no time to celebrate. Another pirate came at him, sword flashing. After parrying several blows, Nicolas decided what was good for one pirate was good for another. Waiting for a downward strike, he purposely caught his attacker's sword in the ridges of his own then delivered a mighty kick to the pirate's groin. As the attacker collapsed, his mouth an exaggerated O, Nicolas grabbed his head and drove his knee into the pirate's nose, which gave under the impact, loudly cracking and spraying blood down the pirate's shirt as he tumbled backwards.

Aware suddenly that someone was behind him, he turned and brought his guard up, too late. The pirate's sword was only inches from his neck when it stopped abruptly, and yellowing eyes in a dirty face widened in surprise and horror. The man gave a single hacking cough, blood spurting from his mouth before he fell forwards. Nicolas stepped to the side so the pirate didn't fall on him, seeing the trident planted in the pirate's back as he hit the ground. That'd been too close. Silva shook her head like a displeased teacher and gestured for him to stay aware of his surroundings. He nodded his thanks before watching Silva grab a passing pirate's arm and snap his wrist with a simple motion so she could claim a new weapon and jump back into the fray. Beyond Silva, Garaz picked a pirate up by his neck, hoisted him into the air, and slammed him into the floor as if it were nothing. The wood visibly buckled.

The realisation that he'd been distracted again was punctuated by a fist catching him a glancing blow to the cheek. The world around him shuddered fiercely as he stumbled backwards, trying to come to his senses. He was vaguely aware of the pirate charging him. Was it one pirate or three? It kept changing. Still, he had the wherewithal to step to the side at the last second. Okay, so it was more of a stumble. The pirate's fist struck the door in front of which he'd been standing, hard. Staggering into his attacker as the man cradled his broken hand, Nicolas delivered a solid blow to the man's kidneys, and he folded to the floor, body spasming in pain. Nicolas kicked him hard in the face to keep him there.

He needed a moment to collect himself, to shake off the fuzz from his mind. Putting one hand out, he leant on the nearby wall and closed his eyes. They opened again, wide in surprise, as a *thunk* echoed in his ear. The arrow, stuck in the wall and still vibrating from the impact, had missed him by inches.

Tracing the line of the arrow shaft, he could see that the archers had taken up a new position on the roof of a nearby building. Beside him, one of Zal's warriors fell, arrow striking him in the chest and penetrating his armour. *Deities.* How much protection did his own armour really give him?

He wasn't the only one who'd witnessed the warrior fall. Zal watched his comrade's body hit the floor grimly. Raising his trident, pointing it in the direction of the sea, Zal chanted. His body shook, strain visible on the merman's face. With a cry, Zal flicked his trident toward the archers, moving it as if it weighed a ton. As it moved, a huge wave appeared, arcing over the top of the nearby houses before crashing down on the archers, washing them from the roof. The several who hit the floor on the side of the building where the battle raged were quickly dispatched by Zal's soldiers.

Zal sagged with the effort of his conjuring and didn't notice the pirate running at his back, knife in hand. Wasting no time, Nicolas charged the pirate, crying out as he did. Driving his shoulder into the chest of the attacker just before the knife hit home, Nicolas lifted the man, carrying him a few steps before slamming him into the unforgiving wooden floor. Two hard punches to the face ensured he wouldn't rise again. Zal gave Nicolas an impressed and thankful nod.

By now, the battle had definitely turned in their favour—around him were more allies than enemies, though a toll had been taken. Across from him, Auron raised a pot and smashed it down on a pirate's unpro-tected head, looking satisfied with his work as the pirate crumpled to the floor. He'd be hearing all about that later, and he looked forward to it, as that meant he'd be alive to hear it.

'Victory!' Zal cried as the last few pirates fled.

They didn't bother pursuing the fleeing dogs. Most likely they were heading toward the dock, where Ramirez's men waited, likely eager for some payback themselves.

Slowly, his senses returned to normal as the adrenaline eased away. He was shaky but thankful to be alive. He reminded himself to thank Silva later, as without her training—not to mention her trident—he would've almost certainly been dead. It appeared he had to thank the Deities as well, and the sloppy aim of an archer. Though judging by the stink of ale, the attackers had been more than a little drunk when they'd sprung their trap.

He looked for his companions, anxious to find them well. Thank the Deities they were. Garaz was tending the wounded, while Silva ensured any stirring pirates stayed down. Shift was bent over, hands on their knees. They gave him a thumbs-up when they noticed his interest.

'Perhaps I should invest in Silva's training after all,' Shift shouted to him across the carnage.

'Yes, you should,' Silva interrupted as she delivered a boot to a stirring pirate's face.

'Nice fight, kid.' Auron surveyed the scene, nodding. '*Nick Carnage* handled himself pretty well, considering.'

'That's strange,' he smiled back, 'because I didn't see him here, only me.'

Auron smiled.

'What about you?' Nicolas asked the spirit. 'You've been playing the ability to throw things pretty close to your chest.'

Auron looked both smug and embarrassed for a moment. 'Well, you were so busy with Ramirez and Silva that I had plenty of time on my hands,' the spirit replied with a cheeky wink.

'You still have much to learn of combat Nicolas,' Silva told him as she passed, checking the bodies. 'But it was not bad.'

'Praise indeed,' he said, raising his eyebrows at Auron.

'Killgore's not here.' The frustration was evident in Zal's voice as he looked around. 'If he was, there's no way he wouldn't have been in the fight.'

That was a fair point, yet they still had Silva kick in the door of his lodge and check it, just to be sure, while Nicolas grabbed the *Dawn Blade* from its hook above the door. It felt good to have the sword back in his hands. It seemed Garaz was equally pleased to have his staff returned, which had also graced Killgore's collection.

For a reason he couldn't really understand, Nicolas brushed the hilt of the sword vigorously, as if to remove the taint of Killgore's hand from it. Drawing the blade, he checked it over. It was still perfect, briefly reflecting the large bruise appearing on his cheek. He'd get Garaz to look at that once the orc had finished with actual wounds.

Silva emerged from the lodge with a look of disappointment, shaking her head just as Hay Sharkbait appeared to tell them that the *Black Death* was missing.

****

Standing on the dockside, they looked at the empty berth where the *Death* should've been.

'They must have left before nightfall.' Zal's voice was as calm as the sea before a storm. 'The princess is nowhere in this...place, so they must have taken her with them.'

And suddenly their victory was soured. There was no Killgore, no faun, and no princess. It *was* a victory, though. They'd taken the pirate's lair and saved the children; that was no small accomplishment. Though the prospect of war still loomed over it all. They weren't done.

'What's our next move?' Nicolas asked, the frustration boiling in him needing some hope of release.

'The *Death* will be at the stand-off,' Zal said thoughtfully. 'That much is assured. We must find her before they enact their plan.'

'I imagine the range of their weapon to be great, judging by its size,' Garaz told them. If anyone would know, it was him.

'Yes, but the faun will want to be close so he can see his handiwork,' Nicolas added. It fit with what he knew of the creature.

'There's still potentially a lot of sea around the two fleets,' Shift said. 'And they're bound to be concealed somehow.'

'Five of my turtles will spread out to cover the area as best they can and hope for some luck,' Zal replied. 'I shall sail to the head of my people's fleet and attempt to talk some sense into them.' Judging by the tone in his voice, Zal didn't fancy his chances.

'What about taking the children home?' Nicolas asked.

'I think if the captive children appear on one of our turtles, your people may shoot first and ask questions later.' He doubted the human fleet would fire on a vessel bearing their own children, but you couldn't be too careful. Besides, he doubted Zal meant literally.

'They can board the *Amora* and be taken somewhere safe,' Garaz said.

'No,' a voice interjected.

Ramirez was approaching them along the dock, walking like a man with a purpose. 'The *Amora* will be hunting these scurvy dogs along with the rest of you. Some of my men will stay here to ensure the children's safety until we return.'

'Are you sure about this?' Nicolas asked the captain quietly, who nodded firmly in response.

'I am,' Ramirez confirmed. 'While I sat out there, watching and waiting, knowing brave men were in here dying, I realised I could no longer stand idly by and let others do my fighting. I have been shamed enough. I will not let the forces of evil prevail while I wallow in self-pity. It is time to take back my name.'

'The more ships in the search the better,' Silva added, looking at Ramirez with something akin to pride. There was certainly affection in her eyes.

Internally, Nicolas sighed. This should've all been so simple. Raiding the pirate lair was supposed to tie up everything in a neat bow—save the princess and the children, capture Killgore and the faun, avert a war. Job done. Now they had the prospect of looking for a ship that could disguise itself in open sea, somewhere near two mighty fleets that were facing off on the brink of war. And here he was, amongst it all, just a village boy with a sword and a can-do attitude. Would it be enough?

His attention was drawn to murmuring behind him, the children were being led out of their cage and into the town. Again, it seemed as if the faun's magic was wearing off. Was it because of the distance from the one who entranced them? He pushed that thought aside. He'd likely go cross-eyed trying to understand how magic worked. Either way his heart went out to them, but at least they'd be home soon enough. Whether he'd be going home soon was a bigger question, and one he couldn't answer right now.

Several of the children began to cry. It was hard to watch, but he imagined their happiness when they were reunited with their parents again.

Provided they don't become war orphans. That thought strengthened his resolve. He wouldn't allow that to happen. They'd find the ship and stop this nonsense before it got any worse.

CHAPTER 22

E ven from this distance, he could tell that the two fleets currently facing off were mighty. The Meridan fleet was comprised of various classes of warships from small to huge, each brimming with ready weapons and, he assumed, men eager to use them. Their flagship was evident, a giant vessel with four wooden towers on its sides, making it look more like a floating castle than a boat. Seeing movement in the towers, he guessed they were loaded with archers ready for battle.

The fleet of the Tidal Kingdom was wildly different, made up of various sizes of sea creature with structures attached to them containing weapons and troops. Their flagship appeared to be a mighty whale-like creature from whose armoured head extended a long, swirling horn. Thick plate armour covered its hide, with a shell-like structure atop it carrying the weapons.

Behind the human fleet was the island of Merida Minor. Everything was framed in shades of red as the sun began to rise to mark a new day. If these two fleets clashed, the sea around the island would be as red as the sky.

'This could get messy quick,' Auron remarked, able to see the vast array of dots on the horizon.

'Indeed,' Garaz said solemnly.

'And all it'll take is one shot from the pirates,' Shift added grimly.

'If they are allowed to take their shot.' Silva sounded way more confident than he felt.

'We have to find them first.' Which would be no easy feat. Besides the two large armadas against the backdrop of Merida Minor, there seemed to be only open sea all around.

'Always the pessimist, kid.' Auron smiled thinly.

Well, I'm not wrong.

There was no telling whether the pirate ship was even on this side of the fleet. They could be concealed anywhere. They could be camouflaged as one of the ships on either fleet, waiting to strike, though that didn't seem very likely. There would be no way to get away before the shooting started and he doubted the faun would put himself directly in the line of fire.

'Camouflaged,' he muttered aloud.

'What's that?' Shift asked.

'The ship was camouflaged when it came for us,' he continued. 'It was disguised as the smaller ship to draw us in.' An idea was forming, but he needed to talk it out. 'But Garaz sensed it before it changed.'

'I felt the magical disturbance, yes,' the orc confirmed. 'I imagine it takes quite a bit of energy to cast such a large illusion.'

'You did, didn't you?' he cried, the idea fully formed now. 'Can't you just reach out with your senses and find a magical disturbance? I imagine it'd be easy to spot, completely hiding a ship that big.'

Garaz seemed to weigh up the idea, which was good—it meant it wasn't getting dismissed offhand and, therefore, could work. 'I can try,' the orc confirmed after a moment.

As the rest of them cleared a space on the prow of the ship, Garaz sat cross-legged on the deck, closing his eyes and steepling his fingers. The orc slowed his breathing, turning it into a rhythmic pulsing of deep breaths in and out, his large form rising and falling with each one. After a few moments, Garaz's brow furrowed with concentration and his fingers trembled. Then his body slowly turned to his left, his fingers, tense, moving slowly downwards until he pointed in a specific direction.

'There.' Garaz released the tension in his body with a deep breath out. 'The *Death* is in that direction. Dead ahead, so to speak.'

Nicolas looked where Garaz had pointed. To the naked eye, it seemed like normal open sea. Putting the looking glass back to his eye, he concentrated on the area the orc had indicated. For a few moments, nothing...then he caught sight of a gull flying through the area. One minute, the bird was flying normally then it seemed to strike something, flapping its wings fiercely to keep from falling into the sea and squawking in surprise. Shaken, it flew in the opposite direction at speed.

'He's right,' he exclaimed. 'She's there.'

Before he'd even put the looking glass down, he was running to the aft of the ship to inform Ramirez.

'Okay,' the captain said quietly as he put down his own looking glass.

'That's it?' he asked, having expected more of a response to the news. 'Aren't we getting underway?'

The look of reluctance on the captain's face didn't fill him with confidence. He seemed to be taking a lot of time mulling over something that, in Nicolas's opinion, was very simple. And urgent.

'I thought we'd talked about this?' He tried to keep the frustration from his voice but failed instantly.

'We have,' the captain confirmed. 'But now we are here, I...cannot. I cannot face him. It is all I can do not to turn the ship around and flee.'

'Of course you can,' he cried. 'You can't come all this way just to give up in the very final moments. So many people are depending on us...on *you*.'

Ramirez still wavered. They had no time for a back and forth on the subject, so Nicolas took a leaf out of the book of a certain dwarf gangster who'd helped snap him from his fear, albeit unknowingly.

Nicolas slapped him across the face.

Ramirez stared at him, wide-eyed. 'What are you—?'

Nicolas slapped him again. 'What's your name?'

'I don't—'

Nicolas slapped him again. 'Your *name*!' he insisted.

'Roberto Ramirez,' the captain whispered, still seemingly shocked by the assault.

Another slap. 'Like you mean it.'

'Roberto Ramirez.'

Slap.

'So the Deities can hear you!'

'*I am Roberto Ramirez, captain of the* Irresistible Amora!' the captain screamed, veins protruding on his neck, face as red as a beetroot. Maybe he'd pushed the captain too far? Was he about to have a heart attack? The man was getting on a bit.

Regardless, Nicolas stomped over to look onto the main deck of the ship, cupping his hands as he did. '*Who is your captain?*' he cried to the assembled sailors before him.

'*Roberto Ramirez!*' the crew cried as one, raising fists and swords.

'Right.' He turned back to Ramirez. 'You remember who you are now. Your crew know who you are. Now go and show *them* who you are!' Nicolas pointed in the direction of the concealed ship they were hunting.

Face set in a snarl, Ramirez walked to the wheel of the ship, relieving the helmsman and turning the wheel passionately as he shouted orders to his crew, who obeyed as if the Deities themselves were commanding them. The ship swung around as air filled her sails and she moved at speed in the direction of the *Death*.

'It is time to take back what's mine,' Ramirez snarled from behind the wheel, cape flapping in the wind and again looking every bit the dashing pirate captain.

'Remind me never to need an encouraging talk from you,' Shift said, half in awe.

'Desperate times...' Nicolas slyly rubbed his sore palm. 'So what's the plan, Captain?' he asked. 'We can't see them, and we need those fleets to be able to before the shooting starts, which could be any second now.'

Ramirez smiled at him through gritted teeth, like a crazed animal. 'We ram them.'

'We *what?*'

'*Ramming speed!*' Ramirez bellowed, commanding his crew.

The ship picked up speed.

It was possible he'd overdone it with his motivational slapping. 'Now hang on a minute—'

A ballista arrow clipped the side of the *Amora*, rocking it violently. As the projectile fell away, a hefty chunk of wood was missing from the side of the deck. It seemed they'd been spotted. Bracing against the nearest rail, Nicolas watched a hail of projectiles emerging as if from nowhere before arcing toward the ship. On the deck, the crew took cover as arrows rained down and ballista shots broke planks and, occasionally, limbs. Some of the arrows' tips were aflame, and the crew frantically put the fires out as soon as they'd caught. Still, something was burning. Black ash fell from above. Nicolas looked up. One of the ship's sails was ablaze, the fire spreading and blackening the white cloth around it as it consumed the sail slowly. Flaming pieces of cloth fluttered down on them. Ramirez didn't flinch.

Judging by the urgency of the barrage assailing them, they were very close and the enemy had worked out what they were doing. The main mast was ablaze now that the fire had finished with the sail. From a distance, it must look like some righteous flaming sword moving toward the enemy to strike them down. Damn if he wasn't getting caught up in this adventuring lark.

Suddenly, he gripped the nearest piece of rigging; if the *Death* was close, so must be the imminent collision. For all the damage the attack from the pirate ship was doing, it wouldn't be enough to stop them. Wincing in preparedness, he crouched, the idea of being thrown over the side of the ship on impact very unappealing.

'*Brace for impact!*' Ramirez roared, laughing like a madman in the face of the enemy barrage. '*I am Roberto Ramirez. Fear my name, scoundrels, for it is the last one you shall ever hear!*'

The world itself seemed to come apart as the ship spasmed violently, its prow striking the *Death*. Wood splintered and everything spun as the *Amora* ploughed into the side of the pirate ship. Water was thrown up from all sides as the ships collided, both vessels rising with the impact then falling back to the sea with a tooth-jarring crash. Holding on to the railing for dear life, for a moment Nicolas thought his arms would be ripped from their sockets or that the wave crashing upon the deck would wash him away, but he held firm. The empty sea in front of him shimmered and changed, and the hull of the *Death* appeared before him.

Wow, we've made a hole.

They'd speared the ship badly, breaking through its port side and opening a terrible wound in the vessel, one he doubted she could recover from. The *Amora* hadn't come away from this impact unscathed, either; her entire prow was a mess of compressed and broken wood. Somehow, amongst the wreckage, he managed to spot a single large breast pointing toward him—all that was left of the ship's buxom figurehead.

As Nicolas looked at the hole a terrible truth dawned on him. The slaves in the galley. He prayed that they'd survived, but knew that at least some of them must be dead.

Those poor souls.

'*At them*, my crew,' Ramirez cried as he staggered to his feet and made for the enemy ship, sword raised and blood up. '*At them*!'

The crew followed him with gusto, bellowing battle cries as they scrambled up the mound of debris to board the *Death*.

What have I created?

Taking some time to steady himself, he followed in the wake of the charging crew, amongst which were his companions. Letting them have all the fun because he was tardy would just be rude. Quickly but carefully, Nicolas clambered up the hill of broken wood until he came to its crest.

By the time he was standing on the railing of the *Death*, the battle was in full swing, the deck already a mass of clashing swords, and shouts, and curses. Holding onto a rope to steady himself, he tried to make some sense of the scene, but found none.

Beside him, Auron grinned. 'Cut the rope and swing down.'

Nicolas raised his leg as a pirate swung for him, sword embedding in the wood of the railing instead of his foot. He kicked the pirate in the face. 'You what?' Auron had a knack for picking the worst times to start a conversation.

'Cut the rope and swing down,' the spirit repeated. 'It'll look really heroic.'

'Like I'm concerned about that?' he shouted over the din of battle.

'You'll miss a hero moment if you don't.'

'I'm quite all right with that.' He scoffed. 'You're just trying to live vicariously through me.'

Auron shrugged. 'So? You'll regret it if you don't.'

Something in Auron's words appealed to the part of him that actually enjoyed the adventuring. And...maybe he *would* regret it if he didn't. By the Deities, he wouldn't allow that. Before he could overthink it, he cut the rope from its fastening on the deck rail. He held it tightly for a moment as he built up the nerve then finally kicked himself from the railing.

'Aaaaaaaaaaahhhhhhhhhhhhh.'

He instantly regretted the decision as he sped through the air, no control over either his journey or destination, the world blurring around him. It wasn't quite as bad as when he'd ridden the cow dragon, but it was close. Crying out the whole time—from fear, not battle lust—he swung right across the deck of the ship. For a moment, he thought he would swing clean off the other side, but his motion was arrested by a pirate who stood in his way. His feet impacted against the pirate, sending him over the side of the ship with a cry. Before the rope could swing back too far, Nicolas let go of it and slumped to the deck, joining the chaos consuming it.

Take a breath, Nicolas. Silva has taught you a thing or two. You can do this.

Picking himself up quickly, he entered the fray.

It was a mass of parrying and striking as pirates came at him, and he fought them back. A very strong part of him was unwilling to kill anyone, and he was worried that would get him killed, but he just couldn't bring himself to take a life knowingly. Who knew what had brought these men to this point of their lives? Was it just mistakes on their part, or things out of their control? Either way, their lives weren't his to take. So he blocked and deflected blows, using his legs, elbows, and fists to overcome his opponents, all of whom were thankfully as inebriated as their fellows at the volcano. Pirates, as a collective, seemed to have a drinking problem. Either that or they'd celebrated their victory too early. His restraint did earn him several nicks and cuts, some of which were very near misses. His own blood was hot on his skin, but that was still better than someone's blood on his hands.

A little blood was okay, though. A fierce-looking, bearded pirate came for him, brandishing a pair of small axes. He didn't like the idea of parrying two attacking weapons, so he simply stabbed the pirate in the foot. The big man cried out in a very unmanly way as the sword went through his instep. When he withdrew the blade, the pirate fell back, howling and cradling his injured appendage.

Another attacker was coming for him, so he stabbed down again. This time, the tip of the *Dawn Blade* struck the wooden deck. The peg-legged pirate looked up at him with a malicious grin, so Nicolas kicked him in his only shin. As the attacker stumbled back, unable to balance himself solely on his peg leg, Nicolas punched him, and he disappeared into the ongoing melee.

He was grabbed and spun around to face a pirate with a single snaggle tooth, who screamed in his face, soaking Nicolas in spit that was mostly rum. Too close to use blades, Nicolas headbutted the pirate, who staggered away, now with no teeth. Nicolas tried to blink away the disorientation of the headbutt. He kept forgetting that was what happened when he used one of those.

As a pirate with a harpoon charged him, he ducked, letting the pirate's own momentum carry him over his back to fall to the floor. Swiftly, he kicked the pirate across the jaw before a familiar green glow caught his attention. Across the deck, Killgore finished off one of Ramirez's crew with his enchanted arm-blade thing. The pirate captain had lifted the man right to his face before gutting him, as if he wanted to watch the life drain from his eyes. Killgore was not a nice fellow.

'*You*!'

For a moment, everyone on the deck stopped fighting, whether to see the source of the disturbance or that they believed the call was directed at them. On the deck, Ramirez stood before Killgore, tip of his sword pointed in the direction of the pirate captain in a perfect fencing stance. Ramirez pulled his cape around him to flap it away again dramatically. Ever the showman.

'My name is *Roberto Ramirez*,' the captain cried with gusto. 'I have pursued you across the seas, awaiting this moment. It is time for me to redeem my vow, and time for you to die, you mangy dog's tick.'

'You've come a long way to be disappointed,' Killgore snarled back. 'Your thirst for vengeance will not be quenched this day. But come at me anyway, little man. I'll take you a piece at a time.'

Ramirez gave a coy smile as he raised a single eyebrow. 'You, my friend, sound exactly like your mother.'

Killgore roared in rage like a minotaur about to charge, something Nicolas was familiar with. As the giant pirate lumbered forwards, Ramirez ran to meet him, his eyes filled with glee and bloodlust at finally facing his nemesis. Swords clashed frantically as the two met. Initially, Killgore used his superior size to press the advantage, until Ramirez utilized his footwork to nullify it and gain the momentum himself.

Watching the blades dancing almost faster than his eye could follow, he suddenly remembered that he was in a fight himself. Just a second later, a sword flashed past where his head had been, Silva yanking him aside at the very last moment.

'When you are in a fight,' Silva chided, dispatching his attacker with a stab to the ribs, '*concentrate!*'

Turning quickly, he blocked a blade cutting down towards the warrior from behind, kicking the attacker in the shin before bringing his fist across the pirate's chin. 'Better?' he asked Silva with a smile.

'Do that another thirty times and maybe it will be acceptable,' the warrior replied tartly, hefting her trident and throwing it into the back of a pirate threatening Shift. 'Or maybe start actually killing them.'

'She's right,' Auron added testily. 'You need to make sure they stay down. You're only half fighting, and that will get you in trouble.'

'Sorry, but I'm not a killer.' It was really difficult to talk and parry strikes at the same time. 'It's not in my nature.'

His concentration split, the attacking pirate slipped in under his guard and grabbed him by the neck. A choked cry slipped from his lips. With a sigh, Auron leant across and poked the pirate in both eyes, before Nicolas kicked the screaming attacker away.

'Finger poke of doom,' the spirit declared dryly, using the name of what he insisted was his *special move*.

Another pirate came at Nicolas in a crazed assault that had him backing away. He only stopped when he came back-to-back with Shift, fighting their own opponent.

'Seems we're dancing after all.' He could barely hear what they said over the sound of his own sword clashing.

He kicked the pirate in the shin, and the attacker howled in pain and hopped on the spot. He was about to strike when Shift's sword appeared from under his armpit, driving into the ribs of his very surprised attacker. Nicolas turned away from the man, unable to watch his attacker die, to find himself nearly face-to-face with Shift, breathing heavily.

Wow, their eyes are really green.

'Perhaps I can handle myself better than Silva thinks?' they said with a wink.

Someone bumped into Shift from behind, and they buckled forwards for a second. Nicolas caught them in his arms. Now they were nose-to-nose.

'Don't get any ideas, Mr Carnegie.' Shift smiled. 'This is Nick Carnage time.'

Awkwardly, he stood them back up, about to respond when a pirate threw himself at Nicolas from the side, knocking him to the floor. As he fell, he managed to roll with the momentum, so he ended up atop his snarling attacker, holding him by the collar. As the pirate screamed at him, Nicolas headbutted him right in the nose. Instantly, the pirate slumped in his grip as his world spun and his head throbbed. How did Garaz make that look so easy? Why would anyone headbutt in a fight?

More importantly, why don't I learn?

At least his attacker was unconscious.

Looking around, the fight was going in their favour. Nearby Ramirez and Killgore were continuing their battle. The two pirates seemed hell-bent on fighting on every single surface of the ship. They fenced up and down stairways, they duelled along on railings, they clashed atop barrels. Currently, they were making their way to the aft of the ship, locked in furious combat. It was hard to tell who was winning—both men looked tired and angry. But then he would've been tired if he'd had to move around so much. Probably angry too. Why couldn't they just pick a spot and stick to it?

'Have at you,' Ramirez cried at regular intervals.

'Die, fornicator,' Killgore would roar back.

A flash of bright cloth in amongst the grubby combatants caught his eye as he turned back to the fray. Oleg—with a bloody gash on his head—was stumbling toward the weapon, which was miraculously still intact. This would all be for naught if that weapon fired. Shoving through the melee, Nicolas scrambled toward the wizard. Looking back briefly, Oleg saw him approach and redoubled his efforts to get to the focusing lens. The two ships crashing together must really have rung his bell as the wizard couldn't move in a straight line. But judging by the blue energy around his hands, he was having no problem channelling his power.

'Stop,' he cried as the wizard grew closer, chains of lightning moving up Oleg's arms.

Oleg turned and threw one of the bolts at him. Thankfully, the wizard's movements were slowed by his injury or Nicolas wouldn't have made it aside in time. Instead, the bolt struck the deck where he'd been, blasting the wood to charred cinders.

The lightning in his hand cracked and fizzed brighter as Oleg turned to the weapon. A pang of failure gripped him as the wizard raised his hands slowly, as if underwater. Was the wizard slowing or was it his perception of time? Throwing himself forward with all his might, he made one last desperate grab for Oleg. He fell short. Aiming to land on his back, instead he thumped heavily on the deck just out of arm's reach of his robe. The wind was knocked out of him, so Deities alone knew how he managed to push himself forwards and grab the wizard's leg, but he did. Yanking just as Oleg stepped, he pulled the wizard to the floor before scrambling frantically onto his back.

'Unhand me, boy!' the wizard snarled as he tried to raise his arm.

Nicolas pinned it back to the deck but was rewarded for his trouble with a shock. His body spasmed painfully, yet still he held on.

'No,' he cried through gritted teeth as the wizard struggled under him. Again, he somehow found the wherewithal to try to grab the raising arm.

But this time, Oleg was ready, driving his elbow back into Nicolas's nose. The world flashed black for a moment with a sickening crunch. Blinking furiously, Nicolas rolled to the side, suddenly limp, and the wizard raised his energised arm towards the lens.

No.

Crack.

An axe struck the centre of the first lens just as the wizard unleashed his spell. The lens cracked, a fissure erupting through the previously flawless glass. The lightning struck it. The entire lens was covered in writhing blue energy until there was a blinding blue flash and a burst of energy which lifted Nicolas and threw him across the deck. His motion was only arrested when Hay Sharkbait threw herself in front of him and half grabbed, half collided with him. The pair fell in a heap on the deck.

Trying to focus on what was going on around him, he looked back towards the weapon. Oleg was gone and the lens was in ruins. Above him, a large trail of energy flew into the sky before exploding like a firework. It had been a weapon; now it was a beacon.

'Still got it.' Across from him, Auron was doubled over, hands resting on his knees. The exertion of throwing something so large had obviously taken a toll, his aura dulled. But he looked so damned pleased with himself.

Nicolas saluted him, and the spirit gave a theatrical bow in return.

A groggy voice got his attention. 'If ye don't mind gettin' off me, laddie.'

He was still on top of Hay Sharkbait. After scrambling to his feet, he offered the first mate, who looked a bloody mess—though it was clearly not her blood—a hand up.

'Thank you for saving me,' he said as he hauled her to her feet.

''Tis nothin',' Hay Sharkbait replied as if it was just business as usual.

A large, wince-inducing thud distracted him. Killgore's body struck the deck, the planks denting under the impact of his mighty frame. The green mist that made up his weapon vanished as the wide-eyed captain breathed his last, his face frozen in a look of sheer surprise.

'It's not a real pirate duel until you are at least up in the rigging,' Ramirez shouted down from the mast above them. Those left of Killgore's men dropped their weapons.

How did they get up there so quickly?

Looking down at them, the captain took off his hat and waved it around, raising his sword into the air as he did and somehow managing to stay balanced on the thin mast. 'The ship is ours!' Ramirez cried. 'Huzzah.'

His crew cheered, as did Nicolas and his companions. The ship was theirs. It was done. They'd won. They'd stopped a war. For a moment, he laughed in disbelief. They'd done it. Deities, he was exhausted.

'This adventuring lark is a lot of fighting,' Shift said, puffing and panting as they came alongside him.

There was only one thing to mar the victory. The faun. Nicolas hadn't seen him on the ship at all, nor his little toad butler. But he'd been sure they would be here. Quickly, he scanned the bodies, because sometimes he missed the obvious, but the creature was nowhere to be seen. As much as he was happy with the outcome, he'd been cheated of his payback. He tried not to let it rile him too much, but he knew he was destined to dwell on it later.

Beside him, Hay Sharkbait casually ran a groaning pirate through before looking up at her captain with pride. 'Suppose I'd best go find where his balls are.' Sheathing her blade, she sauntered off towards Killgore's cabin.

'I'll show you,' Nicolas offered, quickly following the first mate. His action wasn't entirely altruistic. He also wanted to be away from the bloody scene on the deck of the pirate vessel. Mainly though he needed to fulfil his vow to get below decks and free the remaining slaves.

He glanced out to sea before entering the cabin. In the distance, some of the ships from both the armadas were growing bigger as they moved to investigate the source of the sudden burst of lightning in the sky.

CHAPTER 23

Something seemed very wrong with the concept of victory medals. It was like a reward for hurting people, which was something he never wanted to do and certainly didn't feel he deserved a gift for. But he, like the rest of his companions, had been swept up in the celebratory mood. He supposed, in the grand scheme of things, a few dead pirates to avoid an all-out war was...all right. He didn't know; he was happy to leave that sort of cosmological balancing to the Deities.

Though he couldn't deny his own pride. A war averted, the princess saved, the children saved. He'd done some real good here. Thinking back to the slave galley of the *Black Death*, he remembered the sheer joy on the faces of the slaves as their chains were taken off, and the way they mobbed him afterwards, hugging and praising him. Should he be more humble about it? He wasn't Auron, after all. He had no idea how he should really react to it all.

What he did know was that he might've preferred being in another battle to being the centre of attention at a ceremony. The fine clothes he'd borrowed from Ramirez hung slack on his thin frame and were far gaudier than he liked, but he could hardly turn up to an official ceremony in some borrowed armour and a torn shirt.

Standing at the end of the long, carpeted walkway in a grand hall with all the expected finery, he looked at the rows of people upon benches before them, all of whom looked back at him expectantly, sharing whispered remarks. He fought his rising nausea harder than he'd fought on the pirate ship. No way would he ever live it down if he was sick on this fine red carpet. Ramirez might also raise an eyebrow if his clothes were returned covered in dried vomit.

'Do we walk in step with each other or just casually?' Shift whispered, looking equally as awkward, which he found comforting.

'I have no idea.' Nicolas was having trouble looking directly at his companion. The dress Shift wore, again borrowed, was sleek and form-fitting and had this strange magic that made his mouth want to fall open when he looked directly at it, which he wasn't sure his companion would appreciate. It had been bad enough when they'd first come out in it, and he'd been accused of *'gawping.'*

'You may be surprised by this,' Auron smiled immodestly, 'but I've received a medal or two in my time. Just walk up casually, take the knee, and rise. Make sure you look appropriately humble all the way through. Afterwards, turn to the crowd and wave. They love that.'

'A medal or two?' Nicolas asked with a raised eyebrow.

The spirit leaned in close to him with a broad smile. 'Considerably more.'

'Oh no.' Shift seemed unusually concerned. 'They're going to announce our full names up there.'

'So?' he asked. 'Do you have an embarrassing middle name or something?'

'Well, I'm just Shift. That's it. It'll sound a bit poor when it's called out. I don't have a fancy way of introducing myself...unlike some.' Why did everyone make fun of him for being polite?

'Would you like me to come up with a last name for you?' he offered. 'One in keeping with the creativity of the name you gave yourself. How about Shift Shifterson?'

'Shut up.'

'Shift Shiftington?'

'Shut up.'

'Shift Sh—'

'You're one to talk,' Shift whispered aggressively. 'When we get up there, are they going to announce you as Nick Carnage, Shin Kicker?'

'Shin kicker?'

'I've seen you use that several times now,' Shift said haughtily. 'Is that your new special move? All the fancy fighting Silva taught you and you go for the manoeuvre of a child having a tantrum?'

'Oh, ha bloody ha. It works, doesn't it? Besides—'

'Can you two behave?' Garaz whispered irritably. 'This is a moment for the utmost solemnity, and you are fooling around. It is unbecoming.' The orc looked proud and upright, almost awkward himself. He was slyly attempting to smooth a crease from his robe, which Garaz had gone to almost insane lengths to get mended and cleaned before the ceremony.

'Sorry Father,' Shift muttered petulantly, before leaning towards Nicolas. 'This is why he can't take us anywhere nice.'

'If you two feel out of place at this ceremony, feel free to step aside, and I shall claim your medals. I did kill more pirates than the pair of you combined, and I saved each of your lives at least once.' Nicolas stared wide eyed at Silva, as did Shift. Was that...a jest? Nothing in the warrior's face suggested it was, it being set in her usual no-nonsense expression. Nicolas was sure he caught a slight twitch of the mouth, but he couldn't have, surely?

He was suddenly aware that the man on the podium had stopped talking and music had begun to play—an uplifting, epic piece played by an orchestra in the gallery above. That was their cue. Slowly, they walked forward, Nicolas praying not to trip with every step as numerous eyes watched him. The awe in their gazes made his stomach knot with awkwardness. As much as he tried to look casual yet dignified, he was sure his awkwardness was visible to all. Several times, he adjusted his posture, just to be sure he wasn't stooping.

Ramirez had chosen not to join the ceremony, stating that as he was wanted for some *irregularities* in his past, it wouldn't be fitting. As wrong as it felt to Nicolas, none of the officials had argued, undoubtedly preferring not to be seen honouring a professional pirate if it could be avoided. Maybe the captain was lucky they hadn't just arrested him? But then, that would've been very ungrateful. Silva seemed to have no issue walking the red carpet, given her past. Maybe none of her misdeeds had been committed here?

Dammit, his mind was wandering. He needed to focus all his energy on not tripping, not making himself look an ass, and here he was thinking about the motives of pirates and mercenaries. Approaching the podium, he ascended the few steps up to it and kneeled briefly in time with his companions. He tried to control his swelling pride as they rose again.

Before him, both King Garian of Merida and Sea King Vassir of the Tidal Kingdom rose, apparently competing to see who could rise with the most dignity. Even when he'd been standing at the far end of the room, the tension between the two rulers as they sat side by side had been palpable. Yes, they'd averted a war, but the two kings evidently still had long-unresolved issues that weren't about to just fade away. The same went for both sides of the grand hall, humans and merpeople alike shooting disdainful looks to one another not in keeping with the dignity of the ceremony. Behind the throne of the Tidal Kingdom, Janessa stood, watching the group with a thankful expression.

'Honoured people of Merida—' Garian proclaimed.

'And patricians of the Tidal Kingdom,' Vassir added.

'We are here to honour those brave few who stood against the dark forces that would wish us ill,' Garian began.

'Those forces that would visit the ravages of war upon both our peoples,' Vassir added.

Oh Deities, they're going to do the whole thing like this.

It was weird. Especially as each ruler glared slightly at the other when they began to speak.

'Yet these good few stood true in the face of that evil.'

'And through their actions, their nefarious plans came to naught.'

There was a cheer from the crowd.

'That evil was vanquished.'

'And its agents brought to justice.'

Not all of them, he remembered bitterly. The faun was still out there.

'So we shall honour them this day.'

'May their names pass down through history for their deeds.'

'Nicolas Percival Carnegie, Garaz Galgrath, Shift, Silva Destrone,' the crowd chanted together.

Shift winced a bit, evidently still embarrassed at only having a single title.

Huh, Garaz does have a second name.

Both rulers stepped forward as retainers met them and opened the beautifully carved wooden boxes they carried. Inside were the medals they were to receive.

'Never received two medals at once,' Auron remarked, a hint of jealousy in his tone as the group took the knee before the two monarchs.

There was a moment when both rulers jostled to go first, exchanging poorly hidden looks of outrage that the other monarch even dared stand upon the same stage as them. Finally, they decided to start at opposite ends of the party, though practically snarled at each other once they met again in the middle. Twice a silky ribbon was hung over Nicolas's neck. One medal was a bright golden circle with an image on it that he would study later and the other was a star that looked like it was fashioned from some kind of sea flower.

'And there is one more,' Garian declared after the medals were handed out. 'One who is here, but whose presence cannot be felt.'

'Though his actions were still instrumental in this victory,' Vassir added.

'Auron of Tellmark,' the crowd chanted.

'Take this for him,' Garian pressed another medal into Nicolas's hand, as did Vassir moments later.

Auron glanced at him in confusion. Nicolas had talked to Zal hours before the ceremony, explaining the spirit's situation, but that he was as much a part of this victory as anyone. More so, as the spirit had really been the one to stop the weapon firing and saved the day. It was wrong not to honour him. Obviously, his message had gotten through to the right people.

'Still got it, kid.' The spirit smiled cockily, trying to hide the emotion from his face.

Medals on necks, the group were bidden to turn so the sea of faces behind them might behold these newly medalled heroes. Bad enough Nicolas knew the crowd was there, he certainly didn't want to face them. But he turned with the others, and the applause started, beginning as a polite rhythm before gathering in pace and volume until it echoed around the whole chamber, interspersed with whoops and cheers. Despite his awkwardness, he was proud, both of himself and his companions. They'd done a great thing here.

He allowed himself his well earned moment of pride, and he waved to the crowd, letting the beaming smile he'd been fighting back finally escape.

****

Outside, in the elegant gardens that surrounded the palace on Merida Minor, the party was in full swing. The orchestra played gentle background music as people conversed and ate and drank, though the merpeople and the Meriduns kept blatantly apart from one another.

'Is it always like this afterwards?' he asked Auron, both standing to the side of the party somewhat, him because of his awkwardness and the spirit because of his inability to enjoy it.

'Sometimes,' Auron mused. 'Sometimes you just ride off into the sunset. There's no real norm for this sort of thing.'

'At least we aren't getting stranded on a desert island as a thank you.' Nicolas laughed.

Auron chuckled heartily. 'That's true,' the spirit admitted. 'Though it was a good job T'goth sent us there. If not, I'm sure these gardens wouldn't look so elegant.'

'Also true.' Nicolas smiled. 'I suppose we should thank him for sending us where we needed to be.' Looking up to the sky, Nicolas raised his glass in cheers to the Deity before taking a long swig of his drink.

Auron did the same, but with an imaginary glass. 'So, you're pretty reluctant to go home then?' the spirit asked from nowhere.

For a second, he was wrongfooted. Why was he always so surprised that he was easy to read?. 'I'm in no rush,' he replied, looking into his drink. 'There's something about these adventures, now that I know what I'm doing. I mean, I've averted a vampire apocalypse, saved a Deity, and stopped a war. That's not bad for a first timer. I think I can see the good I'm doing, especially here. So yeah. Maybe I can delay going home properly. But I do need to let my parents know I'm okay.'

Auron's pride was glowing as much as his aura. 'Good, because we aren't finished, kid.'

'So we're staying together then?' Excitement jolted through him.

Might as well just give into It, Instead of fooling myself.

The pull of home would never leave him, nor should it. But he knew where he wanted to be. *Needed* to be, maybe.

'I've talked to the others, and there's still work to be done,' Auron confirmed. 'None of this has happened without outside help. Maybe that's something to do with my unfinished business?'

'I did promise I'd help you finish it. Be bad to go back on my word.'

'Correct answer, kid.' The spirit smiled.

'So where to next then?'

Auron shrugged. 'Hunt down the faun and see what he has to say,' the spirit suggested. 'I can't imagine he'll stay quiet for long. At the very least, he'll come after us for revenge at some point.'

'Really?'

'Yeah, they always do.' Auron chuckled. 'So this one time, I wiped out a bandit crew of this guy called Jax...Jar...Jarris or something. He gets away, because he was a coward and bolted while I slaughtered his men. So anyway, he decides to come for me, but wants to train first for our *ultimate showdown.*' Guy spends twelve years studying fighting before he comes after me. When he did, I could't even remember who he was. Drove him nuts. So anyway, we fight.'

'And...'

'And, J-whatever's other problem was that he was nearly broke after I wrecked his crew and reclaimed all his stolen loot. The instructors he'd hired weren't of the finest calibre. Well, you get what you pay for, don't you? I think the fight lasted all of five seconds. And *that* was only because I was tired after a night of ale and merriment.'

Nicolas laughed.

'May we cut into your conversation?'

Beside him, Zal and Janessa had approached. Auron seemed almost upset to have the princess so close but didn't leave.

'I take it you're speaking to Auron?' Janessa asked, somewhat coyly.

Nicolas nodded.

'Then I will make my part in this short,' Zal said. 'I just wanted to thank you for what you did. Lesser men would not have involved themselves, but you and your companions...there is something special about you. If you ever need anything, call upon me, and I shall be at your service.'

Nicolas took Zal's offered hand and shook it firmly.

'Princess, Nicolas, Auron.' Zal nodded before taking his leave.

For a moment, Janessa stared at Nicolas, almost awkwardly. 'If I tell you something, will you pass it to Auron for me please?' she asked finally.

'He can hear you.'

Maybe I should leave? No, if Auron wanted to reply, he needed to be here. *Brilliant.*

Janessa looked around uncomfortably until Nicolas pointed to where Auron stood.

'Auron…I… This feels strange. Talking to you, like this,' the princess stammered. 'But you and I never got a proper goodbye. That weighed heavily on me, and now I cannot ever have that moment with you. I can, however, make the most of this.' Nicolas really wasn't sure he should've been hearing any of this but was trapped. 'Our time together, it meant everything to me. Giving you up for my duty was the hardest thing I've ever done. I wish with all my heart it could've been any other way, but even parted, my heart was always truly yours. There is a piece of it that always will be.'

Oh Deities. He was so uncomfortable right now.

Looking at Auron, he saw so much emotion in those ethereal features, something he'd never seen before. Instead of replying, Auron stood before Janessa and cupped her cheek. She started, clearly feeling the touch, but after the initial shock, she pressed her face closer to his hand, somehow managing to look directly into his eyes without even seeing them.

A tear rolled down Nicolas's cheek, shed because his companion could not.

With a half-smile, Janessa turned and walked away, holding her cheek tenderly. Before she turned, he saw the tears filling her eyes.

'Are you okay?' he asked his companion once Janessa was out of earshot.

'Not even slightly, kid.' Auron didn't take his eyes from the princess as she vanished into the crowd. 'But I will be.'

****

Walking from the firm ground to the heaving deck of the *Amora* the next day did little for his hangover. Once the ceremony was completed, the rest of the day had been a blur of drinking and feasting. The overindulgence had done bad things to his stomach. When he'd woken, Nicolas had been surprised to find he'd made it back to his room, even though he hadn't made it quite as far as the bed. Once he'd managed to collect himself, as much as he'd been able, he'd groggily made his way back to the *Amora*. The war was averted, the praise given. It was now time to say their goodbyes and move on to the next part of their adventure. At least they'd be popping over to Hablock so he could see his parents before that. It was only right for him to let them see in person that he was okay.

They must be worried sick.

Plus a couple of nights in his own bed would be most welcome. Maybe he wouldn't sleep in a proper bed for a while? Then there was the issue with mealtimes. When would breakfast be? Lunch? Dinner? He'd need provisions and…

Shift greeted him on the deck of the ship, looking frustratingly refreshed. 'Good afternoon.'

'It's afternoon?' he asked sheepishly.

'It most certainly is,' Auron replied, a little too loudly. The look on the spirit's face made it clear the volume was raised on purpose.

Looking over at Silva, standing by the door that led to the captain's cabin, he thought he even caught a smirk from her. He must look worse than he'd thought.

'I had a lot to drink yesterday, okay?' he moaned defensively, his voice rising to a volume his head found uncomfortable.

Shift suppressed a smirk. 'Oh, you really didn't.' There was something in their expression, in all their expressions.

Oh no. What did I do?

'You have a beautiful singing voice.' Auron's casual statement caused fits of laughter from him and Shift. Even Silva was sniggering.

Deities, no.

'So who's the *busty barmaid* in your song, Nick?' Shift asked between chuckles. 'Someone special?'

Oh, that *song.*

It was an old drinking song from Hablock. It wasn't a tune he generally joined in with, unless his friend Potter pressganged him into it, so he was surprised he'd even remembered the words, and said as much.

'I really don't think you did,' Auron said with a faux wince.

Shit.

'Where's Garaz?' he asked, wanting to change the subject.

Shift nodded towards the cabin.

'He's performing a…reattachment,' Auron replied diplomatically.

'*Really?*'

'Garaz seems to think so,' Shift replied. 'He said the alchemical solution they were in preserved them well enough that reattachment was a possibility.'

He found himself quite pleased for Ramirez, without wanting to think of the specifics or implications. As if on cue, the door to the cabin opened, and Garaz stepped out, looking displeased. An expectant hush descended over the deck. Men ceased loading new supplies onto the vessel and affecting the repairs she desperately needed.

'The procedure was successful.' The orc's declaration elicited cheers from the crew. He was about to congratulate Garaz when the orc raised a hand to silence him. 'Yes, it is done. Yes, it was successful. Now, I would like to never speak of it again.'

'Okay, big guy,' Shift said with a smile. 'Wouldn't want you getting...testy.'

Nicolas choked back a laugh as the orc glared at Shift.

'I am whole again!' Ramirez cried as he burst from the door to his cabin, grabbing Silva and kissing her briefly but passionately. Nicolas turned away awkwardly.

As the crew revelled in their captain being made whole, Hay Sharkbait ambled up to the group. 'Ye've done some great things.' *We've finally impressed the first mate then.* ''tis only fittin' I give ye somethin' back.'

Slowly, the first mate leaned toward Shift and whispered in their ear. Auron leaned in close so he could eavesdrop. The spirit was the one who'd really wanted to know, anyway. As Hay Sharkbait spoke, both his companion's eyes grew wide and soon enough their mouths hung open. As Hayley stepped back, tale finished, Shift looked at her with pure awe.

'*Really*?' they asked. 'I mean...but...*really*?'

Hay Sharkbait gave a single nod then turned and walked away.

'That's...well...unbelievable,' Auron said excitedly. 'I don't even know where to...I...wow.'

'Come on then?' Nicolas prompted.

Shift and Auron looked at each other then Shift turned back to him, patting him on the shoulder. 'When you're old enough.'

'*Seriously*?' he cried, only remembering he had a hangover after he'd raised his voice. Rubbing his head tenderly, he found an arm around his shoulders.

'My friends, my friends.' The captain was beaming. 'How can I thank you for everything you've done? You helped me get my balls back in more ways than one.' He finished with a cheeky wink.

'*We* have done,' Garaz corrected, much to Ramirez's pleasure. Though the orc refused to look the captain directly in the eye. 'You were as much a part of this as us.'

'No reward necessary.' Shift patted the medals around their neck that they had yet to take off, unlike their dress, which had come off straight after the ceremony.

'I am just sorry I cannot offer you a lift home,' Ramirez said regretfully. 'It should be the least I can do, but the ship will be here for repairs for at least another few days.'

'That's okay,' Nicolas said. 'We've booked passage on a freighter leaving this afternoon.'

Shift looked at the bustling dock around them. 'I'm surprised they let a famous pirate dock here for repairs.'

'They are not so much *letting* me,' Ramirez explained coyly, 'as turning a blind eye for services rendered. That suits me just fine. But in all seriousness, if any of you need anything, you need but call me.'

'Thank you.' He found he'd miss the flamboyant captain but was happy that after one more freighter trip his sailing days would be well and truly behind him.

I'm a...how did Hay Sharkbait put it? Oh yeah, a real landlubber. And proud of it.

'And what of you, my love?' the captain asked, turning to Silva and taking her hand. 'Are you sure I cannot tempt you to sail with me? Think of the adventures we would have. Think of the passion of the high seas.'

Nicolas started. This was the first he'd heard of it. Was she really going to stay with the captain? Nicolas wouldn't begrudge her, but...he was surprised to find he'd miss having her around.

The warrior looked conflicted as she stared at her hand in Ramirez's. 'I...cannot.' Clearly, that was something she didn't want to say. 'I have much to atone for, and I cannot do so while sailing the seas with you. My place is with these people. If I ever do manage to atone, we shall meet again knowing that I've earned it.'

They looked into each other's eyes, many unspoken words passing between them. It was a shame for the warrior when she had a chance at happiness. Despite their different attitudes, and ages, they made a good couple. Nicolas was half tempted to interject and argue, but Silva's mind was clearly made up, and he respected her reasons.

'We don't leave for another few hours,' he added instead.

The pair looked at him for a moment as the ramifications of his words sank in. Within moments they'd had disappeared into Ramirez's cabin, without so much as a *'see you later.'*

'Charming,' Garaz said distastefully. 'If he aggravates any previous injuries, I am not healing him again.'

Shift gave a derisive snort. 'I am so glad he chose her over me. I'm not sure I see what the fuss is about anymore anyway.'

'Spoken like an ungracious loser.' Nicolas smiled.

'Spoken like someone happy they get to keep me for themselves,' Shift retorted.

Nicolas turned and found Shift's green eyes staring into his. Slowly, they leaned forward, their mouth slightly open as they tilted their head to the side. He copied the movement, closing his eyes and moving in toward them, until he found thin air and overbalanced. Opening his eyes, he stumbled to correct himself.

To his side, Shift shook their head, smiling. 'I knew you were in love with me.'

'You ass,' Nicolas cursed as his face flushed red. 'I was just...I didn't...it'd be rude to...I thought...' He had no words.

Beside them, Auron put his hand to his mouth to hide his sniggering as Garaz shook his head slowly.

CHAPTER 24

It felt so good to see land again, proper land, that was connected to other land. He looked over the side of the freighter, leaning against the railing, at the bustling city of Meridus, Merida's capital, stretched out before him. Even in twilight, the port was heaving, traders of all sorts unloading or loading ships, crews making their way to the nearest taverns, the ladies of the evening coming out to do business. Pipe music played nearby. All around them was life. This could all have been burnt to ash were it not for them.

Their freighter had only just docked, and the crew were busy unloading the supplies. He'd come up to the deck early with Shift to watch the ship dock.

'So are you sure about this?' Shift asked, the question having hung over them for a while now.

'Yes, I'm sure,' he replied. 'As much as I want to go home, I also don't want to, if that makes sense. I like travelling with you guys. I like the adventuring, and I like doing good. I'm not quite done yet. We aren't done yet.'

Shift nodded. He expected a sarcastic response or some teasing. 'Good,' was all they said.

'So we're definitely keeping him then?' Auron asked as he approached with Garaz and Silva in tow and saw Shift's face.

'He's a stubborn one,' they replied. 'He just won't go.'

'It's because he secretly loves the name *Nick Carnage* so much.' Auron laughed.

'You wish.' Nicolas smiled. 'Though don't forget we're popping home before we go looking for the faun. I haven't seen my parents since I left for Sarus, and I want to let them know I'm okay...and get a change of clothes.' Who knew when he may have the chance again once they continued their journey?

'Yes,' Auron said, rubbing the bridge of his nose. 'I remember from the other twenty times you mentioned it.'

'It will be good to see your family again,' Garaz added. 'Though I am glad you will continue travelling with us, young Nicolas.'

'Me too,' he replied.

'I can't wait to meet your parents,' Shift said. 'I have questions.'

'You can stay outside.' Nicolas snorted.

'You think I'd make a bad impression?' Shift asked, faux offended.

'Yes,' he replied simply.

'I too am looking forward to meeting your family,' Silva added formally. 'If anyone was going to ask.'

'I thought all you anticipated was battle?' Auron asked.

'I enjoy other things.' Silva bristled.

'Ask Ramirez.' Shift smiled.

'Enough of that,' Silva snapped. Shift teasing Silva about her time alone with Ramirez had been a prominent feature of their trip in the freighter.

'I'll tell you what I'm looking forward to,' Nicolas said seriously. 'Finding that faun and making him pay. I'll be very satisfied to bring him to justice.'

'Silva knows a thing or two about satisfaction.' Shift smiled cheekily.

'*Enough!*' Silva commanded.

'We will need lodgings for the night,' Garaz stated, trying to change the subject to something he was more comfortable with. 'We can proceed when we are fresh in the morning.'

'Maybe we can go wherever that pipe music is coming from?' Shift suggested. 'It sounds nice.'

It did sound nice. Dreamily, he looked around the ship.

'Where've the crew gone?' he asked suddenly.

The deck appeared empty, save for them. He was sure it had been full of sailors just moments ago. Making to step forward, Nicolas realised that he couldn't move. His limbs refused to obey his commands, panic gripping him more tightly with each failed attempt. Beside the group, a nearby crate shimmered and vanished.

'Surprise.' The faun dropped the pipes from his lips, his little toad butler standing beside him.

He wanted to scream and curse, but he couldn't talk. Shift, Silva, and Garaz appeared similarly rooted to the spot, only their eyes able to move.

'All my plans, *ruined*.' The faun shook his head in barely contained rage. 'Years of work, *ruined*. And because of what? Some pesky kid and his friends. And that idiot Killgore, who just *had* to go back to the shipwreck for one of his damned trophies. I should've told him to forget the crown, like he did the first time around, but he was so bloody insistent. Idiot. Dead idiot.'

The faun was practically raving. In one hand, he held a dagger with a curved blade. Even from here, Nicolas could see the green substance coating the tip. The faun walked up to Nicolas and prodded him hard with the edge of his pipes. It felt sharp and painful, but he couldn't say *ow*.

'You see, these pipes let me command the weak-minded, which is why you lot can't move right now. But illusion, that's my real skill, my own magic. Like, for example, hiding a ship from plain sight so it can start a war...until some *idiot* rams into the side of us. It was all I could do to camouflage myself before you fools boarded us. And then I had to make Oleg vanish when he was so...damned...close.' From the way the faun was talking, he and sanity were taking a break from each other. 'Now there will be apologies, explanations, judgement, maybe even repercussions.' The faun shivered. 'I sent Old Hob on ahead. Maybe he can sweeten the Maestro up, or take the brunt of his wrath? Not me, no, not old Ro. I'm going back with something to show for it. The deaths of the interlopers who ruined everything should do quite nicely. Yes, might just keep old Ro's skin attached to his body.'

Maestro? Who's the Maestro? Is he the one behind everything?

The faun gently caressed Nicolas's cheek with the blade of the knife, enough to apply pressure but not break the skin. 'But I admit that part of this is for enjoyment.' Ro nodded enthusiastically. 'Oh yes, I'm going to have a good old time killing you. That's why I got rid of the crew and froze you. I want to savour the moment, every second of it. You won't be able to cry out, no sir, but I'll see the screams in your eyes. Plus, I had enough of your girlish screams when I had you whipped.'

Seemed the faun was going to continue his little show, drag out his victory as long as possible. This was going to be a truly horrible way to go.

'I am so fed up with this guy.' Auron huffed, slapping the instrument right out of Ro's hand. It fell to the deck with force, snapping into two pieces.

Instantly, the hold over him released. As the feeling came back to his limbs, Auron turned and swatted the poisoned knife out of the faun's hand too. It slid away across the deck and fell through a hole into the hold below.

The spirit took a step back as the faun looked at his broken flute in surprise. 'Kick his ass, kid.'

Oh, I'm going to.

The group circled the faun, who desperately looked from side to side.

'No, no, no, *no*,' Ro cried. 'This won't be for nothing.' Ro gestured toward Garaz, Shift, and Silva. 'Naynac, you get them.' Then he pointed at Nicolas and snarled. 'He's mine.'

Every time he'd seen the little toad creature, he hadn't paid it much heed, assuming it would be no issue for him or his companions. That thought evaporated instantly as the creature leapt through the air, simultaneously kicking Silva and Garaz in the side of the head with long green legs. The strike must've been pretty hard as both stumbled back from the blow. Nicolas was so surprised, he didn't see the faun approach until Ro hit him.

Reeling back from the blow, Nicolas managed to get his arm up just in time to painfully block the follow-up strike. Before Ro could throw another, Nicolas swung his fist into the faun's jaw, the hooved menace stumbling back due to the force of the blow. Trying to use the advantage he'd bought himself, Nicolas swung again, but missed. Ro made him pay for overreaching with a punch to the ribs. One side of his body crumpled as the pain ruined his ability to stand up straight. However, there was no way he was about to fail now. He'd waited too long for this already. With a cry, Nicolas drove up with his legs, catching Ro in the jaw with a vicious uppercut that sent the faun reeling into some barrels, which collapsed under the force of the body hitting them.

Nicolas doubled over, trying to catch his breath, but the faun seemed to also need a moment to collect himself, rising and rubbing his jaw as the pair exchanged murderous glares.

Beyond them, the sound of fighting caught his attention. Breathing heavily to try to restore himself, he looked to see how his companions were fairing. It wasn't good. As he watched, the toad creature leapt over Shift's head from behind to land in a handstand position. From there, it kicked up with both legs, catching Shift under the jaw. They fell to the deck, hard. Garaz made a grab for the creature, which hopped aside at the last second and swung a kick that caught the orc across the cheek. Garaz roared in displeasure. Nicolas had never heard him roar before.

'That all you got?' Ro laughed, standing upright again but with obvious effort.

'Kid, do you want me to...possess you?' Auron asked nearby, concern evident.

It had worked once before, the spirit taking over his body and using it to defeat enemies, but he wasn't that guy anymore. He didn't need Auron's help, and Ro needed his comeuppance. Waving off Auron's help, he rose and balled his fists, glaring at Ro, who matched his gaze.

He's mine.

'Come and get some more,' he snarled, the faun now the only thing in his vision.

'Oh, I have plenty left for you...boy.' The last word was spat from the faun's mouth with distaste.

'Your zombies didn't get me. Your possessed children didn't get me. Your harpies didn't get me and neither did your pirates.' Damn, he *had* been through a lot recently. 'And you won't get me either.'

'Zombies?' The faun sneered. 'I don't know what you're talking about.'

Nicolas thought back to the king's ship and the dead aboard who hadn't stayed dead. If that wasn't the faun, why had they risen? He might never know, and now wasn't the time to consider it. Now was just the time to fight.

'Enough talk.' Nicolas focused on the faun.

They charged each other at the same time. Meeting in the middle, their confrontation became a blur of fists and blocks. There were spikes of pain as the faun's blows connected with his body, and spikes of satisfaction as his blows connected with the faun. Though the faun seemed an inexperienced fighter, he was a natural brawler and could more than hold his own. The really fortunate thing was that Silva hit harder when she was pulling her punches, and he was pleased with how many blows he could take, though they were painful and he would've much preferred not to. As fists flew and curses were spat, it was anyone's guess who was winning.

It didn't take long for Nicolas's energy to wane, the pain starting to take over as his body cried out for rest and recovery. He felt swollen skin on his cheek and around his eye where blows had been blocked too slowly and he knew there was blood on his face somewhere, though his senses were scattered enough that he couldn't pinpoint where just now.

On the other side of the fight, the faun was starting to look a bloody mess too, his nose angling to a side it shouldn't have and his lip broken and bleeding. Angry purple bruises covered one of his cheeks, and he seemed to be having as much difficulty moving as Nicolas.

Nicolas would be dammed if he was going to lose this fight.

His peripheral vison was drawn to a thud beside him. It seemed the toad creature had somehow thrown Silva to the deck. He really hoped his friends could handle it, because after this, he'd be in no fit state to deal with it himself.

Ro came at him again, screaming and making obvious the right cross he was sending Nicolas's way. Stepping in as Silva had shown him, he drove another uppercut into the faun's jaw, sending Ro stumbling backwards, following it with a blow to the stomach. Driving all that was left of his might into the punch, it lifted the faun from the deck slightly as Ro grunted hard with the sudden pain.

Ro fell to his knees, coughing and spluttering until the deck beneath him was flecked with blood. And was that a tooth?

Standing over the faun, Nicolas made the mistake of letting his guard down for a second, believing, in his naiveté, that'd he'd won. Ro made him pay for it by jumping up and driving his fist into Nicolas's face. The blow was so fierce Nicolas thought his neck might snap from how quickly his head snapped to the side.

Now it was his turn to spit out a tooth. Seeing it lying on the floor beside him, he remembered the whipping he'd endured, the kidnapped children, the harpies, everything. And all of it because of the faun.

Using those memories, he fuelled himself with determination to win, to make this villain account for his crimes. His strength renewed by his fury, he threw himself at Ro.

Right cross, left cross, right jab, left underhook, each blow connected. The faun's body shook under each impact. Several times, skin tore under his knuckles. In desperation, the faun grabbed his throat, but Nicolas struck him in the pressure point, just as Silva had taught him, and the grip vanished as his arm went limp. Ro stepped back and appeared to be struggling to just stay standing, panting heavily, almost wheezing. Maybe he'd broken one of the faun's ribs. He'd certainly heard a snap and felt something give on one of his strikes.

'You're done,' he snarled quietly in Ro's face.

'Can't...be...for...nothing...' the faun whispered from a bloody, swollen mouth.

With his own burst of energy that caught Nicolas by surprise, Ro tackled him, ramming his shoulder into Nicolas's stomach, winding him and lifting him from the ground to carry him across the deck on clopping hooves. All Nicolas could do was watch as the world blurred by until he was slammed into a cabin door. His back crashed hard into the wood before the force of the faun powered him through it. It was so sudden, he didn't even have time to cry in pain. He suspected he wouldn't be walking for a while as he was driven into the deck. Ro was atop him in an instant. The faun brought a fist down onto his eye. The faun seemed to grow and contract as he lost his depth perception.

'You...stupid...kid.' The faun reached down and clasped his throat, fingers digging into his skin as Ro put all his might into his grip, his eyes crazed as he went for the kill.

'Let go. Let go.' The words came out as choked barks.

The life was being squeezed from him. Images flashed before him, but too quickly to make out any detail. If he didn't do something, he would die. After a few seconds spent trying to break the faun's grip, which proved impossible when he was struggling to breathe, he reached around desperately for some kind of weapon. His hand stopped when he came to a piece of splintered wood from the ruined door. Gripping it tightly, acting purely on instinct, he drove it into the faun's side. Ro's eyes bulged with the impact as he made an ugly groaning sound. The grip on his throat didn't slacken, so he stabbed twice more, his hands growing wet and slippery. Still, the grip held firm. How was he not letting go? Why wouldn't he let go?

Drawing the piece of wood out again, Nicolas thrust it into the faun's neck with a squelch. Ro's head collapsed toward his wound. Blood dribbled from the faun's mouth onto him as his grip finally gave, and he gasped to bring new air into his lungs. Ro looked at him in disbelief, holding his gaze even as the last light faded from his eyes. Then the deadweight of the faun landed atop him.

'Why did you make me do that?' he whispered.

Someone roared in the distance. Nicolas passed out.

****

In the darkness, he heard voices, distant and faint.

'Garaz, what did you do?'

'What was necessary.'

'*That* was necessary?'

'Yes.'

'But you—'

'Enough.'

'No, we need to talk about—'

'I said *enough*.'

The voices got louder.

'Kid? Kid?'

'He's coming around.'

The voice in the distance called him back to consciousness. Remembering what had happened, he snapped his eyes open and cried out in panic. He lay on his side on the cold wood, looking directly into the eyes of the dead faun, who lay next to him.

'Don't look at him.' Shift's voice was soft as their hands moved his head away. He tried to fight it, but he had no energy left. Even as his head turned, he kept his eyes locked with Ro's cold dead ones as long as he could.

'I do not think there's any serious damage,' Garaz said, looking him over. 'Lay still and I will minister to you properly.'

A hand touched him, and he slapped it away. Breathing ragged, he crawled frantically back to the wall of the cabin, curling into a ball and looking again at the dead faun. He opened and closed his hands, but there was some resistance against his skin. His palms were covered in blood. His vision blurred as he tried to focus on the red substance.

'No.' He furiously rubbed his hands against his clothes until they were sore. No matter how much he did, the blood wouldn't come off. Why wasn't it coming off? It was as if his hands were forever stained by what he'd done. His soul was stained.

'What have I done?' he cried hysterically.

'Okay, Nick, you need to calm down,' Shift soothed.

'Calm down?' he asked incredulously. '*Calm down*? I killed someone. I murdered him.'

'It was self-defence, kid,' Auron said calmly. 'He didn't give you a choice, and don't forget, he was a bad guy. No one will weep for him. Besides, you've taken lives before.'

In disbelief, he looked up at his companions, each of whom looked worse for wear, sporting their own bruises and injuries. What were they talking about? He hadn't taken any lives. Were they insane?

'The vampire in the barracks,' Auron said, evidently seeing his confusion. 'You cut his head clean off.'

'That wasn't taking a life,' he protested. 'He was already dead.'

'Are you serious?' Shift muttered.

'What about the guards in *The Grove*?' Silva asked. 'Many of them died because of you.'

What troll crap is this? 'I didn't kill anyone.'

'Nicolas,' Garaz interjected calmly, 'when you purposely release a pack of wild creatures and they kill people, you are responsible for those deaths.'

'No.' Nothing made sense anymore. 'That's not how it works.' They were animals, made by magic, no less. He wasn't responsible for what they did.

'How naïve are you, Nick?' Shift asked incredulously.

'Look who you're talking to,' Auron suggested.

'I'm no killer. I haven't killed before...have I?'

'What about the pirate you knocked off the side of the ship?' Shift asked. 'What do you think happened to him?'

'He swam to safety.'

Shift mouthed the word, *'Wow'*.

'Look, kid, I get this is traumatic, but you need to—' Auron began.

'*No*.' He couldn't be here anymore. Not in this room, with...what he'd done. 'No. What I need is to get away from all of you. *You* made me a killer. I wasn't like this before. Life was quiet. Life was good. Then you came along, and now I have blood on my hands. So much blood...and it won't come off. I'm a *murderer*.'

Shift reached for him as he jumped up. Pushing their hand away, he ran past his companions and through the cabin door, sick at what he'd done. Why had this happened? What had he become? How had he allowed himself to become *this*? It must be because of them. These *companions* of his had drawn him into a life of violence, and now he'd killed. He'd become one of them. Now he was damned to the Underworld for all eternity when he died. He couldn't stand it. He wouldn't stand for it.

'Nick...'

'Stay away from me!' he cried.

Nicolas ran, and he didn't stop running.

EPILOGUE

B o had never seen Mother so enraged, and she was known to be an angry woman. Following in her formidable wake, he winced as she crashed through the doors of the tower like some unstoppable juggernaut. It was a shame; they'd been such nice doors. He understood they were thousands of years old, containing carvings of ancient great deeds. Just broken wood now.

'My Lady,' began an acolyte, bowing respectfully as he approached. 'Forgive us. We did not expect you to—'

Then he was dead. Without breaking stride, Mother sliced his head clean off with her razor-sharp talons. Bo gulped as the head wetly slapped to the floor near him, the end of whatever he was about to say stuck forever in his open, dead mouth. As they continued up the corridor, the headless torso leaked blood over the mosaic floor. There would be some significant clean up needed after she was done, Bo wagered.

Unsurprisingly, no other acolyte in the entrance hall dared approach her. Indeed, they all seemed to have made themselves scarce, moving to the shadows lest they be noticed by the storm blowing through the entrance hall.

Following Mother was like following in the wake of a raging inferno, Bo simply doing his best not to get burned himself. He found himself wishing one of his brothers was here instead of him, but he'd been unlucky enough to be with Mother when she'd gotten the news.

Maybe it wasn't bad luck? Maybe the others knew beforehand...

It was strange how they'd all disappeared so conveniently right before Mother received the message. Yes, the more he thought about it, the more it sounded right. They'd known and chosen him, *The Anomaly*, to be the one to accompany Mother, knowing where she would go and that she would need a voice of reason before she did anything too rash. They also knew that the voice of reason might end up being brutally killed. It wouldn't be the first time. He would get revenge on those goblin anuses...if he survived this trip. Frantically, he began to think of ways out of this, but all he could come up with was to keep quiet. If he turned to leave, Mother would know, even as intent on her path as she was.

At the door leading to the sublevels of the tower, the two guards made the mistake of stepping forward to challenge those approaching, and then they were dead. Bo choked back some sick as he briefly glanced at the patterns of splattered blood on the walls.

Yes, a lot of clean up.

With surprisingly little effort for something so heavy, Mother pushed the stone door aside and continued. *Stone.* A testament to how powerful Mother was.

Beyond was a winding stairway lined with ancient symbols and runes carved directly into the stone itself that Bo didn't understand. They descended at speed, Bo nearly stumbling several times as he tried to keep up with Mother. At the bottom of the stairs was another stone door. Another acolyte approached Mother.

'Forgive us, Great One, you were not expected—'

Slash.

Another one dead. Mother was racking up quite the body count. And it wasn't over yet. Why were none of these acolytes reading her expression before approaching her? Were they all idiots?

The acolyte's companion took a few steps back in shock, so Bo was genuinely surprised when he continued to speak.

'The Maestro cannot be distur—'

Slash.

Mother had actually broken stride to kill that one. With a flick of her wrist, she discarded his lifeless body from her bloody talons, the corpse striking the wall and sliding down it, leaving a blood trail in its wake.

Just like Mother.

Fortunately, the guards by the door itself had the good sense to press themselves as far into the corners of the wall as they could. At least two less would die. The Maestro probably wouldn't take kindly to Mother butchering *all* his servants.

With a snarl, Mother crashed through the final door and into the great chamber beyond.

'And what can I do for you?' greeted the calm voice.

Mother came to a halt just before the couple of steps that led to the raised platform in the centre of the room. Upon the platform was a small fountain containing rippling, metallic-looking liquid, part of which had risen from the fountain and taken a humanoid form. *The Maestro*, as he was known to Bo. He looked down upon Mother levelly as her body heaved with each enraged breath she took. Beyond him were the steps to the gate, which pulsed red. Bo could feel its heat.

'Have you heard,' Mother snarled through gritted teeth. It wasn't a question.

'I was just discussing the matter,' the Maestro replied.

There was something about the Maestro that made Bo's skin crawl. His Mother was terrible, and he'd done no shortage of awful things, but there was something about *him*, some casual disregard for life that chilled Bo worse than any headless corpse.

'The matter?' Mother snapped incredulously. 'That *matter* you so casually speak of is that my son has been killed!'

The Maestro appeared to consider this for a moment. 'That is regrettable,' he said finally.

'Regrettable?' Mother shouted with a dry laugh. 'Regrettable? My son is *dead*!'

'I understand your grief,' the Maestro soothed. 'Take comfort in the fact that his mission did at least partly what it was supposed to do. The damage to the cause was minimal.'

'I take no comfort in that at all,' Mother sneered, nearly frothing at the mouth.

The Maestro was about to reply when his form looked over Mother's shoulder. 'How many of my people did you kill?' he asked calmly.

Mother didn't respond.

'Five.' Bo knew it was stupid to draw attention to himself the second he spoke. Though he thought he'd whispered, all eyes turned to him. He shrank under Mother's deadly glare, bending his will to not soiling himself. Just then the two guards of the second door appeared sheepishly in the opening.

'Fantastic work guarding the door,' the Maestro scoffed. With a flick of his wrist, two globs of metallic substance flew from the Maestro's form. As they passed Bo, they coalesced into two deadly looking knives, their blades perfectly reflective, until they embedded themselves in the guards' necks and became covered in blood.

Bo looked away as the dead men crumpled to the floor.

'So why are you here?' the Maestro asked, returning his attention to Mother.

'I want to know what you're going to do about it,' Mother replied firmly.

'What I'm going to do?' the Maestro echoed.

'The resources you have at your command...' Mother began. 'I want to go to war with this *Nick Carnage* and his friends. I want to burn every piece of land they've set foot upon and butcher any who have affection for them.'

'Hmm,' the Maestro mused. 'That may not do for keeping our work beneath the shadows.'

'I do not care about that.' Mother's voice was a low growl. 'I care about revenge.'

'You could not be naïve enough to believe you could send your children out into the world on these missions for us and have none of them get hurt?' the Maestro scoffed.

'You dare...' Mother took a single step towards the altar.

'Do not overstep.' The sentence was said calmly, but the power behind it made Mother stop and Bo shiver in fear. After a moment, Mother retreated. She had *some* good sense, at least. Praise whoever for that.

'We are a partnership,' the Maestro soothed. 'Let us not forget that and allow our tempers to get the best of us.'

'But what of my son?' Mother asked, the wind taken from her sails slightly but still enraged.

'I was actually just discussing the matter with Koth here, wasn't I?'

Bo followed the Maestro's gaze to a figure he hadn't noticed in the shadowed corner of the room. He felt as nauseated as he always did when faced with that creature. Even Mother took an involuntary step backwards.

'It is so,' Koth confirmed in that whispering, inhuman voice of his.

'This *Nick Carnage* has interfered in our affairs once too often, and now he must be dealt with,' the Maestro declared, addressing the room more than an individual in it. 'But we do not need to go to war for it. Koth is a fixer, and he shall fix this. Won't you?'

'Your will is my command,' the creature replied levelly.

'Yes, it is.' The fact that the Maestro had such a terrible creature as his servant terrified Bo. The sheer will to have power over something like *that*, Bo couldn't begin to understand it. But it seemed the promise of unleashing Koth on this human was enough for Mother to back down, though her body still rose and fell with agitated breaths.

'He suffers?' Mother's tone was almost pouty. It was strange to see Mother, whom he regarded as so powerful and intimidating, overshadowed by worse.

The Maestro looked from her to the creature in the corner. 'The boy suffers. This is my command.'

Koth's cold eyes regarded his mother. 'He shall suffer. For your son.'

'And for being a thorn in our side,' the Maestro purred.

Bo was sure Mother cared much less about that, but she paid the idea the proper lip service. They'd worked long and hard to get where they were and could not allow everything to be undone by a blood feud. Bo knew that but had no wish to try to explain that to Mother in her current state.

'Very well,' Mother said finally, not satisfied, per se, but no longer on the edge of doing something stupid.

'Excellent,' the Maestro said gleefully. 'While you are here, you can update me on the guilds.'

They began to talk, but Bo didn't listen. He found himself staring at Koth instead. He desperately wanted to look away, but his eyes were drawn to the creature. Into him, almost. After a few moments, that inhuman head turned and regarded him back.

Bo's entire soul clenched under that thing's gaze.

Acknowledgments

So here it is. Book 3 is published and released out in the world. January 2022 I had a total of 0 published books, and today I have 3 (or maybe more, depending on when you picked this book up)!

As I finish my first draft of book 8, I'm so pleased to have the opportunity to share my stories, and my dubious attempts at humour, with people like you.

Whether it bothered you or not, I apologise for having Nicolas whipped. If it helps, I felt truly crappy about myself after I wrote it, which is a testament to how much I love him and my other characters. They all live in my head full time now, so when I'm not nice to them it's difficult to look myself in the mirror afterwards.

The other day when I walked in a table leg I actually said *'For Deities' sake'*. So yes, I'm fully immersed in their world now.

Now that you've finished the book, assuming you haven't cheekily flipped to the end first, I want to thank you for joining Nicolas and the others on their journey. They still have a long way to go, but it's going to be very entertaining...for you at least...for them, not so much.

As I've come to expect, my editor Dani did her usual fantastic job of making sure this went from a simple Word document on my computer, to a full blown and coherent novel. Pointers were given, and improvements made, though hopefully with each successive instalment I'm making her job just a little easier.

And how about that cover...Miblart knocked it out of the park this time around. Already I'm filled with ideas for Book 4's cover, and can't wait to see what they produce.

I also need to give a big thank you to my mum and chief proof reader, Christine, who aids me in the continual battle of *'Where exactly do these bloody apostrophes' go?'*.

If you follow my work, it's no surprise that the production costs of this cheeky little novel were raised by Kickstarter. If you contributed to my campaign then thank you so much. What you are reading right now is possible because of you!

3 books...That's crazy.
Soon it'll be 4...where it gets crazier!
Until then,
Keep adventuring!

Andrew

About Author

Andrew Claydon has an imagination, one full of variety.
Sometimes it's funny, sometimes it's adventurous, sometimes it's shock-ing, and occasionally it's outright strange...but it's never boring!
Andrew is a UK author who grew up loving fantasy movies such as Conan, Krull, Beastmaster and Willow. The epic worlds and battles of swords and sorcery therein inspired him to create his own fantasy worlds, adding to them his own brand of irreverent humour; because sometimes it's good to chuckle in between sword fights!
He wants to inspire the imagination of others, just as he's been inspired; with dashing heroes, epic quests and vile villains.
So reader beware, you aren't just opening a book, but a doorway into Andrew's imagination. It'll be a strange journey, but an entertaining one!
When he isn't writing, he loves to read sci/fi and fantasy novels. It's one of the things that inspires him to write himself. He also enjoys playing Warhammer 40,000 and is a keen wrestling fan.
He has degrees in both history and psychology, as well as black belts in several martial arts.
When he isn't creating vast fantasy worlds and populating them with good guys and bad guys to run around fighting each other, he works as a supermarket baker.

Subscribe to my newsletter for the latest publishing news (and get a FREE prequel novella) at: www.andrewclaydonauthor.com
Or follow me on social media:
Facebook: Andrewclaydonauthor
Instagram: @authorandyc
Tiktok: @authorandyc
If you enjoyed the book, then please leave a review with your preferred retailer and/or Goodreads.
Reviews are really important to indie authors to help them get their work out there and create more amazing books for avid readers like you.
If you do take the time to leave a review, thank you.

Also By

Chronicles of the Dawnblade Series
The Simple Delivery
Strange Companions
The Odd Sea
Wrath and Wraiths
Trail of Death
Demons and Disorder

Novellas and short stories
A Grudge is Born
The Gathering
Don't you know who I am?